Monday Girl

Monday Girl

Doris Davidson

First published in Great Britain 2007
by
Birlinn Limited

Published in Large Print 2008 by ISIS Publishing Ltd.,
7 Centremead, Osney Mead, Oxford OX2 0ES
by arrangement with
Birlinn Limited

British Library Cataloguing in Publication Data
Davidson, Doris, 1922–
Monday girl. – Large print ed.
1. Landladies – Scotland – Aberdeen – Fiction
2. World War, 1939–1945 – Social
aspects – Scotland – Aberdeen – Fiction
3. Love stories
4. Large type books
I. Title
823.9'14 [F]

ISBN 978–0–7531–8194–2 (hb)
ISBN 978–0–7531–8195–9 (pb)

Printed and bound in Great Britain by
T. J. International Ltd., Padstow, Cornwall

Part One

CHAPTER ONE

11.02a.m. Sunday, 3rd September 1939. ". . . Consequently, this country is at war with Germany."

Neville Chamberlain's grave words left millions of Britons filled with horror, or openly excited, or believing that they heralded the end of the world. One not quite sixteen-year-old Aberdeen girl, who had taken in only this last sentence of the Prime Minister's speech, brought her private thoughts briefly to a halt, then decided that the coming of war could never affect her life.

Irene Gordon, familiarly called Renee, was blissfully unaware that her own actions would blast her little world asunder in just over two hours. She'd made up her mind to give Fergus one more week, and if he hadn't told her mother by then, she would do it herself. It must be done on a Sunday, when the other three lodgers were away, and she'd have to keep it calm and simple. "Mum, Fergus and I love each other."

That's all she needed to say, and he could take it from there.

Little bubbles of excitement welled up inside her, like fizzy lemonade, at the prospect of being able to declare her love at last, so she was rather annoyed when her lover broke the spell.

"Well, it's here." Fergus Cooper sounded pleased.

Anne Gordon rose to switch off the wireless set. She was the most upset of them. "Don't sound so happy about it, Fergus. I remember the last war, the war to end all wars, and the amount of lives that were lost. What a waste of young men, and what for? So another war could break out in twenty-one years? We don't want to have to go through all that again."

"We won't." His face sobered, to humour her. "This'll all be over in a few months."

Anne still looked despondent. "That's what they said in 1914, and it lasted for years, not months. And remember, Poland and Czechoslovakia were no match for Hitler's stormtroopers."

"That's different. He'll never try to invade Britain, and I wouldn't mind joining the army to see a bit of Europe before it's too late." Fergus stood up. "Would you like me to give the back grass a run over with the mower?"

"Oh, thanks. It's badly needing it."

When Anne went through to the scullery to prepare lunch, Renee was left to organise her jumbled thoughts. She'd said nothing since she'd heard the declaration of war being made, but her brain was turning over furiously, and her heart was aching at the thought of Fergus wanting to leave her.

On the spur of the moment, she made up her mind that she'd have to make her stand today, instead of next Sunday. That way, if he did go into the forces, she'd be sure that he'd come home to her when the fighting was over.

By the time she sat down at the table in the dining room, at one o'clock, her stomach was churning, but she was still determined to carry out her plan. Any unpleasantness which might arise would be past by the time Jack, Tim and Mike came back this evening.

She waited until they finished their broth — it was better that they had something substantial inside them when she sprang it on them — and spoke as her mother rose to bring through the meat and vegetables.

"Sit down, Mum." Her voice quavered a little. "Fergus and I want to tell you something." The planned simple sentence was forgotten, but this would be just as good, as long as she kept calm. Whatever happened, she must keep calm.

Unadulterated fear registered painfully on Fergus's face. "Renee, your mother doesn't want to hear about . . ." He was stuck for words for once — this totally unexpected threat to him had knocked him off balance — but he recovered quickly. "She doesn't want to know what we're planning for her birthday," he finished lamely.

Anne's suspicious eyes swivelled from him to her daughter. "What's going on? My birthday's not till December." She turned her attention again on the man, now cowering fearfully in his seat. "I wasn't born yesterday, Fergus."

"Don't mind him," Renee said, quietly. "This is a new kind of experience for him."

"Yes?" Anne barked the word out and waited for an explanation.

"I'm in love with Fergus, Mum, and he loves me."

It was out at last. She had known there would be some repercussions, but had never, in her wildest nightmares, imagined the explosion that followed.

Even when it was all over, and she was lying on her bed sobbing her heart out, she could hardly believe what had happened.

Fergus couldn't be so low. All the months he'd been making love to her, and telling her he loved her, he'd been doing the same to her mother. It couldn't be true! But he'd actually admitted it. Even if she'd waited another week, it would have come out just the same, and she'd never be able to forget this disastrous Sunday. It was far worse than that other time when her life had been shattered, and that had all started on a Sunday, too. A Sunday six years ago, long before she'd ever known Fergus.

CHAPTER TWO

Renee Gordon's school holidays had been spent at Gowanbrae that summer, because her mother had thought she was looking peaky. "A long spell of country air's what you need," Anne had said, and had written to her aunt to ask if the girl could go there for the eight weeks. Renee hadn't wanted to go. Uncle Jimmy was very nice, but she was rather scared of Auntie Teenie. Christina Durno, however, had left the not-quite-ten-year-old to her own devices, and Renee had revelled in the freedom of not having to wash herself except on Sundays, when the three of them went to church. This Sunday, they hadn't pursued their weekly worship because Anne and Jim Gordon were coming to take their daughter home, so she didn't bother to wash. This was somewhat unfortunate for her, as she discovered later.

When her parents arrived in the green Erskine, Renee had mixed feelings about leaving the cottar house attached to the farm of Gowanbrae. She was glad to see her mother and father, of course, but sorry to be losing the friends she'd made among the neighbouring children. Surprisingly enough, she realised that she would also miss Auntie Teenie.

In the car, she chattered on during the 35-mile journey, until her father laughingly remarked, "And there was Mummy worrying in case you were homesick."

"Oh, no. I was never homesick. I loved it, and Daddy, can I go back next year?"

Looking rather upset that her daughter hadn't missed her, Anne said, "We'll have to see what happens. A year's a long time, and things could change."

"How could they change?"

"Oh, I don't know, and I said we'll see."

To her own surprise, as well as her parents', Renee burst into tears as soon as she went into her own home again.

Anne, on her way to light the gas under the kettle to make a pot of tea, turned round anxiously. "What's wrong?"

"I don't know," the girl sobbed. "I can't help it."

Jim laughed. "She's homesick now. That's what it is. She's so glad to be home, isn't that it?"

"I suppose so."

Relieved, Anne continued through to the scullery, but returned in a few seconds to try to comfort the still-weeping girl. Renee hadn't realised that her tears were to bring retribution for the weeks of glorious neglect to her toilet, but her mother took one look at the grey rivulets leaving lighter skin behind as they ran down the heart-shaped face, and hit the roof.

"Renee Gordon! I thought you were sunburnt, but you haven't been keeping yourself clean, have you? And just look at the state of your knees! The fire hasn't been on, so there's no water for a bath, but use the kettle and scrub yourself properly."

Renee picked up *Little Women*, which had belonged to Auntie Teenie's daughter, and which she'd been told she could keep, and went into the bathroom. She scrubbed her grimy face, hands and knees — only the parts that could be seen — before she sat down on the lavatory seat to read.

After about fifteen minutes, her father shouted to her, "Come on, Renee. What are you doing in there all this time?"

"I'm nearly finished, Daddy," she called back. "Just drying my legs."

"Get a move on, then. I've to get up early in the morning, remember." Jim's irritation showed clearly in his voice.

Pulling a face, Renee turned a page, but in a few minutes, she heard him saying to her mother, "I'll soon get her out."

She wondered fleetingly what he meant to do, but the antics of Meg, Jo, Beth and Amy were so exciting that she lost herself once more in the story, until, without warning, the light went out. She'd always been afraid of the dark, and she shot out of the bathroom like an arrow from a taut bow.

"I knew that would shift you." Her father was laughing as he straightened up from the electricity box after switching the lights back on.

"I hate you for that, Daddy!" she shouted as she ran up the stairs. "I really hate you!"

For a long time afterwards, she was to regret these angry words, because they were the last she ever spoke to him.

She was shaken awake the next morning by her mother, white-faced and trembling. "Daddy's been in an accident with his bike, and you'll have to get up, Renee. Two policemen came to tell me, and one of them's gone next door to ask if Mr Fraser'll go with me to the hospital."

Dressing herself hastily, the girl ran straight downstairs to the living room. Mr Fraser and his wife were already standing there beside the two constables.

"I'll take Renee next door," Mrs Fraser was saying. "And Archie'll go to Woolmanhill with you, Mrs Gordon."

"I don't know how long I'll be." Anne bit her lip with anxiety. "It might be better if you took her to my mother, if you don't mind? It's not far, and Renee can show you the way. You can say I'll collect her as soon as I can."

Renee's young brain had hardly taken in what was happening, but she did grasp the fact that she wouldn't be going to school, even though it was the first day of the new term. Her grandmother was very surprised when they knocked at the door of the tenement flat in Woodside, and was shocked when Mrs Fraser explained why they were there, but her usual hospitality didn't desert her. "Ye'll come in for a cup of tea, Mrs Fraser?"

"It's very kind of you, but I'd better get home. I offered to keep Renee with me — it would have been no bother — but Mrs Gordon wouldn't hear of it."

"Na, na. It's best the bairn came here."

Maggie McIntosh led her granddaughter into the kitchen. "Dinna worry, my pet, yer daddy's goin' to be a' right, I'm sure. Did ye ha'e ony breakfast?" A negative shake of the girl's head made her carry on. "I'll use this packet o' oats, then, for they're quicker than oatmeal, though yer granda doesna think they mak' real porridge." She smiled brightly.

The breakfast duly made and supped, Maggie said, "I'll wash up the dishes, but it would be a big help to yer granny if ye did the dustin'."

Not understanding that this was only a ruse to keep her busy during the suspenseful waiting, Renee dusted everything thoroughly, then sat down at the table to shell the large mound of peas Maggie set out for her. Time dragged interminably for the woman, but the girl was quite unaware that it was almost two hours before her mother and Mr Fraser came back from the hospital.

Anne walked in slowly, her steps mechanical, her face ashen. "Jim died before the ambulance got to Woolmanhill," she said, in a flat monotone.

"Oh, Annie!" The two words conveyed all Maggie's heartfelt sympathy, and she shepherded her daughter into the bedroom to find out exactly what had happened. Anne refused the proffered chair, and held on to the bedpost, while Maggie stood anxiously waiting, afraid to say anything in case she upset the young woman even more.

"The police just told me a van had run into him when he was cycling across Ashgrove Road." Anne's voice was quite steady, but her white knuckles revealed her inner agitation. "Being on a bike, he'd no protection, they said."

"Why did he nae use his car till his work?" Maggie had often wondered about this.

"He said he liked the exercise . . . We went past the place it happened, when we were on the workers' bus, and the bike was still there, in little bits, all mangled up. A man came on at the next stop, and he told somebody he wasn't surprised that van had been in an accident, for the driver always went too fast. He didn't know I'd any connection, of course."

Maggie felt sick at the thought of the torment Anne must have gone through. "Ye'll get compensation, though, when it's proved the van driver was reckless? Nae that it'll be ony consolation, of course, but . . ."

"They couldn't find any witnesses. It was just after six in the morning, remember."

Anne was silent for a few seconds, then she turned round.

"I'm going home now. Mr Fraser's going to arrange for the funeral, and I've told him to make it Thursday, so is it all right if I leave Renee here for the two days?"

"She can bide for as lang's ye want, the wee lambie, but would it nae be better to tak' her hame wi' ye, for company? The shock'll likely hit ye later on." Maggie looked concerned.

"I want to leave her here." Anne's set mouth was obstinate. "I'm very shocked now, and I can't see that I could feel worse."

"I could come wi' ye, an' a'," Maggie persisted, just as determined as her daughter.

"I want time to think, without Renee being there asking questions." Anne gulped, then carried on, resolutely, "Mr Fraser says his wife'll help me on Thursday, so if you bring Renee over early, that's all I ask." She opened the door and went back to the kitchen. "I'm ready, Mr Fraser."

Maggie did all she could to take Renee's mind off the tragedy, even though she suspected that the girl didn't quite comprehend that she would never see her father again, but she, herself, had been very fond of her son-in-law, and needed to keep fully occupied to avoid letting her sorrow overwhelm her.

That afternoon they went out for a walk, and in the evening, after Maggie's husband, Peter, had been told the sad news when the girl was out of the room for a moment, they all played tiddlywinks on the chenille-covered table. Peter had wanted to go to his daughter as soon as he knew of her loss, but had eventually been persuaded that she preferred to be on her own.

Renee was allowed to sleep with her granny in the bed in the kitchen recess, and her granda went into the bedroom which had been shared by Anne and her sister, Bella, before they left home to be married. On that first night, only the nine-year-old had a decent sleep.

Much the same pattern was followed on Tuesday and Wednesday, and, although Renee realised that this extended visit to her granny was not another holiday, she quite enjoyed the unforeseen absence from school.

Only very occasionally did a vague flicker of disquiet assail her, and her grandmother could always dispel it.

On Thursday morning, Maggie supervised her at the kitchen sink. "Ye'll ha'e to gi'e yersel' a right wash the day, my pet, for there'll be a lot o' folk seein' ye, and we dinna want them speakin' aboot ye nae bein' clean."

Renee remembered how she'd been caught out on Sunday, so she washed herself carefully, even her neck, then Maggie made her dress in the bedroom to let Peter have a sponge-down.

On the walk to her home, the girl reflected that her grandparents were dressed almost the same as Auntie Teenie and Uncle Jimmy had been when they went to church, even to the bowler hat perched on Granda's grey head, and that they looked every bit as uncomfortable. Her amusement disappeared as they neared the house, to be replaced by apprehension about what lay in front of her.

When they went inside, she cheered up when she saw her cousin, Peggy, with Auntie Jenny and Uncle George. The two girls, only a few weeks apart in age, were told to sit down and not make a nuisance of themselves, but Renee remembered that there was a pile of *Children's Newspapers* in the lounge, where she had left them before setting off for Gowanbrae several weeks before. That would give them something to do, seeing they weren't allowed out.

Taking time to tell Peggy what she was going to do, she ran into the other room and was brought up short by the sight of the coffin. Seeing her father's porcelain face, eyes closed in unnatural sleep, she forgot her reason for being there, and stood, horrified, gazing down at the waxen hands lying crossed on the white silk until she burst into choking sobs and dashed back to the living room. Maggie caught the full impact of the hurtling figure. "Oh, lassie, ye didna go through there, did ye?" She enveloped the shivering girl in her comforting arms. "It's a' right! It's a' right! Granny's got ye."

It was Renee's first sight of a corpse, and she vowed to herself that she would never, ever, look at another one, come what may. She sat down beside Peggy on the floor, in the corner between the sideboard and the window wall, and huddled closely against her in an effort to shift the icy coldness which seemed to have taken possession of her.

Her terror transmitted itself to her cousin, and they sat in silence, not understanding what had happened, or even what was happening now, but realising that all the people who were arriving had not come on a normal visit.

When the minister came, to conduct a short service over the coffin, the mourners went through to the lounge, but the two girls remained where they were, too scared to move, and no one remembered about them.

The service over, all the men went out — to follow the hearse to the cemetery, Granny told them — and they were allowed to have a glass of milk and something to eat.

The women scurried around, putting sandwiches and biscuits on cakestands and setting out cups, saucers and plates on the table, with both its extensions pulled out. Kettles were placed on the cooker, and teapots were rinsed out with boiling water before tea was spooned into them and they were filled to the brim.

Renee noticed that they were using Granny's kettle and teapot, as well as her mother's, and probably the other ones belonged to Mrs Fraser. They were going to need them, if they were going to fill all the cups they'd laid out.

The men returned, and the room was filled with people, sitting, standing, milling about. It was all too much for the girl, as she and Peggy sat not making a nuisance of themselves, and tears welled up in her eyes. She hadn't really understood when they told her, last Monday, that her father was dead, but finding him lying in his coffin like that had shocked her out of any hopes she'd nursed of ever seeing him again. She knew now what death meant.

The hushed voices of the grown-ups as they went over, one after the other, to speak to her black-clad mother, made her flesh creep, and she prayed that her mother would never die. She could never look at another dead body, no matter whose it was, and the word corpse was the most revolting she'd ever heard.

When she stopped living, she'd be a corpse herself, of course, but she wouldn't have to look at it. All the relatives would gaze on her, and say how natural she looked, like they'd said today about her father, and she'd know nothing about it. A hysterical giggle rose in her throat at her senseless thoughts, and she clutched Peggy's hand tightly.

In ones and twos, the people departed at last, until only Granny and Granda, Auntie Jenny and Uncle George, and Peggy were left. The adults sat down to relax and recover over another cup of tea, although Granda and Uncle George took a glass of whisky first, and it was half an hour later before they were all gone, and Renee and her mother were completely alone.

Anne Gordon sank down on the settee beside her daughter, her mousey hair damp with nervous perspiration. "I'm sorry, Renee. I haven't had time to think about you, or notice what you were doing."

"I was thinking about last Sunday night, when Daddy switched off the lights, remember?"

A faint smile lifted the corners of Anne's mouth. "You came shooting out of the bathroom like a scared rabbit."

"I wasn't scared," Renee protested. "But I told Daddy I hated him for doing it, and now he's dead and I can't let him know I didn't mean it."

After a slight pause, Anne said, in a choked voice, "He knows, don't worry. We all say things we don't mean at times."

She studied the girl then — her daughter who would be ten years old in a few days. The shoulder-length fair hair was curling up at the ends, the bright blue eyes were clouded with remorse and doubt, the sturdy legs were encased in knee-high socks and the blouse and gym-tunic were what had been laid out for her on Monday morning to go to school.

Renee was so like her father that Anne's heart constricted in agony, and she was forced to avert her head, but, after a few minutes, she turned back to the girl. “Oh, God, Renee,” she whispered sadly, “I hope you never have to go through anything like this.”

Not knowing how to reply, Renee took her mother’s hand, and they sat in silence for a long time. At last, Anne stood up. “Help me to lay past the dishes, Renee. There’s only you and me now, so we’ll have to help each other as much as we can.”

The girl had a few private weeps when she recalled her last angry words to her father, but Anne remained dry-eyed, as she had been since the accident, until after the minister called, the next forenoon. The Reverend Graham was an old man, and had made hundreds of visits to the bereaved, but he could offer no explanation when Anne burst out, “Why does God let things like that happen? My Jim was a good man. He didn’t drink, or smoke, or swear, and we went to church every Sunday. Why was he taken from me?”

Looking slightly uncomfortable, the minister laid his hand over hers. “It is not given to us to understand, my dear. The Lord moves in mysterious ways, and only the good are called to the Kingdom of Heaven.”

Anne gave up. How could she argue with that? She felt cheated, betrayed, but it was only after the man left that she found blessed relief in tears, while Renee stood by helplessly. She had never seen her mother weeping before, and the experience was not pleasant.

“It was best for her to let her grief oot, lassie,” Granny said that afternoon, when the girl told her about it. “She needed to ha’e a good greet, an’ she’ll feel the better for it. But ye’ll ha’e to try to keep her spirits up, though ye'll need to be content wi' a lot less than ye've been gettin' up to now." Maggie put her arm round the girl, to let her know she wasn't criticising her in any way, and Renee blinked away her tears as they joined her mother in the living room. She vaguely understood from overheard conversations between Granny and Granda, Uncle George and Anne on Sunday afternoon, that her life was going to be different in future. She had no father to provide for her now, and all his savings had gone to pay the deposit on this house in Cattofield, a fairly new suburb of Aberdeen, where they'd moved only eight months ago. And something called a mortgage had to be paid every month, otherwise they wouldn't even have a roof over their heads.

Renee also gathered that her mother would not receive a widow's pension, because Jim Gordon, in partnership with his brother George in a small butcher shop, had not paid insurance stamps. Apparently it wasn't compulsory for a self-employed man to contribute, and he had never considered the possibility that he could die so young.

Uncle George was going to carry on the shop with the help of Frank Leslie, the young man he'd employed after Renee's father was killed last Monday. He agreed to make Anne a small allowance, but he warned her that it wouldn't be much, after the wages were paid, and all the other expenses.

Maggie McIntosh pursed her lips when she heard this. "I doubt ye'll ha'e to tak' a job, Annie."

"I'm not trained for anything." Anne looked rueful. "And a skivvy's wages wouldn't pay the mortgage and the rates and everything else."

Anne McIntosh had been fortunate in marrying a man like Jim Gordon, everyone had said at the time, with her just being in service and him his own boss, but it was hard to be left like this. "Oh," she groaned, suddenly. "Why did it have to be a butcher? If it had been another kind of shop, I could have served behind the counter, but I don't know anything about cuts of meat, or making sausages and potted head."

"My father used to say he was a flesher and poulterer, not a butcher," George Gordon remarked. "That's what's above the door."

Maggie fixed him with a reprimanding glare as she tutted with disapproval at his facetiousness, and he looked suitably chastened, so she turned her attention on her daughter again.

"Ye've a grand hoose, Annie, so ye could maybe tak' in lodgers. Ye wouldna mak' muckle profit aff them, but it would surely see ye an' yer bairn fed and clad, an' pay for the electric an' gas, as weel as yer mortgage an' rates."

Anne looked horrified. "Jim wouldn't have wanted his house used for taking in lodgers, Mother."

"Maybe no', m' dear, but he shoulda looked ahead an' ta'en oot an insurance on his life, so's nae to leave ye penniless."

"That wasn't Jim's fault. He did speak about it, but I thought we'd have a hard enough time paying the building society for the sixteen years without taking on any more commitments."

Shaking her head until a few long dark strands, and one or two silver, struggled loose from the coil at the back, Maggie said, rather impatiently, "An' jist look far it's got ye. Lodgers are yer only hope, as far as I can see."

"I suppose so." Anne's sigh was prolonged and noisy. "But how do I go about getting them?"

"Tak' oot an advert in the paper, or answer ane, if ye like. There's aye men needin' lodgin's."

When her relatives left, Anne felt easier in her mind, and sat down to look through Saturday's *Evening Express*, where she did find that several men were seeking board and lodgings.

"I could take two, I suppose," she remarked to Renee, "but I'd better let them share the downstairs bedroom."

"Where will you sleep, then?"

"I can take your room, and we'll move you into the loft. Your father lined it with plywood to use as a dark room for his photography, so maybe Granda'll paper it for you."

The girl felt quite excited at the prospect of the change round, especially when she thought that there would be strangers in the house. "How much will you charge them?" She was being more realistic than her mother, or perhaps she was not quite old enough to be affected by the tragedy of the situation. Anne looked bewildered. "I've no idea. I don't know how much lodgers usually pay."

"There's a bit in here about accommodation vacant as well." Renee was looking at the newspaper again. "Some of them say one pound per week, so if you took two, you'd get two pounds. How much do you need for the mortgage?"

"It's four pounds a month, that's one pound a week." Anne frowned in concentration. "With two pounds from the lodgers, and whatever I get from the shop, I might just be able to keep things going. It'll be a struggle, though, with all the other things to pay."

"I'm sure you'll manage." Renee helped her mother to draft a letter, then Anne wrote to the six of the box numbers which seemed to be most suitable. Now that she had burned her boats, she would have to wait patiently for replies, but in the meantime, she had to organise extra beds and bedding, and rearrange the present sleeping quarters. Maggie gave her an old single bed she didn't need, which Granda and Uncle George transported in the shop van, and they repeated the operation with another bed, which one of Jim Gordon's friends offered to Anne. She asked them to move her double bed to Renee's upstairs room, and to shift the girl's single bed into the loft, which Granda had covered with flowery wallpaper to make it more pleasant as a bedroom for the girl.

"It'll be oor birthday present for Renee," he remarked, refusing to take the money Anne wanted to give him to pay for the wallpaper, paste and paint, Maggie and some of her friends donated sheets, blankets and bedspreads, as well as pillows and pillowcases, and Anne rushed about making the downstairs room presentable.

In a few days, she received six letters in answer to hers, and sat down with Renee to see which of the writers, if any, would fit into her household. Some of the notes were quite badly written, but two were worded politely and thoughtfully, so they were the obvious choices.

One was from a William Scroggie, who said he was a gardener in Huntly and had been offered a job with a firm of horticulturists in Aberdeen. He would be going home every weekend, and was twenty-three years old.

"He seems a friendly sort of person, from the way he's written." Anne laid his letter to one side.

"That's one, then," Renee smiled. "What about this Jack Thomson from Peterhead?"

"Well . . . he's very young, just newly sixteen, he says, but he does sound quite nice. He's starting an apprenticeship with an engineering company, though he doesn't say which one, so that's steady work . . . and he'll go home at weekends, too. Yes, I think I'll settle on them."

Anne wrote replies to each letter she had received, four saying that she regretted that her vacancies had been filled, and two stating her terms and hoping that the boys would find her home comfortable. Renee could hardly wait, now, for the lodgers to arrive, because they would be sure to brighten up her existence, and, hopefully, her mother's. Anything could happen with two young men in the house.

CHAPTER THREE

When the boarders made their appearance, Anne Gordon knew she'd chosen well. Bill Scroggie, from Huntly, had a mop of fiery red hair, belying his quiet, serious disposition. He was about five feet eight, and quite stocky, but very polite and friendly. Jack Thomson, from Peterhead, was almost six feet, very slim, and his sandy hair stood up in a quiff at the front. He, too, was inclined to be quiet, especially at first, but he had a strong sense of humour, and his whole face lit up when he smiled, tiny dimples appearing at the edges of his mouth.

They settled in quickly, and Renee soon came to regard them as part of the family, but Anne worried in case she was charging them too much, seeing they went home at weekends. When she mentioned this to Bill, he smiled. "No, Mrs Gordon, we're very happy about it. There's lads paying the same and sleeping four to a room in a tenement."

Renee avidly followed the course of Bill Scroggie's romance with Lena Wilson, and often wished she was old enough to go to the Old Time Dancing in Gray Street, which was where he'd met his girlfriend.

"Why don't you go out dancing?" she asked Jack one evening. He was sitting, as usual, listening to the wireless in the living room.

"I can't afford it, not on my wages."

"Oh, I'm sorry. I didn't think." Even though Jack smiled to let her see she hadn't annoyed him, Renee was annoyed at herself. She should have remembered that her mother had told her he only got five shillings a week, and his widowed mother had to take in dressmaking to pay for his lodgings. He went home every week to see her, so he had little money left to spend on enjoyment, but he never complained and sometimes played Snakes and Ladders, or Ludo, with the schoolgirl when she finished her homework, which passed the time quite pleasantly for both of them.

When Renee was eleven, and attending intermediate school, she started weaving dreams about Jack, now seventeen, waiting for her until she was old enough to be his girlfriend. By that time, of course, he'd be a time-served engineer and making a decent living wage, she realised, with a talent for finance picked up from listening to the discussions her mother had with her relatives.

Every Sunday, George Gordon drove up in the Erskine, which he'd bought for five pounds after his brother Jim died, to give Anne her share of the profits, but he never asked her how she was coping. As it happened, she'd always managed to meet the monthly mortgage, although it was very difficult sometimes, with all her other expenses, and providing meals for four. She'd to scrimp and cut corners, mending sheets and clothes instead of buying new, as she would once have done.

Sometimes Peggy came with her father, and Renee was glad of her cousin's company to let her be free of the boring adult conversation. She felt jealous of Peggy's smart new dresses and skirts now and then, but she never mentioned this to her mother.

Maggie and Peter McIntosh came every Friday evening, to make sure that their daughter and her child were not going short of anything. The difference between them and Uncle George, of course, was that they would have given Anne their last penny if they had suspected she was in need of it. Maggie's legs were beginning to trouble her, and Anne often felt ashamed that they always came to see her, instead of the other way round, but with all the work she had to do, the cleaning, cooking, patching, and letting down Renee's clothes, she seemed to be at it until bedtime every night. Peter, too, was looking older. He would be retiring from his work as a monumental mason shortly, and arthritis had set in to his hands. His back was bowed now and his face was lined with deep furrows, but his white hair was still bushy, like his moustache and eyebrows, though they were not so white, more a gingery grey.

One Sunday, about a year and a half after their circumstances had so dramatically changed, Renee realised that her mother had been standing talking to Uncle George at the door for nearly half an hour, and wondered what they could find to talk about after spending all afternoon in discussion.

At last, Anne came in, and sat down heavily on an armchair, her black dress making her pale face look even paler. "Your Uncle George and Auntie Jenny are . . . splitting up," she said carefully, obviously considering that her daughter was too young to be given any reason.

Renee, however, wouldn't have it left at that. "Why? What's happened?"

Her father's brother was her favourite uncle, handsome and smartly dressed, with his jet-black hair always slicked back neatly, and often telling her little jokes, but his wife, Auntie Jenny, was a dour, thin-faced woman, with a constant expression of disapproval, no matter where she was or who was there.

Anne seemed to be rather relieved to talk about it, after all. "Uncle George has been . . . seeing another woman, and Jenny found out about it. She's told him to get out of their house, and he's got nowhere to go, as his . . . friend's married already."

"Oh! Poor Uncle George!" Renee did not stop to think that it should really be "poor Auntie Jenny", and her mother did not correct her.

"He said he'd pay thirty shillings if I took him in here, that's more than the other two. Of course, he'd be here at the weekends, so that would be full board."

"There's no room for another bed in that room — you're not going to put Jack or Bill away, are you?"

Anne looked at her daughter's apprehensive face. "George doesn't want to share at all. He wants a room to himself."

"Not both of them?" Renee was alarmed now. "Oh, Mummy, you can't do that. You can't put both of them away, you'd have less money than you have now."

"I wish you'd stop jumping to conclusions, Renee. I'm not putting any of them away. As you said, I need the money."

"What's Uncle George going to do then, if you told him he couldn't come here?"

Anne hesitated. "I . . . er . . . told him he could come. He can have my room, and I'll move in with you."

"That's not fair!" The girl's face showed exactly how indignant she was. "I've always had a room to myself, ever since I was old enough. I need it to keep my books, and all my . . ."

"Things have changed, you know that. You've grown out of practically all your clothes, and I can't afford to buy you new ones the way we are just now." Anne brushed a strand of hair out of her eyes. "You'll just have to throw out some of the rubbish you've collected, and make room for me."

Renee's expression of resentment suddenly changed to triumph. "Uncle George'll need a bed, and you can't afford to buy one."

Her mother sighed. "I'm going to put your bed through for him, and take my double bed into the loft for us to sleep on." She held up her hand to avoid further protests. “He’s moving in on Wednesday, so you’d better stop moaning. It’s all settled.”

Renee knew that Wednesday was the shop half-day, because her father, in those never-to-come-again days, had taken them out in the car every Wednesday afternoon in the summertime. They’d visited Teenie and Jimmy Durno sometimes, and, more frequently, her mother’s sister Bella, at all the different places Uncle Willie was fee’d at. He usually worked on a farm for only the obligatory six months he’d agreed to at the Feeing Market in Aberdeen, and then moved on to another, so the Lawries had been in cottar houses all over Aberdeenshire and Kincardine.

In the winters, they hadn’t gone out in the car on her father’s half-days, because he’d played football in the Wednesday League, teams being made up of shopkeepers and assistants who were unable to take part in the Saturday amateur games.

Swallowing the lump which had come to her throat, she realised that her mother had gone upstairs. The noisy thumps and scrapings suggested that furniture was being moved round in the loft. Renee hadn’t really minded having to shift out of her original room, because she’d often been afraid at nights upstairs on her own, and when her mother took it over, the girl had been comforted by the knowledge that only a wall separated them. But this move was an entirely different thing — an invasion of her territory. She’d have no privacy whatsoever, and her precious sanctuary would be cluttered up with the big bed taking up double the space of the single. Worse still, her mother would probably claim half the chest of drawers and half the wardrobe, both of which had been given to them by sympathetic friends when her father died; Renee kept cardboard boxes in them, full of small interesting items, as well as her clothes.

The room which was to be Uncle George's had a box-room off it, with lots of shelves, and a rail along one side for clothes, so he wouldn't need a wardrobe. It had a jute carpet square and varnished surrounds, while the loft had only two threadbare mats on the natural floorboards. It wasn't that Renee actually resented her uncle for further upsetting her life, but she did wish that she could have been left in her little dominion on her own, where she could retreat any time she wanted to spend some time by herself.

Bill Scroggie and Jack Thomson switched the beds around on Tuesday night, and Anne made the single bed ready for her new boarder. The small walnut dressing-table with the triple mirrors and the matching three-drawer chest looked rather feminine for a man — they'd been bought originally for Renee — but there was no money for new furniture, and the room was quite attractive. When she joined her daughter in the double bed in the loft, Anne said, "That's it, then. I hope I've done the right thing. Seeing somebody once a week's not the same as seeing them every day, but I don't think your Uncle George'll be much bother. Anyway, time'll tell."

George Gordon arrived, in the shop van, late on Wednesday afternoon and had unpacked two suitcases of clothes before Bill and Jack came home. They helped him to carry up a comfortable armchair and a small table, which he had bought in a saleroom with the idea of making himself a bed-sitting room. Renee took up some of his other, smaller, belongings. "You've got a lot of good books, Uncle George," she remarked, as she placed them along a shelf in the boxroom. He smiled. "I don't like Westerns or love stories, if that's what you mean. Have you ever read any of these, or are you still on school stories?"

"Not so much now, though I still read them if I'm stuck, but I like *Little Women, Uncle Tom's Cabin, Anne of Green Gables*, and I've had Dickens' *Christmas Carol* out of the school library." She glanced at the row of books. "I've never read *Treasure Island* or *Tom Brown's Schooldays*."

"You don't know what you've been missing, and you're quite free to borrow any of my books, as long as you look after them."

"Thanks, Uncle George. I'm always careful with books."

Like Bill Scroggie and Jack Thomson, George took his meals in the lounge, now called the dining-room, but he had to go back to the shop after teatime, because it didn't close until eight o'clock. If he came home immediately after that, he spent his time in his own room, but more often he did not come home until bedtime.

"He's likely out with his fancy woman," Anne said, unthinking, one evening.

"What's a fancy woman?" Renee had never heard the expression before, and was intrigued by the image it conjured up.

"It's a man's lady-friend when he's got a wife already."

"Was Auntie Jenny not fancy enough for him?" The girl smiled as she thought that "fancy" was the last word she would have used to describe her sour-faced aunt.

"What'll you be wanting to know next?" Anne sounded exasperated by the questions, and obviously wished that she had guarded her tongue. "I'd say Jenny had only herself to blame for the whole thing, though. She nagged about him reading so much, and she couldn't stand him pottering about with his bits of wirelesses. I suppose that's why he started going out — to get away from her nagging."

"I love to see him making the wirelesses," Renee said. "He let me watch him one Sunday. Do you know, he makes cases for them as well, and cuts out a sort of sunray pattern with a fretsaw? It's something like the one we've got. Did Daddy make it?"

Anne's face softened. "Yes, he did. Your father was always pottering about, too. He used to make crystal sets to start with. I think there's still a crystal lying around somewhere. It was funny hearing a voice coming out of it for the first time — that would have been before you were born. The year before — 1922. Wireless was a really marvellous invention, wasn't it?"

"Look for the crystal, Mummy, please, and maybe Uncle George can show me how it works."

Two days later, Anne handed her daughter a small, red circular box, rather like a pillbox. "I knew I hadn't thrown it out, but it had slid down the back of one of the sideboard drawers, and it was just luck I found it."

"What is it?" The girl had forgotten about her previous request, and read the label with interest. "Receptite. The perfect wireless crystal. Guaranteed supersensitive." She looked up, her eyes dancing with excitement. "Oh, great! I hope Uncle George comes straight home from the shop tonight, so he can show me how it works."

"Don't pester him, though."

Renee lifted the round lid and took off the protective layer of cotton wool to look at the small, grey stone nestling in another layer of soft whiteness. "Oh, it just looks like a bit of granite, or something, not like a crystal at all." Her disappointment was only momentary. "It doesn't matter what it looks like, as long as it does the trick."

It was almost half past eight when George Gordon took Renee and Jack, who had also expressed an interest, upstairs to perform the miracle. After fiddling about for quite a while, he succeeded, with the aid of some coiled wire and a pencil, in letting them hear a few faint squeaks. "It needs to be amplified," he said, apologetically. "Earphones, or a loudspeaker."

Going downstairs, just after quarter to ten, Renee wondered why her mother hadn't called up to her, at half past nine, that it was time she went to bed, but soon discovered the reason. Bill Scroggie, who didn't usually come home until after everyone else was in bed, was sitting by the fire, looking very excited. He had already told his landlady his good news, but had to repeat it for the benefit of the other three.

"Lena and me are getting married, and we're not going to wait, for her mother says we can get a room from her."

"Oh, Bill, that's great!" Renee's eyes were shining, although she had not taken the same interest in Bill's romance since Uncle George had come to live there, and hadn't realised that he was so serious about Lena Wilson. Jack Thomson held his hand out to his room-mate. "Aye, that's good news. Congratulations, Bill, and when's the wedding?"

"We're going to see about it the morrow in our dinner hour, but it'll be as soon as we can manage, seeing we've got a place to stay. We canna afford a big wedding, just Lena's father and mother and mine, my brother for best man and Lena's cousin for bridesmaid."

"Make sure you're the boss, Bill." George smiled ruefully as he came forward to shake hands.

Over the next few weeks, Renee and Jack listened eagerly to the wedding plans unfolding, putting forward a suggestion now and then, especially about what Bill should wear.

"You can get a good suit at the Fifty-Shilling Tailor," Jack suggested, one day. "One of my mates at the yard got his marriage suit there, and he was very pleased with it."

"You'll need a grey tie." Renee had studied an article on wedding etiquette in one of the magazines her mother got from Mrs Fraser, next door. "And a white shirt. And, if it's a navy or dark grey suit you buy, remember you'll have to wear black shoes." This caused great amusement, because Bill always wore tan shoes, no matter which other colours he was wearing. They had often teased him about it.

"Tan shoes aye seem to fit me better," he said, "but I'll get black this time, for I must look smart for my wedding."

The big day arrived at last, and Anne and Renee, escorted by Jack, went to Rosemount Church to see the small group going in, and to throw confetti at them when they came out, some thirty minutes later.

Renee thought that Lena Wilson, now Scroggie, was really beautiful in her dusty pink costume and matching picture hat. Her dark hair had been permanently waved, and curled appealingly round her face, which was absolutely radiant. So, too, was Bill's — red, perspiring, but radiant — though he seemed embarrassed when his mother aimed a camera at him. His fiery mop had been tamed with brilliantine, making it much darker, but nobody could say he wasn't smart. His black shoes, uncomfortable though they may be, went very well with his parson-grey fifty-shilling suit; his white shirt, and the grey tie under the Van Heusen collar, were just right for the auspicious occasion. He beamed at his three friends when they scattered their confetti, and Renee reflected, wistfully, that it would be a few years yet before she'd enter the most exciting stage of a girl's life, when love blossomed and ended in a union like Bill and Lena's.

"You'll be looking for another lodger now, I suppose, Mrs Gordon?" Jack remarked when they were going home in the bus.

Anne looked thunderstruck. "Oh, my! With all the excitement about the wedding, I forgot about that, but, yes, I suppose I'll have to."

"I know it's not up to me," Jack began, cautiously, "but one of the lads that works with me was saying he was fed up with his digs, and I said you might be able to take him. But only if it's OK with you," he added.

Anne was glad that she'd be spared the bother of having to find another boarder. "You're the one who'll be sharing a room with him, so if you think he'll fit in, it's OK with me."

CHAPTER FOUR

The newly-weds came to visit quite frequently, and Renee and her mother gradually gathered that their marriage wasn't all moonlight and roses. Coming on his own one evening, Bill Scroggie confided in them. "We've been having a few rows, but Lena and me would get on fine if it wasn't for her mother. She's aye poking her nose in, and Lena gets wild if I say anything."

"It'd be far better if you'd a house of your own," Anne said.

"Oh, aye, but my mother-in-law says there's no need for us to look for another place when she's got plenty of room. She doesn't want Lena to leave her, that's what it is. It's not the money, for Lena's father's got a good job — a riveter with Hall, the shipbuilders."

"If you found another house without telling her," Renee suggested, "she couldn't stop you from moving into it, could she?"

"I wouldna be too sure about that." There was frustration in Bill's voice. "And there would likely be one helluva row. Och, I'm that fed up I feel like emigrating. I saw an advert in the paper last night for a chauffeur/gardener in Canada, and it would suit me fine, if I could get Lena to agree."

"Apply for it, Bill." Anne sounded decisive. "I'm sure she'd go with you if you got the job, and you'll have to do something to save your marriage."

"Aye, right enough. Maybe I will, then." Bill looked much happier when he left.

Anne and Renee discussed his situation until George Gordon came home, about a quarter of an hour later, then Anne went to make him a cup of tea and the girl told her uncle what Bill had been saying. "I hope he gets his Canadian job. Mother-in-law trouble's the very devil — nearly as bad as wife trouble," he added.

"If Lena won't go with him, he could divorce her and go on his own. Maybe he'd meet somebody else over there." Renee felt that her solution was only common sense.

"Getting a divorce isn't as easy as you think," George said sadly. "Your Auntie Jenny won't agree to divorce me, so I'm left high and dry, and there's nothing I can do about it."

"You couldn't marry your lady friend, anyway." Renee blushed, because she had almost said "fancy woman" and, moreover, it was really none of her business.

"Why can't I?"

"I'm sorry, Uncle George. I shouldn't have said anything."

He turned serious. "No, go on. Why couldn't I marry her if I was free?"

She looked embarrassed, avoiding his eyes as she said, "She's married already, isn't she?"

"Oh, that one? I was finished with her before your Auntie Jenny ever found out, but she wouldn't believe me."

"Oh." Renee's sympathies went out to her uncle. "But you've found somebody else that's not married, have you?"

"I have that, Renee." He was smiling now. "A very respectable lady I'd like fine to spend the rest of my life with. She's got her own house, as well, but, as I said, she's very respectable. It's a case of marriage or nothing with her. You understand?"

At thirteen, Renee didn't quite understand the implication of what he was saying, but she thought she'd better not ask. Anyway, she'd other, better things to think about.

The new lodger, who had moved in a week after Bill Scroggie's wedding, was making her heart flutter every time he looked at her with his smouldering, almost black eyes. Fergus Cooper was a Tyrone Power type, with dark brown curly hair and perfect white teeth. He was nineteen, the same age as Jack, and she was just beginning to recognise what lay behind the long mysterious looks he gave her when her mother was out of the room. His previous landlady, he'd told them, was a terrible nag, a terrible cook and a terrible housewife, and he drew such a vivid picture of his dirty room and the awful food that Renee had been most upset for him. She just couldn't understand how anyone in her right mind could treat him like that, he was so nice.

Fergus Cooper now occupied all her dreams, waking and sleeping, and the current speculations about the new king, Edward VIII, and the American divorcee, Mrs Simpson, made them all the more colourful. When the king abdicated for the love of his "Wallis", Renee lay in bed beside her mother, making up romantic fantasies in which Fergus renounced an inheritance before he gathered her in his arms and kissed her, then took her away to an exotic island in the Caribbean to live happily ever after.

Maggie upset her granddaughter quite unintentionally on one of her visits, by remarking to Anne, "I wouldna trust that new lodger ye've got, Annie. He doesna half fancy himsel', an' there's something aboot him . . ."

Anne Gordon laughed. "Rubbish! He's quite a nice lad. He's very good-looking and he knows it, that's all." But Renee had resented the criticism of her heart-throb.

One Sunday, just after teatime, Bill and Lena Scroggie appeared, full of happiness and excitement. "I got that job in Canada I was telling you about," Bill began, "and, would you believe it, Lena was fair pleased?"

"Aye," his wife put in. "I was just as fed up as Bill with my mother interfering, though I tried to stop him from arguing with her, for the sake of peace, but we never told each other what we were feeling."

Bill carried on. "I thought she'd be angry with me for writing about the job behind her back, but . . ."

"We've been to see about our passage to Canada, we've got all the papers, and we sail on Friday." Lena beamed fondly at her husband.

"Aye, we'll be leaving bonnie Scotland on the first day of 1937," he said, his eyes growing serious. "It's something we'll never forget for the rest of our lives, I suppose."

Renee resolutely pushed her own never-to-be-forgotten date, 24th August 1933, the day of her father's funeral, to the back of her mind and said, "It's great, isn't it. I wish I could go to Canada."

"Maybe you will, some day," Bill consoled. "You never know what lies in front of you . . . maybe it's just as well. But we'll be pleased to see you if you ever do cross the Atlantic."

Lena nodded emphatically. "Yes, we will. We'll write and give you our address once we've settled in. There's a house goes with the job, so that's a big relief."

"She's been planning the way she wants the place to look." Bill laughed. "She's even picked the colour of the . . ."

"I want to choose my own colours," Lena explained. "The house is part-furnished, but I want my own curtains and things like that, and we'll have to buy more furniture, and . . ."

"You see?" Bill threw up his hands in mock resignation. "She'll have the whole of my first year's wages spent before I ever get them."

Anne suddenly remembered the real reason for their departure. "What's your mother saying about all this, Lena?"

The girl looked sad. “She’s not very pleased, I can tell you, and she’s stopped speaking to Bill.”

“I’m the black-hearted villain that’s taking her little girl away from her,” Bill said ruefully, and Lena slipped her hand through his arm.

“My life has to be with Bill, though I’m sorry about leaving her, but that’s the way I want it to be.” Her baby-blue eyes looked adoringly at her husband.

Bill smiled. “Well, lass, we’d better be moving. We’ve a few more folk to see yet. Will you say goodbye to Jack for me, Mrs Gordon? I’m sorry I havena seen him, he was a good room-mate.”

Anne nodded. “I’ll do that, Bill, and I’m sure he’ll be disappointed that he’s missed you.”

“This was the only chance we had,” Bill said, “and we can’t wait any longer. We’ve still a lot of packing to do as well.” He stood up, and pulled his wife to her feet. “Well, cheerio, Mrs Gordon, and Renee.” He gripped Anne’s hand for a moment.

“Cheerio, Mrs Gordon, and remember, you and Renee’ll be made welcome if you ever manage to come to see us.” Lena shook hands with both Gordons.

“Thanks, Lena, but I doubt if you’ll ever see us again, unless you two manage to come back.” Anne swallowed. “Good luck, anyway, and bon voyage.”

“Yes, and I hope you’ve a good trip across,” Renee added, unnecessarily, amid rather subdued laughter.

“I hope everything goes well for them,” Anne said when they had gone. “It’s a big step to take.”

They told George about Bill and Lena when he came home, shortly afterwards, and he was genuinely pleased for them. “I’m glad he had the guts to make his own decision. I’m going to have to make up my mind about something, too, so I’m taking a few days’ holiday to think it over. I’ll be leaving on Wednesday, Anne.”

“That’ll be a nice break for you,” she said. “You haven’t had a holiday since you came here, and that’s over a year and a half ago. When will you be back?”

“Next Sunday. The message-boy’s too young to help Frank Leslie in the shop, and the butcher I’m taking on starts another job on the Monday, so I can only take a few days.”

The door opened and Jack Thomson walked in, back from seeing his mother in Peterhead, so he had to be told the exciting news about Bill and Lena, too. “Bill doesna take long about making up his mind, does he?” he laughed. “Well, good luck to them. They deserve it for taking the plunge. It’s never a case of ‘everything comes to him who waits’. Not these days, at any rate.”

“You’re right there,” muttered George, as he turned to go up to his own room.

Anne sat for a few minutes, then rose to her feet. “I think I’ll get off to bed as well. And you’re late, Renee. Remember you’ve got school in the morning.”

“I’ll be up in a few minutes.” The girl was hanging back in the hope of seeing Fergus Cooper before she went to bed.

Jack leaned back in the settee. “I don’t know when Fergus’ll be in,” he remarked, as if he’d read her thoughts. “I saw him down the town just now with a girl.”

Renee's heart sank. She'd never considered the possibility of her hero having a girl already. "Has he been going with her for long?" She tried to sound off-hand, and hoped that Jack would know the answer, since he and Fergus shared a room.

"He changes his girls as often as he changes his shirt, but this one's lasted a few weeks."

"Is he . . . serious about her, would you say?" She had to ask, although she dreaded the possible reply.

"Looks like it. Are you disappointed?" He was only teasing the thirteen-year-old girl.

"Oh, no!" Renee said it rather too vehemently, then felt obliged to prevent Jack from stumbling on the truth. I was only asking. We might have another wedding if we're lucky." Unlucky would be more like it, she thought, but kept a smile on her face. It came back to her how she'd woven fantasies about Jack before Fergus came on the scene, and she realised that she still liked him a lot, but not as much as Fergus.

The sound of a key in the Yale lock made her heart start hammering, and she hoped it didn't show in her expression. "Here's Romeo now," Jack said as the other man came in, his shirt open at the neck although it was the end of December, and his flannels looking somewhat crumpled.

Fergus laughed lustily. "Come off it, Jack. Romeo stuck to one girl, didn't he? I've had dozens."

"What's her name, the one you were out with tonight?" Jack winked to Renee, to show her he was teasing Fergus this time.

"Eleanor. She works in Boots the chemist, and she's a real corker. Lovely fair, curly hair, and not one of your suicide blondes, either, like some of them."

Renee, whose own fair hair had straightened out a bit since she'd pestered her mother to have it cut, felt that she'd hate the name Eleanor for the rest of her life, but she was curious enough to ask, "Suicide blondes? What's that?"

"Dyed by their own hands." Fergus giggled, then had to explain. "Dyed, as in bleached, died, as in snuffed it. See?"

"Well, folks, I'm off." Jack stood up. "Work the morrow, again. I hate Mondays. Goodnight, Renee."

She rose to her feet hastily when he went out. "I'd better go, too, or Mum'll be wondering what I'm doing." She had dropped the childish "Mummy" since Fergus had come to lodge with them.

Giving her his mysterious look, he murmured, "I know what I'd like you to be doing."

With no experience of suggestive remarks, she asked, naively, "What's that?"

"Giving me a cuddle." He gave her a sidelong glance as he placed his arm round her. "You're getting to be a real beauty, Renee, but I wish you were a few years older."

The butterflies in her stomach almost prevented her from breathing. Was she about to receive her first kiss?

Turning her towards him, Fergus looked deeply into her eyes. "Grow up quickly for me. I want to be your very first." He brushed her lips gently with his, leaving her trembling when he went out, and wishing the next few years of her life away. She was disappointed that he hadn't kissed her properly, like in the love stories she sometimes read now, when she imagined that Fergus was the hero and she was the heroine, but that near-kiss would do to be going on with. A promise of things to come? What had he meant when he said he wanted to be her very first, though? First what? First boyfriend? First man to kiss her? Either way, it would be Fergus, whatever happened.

George Gordon set off on Wednesday morning, with two boxes and a suitcase in the boot of the old Erskine, so Anne took the chance to spring-clean his room. She washed his blankets and bedspread, then the curtains, and even gave the jute carpet a shampoo with yellow soap after she brushed down the ceiling and walls. It was hard work, but she liked things to be clean.

Fergus made no further advances to Renee, nor any attempts to get her alone, and a sick jealousy took possession of her each time he went out, presumably with his Eleanor, the corker who worked in Boots, and who didn't bleach her hair or snuff it, whatever that was, and so wasn't one of those who were suicide blondes. She couldn't divulge her feelings to anyone — not to Jack, who would probably laugh at her, and certainly not to her mother, who would be horrified — but her dreams were always of Fergus, his dark eyes full of love as he looked at her, and his firm lips pressed passionately against hers.

George Gordon did not return on Sunday, and, by the middle of the week, with no word from him, Anne began to fear that something had happened to him. On

Thursday morning, she asked Renee to go into his boxroom with her. She hadn't liked to go in there before, as it was where he kept all his personal belongings, but an uneasy suspicion was forming in her mind.

Renee was amazed when they opened the door. "He's taken all his things! There's just a few books left, and odd bits of wirelesses and old rubbish."

"I'm not really surprised," Anne said sadly. "I was beginning to think he'd done a bunk."

"He wouldn't go off like that without telling you, Mum."

"Oh, yes, he would, if it suited him."

"Look at this." Renee pounced on a small bottle. "This is black hair dye. Did you know he dyed his hair?"

"He only did his sideburns." Anne shrugged her shoulders. Her brother-in-law's hair was the least of her worries.

"What's sideburns?" Even at a time like this, when she knew that her mother was upset, the girl had to ask about anything which puzzled her.

Anne clicked her tongue, but pointed to the front of her ear. "It's the bits down here. For goodness sake, put that bottle down. We'd better go downstairs, for there's nothing we can do about this." She closed the boxroom door, and leaned against the bedroom wall, breathing deeply for a minute, before she walked to the top of the stairs.

Renee followed her mother, noticing that Anne's hands were shaking as she laid them on the bannister. What on earth was going to happen now?

"George has taken all his stuff away, except for a few odds and ends," Anne said quietly, when she went into the dining room, where Jack and Fergus were having breakfast. "He'd never meant to come back. I bet he's away with his fancy woman — that had been the decision he said he'd to make."

"Good for him," Fergus said, grinning. "That's the way to do it. Take the bull by the horns, and to hell with everything."

Renee didn't know whether to be happy for her uncle or not, but she felt obliged to set her mother straight about one thing. "It wasn't the fancy woman, Mum. Uncle George told me he'd been finished with her before Auntie Jenny ever found out, but she wouldn't believe him. He said he'd met a very respectable lady who wanted marriage or nothing, so *she* wouldn't have gone away with him — not if she knew he was a married man."

Fergus burst out laughing. "Maybe he didn't tell her. This gets better all the time. Marriage or nothing, that's great."

Anne drew her brows down angrily. "He could at least have told me what he was going to do. I wouldn't have told Jenny, and now I don't know whether to let his room or not. I'd a feeling something wasn't quite right, and I can't afford to hang on much longer."

Silent until then, Jack asked, gently, "What about the shop, Mrs Gordon? Will the man who was left in charge manage to run it on his own?"

"Oh, my God!" Anne moaned, the anger in her face replaced now by anxiety. "I'd forgotten about the shop. No, Frank Leslie won't manage to run it on his own. You see, somebody's got to go to the meat market every morning, and it's all got to be cut up, and there's mince to be made, and sausages and potted head . . . No, no, he couldn't. What am I going to do?"

Jack stood up. "You'd better speak to this Frank, I think. He might be able to suggest something, and, anyway, you'd find out exactly what's what. Maybe George told him what he was going away for. I'm sorry, but I'll have to go now, or I'll be late. Are you ready, Fergus?"

"Sure thing." He pushed back his chair. "Don't worry, Anne, it'll all come right in the wash."

Renee worried about her mother while she was getting ready for school, until it came to her that Fergus had said "Anne", not Mrs Gordon as he usually did. Why the change? She couldn't fathom it out, and the seed of jealousy was sown.

After her daughter went out, Anne washed and dressed, to go to the shop to talk to Frank, as Jack had suggested. She was lifting her coat out of the old wardrobe in the loft, when the doorbell rang, so she ran downstairs, wondering who could be calling at that time of day.

It was Frank Leslie, in the shop van. "Can I speak to you, Mrs Gordon?" His voice was urgent.

"I was just coming to see you." Anne held the door open for him. "I think George has left for good."

"No 'think' about it. He's left for good, right enough." The young man sat down wearily, though his hands were moving restlessly. "And he's left a right mess behind him."

"A mess? What d'you mean?" Her abrupt words conveyed tense alarm.

"He hasn't paid the meat market for weeks, and he's away with all the cash. He must have planned it all out."

"What?" Anne collapsed into the other armchair.

"The man he took on to help me the time he was away was only there till Saturday night, so I've had to close the shop every day this week to go for the meat."

"Yes?" She had difficulty in saying even the one word.

"Well, I thought they were a bit funny the first three days, but this morning the manager told me we wouldn't get any more till we paid the hundred and fifty pounds that's owing. And we can't pay, Mrs Gordon, for there's no money."

"But, surely, if they gave us time, we could . . ."

"We couldn't, there's nothing to sell." Frank stared at Anne as if he hoped she could perform a miracle.

"Oh, my God! I never thought things would be as bad as this." The tears were not far off, and she swallowed repeatedly, so as not to break down in front of him.

"I'd have worked for you for nothing, Mrs Gordon, till the shop got back on its feet, but if we can't get meat, we're absolutely sunk." They looked at each other helplessly, each trying to find strength from the other. It might as well have been a thousand pounds owing, for all the chance they could see of settling the debt George Gordon had amassed.

Anne was first to break the silence. "What can we do, then? How can we pay off all that?"

Frank straightened up. "There's only one thing we can do, and that's to sell up everything — the van, the machines, the message bike, the till, everything. Even at that, it'll be touch and go if we get enough, and it's the end of the shop."

After sitting deep in thought for a few minutes, unwilling to take this drastic step, Anne nodded slowly. "It'll be the end, but it's the only thing we can do. Where can we sell them, though, and how do we start?" The shock of learning the predicament was bad enough, but disposing of the shop which Jim's father had built up made her feel very guilty. The young man knew exactly how she was feeling, so he said, gently, "I haven't much idea about it myself, but I'll put word round some of the other butchers for a start, and they'll maybe buy some of the stuff. It's not your fault, Mrs Gordon, and nobody can blame you for it."

"I suppose not, and thank you for trying to help. I wouldn't have known where to begin."

"That's OK. I'll let you know what happens, but I'd better get back to the shop now and sell off what little there is left. Then I'll make up a list of all the equipment."

When Renee came home from school at lunchtime, she found her mother, with red-rimmed eyes, setting the table. "What's wrong, Mum?" she asked, fearfully. "Has something happened to Uncle George?"

"Nothing'll ever happen to your Uncle George," Anne said, sharply. "He's got the luck of the devil himself. He's cleared off with all the money from the shop, and owing the meat market a hundred and fifty pounds."

"What'll they do about that?"

"They expect the shop to pay, but there's no money, and no meat. Frank Leslie was here this morning to tell me about it, and we're going to have to sell up everything and give up the shop. It's all that's left to do."

Renee was outraged. "I never thought Uncle George would do a thing like that. He was always so thoughtful and kind."

Anne pursed her lips briefly, then shook her head. "I suppose we can hardly blame him, really. His life hasn't been up to much for a long time, but he hasn't thought about anybody but himself now. He'll likely not even support Jenny and Peggy, and, with the shop finished, there'll be nothing for them, or for us, either. I don't know how I'm going to manage."

"We'll manage. I'm sure we'll manage. We've come through all right so far, haven't we, and you thought we couldn't, when Dad died, remember?" Renee looked hopefully at her mother. "What about asking Granny and Granda if they'd help you to pay off the . . .?"

"They haven't got that kind of money, and besides, I couldn't tell them how bad things really are, they'd worry themselves sick. They never thought much of George Gordon, anyway."

At teatime, when Jack and Fergus were told what had happened, they showed totally different reactions. Jack was horrified at Anne's plight. "The selfish bugger! Oh, I'm sorry, Mrs Gordon, but I couldn't help swearing. You'll have to put up our board, and I'll ask at the yard if anybody's needing good digs. If you got another single bed, you could take in two."

"Well, I admire him." Fergus chuckled lightly. "It takes a lot of guts to walk out on everything like that, and what had he here, in any case? He wasn't really married, but he wasn't free. It was the best thing he could do — chuck the lot." Renee was disappointed in her heart-throb, but, when he turned and winked to her, she would have forgiven him anything.

The following afternoon Anne's spirits, already at a very low ebb, slumped even further when she was visited by her sister-in-law, who barged past her when she opened the door.

"I went to the shop to find out why I didn't get any money last week." Jenny's voice held more than the usual complaining tone. "It knocked the feet from me when Frank Leslie told me what had happened, for I've been using what I'd laid past for the rent. Mind you, I'm not surprised that George just disappeared like that — he never considered me at all — but what's going to happen to me now? You'll have to give me my share of whatever you get when everything's sold up."

"There won't be anything left to share." Anne had never liked this woman, but could feel sorry for the way things had turned out for her. "I don't even know if we'll get enough to pay what we owe to the meat market."

Jenny frowned. "It's all right for you. You've a fine, big house, and can take in lodgers, so you weren't really depending on the shop." Her sneering expression made it evident that this was something which rankled in her mind.

Feeling her hackles rising Anne snapped. "My house has still to be paid up, and what I get from the lodgers has to feed Renee and me as well as them. I've had a bloody hard struggle to keep things going since Jim died, and it'll be a lot worse without the money from the shop."

Jenny brooded over her own trouble for a few minutes, then said, plaintively, "My sister in Chicago often says in her letters that she'd be willing for Peggy and me to go and live with her, but I can't afford the fares. Could you . . . ?"

"I'm sorry, Jenny," Anne said, hastily, "but I hardly make enough to cover my own expenses, never mind give any away."

"Nobody cares about me." Jenny sounded mournfully accusing. "Peggy and me could starve and nobody would worry."

"Oh, come on, Jenny. That's not true." Anne's sympathy, already sorely stretched, was fighting a losing battle against her impatience at her sister-in-law's attitude. "I do worry, but I'm not any better off than you, you know. I'd help you if I could, but . . ." Her hands rose in a gesture of hopelessness.

Jenny sighed. "That's it, then. There's nothing left for me to do but go on the Parish, like all the other destitute women." Going on the Parish was considered a disgrace, a last resort, so Anne knew that the other woman was attempting moral blackmail, trying to force her to do something, but she was in no position to help. Her own circumstances were every bit as bad, if not worse, because she'd taken on the responsibility of paying off the debt which Jenny was conveniently ignoring.

"You could look for a job," she said, after a slight pause. "You worked in an office before you were married, didn't you? Your wages would be enough to keep Peggy and you, I'd think."

"Oh Anne, I couldn't go out to work again. My God, it's been sixteen years."

"You could, if you wanted to . . . Anyway, I'll let you know what happens about the shop." Anne stood up and opened the living-room door, so Jenny took the hint, and stalked out.

Everything was sold within a few days, even the errand bicycle and the van, both long past their prime. The other butchers in the city, who had known and respected Jim Gordon, had made a point of paying more for the items they bought than they were really worth, and the man who would be leasing the premises had even agreed to accept responsibility for the gas and electricity consumed since the last bills had been paid — fortunately, only a few weeks previously.

Frank Leslie was elated when he came to inform Anne of this. "The sausage machine, the mincer and the slicer all sold for about half as much again as I thought we'd get. And I was surprised when Jock Reid paid fifteen pounds for the van — it's just fit for scrap, really."

When everything was totalled up, they were only five pounds, two shillings and ten pence short of the amount due to the abbatoir, but Anne could see no way of finding the rest of the debt.

"I can't even buy a threepenny raffle ticket at the door nowadays," she observed ruefully, "so God knows where I'll get five pounds odd."

Frank looked at her sympathetically. "I'm sorry I can't afford to give you anything, Mrs Gordon."

"No, no." She was appalled at the very idea of it. "It shouldn't be your worry. If the meat market would let me pay up the rest a little bit every week, I might manage if I took in another two lodgers, though it'd be hard going."

Anne was very grateful to all her benefactors, but that was nothing compared with the deep relief she felt when Frank Leslie returned that evening to tell her that the meat market had accepted the amount of money he had taken in, and had agreed to write off the balance. "As a mark of respect to your husband, the manager said."

"Frank, I can't thank you enough for what you've done. I don't know how I'd have managed without you, and I hope you find another job soon."

"I was glad to be able to help you, Mrs Gordon, and I'm starting on Monday with Kenny Wilson in the market. He offered me the job when he was in looking at the things, and it's five shillings a week more than I was getting."

"Oh, Frank!" Anne's expression showed exactly how upset she was. "Wages! I'd forgotten about paying you, and I've nothing to . . ."

"Look, Mrs Gordon, it was no bother, and I'm not needing paid for anything."

"But you haven't . . . did George leave wages for you?"

"Don't you worry your head about that," he laughed.

"He didn't. I can tell by your face. Oh, Frank . . ."

"It's just one of these things." He shrugged his shoulders. "I'd a wee bit laid by, and we managed. I took a bit beef home to the wife sometimes, out of the shop." He looked at her anxiously. "I hope you won't think I was stealing."

"No, no. I'm glad you did. Oh, I'm so mad, I would kill that George if I could get my hands on him."

Frank smiled wryly. "Just forget about it, Mrs Gordon. There's nothing we can do about it now, and everything's settled, so you'll have no more worries."

"No more worries," Anne said bitterly, when she came back from seeing him out. "There'll be no more money from the shop, and I'll have to find another bed before I can take in two more lodgers."

"You'd manage once you had four, though, wouldn't you?" Renee asked, hopefully. Her mother heaved a huge sigh. "I'll have to, and maybe you'll be allowed to leave school at summer if I apply, under the circumstances. The deadline is 31st August, but your fourteenth birthday's just days after that."

"Oh, great! That's just a few months, then I can take a job. That'll help, won't it, Mum?" The girl had visions of being the mainstay of the household with her wages.

"For all you'll get . . ." began Anne, then saw the naked disappointment on her daughter's face. "Yes, Renee, it will help. Every single shilling makes a difference."

Jenny Gordon's expression darkened when Anne went to tell her the outcome of the sale. "There's George away with another woman, and he's left me nothing except the furniture."

Anne felt no sympathy for her this time. "You've only yourself to blame for him going off the rails, you and your nagging. George was happy enough with his hobbies, till you went on and on at him about them. And you're lucky in a way. You're only paying a few shillings a week rent for this house, but I've to find a pound a week for the mortgage on mine. I've taken in lodgers, and worked from morning to night to keep things going, but you're just sitting back feeling sorry for yourself."

Not unexpectedly, the other woman's eyes filled with tears. "My God, Anne, you're hard, and I'll never forget the awful things you've said." She began to snivel.

"I've had to learn to be hard, and you'll have to do the same if you want to get over this." Anne stamped out of the house and banged the door behind her. She walked to the bus stop, regretting her bluntness now, but hoping that Jenny would have the common sense to look for a job. When Peggy left school in June, her wages would help them out a little bit.

Jack Thomson had kept his promise to ask his workmates if they knew of anyone requiring lodgings, but nothing had come of it, and he was just as worried as Anne.

When Maggie eventually learned that George had left, she was very angry. "Did he owe ye onything when he took off? Had he paid his board?"

Anne's eyes dropped. "He didn't pay me the week before he went away, so it's only a week and a half he was due me." She pulled a face. "It could have been worse."

"It was still forty-five shillin's." Her mother sounded most indignant. "It just shows ye. Ye canna trust onybody these days. But ye'll easy get another lodger, Annie, an' wi' the money from the shop, ye'll be . . ." Maggie stopped in dismay when she saw Anne's set expression.

"There'll be nothing from the shop, Mother, we've had to give it up."

"Gi'e it up? But that was jist plain daft. Why in the name o' heaven did ye gi'e it up?" Anne had to tell her the whole truth then, but hastened to explain that the debt was all settled.

"Annie, ye shoulda tell't me at the time — we'd ha'e tried to help ye. What a worry ye musta had."

"It was pretty bad," Anne admitted, "but it's past now."

"How are ye goin' to manage, lass? Ha'e ye got somebody else for his room?"

"Not yet, but Jack's still trying."

"Ye'll ha'e to put an advert in the . . ."

"I can't afford it."

"Oh." Maggie stared at her hands for a few seconds, wondering what she could do to help. "Look, I think I've got a pound in my purse." She opened the old black handbag which she'd carried around with her for years.

"No, Mother. You can't afford it, either."

"Ye could answer some adverts then, like the last time?" The older woman closed her purse and replaced it in the bag.

"I can't think straight about it yet, and that's a fact." Anne was near to tears now. "Something'll turn up."

"Tak' this, ony road, it'll buy something for ye to eat." Maggie pressed into her daughter's hand the pound note she'd slyly slipped out of her purse a minute before. "Nae arguin', noo, me an' yer father dinna need so muckle nooadays."

Knowing that her mother would be offended if she refused to take the money, Anne accepted it gratefully. It would enable her to stock up her store cupboard, which was almost empty, so they wouldn't go hungry for a few days yet.

At teatime, Jack Thomson blurted out his good news before he was properly inside the room. "The yard manager asked me this morning if my landlady could take in a new apprentice that's starting a week on

Monday. His mother had asked the yard to find digs for him."

Anne's jaded eyes lit up with relief. "Oh, Jack, that's good. Did you say it would be all right?"

"I did that, and he gave me their address. You've to write and let the laddie's mother know, and tell her your terms."

Anne's letter was answered by return. The boy's mother thanked Mrs Gordon for writing, and asked if she could possibly make room for her other son, who had been working with the same firm for a few months, but wasn't too happy with his present lodgings and would prefer to be with his brother.

"They would be willing to sleep in a double bed, like they do at home," her letter finished up.

Anne looked rueful when she folded up the sheets of paper. "I'd easily manage to take the two of them if I'd only got another single bed."

"You could get one on the instalment plan," Renee suggested.

"I've never done anything like that in my life!" Anne was outraged. "We weren't brought up like that. Your granny never got anything unless she could pay cash for it."

The girl laughed derisively. "That's old-fashioned. A lot of folk buy on tick nowadays. It's no disgrace, and you'd be able to pay it up seeing you'll have an extra lodger."

"I suppose so." Anne sounded none to sure about it, but an even better plan had just occurred to her daughter.

"If you got a double bed, like their mother says, I could have the single one — it was mine once anyway

— and we could shift the furniture round in the loft to make room for it."

Anne's troubled eyes softened. "Oh, I see what you're getting at. You want a bed to yourself again?"

"Please, Mum?"

"But it would be dearer, and . . . well, all right. I'll go and see about it tomorrow."

A brand new double bed was obtained on a deposit of half a crown, which Anne could ill afford off the board money she'd received from Jack and Fergus the night before, but she had twelve months to pay off the balance. Renee was delighted to have her old bed back, but the attic bedroom was really overcrowded now.

The Donaldson brothers, from Turriff, took over George's room the following Sunday. Tim, the sixteen-year-old apprentice, was very blond, his mischievous blue eyes danced between surprisingly dark lashes. He wasn't much taller than Renee, but his outgoing personality and impish sense of humour made up for his lack of inches. Mike, nearly twenty-two, was a storeman, taller and much quieter than his brother, but his shy, serious eyes were transformed when he smiled. His hair was just as blond as Tim's, but his eyelashes were lighter, and it seemed, at first glance, as if he'd none at all. They slipped quite easily into Anne Gordon's household, Fergus Cooper being the only one who took some time to accept them. When he realised, however, that they were no challenge to him as the most handsome male in the house, he came round and treated them as friends.

Renee and her mother were interested in the discussions the four young men carried on and were amused by their differences of opinion, and only very occasionally did Anne have to step in to prevent an argument getting out of hand. Their controversies ranged from football to films, current affairs to clothes, but Anne made a firm rule — "No politics or religion". She had found that tempers were apt to get frayed when these subjects were raised. Tim Donaldson, being nearest Renee's age, teased her quite a lot, but she developed the knack of giving as good as she got, egged on by Jack and Fergus.

A few weeks after her visit to Jenny, Anne received a short note from her.

Dear Anne,

I'm sure you'll be pleased to know that my sister has sent me the money to pay our fares to Chicago. We're sailing to New York the day after Peggy leaves school, and apparently there'll be no difficulty in both of us getting jobs when we arrive. So you see, I'm not feeling sorry for myself any longer, and I mean to make a decent life for us.

I'm not going to ask you to keep in touch, because we were never that close, but I hope everything goes well for you.

Yours,

Jenny Gordon.

P.S. I hope Renee gets a good job.

Anne took a deep breath and exhaled it slowly. "Well . . . I'm glad about that. It'll do Jenny the world of good."

Renee twisted her face to show what she thought of her aunt. "I'm sorry I'll never see Peggy again, though, but I'm pleased for her, because she'll have a chance of a better job over there. America's supposed to be the Land of Opportunity." It crossed her mind, then, that she had lost several friends and relatives in this year of 1937 — first Bill Scroggie and Lena off to Canada on New Year's Day, then Uncle George off not long after to who-knew-where, and now Auntie Jenny and Peggy off to Chicago — but finding a job, within a week or two, would be the highlight of the year for her. She studied the Situations Vacant columns in the evening paper every night, and, on a Saturday morning, called to see R. Mackay, Wholesale Confectioner, who had advertised for an office girl. "School leaver," he had stipulated, so she felt quite confident of the outcome when she set off.

Anne had tried to make her understand that there would be other girls after the job, and not to pin her hopes on it, so she was very relieved when her daughter came back smiling. "I start the Monday after the term finishes, and I'll be getting seven and six a week." Renee danced round the room in great exultation, while her mother shook her head fondly.

"It's nine to six, with an hour and a half for my dinner," the girl went on, almost singing the words in her excitement.

"You'll have plenty of time to come home, then, that's good, but you'll be a bit late for your tea. Oh, well, it can't be helped." Anne suddenly felt a touch of sadness that her daughter would soon be entering the adult world and leaving her schooldays behind.

"Settle down, for goodness sake," she said, sharply.

"I was counting out what I'd need for my fares, Mum, and I'll manage to give you five bob for my board, for I won't need to spend much on other things, will I?"

"No, I don't suppose so." Anne considered what this promised contribution would mean to her. It would make the household finances better than they'd ever been since Jim Gordon died — four pounds five shillings — it was riches compared with what she'd taken in at times.

"Thanks," she said, at last. "That'll be a big help, and once I've got the bed paid up, we'll be better off still. I only hope nothing happens to spoil things this time, now we're all one big happy family."

CHAPTER FIVE

The tiny office was quite cramped, the only furnishings being one huge desk, with deep drawers down each side, two high stools, and a table where the samples of sweets were laid out for customers.

When Renee Gordon went for the interview at the wholesale confectioner's, Mr Mackay, the owner, had asked if she had good teeth, and had laughed at her bewilderment. "They won't be good for long in this job," he'd laughingly explained.

Once she started working as office girl, she understood why. When the manufacturers' representatives came in with new lines, they always asked Miss Maitland and Renee to sample their wares first. If their reaction was favourable, Mr Mackay placed an order, so their judgement was valued by the visiting men.

Miss Maitland, in charge of the office, was a cheery, even-tempered woman, whose age Renee found it difficult to assess, but guessed at around forty. They got on very well together, and sat side by side at the oak desk in front of the window.

Rather Victorian in his ideas, Mr Mackay didn't believe in allowing his staff to have a break in their working hours, but, because he was often out canvassing for orders, they kept bottles of soft drinks in the deepest drawer of the desk, behind the leather-bound ledgers. With that, and the sweets from the travellers, they managed to keep their strength up.

Renee's job entailed folding accounts so that the addresses showed in the window envelopes, and taking orders through to the store. Sometimes she was allowed to answer the telephone, and to write the customers' requirements into the order book, but although they were mostly fiddly little tasks she was given, she enjoyed it all. Sweetshop owners and newsagents came in, to settle the bills for the confectionery they'd bought, or just to have a look round for anything new which might have been introduced, and it was all strange and exciting to the girl at first. Receiving a wage every week gave her a feeling of independence, and handing over five shillings to her mother made her proud, though she often wished it could have been more. It was a pity she'd so little left to spend on herself, but she felt no real sense of deprivation.

If they weren't busy, Miss Maitland let the girl experiment with the typewriter, and she was soon tapping away merrily. She wasn't proficient enough to use all her fingers, but the end result was fairly presentable, and she was thrilled when she was allowed to type some invoices. She took time over them, and they seemed to meet with Miss Maitland's approval.

It took less than a year for the novelty to wear off, and Renee began to yearn for something different. There was no likelihood of promotion, as Miss Maitland had been there since she left school, and appeared to be one of the fittings. Renee carried on with her now rather boring work until just before her fifteenth birthday, when she saw an advertisement in the newspaper one night for a junior clerkess, aged fifteen to eighteen. "Wages twelve shillings and sixpence," it said. "I'm going to apply for this," she told her mother, handing over the paper and pointing to the place.

Glancing at it, Anne smiled. "That's a good idea. Mr Mackay's never mentioned raising your wages, has he?"

"No. You see, he just takes on a girl straight from school for about a year, then gets another one. That's what Miss Maitland says, anyway. He can't afford to pay higher wages."

She carefully wrote out a letter of application, stating where she was employed and that she could type, omitting to mention that she used only two fingers on each hand. In a few days, she received notification to call for an interview, and, when she asked Mr Mackay if she could have time off, he seemed quite relieved that she was looking for another job. "I can't really pay two clerkesses, I'm afraid, and all my office girls move on after about a year. Give me a full week's notice, that's all I ask."

Realising that several other girls must have applied for the same position, it came as a very pleasant surprise to Renee when the interviewer asked when she could start work. "I've to give a week's notice, so I could come a week from Monday, if that's all right?"

In September 1938, therefore, Renee began as a junior clerkess with Brown and Company, a branch of a national wholesale food distributor, and the manager called her into his office on her first morning.

"We expect our juniors to get certificates in shorthand and typing, Renee," he told her. "We pay the fees, but you must attend evening classes regularly."

"That's all right, Mr Murchie. I'm quite prepared to work hard, and I won't let you down."

"Good. We expect you to pass the Royal Society of Arts at the elementary stage the first year, the intermediate the following year and the advanced in the third year. Depending on that, your salary will rise every year, on your birthday, until you reach twenty-four. That's the top of the scale."

An excited Renee told her mother all this at lunchtime, and Anne was suitably impressed. "I thought twelve and six was very good for your age, but if it's going up automatically every year, that's the right kind of firm to be with. You'll just have to make sure you pass all your exams." Towards the end of September, when the girl went to the grammar school to enrol for the evening classes, she found that the shorthand course involved two hours every Monday, and the typing occupied only one hour each Wednesday. The second hour was devoted to book-keeping, she was told, so she enrolled for that, as well. It might come in handy in the future.

There were two others in the office of Brown and Company. Miss Esson, the cashier, was the person who had engaged Renee as junior clerkess, and was another lady of indeterminate age. She could have been slightly older than Miss Maitland, but it was difficult to judge.

Sheila Daun, the clerkess, was only a year older than Renee, so they quickly became good friends, talking to each other so much that Miss Esson sometimes had to admonish them. "I don't mind the two of you chattering twenty to the dozen when you're on your teabreak, girls," she said one forenoon, "but not when we're working. I can't concentrate for the noise."

"She can't concentrate because she's frightened she misses anything," Sheila whispered, but they stopped talking.

The evening classes, which started in the first week of October, were very interesting for Renee. She didn't attend on the same nights as Sheila Daun, who was in her second year, but she quickly became acquainted with most of the girls, and one or two of the boys, in her class. The atmosphere was far more conducive to learning than it had been in school, each student being anxious to pass the coming examinations, so she found that the two-hour sessions passed rapidly.

It was on the third Monday that it happened. Coming out of the building, laughing and talking with some of her classmates, she bade them goodnight and turned to walk home alone, as no one else went in the same direction. It was very dark, and the street lights were fairly dim, so she didn't see the figure standing in the shadow of the wall until she was almost abreast of him. When the man stepped out in front of her, she had a momentary stab of panic, until she realised that it was Fergus Cooper.

"Oh," she gasped, quite taken aback. "What on earth are you doing here?"

"Waiting for you." He walked alongside her, up the hill to Rosemount Place, across into Watson Street, and she was too tongue-tied by the shock of him being there to say anything, although his presence had sent thrills all through her.

"This was the only way I could think of to get you on your own," he said, breaking the silence at last.

"Oh," she said, again, but her heart was jumping madly.

"You see, I've been dying to give you a proper kiss, and there's no way I can do that in the house."

Not sure of how she should reply, Renee kept her head down.

"Aren't you going to tell me what you think of that?" Fergus asked, pettishly. "Don't you want me to kiss you?"

"Yes, I do," she breathed, "but you said I wasn't old enough." She wished he'd stop speaking about it, and just do it.

"That was over a year ago, remember, and you've grown up quite a bit since then. Have you ever been kissed yet?"

"No." Feeling that she shouldn't have admitted that, she added, "I didn't want anybody else to kiss me, just you."

"That's more like it."

They had reached the foot of Watson Street, where the houses gave way to the railings of the Victoria Park, and, there being no one about, he led her through the gates, out of sight of the road, and put his arms round her.

Renee ran her tongue over her dry lips, and waited expectantly, not knowing if she was expected to do anything or not.

She hadn't long to wait. Fergus bent his head and placed his lips on hers, gently and experimentally, but removed them quickly. She was very disappointed. She'd felt no great thrill, and began to suspect that kissing wasn't all it was made out to be if this was the proper kiss Fergus had promised.

His second kiss dispelled all her doubts, and she gasped for breath when it was over. Her heart was pounding, her legs were trembling, and, before she had recovered, he was kissing her again . . . and again. His body was pressed tightly against hers, and his hands were sliding up and down her spine.

"Oh, Renee," he whispered. "You're wonderful."

They stood there for just over ten minutes, then Fergus said, "Come on. We'd better stop, before I do something I shouldn't."

She would willingly have stayed there for hours, although she shivered with cold when he removed his arms, but he took her hand and guided her back to the street. They walked hand in hand until they were almost home, then he stopped and turned her to face him.

"I can't come in with you, Renee," he said. "We don't want your mother to know about this, do we? I'll meet you next Monday."

"What about Wednesday?" she asked, hopefully. "That's my other night for the classes, Fergus."

"Sorry, but I play billiards with my pals every Wednesday . . . It'll have to be Mondays, I'm afraid." He walked away from her then, without even kissing her again, and she stood for a minute, frustrated, and rather indignant that he preferred playing billiards on Wednesdays to meeting her.

She let herself into the house, hung her coat on the hallstand and looked at herself in the mirror. Apart from being slightly flushed, she showed no sign of her experience in the park, but she went into the bathroom and splashed her face with cold water before she joined her mother.

"You're a wee bit later, tonight," Anne remarked.

"The shorthand teacher was showing us some new shapes, and we've to practise them for next week." The false excuse had come to her in a flash.

"See that you do, then."

Renee set off eagerly to her evening class the following Monday, but couldn't concentrate properly on the shorthand lesson for thinking about Fergus waiting for her when she went out. She wasn't disappointed in his kisses in the park this time, and when he drew away from her at last, she tried to pull him back.

"Please, Fergus, don't stop yet."

"This is getting too much for me, Renee," he said thickly, dropping his arms. "You're tormenting me, and making it harder." He laughed suddenly. "You've definitely made it hard."

She couldn't understand why he was laughing, because she could see nothing amusing in what he'd said, so she asked, "What's hard, Fergus?"

He put his hand under her chin and kissed her lightly. "You'll find out. Some day soon . . . very soon."

She had to be content with that, and they left the park to start their walk home.

Next evening, when she was alone with Jack Thomson in the dining room for a few minutes, he said to her, "I saw you walking up the road with Fergus last night. Watch yourself with him, Renee. Don't trust him, whatever he says, for he's fooling around with other girls as well."

"Don't be daft, Jack," she snapped, angry at having been seen, and angry with him for interfering. "Of course I trust him. He told me he's only going out with them till I'm old enough for him to ask out properly."

Jack frowned. "Don't believe him. He's a waster. I've heard a few stories about him, and I'm sorry I ever told him about the digs. His folk live in Aberdeen, you know, and they put him out, so I've been told."

"Jack Thomson, you're just jealous of Fergus with all the girlfriends he's had." Renee looked at him defiantly.

His responding glare softened suddenly into a long penetrating look which made her blush. "Aye," he said, quietly. "I am jealous, but not for all his other girls, just one."

"Oh." Renee felt uncomfortable, knowing he meant her. She liked Jack, she liked him quite a lot, but she couldn't flirt with him like she did with some of the boys at the classes. "Fergus is serious about me," she said, at last, "and I'm serious about him."

"Don't say I didn't warn you, then." Jack strode out of the room as Anne came in.

"What's wrong with him? He'd a face like thunder."

"Why should there be anything wrong with him?" Renee was still angry that Jack had said those awful things about Fergus.

"Well, he looked upset about something."

"I don't know what it is," Renee said, acidly, as she rose to clear the table. "What's happened to Fergus, tonight? He's a bit late, isn't he?"

"He came home early, and washed and dressed himself, and went out without his tea."

"Where was he going?" Renee half expected her mother to tell her it was none of her business, but she had to ask.

"How should I know? He doesn't tell me what he's doing." The sharpness of Anne's voice made Renee study her. Her mother was taking more care with her appearance these days, and had been brighter than usual recently. Could there be a special reason? Surely she wasn't . . . ? Surely Fergus hadn't . . . ? No, no! That was ridiculous. Then she remembered that Fergus had called her mother "Anne" the day they realised Uncle George wasn't coming back, and the seed of jealousy which had been sown at that time, but had lain dormant ever since, began to germinate.

He'd only been trying to be kind at that time, she thought, hastily. Later on, though, he'd said he admired George for going away, and that wasn't being kind to her mother. It was very puzzling, and she decided to ask Fergus about it when she met him next Monday. There was probably a perfectly reasonable explanation. There must be!

As soon as she came out of the grammar school the following week, she tackled him about the use of her mother's Christian name.

"Good God! What made you remember that? The day your uncle drove off into the sunset? But that's more than a year ago." Fergus laughed as he tucked her arm through his. "Let me think. I suppose it must have been hearing George calling her Anne. I didn't even realise I'd said it. You're not jealous of your own mother, are you? She's more than seventeen years older than me, for heaven's sake."

"I'm sorry." Renee was contrite. "I just couldn't help wondering about it, but it's all right now, and I won't be jealous any more."

"I bloody well hope not. I've enough on my plate just now without you starting. Lily's getting too serious for my liking, and I'm trying to shake her off."

"Lily?" Her newly assuaged fears were turned in another direction. "What about . . . Eleanor?"

"Eleanor's in the dim and distant past. There's been quite a few since Eleanor, but Lily's my Tuesday girl, the same as you're my Monday girl. See?"

"Fergus Cooper! You haven't got a different girl for every night of the week, have you?" Renee did her best to sound lighthearted, but her heart was as heavy as lead at being classed as one of his many conquests.

"I told you — it's only till you're older. You know we've to keep this a secret just now. Your mother would go mad if she thought you were going out with an old man of twenty-one, and you not long fifteen." His eyes were tender and appealing.

Renee believed him. She had to believe him, otherwise her life wouldn't be worth living. "I'm fifteen and eight weeks," she reminded him, as if the extra time made a difference.

"Look, I'll prove how much you mean to me." They had reached the park gates, so he took her in and guided her towards a clump of bushes near one of the huge trees. Taking off his coat, he spread it on the grass and pulled her down on to it.

"You're the only one I really love, honest," he whispered. "You know that, don't you?"

"Y . . . yes," she said, doubtfully, "but . . ."

"I just know." He laughed softly as he took her hand and slid it down his body. "That's what I meant was hard, last week. Feel it, it's sitting up and begging for you to let it out."

Now she understood, but she panicked suddenly when his hand crept under her skirt and up her thigh. "No, Fergus, please!"

"Say yes, Fergus, please." He was under her French knickers by this time, and his breathing, like hers, was a series of short gasps. "Say I'm the very first for you. I must be your first, Renee." He heaved himself on top of her and forced her legs apart.

Her fear of the unknown made her tense, so he moved himself around a little until, with a sigh, she relaxed to receive him. He entered her slowly, and when she moaned at the pain, exquisite though it was, he kissed her fiercely.

"It's all right, it's all right," he panted, thrusting deeper. "I won't hurt you, and you really like it, don't you?"

He climaxed very quickly and collapsed by her side, leaving her ashamed of the feelings he'd aroused in her, and which were still clamouring to be satisfied.

In a few minutes, he sat up. "Now you'll always belong to me, because I know I'm the first man to have you, and you're my Monday girl, because you're the first girl for me."

"Your first time, too?" Renee wanted to believe this, but needed his assurance that it was true.

He looked at her with a wry smile. "No, I can't say that. At my age, you couldn't expect me . . . I've had sex with quite a few girls, but you're the first, the most important to me, now, and Monday's the first day of the week, so that's why it's right that you're my Monday girl."

She smoothed down her clothing and sat up, still trembling, but he only kissed her gently before he pulled her to her feet to resume their homeward walk.

Later that night, Renee was glad she had her own single bed where she could relive the wonderful time in the park, the kisses, the words of love, the . . . She could feel Fergus there inside her, and desire for him rose again. It was a good thing her mother couldn't sense the innermost thoughts of her fifteen-year-old daughter, otherwise there would be trouble.

During the following evening, the girl was unable to settle to anything for thinking about Fergus out with Lily, his Tuesday girl. Over and over again, she consoled herself by remembering that he'd said he was trying to shake Lily off, but she kept torturing herself by imagining him doing to the other girl what he'd done to her the previous night. Jealousy ate into her very soul, like a canker, and she was sure she'd never be able to bear this uncertainty until she was old enough to tell her mother how she felt about him.

All through the winter and spring, they made love on Mondays in the Victoria Park; mad, passionate love, until Renee could hardly keep their secret to herself. She wanted the whole world to know how much she loved Fergus, and how much he loved her, but it wasn't possible, at her age.

Once she was sixteen, though, it would be different. After all, in Scots law, girls could marry at sixteen without parental consent, so she could make her feelings public and her mother couldn't do a thing about it. She meant to tell Fergus what she intended to do, but their time together was so precious, so intense, that she never remembered about it when they were alone, and there was no opportunity inside the house. The light summer nights made things more difficult for them, however, because he worried that someone might see them and pass the information on to Anne.

"I don't care who sees us," Renee said, indignantly, one night, annoyed that his fears were damping his ardour.

"It's you I'm thinking about, darling," he protested, but she was stung into action when he lay back, not having attempted to do anything except kiss and caress her. She surprised herself, and Fergus, by pulling him towards her again, and kissing him wildly until she felt him responding. His hands went willingly now to where she had ached for them, and he muttered, "You've asked for it, Renee, and by God you're going to get it."

His frenzied penetration alarmed her into fearing that he might rip her apart, but, in a few seconds, she, too, was caught up in a great tide of passion, and she forgot everything except the blinding need for the gratification of her desires.

"Oh, Fergus, I love you," she moaned, just before they peaked together.

"And I love you," he panted, digging his nails into her arm.

He had just turned on to his back again, when they heard footsteps coming along the path towards them, and he averted his head as a young couple passed. "I don't think it was anybody we know," he muttered as the sound of their feet died away, then he grinned. "God, that was good, Renee. We're absolutely made for each other." Her irritation at his first reaction vanished. They were made for each other, that was what was so wonderful for her.

That Wednesday was the last of her classes until after summer. She had forgotten, in the torrid passion of Monday night, to tell Fergus that they wouldn't be able to meet outside the grammar school until the evening classes resumed in October.

Over three months! She turned cold at the thought. She must find a way to keep their weekly assignations carrying on. Perhaps she could tell her mother that she was going out with a friend? That way, she could spend a few hours with her lover instead of the snatched twenty to thirty minutes they'd had until now, but she'd have to pave the way with her mother, and arrange it with Fergus. Letting him know was going to be almost impossible with the other three lodgers in the house, so the only way to do it would be to scribble a note to him, and to find an opportunity to give it to him before Monday.

On Thursday evening, when they were all seated round the dining-room table, she made her first real move into the sordid world of lies and deceit. "I met Phyllis Barclay when I came out of the office tonight, Mum. Remember, she was in my class at school?"

"Oh, yes." Anne waited until her mouth was empty before she went on. "You used to speak about her quite a lot. Where's she working these days?"

"She's in a solicitor's office in Bon Accord Square, and she gets better wages than me. She went to Webster's Day Classes for six months when she left school, so she's a shorthand-typist."

"You'll maybe have better wages than her, in the long run." Anne smiled. "You're getting yours up every year until you're twenty-four, so you should end up with a really good salary."

"I suppose so . . . Anyway, Phyllis asked if I'd go to the pictures with her on Mondays, now that my classes are finished." The falsehood tripped off her tongue as if by magic. She hadn't even thought of what she would say. She saw Fergus raise his eyebrows, but she couldn't explain to him. It was all in the little note tucked up her sleeve, and which she was intending to slip to him when no one was looking.

"That'll be nice for you," Anne remarked. "But, remember, I don't want you to be too late in coming home."

"OK, I'll remember. I'll come straight home every week." Renee rose to go through to the scullery to refill the teapot, and, as she passed behind her mother, she looked over to Fergus and pulled the edge of the note into view, to let him know what to expect. He couldn't give any sign that he had understood, because he was facing Anne, but she trusted that he had realised what she meant.

Later, when she saw her mother deep in conversation with Mike Donaldson, she looked enquiringly at Fergus, who gave a slight nod and puckered his lips in a make-believe kiss. She noticed then that Jack Thomson had seen the by-play and was frowning at her. She didn't care, it was none of his business what she did or who she went out with. Fergus remained at the table after the other boys left, so Renee was able to slide her piece of paper under his plate just before her mother came back into the room. He retrieved it at once and pushed back his chair.

"I'll have to hurry if I'm going to beat that three to the bathroom. I've to spruce myself up tonight — it's my Thursday girl." He laughed and winked as he went out.

Renee turned round quickly to see if her mother had noticed, and was horrified to see that Anne was right behind her, and was blushing like a young thing. My God, the girl thought, she must have believed he was winking to her.

Over the weekend, Renee was very excited at the prospect of a whole Monday evening with Fergus — a real date. He had slipped his reply into her hand on Friday, when she passed him in the dining-room doorway, and she'd gone into the bathroom to read it.

"Darling," it said. "Half past seven Monday outside Woolies. Love, Fergus."

She had been in a state of euphoria ever since, and her spirits were not in the least dampened on Monday morning, when she saw the rain lashing down. It couldn't last all day. Half past seven! Half past seven!

The words went round and round inside her head, even after she started work.

She kept glancing out of the window, but the rain hadn't stopped, then she remembered a little rhyme her granny used to say to her on wet days when she was a small girl.

Rainy, rainy, rattlestanes, dinna rain on me.
Rain on Johnny Groat's hoose, far across the sea.

She repeated the jingle to herself during the rest of the forenoon, crossing her fingers childishly whenever she could, to make sure it worked. It was still raining when she went home at lunchtime, but not quite so heavily, and by half past five it was off altogether. She'd been sure that it would be.

After teatime, she quickly helped her mother to clear up, then rushed to wash as soon as Jack came out of the bathroom, before anyone else went in. She dressed herself extra carefully in the green Grandholm flannel dress she had made at school, and which she kept for best. Then she rubbed a little Pond's Vanishing Cream into her face before powdering it and applying a touch of lipstick. She imagined that the Tango shade was a bit too orange for her, so she flapped her powder puff over her lips to tone it down.

Her hair had grown again and was curling under at the ends in a lovely stylish page-boy, but she swept the sides up and pinned them with kirbigrips. Perfume now. She hadn't used much of the "Evening in Paris" that Granny and Granda had given her at Christmas, so she tipped it on to her finger and dabbed it behind her ears.

Her heart was palpitating as she walked down the stairs. There was no sign of Fergus — he must be getting ready to meet her — but Jack's eyes lit up when she walked into the living room.

"You're looking really bonnie, Renee," he said. "I think it must be a lad you're going to the pictures with tonight."

She couldn't meet his admiring, teasing eyes. "Don't be daft. I don't have to be meeting a lad just because I've tried to make myself look nice."

"You don't have to try to look nice," he said softly, but Mike Donaldson came in at that moment and prevented him from saying anything else.

"If you hang on a minute, Jack," Mike said, "Tim's nearly ready, so we can all get the same bus."

Jack smiled pleasantly. "OK. There's no desperate rush for me. What time are you meeting your chum, Renee?"

"Half past seven, but I want to be there in plenty of time. I hate having to wait for other people, so I try never to be late myself. I'll just go and wait for the bus, in case you lot don't make it."

She'd been standing at the stop for a few minutes when she saw the bus coming, and heaved a sigh of relief that the three boys wouldn't be in time to catch it, but they came racing round the corner and jumped on as it was moving off.

"Phew! That was close." Jack was puffing as he took the seat beside Renee, while the two Donaldsons sat down in front of them, laughing breathlessly.

Tim turned round and spoke to Jack. "Is Fergus going out, or is he staying in again to keep Mrs Gordon company?"

Renee had noticed the amused glance that had passed between him and his brother, but she was afraid to look at Jack, though her stomach was sinking at what Tim had implied. "What d'you mean?" she demanded. "Do you think something's going on between Fergus and my mother?"

"Tim's just blethering." Jack's voice held a note of warning. "He should keep his stupid jokes to himself." Tim coloured as he turned to the front again.

Jack nudged the girl and laughed. "He's a great comic, Renee, take no notice of him. You know what he's like. Where are you meeting your pal?"

"Outside Woolies," she replied, without thinking, her mind still preoccupied by what Tim had hinted. Had Fergus really stayed at home with her mother all those other Mondays, before he met her at the classes?

She felt sick at the idea of what might have been going on, but tried to make excuses for him. He'd only been passing the time until half past nine, and he'd been sitting talking, that was all. She was his Monday girl; she was his first, most important one, not her mother.

Tim and Mike went off the bus at the stop before Woolworth's, and Renee wished that Jack had done the same. It would be awful if he came off at the same place as she did. But that was how it happened, and she wondered if this was where he had originally meant to go, or if he suspected the true identity of her "pal".

They crossed the tram lines on Union Street, and walked along until they came to the first entrance into the store which boasted "Nothing Over Sixpence".

"I'll just leave you, then," Jack remarked. "One of my mates works in the Club Bar in Market Street a few nights a week, and Monday's aye slack kind, so I promised I'd go in to keep him company." Whistling, he walked away. Renee was grateful for her narrow escape. He hadn't been checking up on her, after all. Not that it mattered, really, because he already knew how she felt about Fergus, but it was safer for her if he didn't find out about this meeting.

She watched the passers-by hurrying to keep a date, or strolling arm in arm already partnered. She felt very grown up, waiting for a boyfriend, and there were only a few weeks left until she'd be sixteen and could broadcast her love to the world, or, more specifically, to her mother.

When the next bus from Cattofield drew up, she watched hopefully, but Fergus didn't come off. Nor the next bus, nor the next. At eight o'clock, she walked a little bit along the pavement, to save people thinking she'd been stood up, but she kept turning round to watch the bus stop at the other side of the street. She was certain that he'd come, but why was he so late? Tim's remark came back to her, but she laughed it away. Fergus and her mother? Never in a million years!

The Town House clock had chimed quarter past before he ran round the back of a bus and across the street. "I wondered if you'd still be waiting," he said. "A button came off my only decent shirt, and your mother offered to sew it on."

Renee rejected the unwelcome thought that sewing on a button shouldn't have taken three quarters of an hour. "I thought you'd changed your mind," she pouted.

"Oh, no! My God, Renee, I've been counting the minutes till I could have you all to myself again. Your mother kept me speaking for a while, that's all, and I couldn't get away without being downright nasty to her."

His black eyes bored into hers, and her heart melted. She couldn't suspect him of . . . anything like Tim had suggested. It was impossible. "What are we going to do?" she asked brightly. "How about going to the Bay of Nigg? There shouldn't be so many folk there." He took her hand and led her back across Union Street to wait for a bus.

On the journey, Renee told him that her father used to take them to the Bay of Nigg in the car. "That was the Erskine that Uncle George had eventually, but it was my favourite evening run. Through Torry, down St Fittick's Road, then up past the lighthouse and the Torry Battery. Dad told us that it was full of soldiers during the war. I don't think he was ever there himself, though. He was mostly in France and Belgium."

"Your mother doesn't speak about him at all."

"She wouldn't, would she? It's a long time since he died — 1933, that's six years ago — and it would be like asking people to pity her, and she's not like that."

"No, she's not like that. Did he take you right round to Sinclair Road and into Torry again? Because that's what we'll be doing tonight."

"Yes, that's the way we always went, and it just used to take us about twenty minutes in the car."

Fergus smiled. "It'll take us a lot longer than that, though, going on our own feet."

"It was always my favourite run, but it'll be my extra-special place after this."

They were the only two people still on the bus when it reached the terminus, and the conductor winked knowingly when they went off. "The grass'll still be too wet for lying on."

"We'll find a dry bit, don't you worry." Fergus laughed and winked back.

Renee's face had turned red with the embarrassment of what they were meaning, and she was very relieved when the vehicle turned round immediately and went back towards the city centre. Fergus also seemed more relaxed now that they were away from the crowds, and slid his arm round her waist possessively.

The sea, to their right, foamed white and angry amongst the huge rocks in the bay, and the wind whipped their faces with a force built up during its uninterrupted passage from the north.

Renee shivered in her lightweight coat, so Fergus drew her closer against him. "I can see I'm going to have to heat you up, my little Monday girl," he murmured, then stopped to kiss her before they rounded the bend to Girdleness Lighthouse, where he led her off the road, towards its high surrounding wall. "If we stay at this side, we'll be away from the wind," he told her, "and it won't be so wet, being sheltered. I've been thinking about this since Thursday."

So had Renee, and she waited, trembling with expectancy as much as the cold, while he spread his coat on the still damp grass, then flopped down and held his hand out to her. She lay down beside him, to be transported away from their wild surroundings by his searching and equally wild love-making. After it was over, they lay for a few minutes, then Fergus stood up. "It's getting too cold now. Come on, my darling, my first day of the week, first before anyone else, Monday girl. We'll walk right round and into town, then it'll be time for you to go home. The pictures would be coming out about half past ten, so you should be home about the right time if we put a step in."

The girl would have been quite happy to stay there and let him make love to her over and over again. She felt that she could never have too much of it. She was the luckiest girl in the world to have such a lover. Who else but Fergus would ever have thought of making love in the shadow of a lighthouse?

"Come on, Renee," he said. "If we don't get moving, you'll be late, and your mother won't let you out again."

That was true, she realised, so, not wishing to jeopardise her future opportunities of being with him like this, she jumped up, and they carried on walking along the barren road. When they reached Market Street, Fergus stopped. "One of my pals lives over there, Renee. You'll manage to get the bus OK if I drop in on him for a while, won't you? I can't take you right home, anyway."

She was disappointed that he wasn't going to see her on the bus, or even just to the bus stop, but tried not to let it show. "I'll manage," she said, forlornly, and watched him as he walked across the street and disappeared inside the doorway of a high tenement.

Before she turned to carry on up the hill, a familiar voice spoke softly behind her. "So it was Fergus, after all." Whipping round, Renee saw that she'd been standing in front of the Club Bar, and Jack Thomson must have seen and heard them.

"I thought it might be," he added, wryly, "but I thought you'd have more sense than to be taken in by him."

"You've been spying on me!" She felt very indignant. "Why can't you leave me alone, Jack Thomson? It's nothing to do with you if I want to go out with Fergus or anybody else."

"I wish it was. And I wasn't spying on you. I came out with Alfie, that's him up there, and I saw Fergus leaving you, so I thought I'd better take you home." She tried to shake off his hand, but he gripped her elbow firmly as he took her up on to Union Street. "It's not a very great place for a young lassie to be walking about on her own at this time of night," he added.

She sat in the bus, silent and resentful, and when Jack glanced at her, she became conscious of her creased skirt and untidy hair. He would know what she'd been doing with Fergus. What could he be thinking of her?

He spoke then, apologetically. "Look, Renee. I know it's none of my business, as you told me yourself, but you're a young, decent girl, and I don't like to see him making a fool of you."

"Fergus isn't making a fool of me!" She was angry now.

Jack carried on with his lecture. "You've never come up against anybody like him before, and no more had I till I came to the town to work, but I'm telling you, he's bad, through and through. He's only playing with you, like a fisherman plays with a fish, and once he's caught you, he'll throw you back and start trying to catch some other young, innocent lassie to do the same to her."

Renee's temper had been rising all the time he was speaking, and she burst out now, her eyes blazing, although she tried to keep her voice low to prevent the other passengers hearing, "You're just jealous because he's had a lot of girlfriends and you haven't any, but he's only serious about me, not any of the rest of them. He told me that himself."

"He's a liar, and you shouldn't believe him."

"I know he's telling me the truth, and he's only going out with them till my mother agrees to him going with me. When I'm sixteen, it'll all be out in the open, and you'll all see it's me he really loves. He won't need any other girls once I'm old enough."

Jack shook his head. "Oh, Renee, Renee. That's the trouble. You're not old enough to understand what he's at. You said I was jealous. Well, I *am* jealous, and angry, but it wouldn't be so bad if it was a decent bloke you were going out with — somebody that would respect you and treat you right — but Fergus . . . That's it. I'm saying no more. I've warned you, and that's all I can do." He ran his fingers through the front of his hair, making his quiff stick up jauntily. "I'm only trying to save you from getting hurt, for you *will* be hurt if you carry on with him."

The silence which fell between them then lasted until they went into the house, but, when she switched on the hall light to hang up her coat, he whispered, "There's grass in your hair."

She went into the bathroom, without any word of thanks for the warning, and combed out the offending green blades, then poked her head round the living-room door. "I'm going to bed, Mum. I don't want anything to eat."

She went upstairs, sure that Jack would keep her secret, but her confidence in her lover was wavering. Jack had seemed so sure of what he was saying, yet she didn't want to believe him. She undressed slowly, her thoughts in a feverish turmoil. Fergus wasn't a liar. If he said that she was the one he loved, it must be true. He was only going out with the other girls for company. Jack was making it all up, out of jealousy. But a niggling doubt had arisen in her mind. He'd said that once Fergus caught her, he would drop her and start with some other innocent girl. Was that why he had been so anxious to be her very first? Was that what he did? Did he try to be the very first for every girl he went out with? No! No! That was a horrible thing to be thinking.

By the time Anne came to bed, Renee was reassuring herself by recalling all the declarations of love which Fergus had made to her. Once a week for months he had said that she was the only one for him, that she was the first, most important one. He couldn't have been lying all that time . . . could he?

Her doubts vanished next morning as soon as Fergus Cooper looked at her. His love for her seemed to shine out of his dark eyes, and Renee was sure that the others must see it, but she wanted to prove to Jack that he hadn't succeeded in making her stop her relationship with Fergus.

"Phyllis was really pleased that I'll be going out with her every Monday, Mum," she said, clearly, for the benefit of both Jack and Fergus. "You see, her other chum doesn't like the same kind of pictures as she does, but I do."

"That's nice." Anne was smiling. "It'll do you good to enjoy yourself for a change, after going to the classes twice a week all the winter."

Renee noticed that Fergus had looked down at his plate, and that Jack was regarding her with a touch of contempt, but fortunately Tim created a diversion.

"Your classes have definitely stopped, have they, Renee?"

"Yes, till the beginning of October." She eyed him suspiciously. "Why were you asking?"

A broad grin came over Tim's face. "Well, you see, Mike's met this girl, and he wants . . ."

"A girlfriend? Oh, Mike, that's great." Renee turned to smile at the shy, red-faced young man. "Have you asked her out?"

"Eh . . . aye." Mike fiddled with his knife.

"That's the trouble," Tim chuckled. "He's not a lady's man like Fergus there, so he's asked her to the Palais in a foursome, with me and . . . you, Renee, if you'll come?"

"Oh." Renee felt most embarrassed. This was a complication she hadn't foreseen, and she couldn't think how to extricate herself. "But I can't . . ."

"Yes, you can." Anne leaned forward eagerly. "It's time you started mixing socially with boys, and you know Tim well enough by this time, surely?"

Renee was desperate. "It's not that, Mum. It's . . . oh, Tim, I don't think . . ."

"I'm not going to eat you," Tim said quickly. "It's for Mike's sake I'm asking, so he can build up his confidence."

"You'll have to go with them, Renee, or else you'll spoil things for Mike." Anne frowned at her daughter then turned to Tim. "When's this double date coming off?"

It crossed Renee's mind, then, that if her mother was encouraging her to go out with Tim, she could hardly object to her going out with Fergus, so this might be a good move. "Next Monday," Tim was saying. "If that's all right with you, Renee?" He looked at her appealingly. "I know you said you'd arranged to meet your chum, but you could phone her at her work and explain, couldn't you?"

Fergus stood up. “Yes, Renee, you should go with them. You’ve got to start going out with boys sometime.”

Anne smiled to him. “She’ll maybe listen to you, Fergus.”

Renee was deeply hurt until she realised that he might have been thinking along the same lines as herself, that there would be no problem about him asking her out after this. “OK. I’ll phone Phyllis and cancel next Monday.”

Tim rubbed his hands together in glee. “That’s all settled, then. Mike, you’re on your way with . . . what was her name?”

“Babs Sandison,” his brother mumbled, his face even redder than before. “Thanks, Renee. Once I get this first date past, I won’t feel so tongue-tied. It’s just . . . oh, I’m sorry for being such a big sheep.”

Everyone laughed, good-natured Mike as loudly as any of them, then Anne pushed her chair back. “Once Renee gets *her* first date past, maybe she’ll think about getting a steady boyfriend.” She winked to Tim to let him know that she would be quite happy if he was the one, then piled the cups, saucers and plates on the tray.

Renee picked up the sugar bowl and the milk jug and followed her mother through to the scullery. “I thought you’d say I was too young to be going out with boys.” She wanted to hear Anne commit herself irrevocably, and she was pleased when Jack Thomson carried in the teapot. He could be her witness.

Anne laughed. "You'll soon be sixteen, and as long as you don't start getting serious about anybody, I'm all for it."

She went back to the dining room, leaving Renee almost jumping with joy. It was going to be all right. She'd be able to date Fergus openly very soon. She gradually became conscious that Jack was still standing beside her. He deposited the teapot on the draining board and turned to her. "I'm glad you've agreed to go out with Tim, and remember, I'll be available if you want another date." He walked away, whistling merrily.

Renee wished with all her heart that it had been Fergus who had come through to ask her out. Her mother would have to agree now. But that was still to come. It *would* come!

CHAPTER SIX

Several times during the week, Renee had doubts about accepting Tim's invitation. It wasn't that she didn't like him — nobody could help liking him — but he was a bit too young. He was still only eighteen, a boy, really, and she preferred men at least six years older than she was. And what if he took it for granted that she'd want to make the outing a regular thing? She couldn't tell him she loved Fergus, not yet, so it would be difficult to turn Tim down without offending him. She was piqued that Fergus had shown no signs of jealousy, although it would have been difficult for him in front of her mother, but he could surely have given her just one little hint of it.

On Friday evening, when Peter and Maggie McIntosh paid their weekly visit and asked how things were, Anne smiled. "Everything's just fine here. Mike's found himself a girl, and Renee's going out with Tim on Monday night."

The girl butted in quickly, to save any misunderstanding. "It's only a foursome with Mike and his girlfriend, Granny."

Maggie's face creased into a smile. "It's a start, ony road, an' I'm real pleased to hear it. Ye could dae a lot worse for yersel' than Tim Donaldson."

At that moment, Fergus poked his head round the door, and beamed at the visitors. "I'm off, folks."

Maggie frowned. "Like him, for instance."

"I don't know what you've got against Fergus, Mother." Anne looked displeased. "He's really very nice."

The older woman said no more about him, but when Renee walked a little bit with them on their way home, Maggie said, "You stick to Tim, lassie, or Jack, but ha'e nothin' to dae wi' that Fergus. I can see through him if yer mother canna."

Her granddaughter's laugh was somewhat forced. "Oh, you. You've got some stupid ideas, Granny, and I'm not intending to stick to Tim. I'm only going out with him as an obligement to Mike. He was too shy to go on his own, that's why we're going in a foursome."

Peter stopped his wife from upsetting the girl further by remarking, "It looks like rain, Maggie. We'd best get hame."

On Monday morning, the girl was still debating whether she'd made the right decision, but the more she considered it — going dancing was one of her old dreams coming true — the more she found herself looking forward to it.

Her excitement mounted all through their evening meal, in spite of her earlier misgivings. She had never possessed a dance frock, but her mother had unearthed one of her old ones — so old that it was almost back in fashion — which Renee had altered until it fit her perfectly. She could hardly wait to put it on, and rushed to get ready as soon as she could. When she came out of the bathroom, Fergus was waiting and handed her a slip of paper before he went in to wash, so she unfolded it as soon as she went upstairs. He'd written only five words: "Remember you're my Monday girl." She stuffed the note into her handbag, to be read again later before she destroyed it. It was too dangerous to keep these little billets-doux, in case her mother found them, and, in any case, she needed no reminding.

She slipped the lemon taffeta dress over her head and fastened the three tiny pearl buttons at the back of the neck, then stepped up to the old wardrobe to look at herself in the full-length mirror. The silvering had worn off in places, but, even in the far-from-ideal reflection, the effect was satisfactory.

The loose, cape-like sleeves, which she'd fashioned out of the original, tight long ones, came to just below her shoulders, and showed her arms to their best advantage. The bodice was pin-tucked with an edging of lace round the neck, and the waist fit snugly, giving her a smooth, slenderly curved neatness before the gores of the skirt opened out over her hips. It was unbelievable the difference it made to her appearance.

She pirouetted daintily and the fullness swirled around her legs, rustling against the fully fashioned silk stockings her mother had lent her. No one could ever guess that this lovely creation was a make-down, it was so beautiful, and there wouldn't be another one like it.

She brushed her fair hair until it shone, then applied some make-up. The tango shade of the lipstick, the only one she possessed, went well with the deep lemon of the dress — oranges and lemons, came the childish thought — and she felt on top of the world as she went down the stairs.

Mike and Tim, in navy pinstripe suits, were waiting for her, and Tim said, "What a transformation. You look like a fairy doll. I'll be scared to touch you in case you break."

She flashed a smile at him, delighted with his admiration, and slipped into the coat he held up for her. Then he took her hand and they followed Mike out. Renee hoped that Fergus was watching from the window. It might make him jealous enough to ask her out in front of everyone in future.

The Palais de Danse impressed her — the lights, the glittering decor, the whole heady atmosphere. The fourpiece band was playing a quickstep when the two girls came out of the cloakroom, and Mike danced off with Babs Sandison, but Renee looked apprehensively at Tim.

"I can't dance, you know," she said sorrowfully. "This is the first time I've ever been."

He smiled reassuringly. "I know that, but it's really easy and you'll soon pick it up. The quickstep's just slow, slow, quick, quick, slow, and the slow foxtrot's the same, only slower." He laughed as he put his arm round her in a firm hold and swung her out on to the dance floor.

Under Tim's expert guidance, she was soon following his steps without having to think about it, and she thrilled at the marvellous sensation of moving in perfect unison with him. When he saw that she was relaxed and coping well, he loosened his grip on her.

"Jack tells me you've been meeting Fergus on the q.t."

"He'd no right telling anybody," Renee snapped, hoping that Tim wasn't going to spoil her evening by warning her off Fergus, too, like Jack and Granny.

"It's up to you, Renee, but Jack's really worried about you, and I don't like the idea much myself. He's a proper lady-killer, Fergus, and not all that fussy how he treats them, either."

"I'd rather not discuss it, Tim, if you don't mind." Her voice was cold.

"OK. 'Nuff said. What d'you think of the Palais?"

"It's super! A great band. Do you come here often?"

Tim burst out laughing and had to explain to her, "It's usually the boy who says that, when he's dancing with a girl he's just met, but don't worry about it. Aye, Mike and me have been coming here nearly every week for a few months now." During the break, the foursome sat together and had iced drinks to cool them down after their exertions.

"Are you enjoying yourself, Renee?" Babs asked.

"Oh, yes, and dancing's not nearly so difficult as I thought it would be."

Mike was also more at ease now. "You've got a fine teacher, though. Tim's reckoned to be a very good dancer."

Tim slipped his arm round Renee's shoulder. "You're only saying that because it's true, Mike, but she's a quick learner, this girl, and I can hardly wait for a tango, to see what she makes of that."

When the band struck up again, Mike took Renee up to the slow foxtrot. "I'm glad you came with us," he said, when she got into the rhythm of it. "Tim's quite shy underneath, though he clowns around a bit to cover it up. He's been wanting to ask you out for ages, but he couldn't pluck up the courage. You'd be better with him than Fergus, you know."

"Oh, Mike. Not you, too?"

"Sorry. I didn't mean to say anything, it just slipped out. What d'you think of Babs?"

"She's nice, Mike. I like her a lot."

"So do I."

Tim had been dancing with Babs, but when they all returned to the side, and the lilting music of a tango began, he pulled Renee back on to the dance floor. "Now then, my fine beauty, let's see how you manage with this. You've to act the goat a bit, but we'll have a wee practice in a corner, first."

She felt self-conscious to begin with, but soon mastered his intricate footwork, and they mingled with the other dancers, exaggerating their steps until they ended up giggling. All too soon, the last waltz was announced. "Have you really enjoyed yourself, Renee?" Tim laid his cheek against hers under the dimmed lights.

"Oh, yes. I never thought dancing would be like this."

He tightened his arm round her waist. "We could maybe do it again some time? Just you and me? I don't think Mike'll need us, after this, he seems to be doing fine with Babs."

"I'll think about it, Tim." Content with that, he grabbed her hand after she collected her coat. They had to walk all the way home, because it was well after time for a bus, but he kept up a running fusillade of jokes, and it didn't seem long.

When they neared their street, Tim halted, and gently maneouvred her against a wall. "Wait a minute, Renee. There's something I've been wanting to do all evening."

As his head came towards her, she turned her face away. "No, Tim. Don't spoil everything now."

He looked at her quizzically. "Don't you think I deserve just one teeny weeny kiss for teaching you to dance?"

His eyebrows were raised so high that she laughed and gave in. "I suppose you do." She planted a light kiss on his cheek, but he brought his hands up to steady her head, and kissed her firmly on the lips.

"That wasn't so bad, was it?" He was joking, but his eyes were serious for once. She had actually quite enjoyed it, and, looking at him now, eyes regarding her affectionately, one lock of blond wavy hair falling over his forehead, she decided that he was really quite good-looking, though she'd never noticed it before, being so involved with Fergus. She let him kiss her again, then drew back to catch her breath.

Hugging her tightly, he murmured, "You're a lovely girl, Renee. Too nice to waste yourself on a rotter like . . ."

She stiffened. "Tim, not again."

"Sorry, but I can't help it. He makes my blood boil. I wouldn't play around if you were my girl."

"Well, I'm not your girl, and I understand why Fergus plays around, as you put it."

He looked apologetic. "Forget I said anything, please. I've enjoyed my night out with you, and you turned out to be quite a good little dancer."

"Only quite good?" She pretended to be offended, but was relieved that he'd stopped criticising Fergus.

"You could be very good, after more practice with me." His forefinger traced the outline of her lips. "D'you know what they say? Generous mouth, loving heart."

"Tim Donaldson! Are you telling me I've got a big mouth?" She laughed, to show that she knew he wasn't.

"You've got a perfect mouth. Perfect for kissing." He kissed her again to prove it — a long, melting kiss, which made her heart pound in spite of herself.

"Well, well! Love's young dream!" The sneering voice belonged to Fergus, who was standing behind Tim with a nasty smile on his face. "You might have taken her to somewhere more private, Tim. Under a lamp post? I could see you from away down the road."

"Fergus, it's not what it looks like," Renee pleaded, mortified that he'd caught her out like this. "There's nothing in it, is there, Tim?"

"Apparently not." Only then did he let his arms drop.

She knew that she'd hurt him deeply, but was so confused she couldn't think how to extricate herself from the awkward situation. "I'm sorry, Tim," was all she could say. She trailed behind them as Fergus led the way round the corner to the house.

"I found these two lovebirds kissing and canoodling back there," he announced to Anne, who was still sitting by the fireside, although it was nearly two o'clock in the morning.

Muttering "Goodnight", Tim went straight upstairs.

"You sounded a wee bit jealous." Anne looked keenly at Fergus as he flopped down on the settee, but he snorted with derision.

"Jealous? Me? That'll be the day! I just thought you wouldn't be very keen on the idea of them kissing, and God knows what else, when she's only fifteen."

Renee's eyes flashed. "I wish you wouldn't speak about me as if I wasn't here, Fergus, and we were only kissing."

She slammed the living-room door as she went out, but could hear Fergus and her mother still laughing when she was in bed, and felt like weeping at the injustices of life. Why did he have to turn up at that particular time? In another few minutes, they'd probably have been inside the house. Now everyone would all be laughing in the morning about how she'd been caught kissing Tim in the street, and what would Jack think of her, after she'd told him she loved Fergus?

And Fergus himself must be upset, although he'd tried to joke about it to her mother. He wouldn't want to have anything more to do with her after this, and he was only laughing now to cover up the hurt he'd suffered because his Monday girl had cheated on him, for that's what he must think. She could feel sorry for poor Tim, as well. She shouldn't have let him kiss her, although she'd enjoyed it at the time. Now he'd be thinking she'd just been making a fool of him, after he'd been so kind to her at the Palais.

She closed her eyes and pretended to be asleep when her mother came to bed, but lay awake for hours, worrying about the terrible tangle she'd landed herself in. And, try as she would, she could see no way of getting herself out of it.

CHAPTER SEVEN

It was late next morning when Renee rose, but she couldn't have eaten breakfast in any case, with this awful sickness still gnawing at the pit of her stomach. The four lodgers were leaving when she went down, but neither Jack nor Tim spoke to her, and Mike just murmured, "Morning, Renee," as he went out.

Fergus, last as usual, wore an annoying smirk. "Farewell, Delilah."

"Don't tease her, Fergus." Anne's voice was sharp.

His dark smouldering eyes turned on her. "Sorry, Anne," he said, before following the others outside. It was as if he'd thrust a dagger into Renee's already bruised heart. He'd said "Anne" again. He'd done it on purpose, this time, and if his intention had been to wound her, he'd succeeded perfectly.

"Don't worry," her mother said, kindly. "He'll stop tormenting you in a day or two."

Renee's work suffered that morning, her mind being on her own troubles, and Miss Esson had to reprimand her twice.

"Problems with a boyfriend?" whispered Sheila Daun, the other clerkess. She was a tall, slim redhead, with brown eyes now looking sympathetically at Renee.

"Yes." The girl felt she had to confide in someone. "Two of them, actually."

"Two? Tell me more."

"Well, you see, we've got four lodgers in our house, and . . ."

"Four? God, you lucky thing!"

"They're all very nice, but I'm in love with Fergus Cooper. He's very nearly twenty-two, and he's only waiting till I'm older before he tells Mum he loves me. And I only agreed to go out with Tim Donaldson in a foursome because Mike was too shy to go out with Babs on his own."

"That's as clear as mud," Sheila giggled, "but go on. How old's this Tim, by the way?"

"Not long eighteen, and quite good-looking."

"How good-looking?"

"Blond, wavy hair and blue eyes, but Fergus's hair's black and curly, and his eyes are dark, dark brown, and his teeth are lovely, and . . . oh, he's just perfect."

Sheila grinned. "You've really got it bad, haven't you? And if you're not wanting Tim, I wouldn't refuse if you passed him over to me. But what's the problem?"

"Mike saw Babs home from the Palais, so Tim had to take me home by himself."

"So? What was wrong with that?"

"Well, I let him kiss me a few times because I'd enjoyed dancing with him, and, of course, Fergus just happened to come past and saw us. Now he's being sarcastic about it, and I don't suppose he'll ever want to go out with me again."

“Ah, now I understand. But what’s your mother saying about you going out with two boys at your age?” Sheila was intrigued by the situation.

Suddenly ashamed, Renee’s eyes dropped. “She doesn’t know I go out with Fergus. He started meeting me after the evening classes last October, but now I tell her I’m going to the pictures with a girl I went to school with.” She dabbed away a tear which was trickling down her cheek.

“Secret assignations? And you’ve never told me before? God, Renee, you’re a dark horse.” There was grudging admiration in Sheila’s eyes, but she suddenly voiced the question which was niggling at the back of Renee’s own mind. “But why can’t Fergus ask you out openly? If your Mum thinks you’re old enough to go out with Tim, she couldn’t have any objections to you going with Fergus. It’s not as if he was somebody she didn’t know. That would have been different. I can’t see why he doesn’t ask her. Unless he’s scared she’d think he’s too old for you.”

The old suspicion returned. If something *was* going on between her mother and Fergus, he’d hardly be likely to ask her if he could take her daughter out.

Sheila carried on, quite unaware of the hornets’ nest she was stirring up. “He maybe doesn’t want to take you out openly at all. There are some men like that, you know, who get a bigger thrill when everything’s underhand, and prefer young innocent girls, until they’re not innocent any longer.”

This was so near to what Tim and Jack had been hinting that Renee burst into tears. “No, no. It’s not like that at all. Fergus really loves me. He told me I'm his Monday girl . . ." She stopped — Sheila would never understand about his other girlfriends. "I mean," she sobbed, "he says I'm the first girl for him, and . . ."

"He told you he's never had a girlfriend before? At his age? Do you honestly believe that?"

Sheila had jumped to the wrong interpretation of the words "first girl" and Renee deemed it best not to enlighten her. To mention the other girls he went out with would show Fergus in a poor light to anyone who didn't understand him like she did.

"I believe what he tells me," she said evasively, scrubbing her eyes with her damp handkerchief. "He wouldn't tell me lies. He loves me."

Sheila grimaced, but her eyes were full of pity. "I've heard that love's blind, but you're burying your head in the sand, Renee. Still, it's your lookout. You'd better go and wash your face, or old Bill will be wondering what's wrong."

Old Bill, as the girls affectionately called Mr Murchie, the manager, had already noticed the little scene through the glass walls of his small office, but he was a warm-hearted man with a seventeen-year-old daughter of his own, and guessed that Renee Gordon was probably upset because of some boy, so he said nothing, and was pleased to see the girl emerge from the cloakroom in a few minutes, looking more composed.

"She's a bonnie wee thing," he remarked to Miss Esson, who was going over some figures with him. "But she'll likely think her heart's broken a few times before she settles down."

"No doubt," the cashier replied dryly. "Are you ready to carry on?" They bent their heads to their work again.

On the way home at teatime, Renee was dreading the teasing she would have to face, but Sheila's last words to her, before she left the office, were making her think.

"Enjoy yourself, Renee," the other girl had said. "Go out with lots of boys and make this Fergus jealous. Maybe that'll bring him to his senses and force him to make everything above-board."

She might just try it. Nothing could be worse than the muddle things were in at present.

At the table, however, no one mentioned the previous night's indiscretion. She was too embarrassed to look at Tim, but Jack, sitting next to her, caught her hand under the tablecloth and gave it a quick, sympathetic squeeze. She returned the pressure to show that she was grateful, but glanced at Fergus in case he had noticed.

No one else happened to be looking in his direction at the time, and he surprised her by puckering up his lips in the make-believe kiss that he sometimes made for her. It was all right. He wasn't angry with her any longer. The relief of that, and her lack of breakfast, gave her a hearty appetite, and, the talk being quite general, she was able to enjoy the meal after all.

Mike Donaldson was the first to make a move. "I'd better get washed and dressed. I'm meeting Babs again tonight."

"No chaperones required this time, then?" Fergus laughed to hide his sarcasm.

Mike smiled pleasantly. "Not now. We got on like a house on fire when I saw her home last night."

"Tim and Renee got on like a house on fire last night as well, of course." Fergus just couldn't resist the dig.

Unexpectedly, Tim answered for himself as he stood up, his hair falling over his brow again. "Aye, Fergus, we did that, till you came and poked your nose in."

Fergus smirked. "I'm sorry I spoiled your little bit of fun for you, Tim." Renee saw Tim's hands clenching, but Anne stepped in before there was a nasty scene.

"Leave it, Fergus. You promised me. There's nothing wrong in Tim kissing Renee, is there?"

He assumed a hang-dog expression. "No, Anne, I suppose not. Sorry again. Me and my big mouth."

Tim turned and walked out; Anne picked up the empty tureen and casserole dish and Jack held the door open for her before he followed her through.

Fergus leaned towards Renee and whispered, "But you liked him kissing you, didn't you?"

His sneer caught her on the raw. "Yes, I did. So what?" She kept her eyes on the plates she was stacking on the tray.

"So warn him off, or else you won't be my Monday girl any more." His brows were down as he pushed his chair back, but he was on his feet and smiling when Anne returned. Renee carried out the tray, but curiosity made her stop in the hall. She wanted to hear what Fergus and her mother would say to each other when they were alone.

"I told you not to tease them." Anne's voice was low and angry. "I know Renee thinks she's in love with you — I've seen the cow's eyes she makes at you when she thinks I'm not looking — but I don't want you encouraging her. I've warned you what I'd do if I found out you were trying anything on with her behind my back."

"Tell her, then." Fergus sounded cocky. "She won't believe you, anyway."

"Fergus, please don't be so cruel." Anne was pleading now. "You know I'm jealous of her as far as you're concerned."

He laughed then. "You've no reason to be jealous of Renee, my dear Anne. She's only a kid, and I've told you before — you're my Monday girl, remember. The first woman in my life."

Renee's legs almost buckled under her as she turned to walk across the hall. It was true. There *was* something going on between Fergus and her mother — much more than she'd ever suspected or imagined. They must have been making love every Monday, before he'd come to the grammar school at half past nine, and . . . Oh, it was horrible!

The sickness had returned to her stomach, a thousand times worse than ever before, and, by the time she had walked through the living room into the scullery, she felt like going back and bursting in to confront them, to shout to her mother that it was she, Renee, who was his Monday girl, and that Fergus was in love with her. But it was as if she were chained to the spot, and she doubted if her legs would have carried her, anyway.

In a few minutes, Anne came through with the rest of the dishes, and started drying what Renee had already washed. The girl watched surreptitiously as her mother laid each item past. She was still an attractive woman, her figure perhaps a little on the plump side now, and she had given her hair a henna rinse lately, so it didn't look so mousey, just thick and healthy. She had stopped wearing black altogether, and the blue jumper and skirt really suited her. She must want to look good for Fergus, Renee thought, because she never slopped around in old clothes when he was there, and appeared to have new clothes all of a sudden. Maybe he'd even bought them for her. And she looked very pleased with herself now, so he must have kissed her . . . or something.

The more the girl let her imagination run riot, the deeper the pain bored into her, and she was willing to clutch at anything to ease the terrible gnawing at her heart. Fergus couldn't possibly love her mother. She was an old woman, thirty-nine on her next birthday, and he would only be twenty-two in a week or two. Maybe her mother was in love with him, but he definitely couldn't be in love with her. He had only one love in his life, a girl only six years younger than he was, Renee herself. She had to believe that. Her life would be meaningless if she thought he loved anyone else.

She dried her hands when she finished washing up, and went into the living room, where Jack and Tim were playing cards at a small, green-baize-covered table.

"Oh, good," Tim said. "We're fed up playing Pelmanism, and my memory's like a sieve. Would you and your mother sit in so we can have a few hands of rummy or whist?"

"You'd better ask her yourself," Renee replied, abruptly.

"Ask her what?" Anne came in, pulling down her sleeves.

"Would you like to play whist with us, Mrs Gordon?" Tim gathered up the cards, hopefully. "Mike's out with his Babs, and Fergus is going out as well, but Renee and you could make up a four."

"Righto." Anne drew in another chair, to sit opposite Jack, leaving Renee to partner Tim.

The girl couldn't concentrate on which cards had already been played, because she'd remembered that this was Tuesday — Lily's night, if Fergus hadn't succeeded in brushing her off — and also because of her bitter thoughts against her mother, but Tim never once reprimanded her for the stupid mistakes she made, and Jack happily counted up the scores in a little notebook.

They played for over two hours, and neither Mike nor Fergus were home when Renee went to bed at ten past ten, her eyes heavy with the sleep she had lost the night before. Her tortured thoughts gave way quite soon to the deep slumber of youth, which caught up with her in spite of herself, and she never heard her mother coming to bed, nor the two men coming in.

On Wednesday morning, she scribbled a short note to Fergus before she went down to breakfast, asking him to meet her somewhere to talk, and managed to hand it to him, unobserved, when she cleared the table.

It was Thursday at teatime before he gave her an answer. "Darling Monday girl — Monday 7.30 same place. *All* my love, Fergus."

Her first reaction was anger that he was making her wait until Monday, and that he had called her his Monday girl after what he'd said to her mother. She wouldn't go! That would show him! Or perhaps she should leave him waiting for a long time, like she'd been made to wait the last time. But she was afraid that Fergus wouldn't wait if she was late, and she loved him too much not to keep the appointment. Then she looked at the last four words on the note again. "*All* my love, Fergus" and the "All" was underlined. Her spirits soared upwards. It was just a mistake about her mother, wasn't it? There must be a perfectly reasonable explanation for what she'd overheard, possibly misheard, and she stifled the doubt which remained in her besotted heart as quickly as she could.

That evening Fergus was out, but the other three young men were in the living room when their landlady and her daughter finished tidying up. "Does anybody fancy going out for a walk?" Tim looked round them all expectantly. "It's too fine a night to be sitting inside."

Renee would have loved to get a breath of fresh air on the lovely July evening, but hesitated to go alone with Tim, after what had happened on Monday.

Jack stood up. "I'm on. How about you, Mike?"

"No, I think I'll stay where I am. My library book's due back tomorrow." Mike stretched out his legs.

"Renee?" Tim was standing beside Jack.

"OK then." She felt safer with Jack going along, too.

"Mrs Gordon? I'm sure you'd like to have the cobwebs blown off you?" Tim looked at her questioningly.

Anne shook her head. "No, Tim. Thanks all the same, but I've some mending to do, and a few other things to attend to, and the back grass needs cutting."

"I'll do that for you." Mike smiled lazily. "After I've had a half an hour's rest. It won't take me long to give it a run over with the mower."

Anne looked relieved. "Thanks, Mike, if you're sure you're not too tired?"

"I'm not really tired, just bone idle." Mike laughed and pretended to yawn.

"Right, then." Tim stepped forward and stood with his back to Jack and Renee. "Troops . . . forward . . . march!"

They "marched' off, laughing, as Mike said quietly, "I think it won't be long before we'll all be marching off . . . to war."

"Oh, surely not," Anne said. "It'll never come to that."

Outside, Tim turned to Jack. "What about taking the bus to the Bay of Nigg and walking right round, back to Torry?"

Jack nodded eagerly. "That's a good idea. We'll get a right blow of fresh air down there."

Renee remembered, with an ashamed lurch of her insides, what she had been doing the last time she was there with Fergus. But it was a lovely walk, and there were two young men with her. Safety in numbers, they said, and neither Tim nor Jack knew about what had gone on beside the lighthouse.

When they set off on the walk along her favourite part of Aberdeen, the sea air was bracing, and the smell of the tangle lying on the rocks was so refreshing that she stepped out briskly alongside her two escorts. They were joking and giggling as they approached Girdleness, but she felt herself tensing up, and her inner guilt made her giggle more. They walked past the gates and she glanced idly along the side of the wall, where she had lain on the damp grass with Fergus. Her involuntary gasp made her companions follow her gaze, and Tim let out a long, low whistle.

"Wow! That's Fergus, and he's fairly enjoying himself."

Jack grasped Renee's arm. "I'm sorry, lass. God, I'm sorry. I wish we'd never come down here . . . I never thought . . . Oh, Renee!" He pulled her along the road, while Tim, looking contrite, hurried after them.

"I'm sorry, Renee. I clean forgot about you and him. The last thing I'd want to do is hurt you like that." Feeling that her heart had stopped altogether, she tried to keep the boys from seeing how much she'd been affected by the sight of Fergus — her Fergus — making love to another girl. And he'd been so engrossed in what he was doing, he'd been completely oblivious to any passers-by. He must have been murmuring the same words of love to that . . . person, as he'd murmured to her, she thought, and wished she was dead. Becoming aware that Jack and Tim were still regarding her with deep concern, she whispered, through frozen lips, "Don't worry about me," but their anxious expressions didn't alter.

"We're as well to keep going." Jack squeezed her arm. "We're about halfway round."

Tim nodded. "Aye, there's no point in turning back now. Try not to think about it, Renee, that's the best way . . . A funny thing happened in the yard this morning . . ." He launched into an account of a not-very-funny incident, then Jack told an equally unamusing story about something that had happened to him that day, both transparently doing their best to keep her mind off what she'd just seen. Grateful for their inconsequential chatter, Renee was also very relieved that neither of them had said, "I told you so."

When he came to the end of another anecdote, Jack noticed that the girl was trembling. "Here, take my jacket, you're cold."

"I'm not cold. It's just . . ."

"Aye, I know. Don't let it get you down, though. You're doing fine. Just keep your chin up and you'll get over it." He squeezed her arm again.

"I've been thinking," Tim said, brightly. "How about the three of us going to the Palais tomorrow night? Will you manage, Jack, or had you something planned?" He obviously didn't want to make it appear that he was asking the girl on her own.

Jack looked at her. "It's the best cure, Renee, and it could be great fun, the three of us."

"All right." She didn't really care what she did, as long as it would take her thoughts away from the horrible tableau she'd inadvertently witnessed.

"That's my girl!" Tim turned red the minute he said it, in case she misunderstood.

Jack came to his rescue. "That's my girl, too," he said, and they all laughed, although Renee's mirth verged on hysteria.

The two men kept up a steady flow of jokes, so there wasn't one minute of awkward silence during the rest of their walk, and when they arrived home, Mike glanced up from his book.

"Did you enjoy your outing? Where have you been all this time?"

"We walked round the Bay of Nigg, it's a beautiful walk on a night like this." Renee never knew where she found the courage to sound so normal, and noticed that Jack and Tim were relieved by her response. She sat down on the pouffe at the side of Mike's chair.

"You'll have worked up an appetite with all that sea air," Anne remarked. "Do you fancy a sandwich, or something?"

"Thanks, Mrs Gordon, but we're not really hungry." Jack sat down on the settee beside Tim. "A cup of tea and a biscuit would go down a treat, though."

When Anne went to put on the kettle, Tim turned to his brother. "Did you get the grass cut, Mike?"

"Oh, aye, no bother. It's just a wee bit of a back green."

Nothing more was said for a few minutes, but when Anne came through with the tray, Jack jumped up and handed round the cups. "We got on so well on our walk, we're all going to the Palais tomorrow night."

"A threesome?" Anne laughed. "Remember what they say — two's company, three's a crowd."

"This three won't be a crowd." Tim winked to Renee. "We're not going to be tied to each other, so we can dance with whoever we like, isn't that right?"

"You're going to be left on your own, then, Renee." Mike nudged her playfully. "If these two take a fancy to somebody, they'll leave you sitting like a wallflower."

"I'll maybe take a fancy to somebody myself." She forced herself to sound jocular, knowing quite well that Jack and Tim would make sure she was never left on her own.

At last, she felt free to go to bed, but lay all night trying to banish the picture of the two figures merged into one, making love in the lee of the lighthouse wall, but it kept manifesting itself graphically in her brain. At times, she felt angry, even murderous, but more often she was engulfed by self-pity, and she had to bite her lip to stop her from crying, in case her mother heard her.

Of one thing she was certain. She would definitely keep that appointment with Fergus Cooper on Monday night, to have it out with him. He'd a lot to account for: first, her mother, now this other girl. He was a rotter, like they said, a philanderer, a sex-mad beast, but . . . she still loved him, God help her. She couldn't help herself.

Next morning, she felt tired and dispirited. She was quite confident that neither Jack nor Tim would let Fergus know that he'd been seen, but was afraid that Mike, or her mother, might let it slip about the walk last night. She didn't want Fergus to be warned, and so have an excuse ready. What excuse could he make for what she'd seen with her own eyes, anyway?

When he appeared for breakfast, Fergus was his usual charming self, and she thought, savagely. He doesn't know what's in store for him on Monday night. Then a chance remark of her mother's made her hold her breath for a moment. "Jack and Tim took Renee out for a walk last night, and they enjoyed each other's company so much they're all going to the Palais together tonight."

The relieved girl noticed, with sadistic pleasure, the surprised flicker of resentment which Fergus quickly veiled. "A love triangle?" he asked, sarcastically.

"Could be," Tim said flippantly.

Raising his eyebrows, Fergus pulled a face, then Mike, sensing the undercurrents, adroitly changed the subject, and the precarious moment passed.

At the office, Sheila Daun saw that something was upsetting Renee. "Had a row with your two boyfriends?" she asked, with sympathetic intent. "Or maybe just one of them?"

"I don't want to speak about it. I'm sorry, Sheila, and I hope you understand. It's too . . ."

"Sure. My lips are sealed. I'll ask no questions, though I'm just dying to know."

Renee mustered a faint smile, and the day dragged on until it was time to prepare for the Palais. She wasn't looking forward to it, but knew it would be better than sitting moping at home. She took no pleasure in dressing, and applied her make-up rather haphazardly, but, when she went downstairs, she tried to summon up a little enthusiasm, in order not to spoil the evening for her two escorts, and they set off in seeming high spirits. Jack and Tim were determined that she was going to enjoy herself, come what may, and she found herself entering into their teasing banter and going up to nearly every dance with one or other of them, and even with several unknown boys who asked her. On the way home, they sang and danced and joked, and entered the house shaking with subdued laughter, to find Fergus sitting on his own with a face like thunder.

"Renee was the belle of the ball." Tim smiled broadly. "It was Jack and me that were left sitting like wallflowers."

She steeled herself to carry on the joke. "Yes, I was sorry for the two lost souls, waiting patiently for me to go back to them, but I'd a really great time."

"That's all that matters, then." Fergus got up out of the armchair. "I'm off to bed. I need my beauty sleep even if you three don't." His voice was dry, and he stamped out leaving Renee unsure of whether to be glad or sorry at his reaction.

Jack laid his hand on her shoulder. "Good for you, lass. That's the way to handle it."

Tim nodded as he sat down to pour the tea from the flask which Anne had left for them. “Aye, let him see you don’t need him.”

When Renee went upstairs, her mother was curious to know how the evening had gone, so it was another fifteen minutes before she got a chance to think over what had happened, and to analyse what she felt about it. She *had* had a great time. Jack and Tim were good company, and had been very impersonal, so she hadn’t felt cornered by either of them making advances to her. Platonic, that was the word, and it was an easy, comfortable relationship. To hell with Fergus and his hole-in-corner affairs . . . No! She couldn’t honestly tell herself that she didn’t care. She did care, very much. Love was like a seesaw — up in the clouds one minute, then down in the depths the next — and she still loved him.

As was their custom, Jack and the two Donaldsons went straight from their work to the country buses on Saturday at lunchtime, and Fergus, usually delighted to be the centre of attention over the weekend, made himself scarce both days, so Renee was spared the ordeal of making polite conversation with him in front of her mother. It gave her a wicked satisfaction to think that he was angry and jealous because she’d gone dancing with Jack and Tim. It served him right that he should suffer for a change. Her mind skated over the unwelcome thought that he might be consoling himself with that other girl. It must have been a once-only affair — it must!

On Monday evening, she deliberately took her time over dressing, and waited until the last minute before she left the house, Fergus having gone out much earlier. She just missed the bus she'd meant to catch, so she was pleasantly surprised to see him still waiting for her outside Woolworth's at twenty to eight, ten minutes after their arranged time.

"We'll have to go somewhere quiet, if you want to talk," he said, brusquely. "I suppose you're wanting to make excuses about you and Tim last Monday?"

Renee ignored the question. She'd almost forgotten that fiasco, it seemed so long ago, now. "We can go to the Duthie Park. We'll get a seat there." It was also well away from Union Street, the Victoria Park and the Cattofield bus route.

He seemed surprised that she'd taken the initiative, but walked with her to the appropriate bus stop, and sat beside her in moody silence until they reached their destination.

"Well?" he began, rather belligerently, when they were seated on a secluded bench in the park. "What d'you want to say?"

"Quite a few things, really, but first, I will tell you about Tim and me last week. He'd been so good to me the whole time at the Palais, and he'd taught me to dance and was very patient, so I felt I should show my appreciation. We were only kissing, whatever you tried to hint to my mother."

"You were enjoying it when I saw you," he taunted.

"Why shouldn't I?" Renee kept her voice low, though she could feel an angry bitterness rising within her. She wanted, desperately, to keep calm. The whole effect would be ruined if she started to shout or weep, but what right had he to criticise her giving Tim a few kisses, after the awful things he'd done?

"You shouldn't enjoy kissing anybody else, because you belong to me, my Monday girl." His caressing voice, as he put his arms round her, almost made her apologise for hurting him. Almost, but not quite. She accepted his kiss passively, he dropped his arms in obvious annoyance.

"So you want to start playing hard to get now, do you? That won't work with me, my lady, and you weren't so hard to get with Tim." He scowled darkly. She allowed the insinuation to pass. Her whole body was aching for him, for his kisses, for his declaration of love, for him to make love to her there and then, but she fought against giving in to him so easily. She must find the reason for the cruel things he had done.

"I really am your Monday girl, am I?" she asked sweetly, deceptively. "Really and truly?"

He softened slightly. "You know you are, my darling. I've told you before. You're the first girl in my life."

Her temper almost snapped at this repetition of his words to her mother, but she took a deep breath. "Do you say that to all your girls?" she got out at last.

"You knew about the other girls, Renee." Fergus was on the defensive for once. "I told you all about them, but there's none of them my Monday girl."

"Except my mother." She watched his chin drop as his mouth opened in amazement, but his discomfiture gave her no pleasure, and she waited for him to bluster his way out of the accusation. She prayed that he could tell her it was all a silly joke, a misunderstanding on her part. She'd be willing to doubt the evidence of her own ears, and perhaps she'd only imagined the overheard words, in any case. His face revealed the furious searching of his brain to find an answer.

"I think a lot of your mother," he said, very carefully. "She's been very kind to me, and . . ." He found his inspiration in the excuse she'd given him for kissing Tim. "I wanted to show my appreciation for all she's done for me, and keeping her sweet's the only way I can. She's taken a fancy to me, you see, and I can't hurt her by telling her I don't feel the same about her."

It sounded reasonable to the agonised girl, and it was what she wanted to hear. "But you called her your Monday girl, the first woman in your life." How could he explain that?

He smiled then. "So that's what all this is about, is it? You've been listening at the keyhole, have you?"

"I couldn't help it, Fergus." Renee was on the defensive now. "You keep calling her Anne, and she's different when you're there. I was jealous, and wanted to find out what you said to her when you were together."

"You've no need to be jealous, my darling." His arms slid round her again. "There's nothing between your mother and me. You're a silly little goose, aren't you?" His lips brushed her nose, her eyes, then came down heavily on her mouth. She capitulated and returned his kisses hungrily, believing him because she wanted to believe him although he'd glossed over what he'd said to her mother. She couldn't break off with him . . . not because of her mother . . . not because of . . .

The repugnant memory of what she had witnessed on Thursday night came flooding back, and she drew away from him abruptly.

"Come on, Renee," he coaxed, all his charm and guile turned on again in the knowledge of the power he held over her. "I've told you. You're my Monday girl, my special girl — God's honour. What is it now?"

She licked her dry lips. "What about your Thursday girl?" she whispered. "She must be special, too."

"My Thursday girl?" He looked bewildered and apprehensive.

"The one you took to the Bay of Nigg last Thursday, and I don't know how many Thursdays before."

"How did you find out about that?" His voice was sharp, alarmed.

"I saw you," she said wearily. "So there's no use denying it. When I was out for a walk with Jack and Tim. We all saw you, making love to her as if your life depended on it. You never even knew we were there."

He was scowling as he moved along the bench, away from her, and he kept his head turned to the front when he spoke. "Spying again, were you? You, going down there with your two boyfriends? You've no room to speak."

"They've never made love to me. I've never even kissed Jack, and only last Monday night with Tim. Just the few kisses you saw." She was on the defensive again, and despised herself for her weakness.

His top lip curled up for a second. "So you say." The accusing note in his voice changed to hurt sadness. "Now you know how I felt that night."

"It's not the same thing at all," she burst out. "We were just kissing, but you were . . . you and that girl were . . ." The words stuck in her throat.

Fergus took her hand in both of his. "Listen, Renee," he said, persuasively. "I never made any secret of the other girls, and I'm only human, after all. I can't refuse when some fast piece hands it to me on a plate. Do you understand what I mean, because it wasn't my fault?" She shook her head, too angry and sick to answer.

He patted her hand, then held it firmly again. "No, I suppose you're too young to know what I'm getting at, but a man's attitude to sex — sexual intercourse," he added, to be sure he was making himself clear, "is different from a woman's. It's just a release for us, a bit of fun, a quick thrill."

Renee's dismayed face made him hasten to qualify what he'd said. "But when a man loves a girl, like I love you, it's different. It means something. I was proving my love to you, so it meant everything — especially when I knew I was first."

She wished fervently that he had not added the last few words. It reminded her of what Jack and Sheila Daun had said about him, but she could at least understand now why he'd been lying beside the lighthouse wall that night, doing what he'd been doing. She didn't feel any happier about it, but had to admit that his explanation was feasible. Fergus was regarding her anxiously. "The other girls don't mean anything to me, Renee, honest, and I'd only been out with that one the once. I wouldn't need anybody else if I could be with you every night."

"Why can't we be together every night?" She leaned against him, and looked up with pleading eyes. "I'll be sixteen in less than three weeks, and my mother didn't object to me going out with Tim."

He bent his head to kiss her again. "She wouldn't let you go out with me, darling. I told you, she thinks she's in love with me, and jealousy's a terrible thing. I've had to swear to her that you didn't mean anything to me and that I don't love you."

"Oh, Fergus!" The shock made her lift her head from his shoulder. This was disloyalty, betrayal of the first magnitude. "You didn't . . . did you?"

His lips touched her eyelids. "I had to, Renee. I have to keep her from suspecting about us till I can find a way to let her down gently, and show her it's you I really want. You'll just have to be patient, my darling."

The reassuring endearments were balm to her buffeted heart, and she placed her arms round his neck, the manly smell of him filling her nostrils as she whispered, "Oh, Fergus, I love you so much I can hardly wait."

He glanced quickly about them, then began to caress her, until she murmured, urgently, "Go on, go on . . . please!"

All the mixed emotions — the doubts, the hatred, the jealousy, the love — which had been pent up inside her, burst to the surface in a show of passion which delighted and excited him, and he took her roughly without further preliminaries. When it was over, his fierce needs satisfied, his kiss was tender. "Have I proved now it's only you I love?"

"Yes, oh, yes," she breathed, banishing the hateful memories that had haunted her over the past few days.

"I bet Tim and Jack could never make love like that," he said suddenly, childishly.

She laughed contentedly, his little show of bravado being the final proof to her of his love. Arms round each other, they walked back to the centre of the city, and Fergus boarded the bus to Cattofield with her. "I'll come all the way home with you tonight, my darling, and your mother can think what she likes."

With a rush of tenderness towards him, Renee thought that this was a new beginning, and snuggled up to him, unconscious of the interested, amused glances of the other passengers.

When they went in, Anne looked suspicious, and her face didn't change when Fergus proferred his glib excuse. "Renee came on to the same bus as I was on."

Having no idea of how much her shining eyes gave her away, the girl was slightly put out when her mother ignored her and began to bombard Fergus with questions as to where he'd been and what he'd been doing.

"I was with an old mate of mine I haven't seen for ages. He's married now, and he took me home with him to meet his wife, and to have a few drinks." His answer came so easily, and sounded so genuine, that Renee had a strange pang of sad irritation at how smoothly he could lie. Had he been lying to her all evening? The doubts came flooding back and she came to a firm decision. Once her birthday was past, she'd wait a week or two to give him a chance to end her mother's attachment to him, and if he hadn't done anything by then, she'd force his hand and tell her the whole truth herself.

She wouldn't mention the wonderful love-making, though. That was a secret to be shared only with Fergus. She'd just say, quite calmly, that they loved each other, and she'd say it in front of him, so he couldn't deny it.

Renee hadn't noticed Jack sitting by the window, and when she did, he was staring at her speculatively, and she could tell from his face that he knew exactly what she'd been doing with Fergus that evening. Well, she didn't care.

In a few weeks, they would all know, and if her mother made a scene and forbade them to meet outside the house, she'd run away with him. At sixteen, she'd be old enough in Scots law to marry him without parental consent, and they could live happily without any interference.

Jack went to bed first, followed closely by Fergus, making Renee suspect that he didn't relish being faced with more questions from his landlady, who now focused her attention on her daughter.

"And what were you doing that you came in all starry-eyed, and looking like a cat that's been at the cream? You weren't out with Phyllis, that's one thing sure."

The desperation to avoid being found out too early gave Renee the deviousness to say quickly, "No, I wasn't with Phyllis. She sent her brother to tell me she wasn't feeling very well, so he came into the pictures with me instead. He's very nice. You remember him, Mum? He's a year older than me."

"Oh." Anne gave a nervous laugh; she hadn't known that Phyllis Barclay had a brother. "Another string to your bow? You're getting to be a real flirt, aren't you?"

Renee thought ruefully that she was getting to be a real liar, anyway, a perfect pupil of the true master of deception — Fergus Cooper.

CHAPTER EIGHT

On the next two Monday nights, Renee's suspicions about Fergus were allayed. He was waiting for her when she arrived at Woolworth's at half past seven and tucked her arm through his while they were walking, which made her very proud and happy. His whole attitude was tender and caring, and she reflected that this was how it should be all the time and would be, very soon, once their love was made public.

Both weeks, they walked all the way to Hazlehead, and found a clearing in the trees near the golf course. They were lying on the mossy ground, their love-making over, on the second Monday, when Renee remarked, idly, "My birthday's on Thursday."

"I know. Mine was a week past Friday." Fergus turned over, to lie on his stomach. "I'm an old man of twenty-two now."

"But I'll be sixteen, and you know what that means, don't you?" She looked at him hopefully.

"Mmmm. It means that for nearly two weeks I've been seven years older than you, but from Thursday I'll only be six years older." Poking in the moss with his finger, he hadn't lifted his head while he was speaking.

Renee ruffled his dark curls. "Be serious, Fergus. I meant that from Thursday I'll be old enough to go with whoever I want, so you can take me out openly."

"I am taking you out openly. Anybody could see us."

"I meant openly in front of my mother."

"I told you before, Renee, I need time to . . . explain to her, and brush her off gently."

"You've had plenty of time already. It's two whole weeks since you said you'd do it, and you could have told her by this time, if you'd wanted to."

"You know I want to tell her, but . . ." He squeezed her hand. "It's very difficult. I can't just tell her straight out to stop pestering me because I don't love her."

"Why not?"

He regarded her mournfully, his dark eyes widening. "That'd be cruel, Renee. I'll have to let her down easily, lead up to it gradually, be diplomatic, or else she might throw me out. She *is* my landlady, remember?"

"I'm telling you, Fergus, I'm not going to wait long. If you don't tell her, I will." She withdrew her hand and made a move as if to get up, but he gripped her arm.

"I'll try, Renee, honest, I will. Don't say anything yet, for God's sake. You'll just make things worse."

Worse for who? she thought ruefully, but let him kiss and stroke her body again until she forgot everything except her aching need for him.

On Thursday morning, she received several birthday cards in the mail, also one large brown envelope, which she opened first.

"Mum!" She ran into the scullery. "It's my certificates from the RSA. I've passed the Elementary in the whole lot — shorthand, typing and book-keeping."

"That's good." Anne was washing the breakfast dishes, but looked up with a smile.

The cards were from Granny and Granda, Sheila Daun, Jack, Tim and Mike, and her mother, but she was disappointed that there wasn't one from Fergus. "Thanks for the card, Mum," she said, propping them up on the mantelpiece.

Anne came into the living room, drying her hands. "That's OK." She lifted a parcel from the sideboard and handed it to her daughter. "Many happy returns, Renee. I'm sorry it's not much."

Renee took off the paper and gave a cry of delight when she saw the powder compact and lipstick. "Oh, that's lovely. Thanks again, Mum."

"I'm glad you like them. You'd better get a move on or you'll be late for work."

At teatime, there was a card from Fergus on her plate, so she happily thanked all the boarders for remembering her birthday, and Tim led them in singing "Happy Birthday" to her.

Anne produced a small cake, which she had baked and iced, and cut in six so that everyone could have a piece.

When he finished eating his, Fergus stood up. "That cake was absolutely delicious, Anne."

"Yes, Mrs Gordon. It was really great." Mike excused himself and followed Fergus out of the dining room.

Tim looked across at Renee. "How does it feel to be sweet sixteen?"

Her high spirits had flagged somewhat at hearing Fergus still calling her mother "Anne", but she smiled and said, "No different, Tim, unfortunately. I wish I was twenty-one."

Jack, sitting next to her, laid his hand over hers for a second. "Don't wish your life away, Renee. Sixteen's a great age to be. I wish I was sixteen again as well."

Anne stretched over to lift the empty cake plate. "I wish I was sixteen again, too," she said, ruefully.

Mike went out later to meet Babs Sandison, and Fergus went out about five minutes afterwards, but he didn't divulge which of his girlfriends he was going to meet. Renee reflected dismally that it was probably his Thursday girl, the one who offered it to him on a plate, and felt a horrible churning inside her stomach.

Then Jack and Tim came through together. "We're going out for a walk. Would you like to come, Renee?" Tim asked.

Oh, no, she thought. Not a repetition of what happened that other Thursday? "Sorry," she said quickly. "I want to wash my hair, and, anyway, Granny and Granda might come across, seeing it's my birthday."

"Oh, aye, they likely will."

Jack turned to Anne. "Would you like to come, Mrs Gordon?"

"No, I'd better be here in case my mother and father do come."

"Oh well, cheerio then." Jack preceded Tim to the door.

"We'll maybe go in somewhere for a drink, seeing we've no ladies with us," Tim said, over his shoulder. "But we won't be late."

Anne picked up her mending basket and sat down, and Renee went into the bathroom. She hadn't really intended to wash her hair that night, but having said it, she felt obliged to do it. She was sitting on the floor in front of the fire, reading to pass the time until her hair dried, when someone rang the doorbell. Maggie and Peter McIntosh had not forgotten to bring their granddaughter a birthday gift. The old lady extricated a bulky parcel from her shopping bag when she was seated on the settee, and handed it to Renee. "We came the night instead o' the morrow, to gi'e ye oor present."

"Oh, a handbag! Just what I was needing," the girl exclaimed as soon as she removed the paper. "It's really beautiful, Granny, and it matches my new coat."

"I hoped it would." Maggie beamed. "I mind ye showin' me yer coat a week or so back, and it fair suits ye."

Renee laughed. "It wasn't bad for twenty-five bob, was it? Thank you very much, Granny, and you, too, Granda," she added to Peter, sitting, as usual, in the background.

His eyes were twinkling. "Ye'd better tak' a look inside to see if it's big enough for a' the rubbish ye cart aboot."

The girl obediently undid the two metal clasps. "Oh, you two pets. There's a bottle of Californian Poppy inside. That's just great, because the Evening in Paris you gave me at Christmas is just about finished. Thanks again." She rose and kissed them both on the cheek, and they appeared very proud that she was so pleased with their gifts.

"Ye're gettin' to be quite the young lady," Peter remarked. "The next thing is ye'll be gettin' a lad."

"She's been out with Tim Donaldson already," Anne told him. "And with Tim and Jack another night, and she went to the pictures with her chum's brother once, as well."

Maggie nodded approvingly. "Ye're best wi' a few, so ye can pick an' choose. Ye're young yet, an' it'll be a puckle years yet afore ye meet the right lad."

Renee hugged to herself the thought that she didn't need to wait a "puckle years" to meet him, and that it wouldn't be long before she could shout it from the rooftops. When her grandparents went home, she went a little way with them, and, when Peter walked on in front, she couldn't resist saying, "I've got the right lad already, Granny, but don't let on to Mum yet."

Maggie smiled encouragingly. "Jack an' Tim are baith nice laddies. Which ane is it? Or is it yer chum's brother?"

"It's none of them." Renee laughed with delight.

"As lang's it's nae that Fergus Cooper." Maggie eyed her keenly. "He's a bad lot, if ye ask me."

"Nobody's asking you, and you don't know anything about him!" The girl had unwittingly revealed the truth by her sharp retort and wondered why her grandmother seemed so disapproving. She returned home, angry with Granny for the first time in her life. She was also annoyed because Fergus had apparently made no effort to break with her mother, which made her doubt if he'd any intention of doing it at all. Still, as he'd said, it was difficult for him, so she'd need to have patience — but not for too long. She'd wait another full week, perhaps until the Sunday after that, when the other three boarders would be away, then she would make her big announcement, calmly, quietly and simply.

"Fergus and I are in love," she would say, or something like that, and let him take it from there. Roll on Sunday, the — she counted it on her fingers — 10th September 1939. It would be a date to remember.

A week before the great day, she sat down along with her mother and Fergus, to listen to Neville Chamberlain's special broadcast at eleven o'clock. Not that she was really interested — it was probably just another warning of the impending doom which never materialised. Her mind was preoccupied with what she meant to do the following Sunday, but her mother's sharp intake of breath made her concentrate on the final sentence.

"Consequently, this country is at war with Germany."

Renee was surprised, and rather indignant. What an effrontery the man had, after promising, about a year ago, that there would be "peace in our time". But this couldn't affect her plans? The British Army, the Royal Navy and the RAF, of course, would naturally be involved, but nobody else. Confident of that, she relaxed and returned to her own train of thought, to pre-live, for the umpteenth time, the excitement of openly declaring her love for Fergus, but his voice intruded on her daydream.

"Well, it's here." He sounded pleased.

Anne, looking very upset, rose to switch off the wireless. "It's nothing to be happy about Fergus. Look at the lives that were lost in the last war."

"It'll all be over in a few months this time."

Feeling better, Renee closed her ears to the discussion, until, without warning, his words filtered through.

"I wouldn't mind joining the army . . ."

Oh, no! He couldn't want to leave her now? She couldn't say anything, and watched him going out after Anne had accepted his offer to cut the grass. Her mother rose in a few minutes, saying, "Well, I'll have to get on with the dinner, war or no war."

Renee was left alone, her heart aching and her brain furiously trying to cope with these new developments. If Fergus joined the army and was sent to fight the Germans, where would that leave her? She couldn't tell her mother anything if he wasn't there to endorse it, and he might stay away and never come back.

There was only one thing to do. It would have to be today, not next Sunday, and she'd be sure he'd return to her when the war was over. Of course, it would have to be done before Jack, Tim and Mike returned in the evening.

She pottered about in the loft until just before dinner-time, tidying up drawers and folding her clothes neatly, glad that her hands had something to do. When she went down to set the table, she was convinced that now was the time. If there was any unpleasantness — she was sensible enough to realise there might be — it would all be over by the time the other three turned up. She waited until they finished their broth, then, steeling her churning stomach, she spoke as her mother rose.

"Sit down, Mum." Her voice quavered a little. "Fergus and I want to tell you something." It wasn't exactly the words she'd meant to use, but it didn't matter, as long as she kept calm. Fergus looked rather alarmed. "Renee," he murmured. "Your mother doesn't want to know about . . ."

Poor Fergus, she thought. He doesn't know what to say, but he'd be grateful to her for helping him out, once she'd said her piece.

"She doesn't want to know what we're planning for her birthday," he finished, lamely.

Anne looked suspiciously from him to her daughter. "What's going on? My birthday's not till December." She turned her attention again on the man who was now cowering rather fearfully in his chair. "I wasn't born yesterday, Fergus."

"Don't mind him." Renee was quietly amused. "This is a new experience for him."

"Yes?" Anne barked out the word.

"I'm in love with Fergus, Mum, and he loves me."

It was out, at last. She'd known there would be some repercussions, but had never, in her wildest nightmare, imagined the explosion that followed.

"You stupid little bitch!" Anne's eyes were blazing as she moved her white face close to Renee's. Her hand came up, as if to strike the girl, then she turned on Fergus, slumped helplessly against his seat.

"Tell her the truth, Fergus! Tell her you love me, and we've only been waiting till she found a boyfriend before we got married. Go on, tell her!"

"Anne," he began, haltingly, but she was beside herself with fury, and newly kindled jealousy.

"Tell her!" she screamed. "Tell her we made love every Monday night all the winter, when she was out at her evening classes. Tell her she's only a kid, and you laugh at her behind her back. Tell her it's me you love!" She was sobbing loudly now. "Go on, Fergus! Tell her!"

Renee's mouth had fallen open with shock, but now she blurted out, "He's made love to me every Monday. Before the classes stopped, and after, as well." She couldn't believe what she'd just heard. "Tell my mother that, Fergus! Tell her you felt sorry for her, and you were only trying to show your gratitude for what she'd done for you. Tell her you love me!" Her voice had risen until she was screaming as loudly as Anne.

Fergus had said only the one hesitant word since his abortive attempt to stop Renee overtaking him. He had no answer to this predicament and made to rise from the table to get away from the two distraught females, but Anne jumped up and pushed him roughly back.

"You two-faced bugger! Who else have you been sticking it into, you bloody liar?" He hung his head and remained silent, and Renee, who had never seen, nor heard, her mother swearing before, burst into hysterical sobs, remembering the other girl at the Bay of Nigg, who had, no doubt, also believed his seductive lies. The trouble was, he was so convincing and persuasive that any girl would have trusted him.

"Well?" Anne demanded again. "Who else?"

He lifted his head slowly. "I haven't been with anybody else, Anne," he said earnestly. "Just you and Renee." He glanced at the girl, as if willing her to keep silent about what she'd seen on her walk with Tim and Jack.

"So you were sorry for me, were you?" Anne shouted. "A broken-down middle-aged widow, with nobody to protect her? And a fifteen-year-old virgin for afters, was that it?"

"No, Anne, it wasn't like that," he mumbled, but she didn't let him go any further.

"I could have you up for that — interfering with an underage girl . . . you . . . you . . ."

"She was asking for it," he interrupted, before she could find a word strong enough to express her contempt. "I couldn't help it, she was always after me. Writing little notes, asking me to meet her, and she wasn't a virgin!" His desperation made him say anything to save himself.

Anne turned on her daughter. "Who else have you been with, you little tramp?"

Renee sobbed even louder. "Nobody else, Mum, I swear to God. I was a virgin, and I'd never have let him touch me if he hadn't said . . . He said he wanted to be first for me, so I'd always belong to him."

Anne started pummelling the man's head. "You filthy . . . low-down . . . lying . . . beast!" At every word, she punched him again, and he sat with his hands up, trying to shield his face.

Anne continued her vicious attack. "You can't . . . find . . . anything . . . to say . . . can you . . .?

"Stop it! Stop it!" Renee rose blindly and ran to the door. She hardly knew how she got up the stairs, but threw herself on top of her bed, sobbing uncontrollably.

CHAPTER NINE

Renee couldn't tell how long she'd lain there, trying to shut out the noise below, her thoughts in such a turmoil she'd been afraid, for a time, that her head would split wide open. The absolute stillness now terrified her. Had her mother, in her irrational anger, murdered Fergus with a table knife? Or had Fergus stabbed her mother? She swung her legs to the floor, and crept on to the landing, her ears straining to pick up any sound. There was nothing. They surely couldn't both be . . . unless one had killed the other, then committed suicide?

Her right foot was hovering uncertainly over the top step, when she heard the living-room door being opened and drew it back fearfully. Which one was it, and was whoever it was coming to kill her?

"Renee, come down and listen to this." Anne's voice was much calmer, but it took the horror-struck girl a full twenty seconds to obey the softly spoken command.

She entered the room in fear and trepidation, although she felt that nothing would surprise her, and her shock at seeing Fergus still sitting at the table, with his head in his hands, was all the greater — an anticlimax. She didn't want to hear what either of them had to say.

It was Anne who set the ball rolling. "I told him to get out," she said slowly, her eyes red and swollen, "and he's changed his tune. Now, Fergus, tell Renee what you've just told me. It might make her feel better, though I doubt it."

He looked up, and the girl was shaken when she saw that he, too, had been weeping. "I'm sorry for everything," he began, quietly, "and I'm apologising to both of you."

Renee's stomach muscles contracted. Was this what she'd been called down to hear? A bare apology? He couldn't honestly think he'd get off so lightly? His eyes were on her now, tortured and pleading. "I'm sorry for saying you weren't a virgin, Renee, because you were. I must have been mad, I didn't know what I was saying. I truly love you, but . . . I love your mother, too. You'll maybe think it's impossible to love two people at once, but it's true." He gulped, and transferred his gaze to Anne, begging her to believe him.

She sighed hopelessly. "It sounds like the baying of a cornered fox to me, but you'll have to make up your own mind, Renee. Do you think he's telling the truth this time?"

"I don't know," the girl faltered. "It's so . . ."

"It's the truth, just the same." Fergus looked from one to the other. "I fell in love with you first, Anne. Maybe because I was grateful to you for taking me in, like I told Renee, but it soon developed into real love, and I needed you desperately. I didn't make love to you just for kicks, I really wanted you."

He shrugged his shoulders pathetically. "But you were growing up, Renee, and more beautiful by the day, and I began to love you, too, and started meeting you after your classes, until I had to make love to you, as well. I thought I was safe enough — you'd never tell each other what was going on — and I could go on having you both." His head dropped again.

Anne rested her elbows on the table. "Needing you, wanting you, making love to you, having you — that's not all love means."

"I love you — both of you," he said, without looking up. "I want to be near you as much as I can, but . . . sex is part of love, for me, anyway. Don't send me away, Anne, please!"

She looked at his bowed head for a few seconds. "I want to believe you," she whispered. "I want to, because I loved you, and because I don't like feeling I've been made a fool of. Renee probably thinks the same, but the whole thing's impossible. I can't share a lover with my daughter. It's unthinkable, obscene." She paused briefly. "I'll let you stay on here till you find somewhere else to go, but only on condition that you promise never to touch either of us again, or say anything that . . ." She straightened up. "It's the only sensible way to deal with it, and, Renee, I'm trusting you not to go behind my back, either."

"I won't." The girl found her voice again. "I don't want to have anything more to do with him."

"I promise I'll never do anything out of place again." Fergus met Anne's eyes steadily.

"That's settled, then." Anne leaned back, still rather shaky. "Remember, Fergus, it's only till you find other lodgings, and we'd better not say anything to the other boys about why you're leaving. They'd only think we're all mad." She swallowed, then gave a short, dry laugh. "My God, maybe we are, at that."

We must be, Renee thought. After the terrible things he'd done, he was getting off scot-free . . . well, almost.

A vestige of his old, charming smile lurked at the edges of the man's mouth when he lifted his head again. "Thank you, Anne . . . Mrs Gordon, but if I promise to behave myself, wouldn't you . . ."

"No!"

"I swear I'll never . . ."

"You won't get the chance," Anne said firmly.

His shoulders dropped dramatically, as he stood up. "All right. I'll try to find new digs as soon as I can." He walked to the door, turning, before he went out, to say, "I won't be in for tea, but I'll be home . . . back at bedtime."

Aware that her mother was holding her breath until the outside door shut quietly, Renee bowed her head as Anne murmured, "What a mess."

With what remained of her heart, Renee wished that she could be transported away from this terrible house; away from her mother — her horrible, despicable mother, whose very existence had turned all those wonderful dreams into nightmares — but she couldn't move. It was as if she were riveted to her now, her legs and feet paralysed, her innards frozen, her brain, unfortunately, still fiercely active. If only she'd left things as they were, but how could she have known what had been going on behind her back? She should have been warned by what she'd heard when she listened at the dining-room door, but she hadn't wanted to believe it and Fergus had laughed away her fears. What a liar he was. How could he have looked her in the face and sworn that it was all on her mother's side, when he'd been . . . oh, it didn't bear thinking about — but she couldn't get it out of her head. Fergus and her mother!

Jack had been right about him — and Granny . . . and Sheila Daun. They'd all warned her and she hadn't listened. It was all her own fault, which made it a thousand times worse. If only she could stand up now and walk out, calmly and with some dignity, but she couldn't. And where would she go in any case? She couldn't afford to go into lodgings, she couldn't go to Granny, she'd be shocked and disgusted if she ever learned what had been going on.

A flood of self-pity welled up in Renee then, and she glanced up to find her mother regarding her with eyes filled with . . . not hatred, nor pity, but — sorrow? Well, it was too late to be sorry.

"We have to speak Renee," Anne said softly. "Even when . . . Fergus leaves, we'll still have to stay together, in spite of what's happened. We can't just paper over the cracks."

Her head down again, the girl muttered, "I don't want to speak to you ever again."

"I don't blame you, Renee," Anne went on. "He could twist any woman round his little finger, but I was old enough — I shouldn't have been taken in by his blarney. They say there's no fool like an old fool, but I wouldn't believe a single word he said, now."

Renee kept silent, praying that her mother would take the hint and leave her in peace, but Anne was not to be deterred. "I should have suspected you'd been going out with him, when you were supposed to be with Phyllis Barclay, but it never crossed my mind that you didn't have the money to be going to the pictures every week — that's how much a blind fool I was. I knew you were attracted to him and I knew he didn't do anything to stop you, but I never dreamt he'd been . . ."

Her head jerking up, the girl burst out, "And I never dreamt he'd been carrying on with you. It makes me sick, just thinking about it — you and him? He told me he loved me, and now I find out he'd been telling you he . . ."

"We've been a pair of bloody fools. We'd better get this cleared up. We'll leave the rest of our dinner till teatime — I don't suppose you feel any more like eating than I do. You know, if your father had been alive, he'd have killed Fergus Cooper for what he's done to us."

If her father had still been alive, Renee thought, bitterly, this situation would never have arisen. Her mother wouldn't have needed Fergus to make love to her, and he'd have been . . . She came to an abrupt halt. He wouldn't have been lodging here at all, and she would never have known him.

Gathering up dishes noisily, her mother said, "I could do with a cup of tea, though. How about you?"

"Yes, please. Er . . . Mum, I'm sorry it was my fault that everything came out like that today." Renee lifted the rest of the dirty crockery and followed Anne into the scullery.

"It had to come out sooner or later, so it was as well to come out today and I'm sorry for the things I said to you. I'm not in the habit of using language like that, but it shows up my lower-class beginnings."

An awkward restraint fell between them while they washed up then had their cup of tea, each of them regretting what they'd said that day, until Renee felt that she must get out of the house. Where would she go, that was the problem? She couldn't go to Woodside, because her Granny would see straight away that something was wrong, and Maggie was the last person Anne would want to know about her stupidity.

"Renee," her mother sounded apologetic, "if you've nothing else to do, maybe you'd do a bit of weeding in the back garden. I'd have done it myself, but there's two pairs of sheets needing to be turned, for they're getting thin in the middle."

Collecting a small trowel and fork from the shed, which had once been the garage, Renee tackled a patch well away from the house, glad that the sun was dimmed by a slight haze. Her physical efforts didn't prevent her brain from going over every sordid detail of the dreadful drama she'd brought on herself by her determination to have her lover declare himself openly.

Why hadn't she left things as they were? Now she knew, without a shadow of a doubt, that he'd been . . . But he couldn't really love a woman so much older than himself? It must only have been for sex. Digging out a clump of dandelions, she threw it viciously on the path beside her. She was still burning with anger, with hurt, with jealousy, but . . . she couldn't stop loving Fergus. A person couldn't turn love off like a tap, no matter what.

After an hour, exhausted by her back-breaking task, she went on to the square of lawn — back green, as Mike had called it — and lay down. The sun was brighter now and she stretched lazily, to let the warmth permeate her body, until the smell of the turf stirred memories of the times she'd spent with Fergus, at the Victoria Park, the Bay of Nigg, the Duthie Park, Hazlehead. She'd never be able to forget him, she reflected, then turned cold as it struck her that they'd never lie anywhere together again. She scrambled to her feet and went back to the house, where Anne dried her eyes surreptitiously as soon as she appeared.

They tried to act naturally with each other throughout their meal, but the unacknowledged antagonism between them could not be ignored, and it would be a long time before they could return to a normal mother — daughter relationship. The jealousy and resentment each felt towards the other was too great, too consuming, to be overlooked and forgotten. They spent the evening in an uncomfortable silence, not really listening to the wireless playing softly in the background — although the Palm Court Orchestra was

Anne's favourite programme — nor concentrating on reading the Sunday newspapers, until Mike and Tim came in just after nine o'clock.

Mike's face was grim as he sat down. "It's terrible about the war, isn't it? I thought it was coming, though, a while back. What do you think about it, Mrs Gordon?"

Anne shook her head slowly. "I'm afraid it's going to be another long struggle like the last one." Renee had completely forgotten about Chamberlain's morning announcement, so much had happened since then. The threat of what the war would bring had been overshadowed by the greater tragedy of learning the truth about Fergus, but she felt herself turn cold again at the thought of him having to go and fight.

"It won't last nearly so long this time," Tim said, quite cheerfully. "We'll bomb the Jerries off the face of the earth. We've got the aeroplanes, the tanks, the guns, and . . ."

"So have they." Mike sounded worried. "Germany's been preparing for war for years, but Britain's just buried her head in the sand."

That was what Sheila Daun had said about her, Renee recalled, and it had been true. She'd ignored all the warning signs, and she shouldn't have been so shocked by what had been revealed at dinnertime. The discussion about the war was three-sided for a time, until Tim turned to the girl, who had said nothing so far. "What do you think, Renee? A war should put some excitement into our humdrum lives, shouldn't it?"

Her dulled senses told her that she'd had enough excitement today to last her for the rest of her life, but she forced a smile. "I suppose so." She could see that Tim was put out by her response, but she didn't care. She wasn't interested in the war, it was the least of her troubles. There were other issues, far more important to her, to fill her thoughts.

Tim gave up trying to include her in the conversation. He'd noticed that his landlady was also less talkative than usual, which he'd put down, at first, to the news about the war, but now suspected that mother and daughter must have had a row about something earlier on.

The speculations began again when Jack appeared, some twenty minutes later, but only between Tim and Jack. Anne and Renee, and Mike, remained silent. By the time they all dispersed to bed, Fergus still hadn't come home, and the girl, lying wakeful far into the night, heard him creeping in at ten past two. Where had he been all this time? Where had he gone to gather his shattered senses, and who had been the recipient of his whispered words of love?

Renee clenched her fists until her nails dug into her palms. It was no use! She couldn't break away from him. She loved him as much as ever, in spite of what he'd done.

CHAPTER TEN

All through breakfast, Fergus Cooper was very subdued, and scarcely made any attempt to eat. Renee wondered if the other three boarders could feel the crackling tension in the air, and it crossed her mind that Tim and Jack would knock him senseless if they ever found out about his duplicity and unscrupulousness. When he left with the others, to go to work, Fergus stopped at the door and said, "I won't be in for tea tonight, either, Mrs Gordon."

With a sinking feeling at the pit of her stomach, Renee remembered that it was Monday, and that she would never be his Monday girl again. Her eyes filled with tears, and she held her head down to prevent them being seen. Her love for him was so great, she could forgive him for everything, but there was no way she could let him know. Fergus had promised her mother that he would never touch either of them again, and she, herself, had promised not to do anything underhand, but was she strong enough to keep that promise?

She could hardly believe it when she found a note in her coat pocket, but she drew it out with trembling fingers. "7.30 inside Playhouse. Please!" A quivering sigh escaped her. Fergus was actually pleading with her, but there was no chance of anything other than secret meetings now.

When she told her mother, at lunchtime, that she was going to the pictures that night with Sheila Daun, she crossed her fingers that Anne wouldn't suspect the truth, but she was unable to use Phyllis Barclay's name any more. She had exposed that alibi herself, unfortunately. But her mother appeared to trust her, even seemed glad that she was going out. It was Jack Thomson who caused a problem later, by catching the same bus into town. The tryst was inside the cinema, though, so even if he came right to the Playhouse with her, he wouldn't see her meeting Fergus.

"Which picture are you going to see?" Jack asked when they were seated.

Renee hadn't had time to look at the evening paper to find out which film was showing, and she wasn't really bothered, anyway, as long as she was with Fergus. She tried to sound off-hand. "We're going to the Playhouse, but I don't know what's on. It's something that Sheila wants to see."

"Oh." He sounded disappointed. "It's Barbara Stanwyck in *Stella Dallas*. Quite good, but not my cup of tea. I'd have come in with you if it had been anything else, but I saw that when it was on at the Capitol a while back."

She heaved a sigh of relief at her narrow escape.

"I'll walk up Union Street with you," he said, when they came off the bus. "Then I'll carry on round to the

Regent. It's a man's picture on there — Humphrey Bogart."

When they reached the Playhouse, he stopped. "I'll keep you company till your chum comes, if you like."

"Oh, no, it's OK." Why did he have to be so considerate? "Sheila said she'd meet me inside, in case it was raining." She hoped desperately that he'd take the hint and leave her alone.

"Fair enough. Be seeing you." He saluted and walked away. It was horrible having to lie to him, but she felt a surge of exhilaration at having come through the ordeal so well. She could understand, in a way, how Fergus could get a thrill out of living a life of deceit. It was like pitting your wits against a stiff opponent in some kind of deadly game, and praying that you'd come through unscathed.

Walking over to the cash desk, she bought a ticket for the back stalls. A whole shilling! It was a bit expensive for her, but she took it for granted that Fergus would want to sit in the back row, where all the courting couples went.

There was no sign of him in the foyer, so she walked round, looking at all the posters advertising the coming attractions, then went round them again. She felt that she'd been there for hours, but her watch showed only five to eight. Only? He was twenty-five minutes late already. Had he really meant to come, or was he punishing her for the fracas she'd triggered off yesterday?

The over-sweet smell of the air-freshener which the usherettes were puffing from their syringes suddenly cloyed in her nose. Conscious of the cinema staff looking at her, obviously pitying her for having been stood up, she could stand it no longer. She would go to the street entrance to get some fresh air, and to check if Fergus was anywhere in sight. If he wasn't, she'd go in and see the film on her own, for she couldn't waste her ticket, though she was so upset she probably wouldn't enjoy it.

With an effort, she walked nonchalantly past the cashier again and took large gulps, as she stood on the steps. When her nausea passed, she stepped on to the pavement to look down Union Street. No familiar face met her searching eyes, and all her hopes drained away. He'd never meant to meet her, and she could hardly blame him.

Immersed in chagrin and self-pity, she jumped nervously when a hand fell on her shoulder. Fergus had come in the opposite direction from the one she'd expected. "I was beginning to think you weren't going to turn up," she complained.

"I'm sorry, Renee. I was early, so I walked up Union Street, and Jack Thomson caught up with me at Holburn Junction. He was going to the Regent, but he asked me to go into the Glentannar Bar with him for a pint first. I didn't like to say no, in case he suspected I was meeting you."

"Thank goodness you did go," Renee said quickly, "for he'd just left me here, and he'd have put two and two together if you'd refused to go with him."

"That's OK then. I was worried about keeping you waiting again, after . . . I told him I was meeting one of my mates at eight o'clock and hurried as fast as I could. I'll get the tickets now. Come on."

"I've bought mine already. Back stalls."

He smiled. "Good girl, but you can't afford that. Here, take this shilling. No," as she shook her head, "I'll just stand here till you take it, so you'd better hurry, or we'll be here all night."

She laughed and slipped the coin into her pocket gratefully. They found the rear seats relatively empty, it being a Monday night, and he led her into the very back row at the far side. "I wondered if you'd come," he said softly. "Why on earth did you tell your mother everything like that yesterday? She nearly threw me out on my ear."

"Oh, Fergus, I'm really sorry about it, but I wanted everything out in the open. I wanted her to know about us so she would stop pestering you. I didn't realise how you felt about her, you see, and I never expected things to be so bad."

He took her hand. "I did try to warn you, and I don't know what to say to you now."

She looked at him sadly. "I shouldn't really have come here tonight, we both know that. I only hope she never finds out — she'd go absolutely mad."

"I had to speak to you, Renee, to try to explain, in case you were hating me. I do love you, my darling, more than you'll ever know, but . . ."

"You love my mother, too — you've already told me." Her voice was cool, but the pressure of his fingers was sending the usual shivers up her arm.

"I had to say that, in front of her." He employed the look which could turn her heart to jelly. "I'm not denying that I made love to her, but it all happened before I started loving you. I just sort of drifted into it with Anne, no great passion, just a sex release, like I explained before about that other girl. But you were growing up into a beautiful young lady, and I fell in love with you, and wanted you to love me, too. I never got any affection at home from my mother and father, that's why I left, so I suppose I was craving to be loved. Please say you haven't stopped loving me, Renee." He kissed her before she could reply, a kiss which made her forget the excruciating heartache he had caused her.

"I still love you, Fergus," she whispered, as soon as she could. "I'll always love you, I can't help it. As long as it's all finished between you and Mum, that's all I ask." Her eyes implored him to reassure her.

"That's all finished, Renee, I swear. She wouldn't have anything more to do with me even if I wanted it, which I don't. But there's no future for us now, you realise that? After what's happened, she'll never agree to me marrying you."

She felt desperate. "I know Mum would never agree to it, but couldn't we run away?" She would have gone anywhere with him, that very minute, if he'd consented.

"I've something to tell you, my darling."

The serious note in his voice effectively applied brakes to the girl's fast-accelerating heart, and she looked at him anxiously. "What is it?" she whispered.

"I thought about this all day yesterday after I left the house, and I made up my mind to do it today. I signed on for the army at dinnertime, and I leave next Monday."

"No! Oh, no, Fergus!" Renee's pupils dilated and her eyebrows rose in shocked disbelief. This was what she'd been dreading. This was why she'd blurted out the truth to her mother and ruined her own life so unwittingly.

His grip on her hand tightened until it was almost unbearable. "It's the only thing I could do, and I haven't told anybody else yet, so pretend to be surprised when I tell them at home." His kiss was slow and deliberate, making her confused, incoherent thoughts swim in the raging torrent of her need for him as he slid his tongue between her teeth. The aching desire was so overwhelming, she was glad when he drew away.

"Oh, God!" he moaned. "It's my last chance to let you see how much I love you, but I can't, not in here. Come on."

The story of *Stella Dallas* was still unknown to Renee as she followed him outside. "Where are we going?"

"Where we started." He hurried her across Union Street, Huntly Street to Esslemont Avenue and past the grammar school and up to Watson Street, to the Victoria Park; where their final declarations of love were made with mounting ecstasy.

Resting against the gnarled tree trunk, exhausted, but fulfilled, Renee said, hopefully, "I could try to meet you another night before you go away. Please, Fergus? I can't bear it if this is the very last time."

"It has to be, my darling. It would look too suspicious if you went out again this week." He stroked her cheek lightly. "I can hardly bear it, either, but I'll never forget you. Promise me you'll think of me every Monday, and don't ever forget you're my Monday girl."

Pushing aside the thought of his other Monday girl, she groped for his hand. "I'll remember you every day, not just Mondays." She paused, then sat up abruptly. "Fergus, I hope you've given me a baby tonight, because then I'd always have something of yours with me."

He straightened up in alarm. "Christ, Renee, I hope I haven't. That would be the last flaming straw. God Almighty, I've got enough on my plate just now, without having to worry about that as well."

Assuming that he was worrying about the possibility of him being wounded or killed, she hastened to reassure him. "Don't say that. You'll come through the war all right, I'm sure."

He laughed then, a peculiar, bemused laugh which she was to remember much later. "Oh, I'll come through OK. I've the luck of the devil, so everybody tells me."

They walked together to within a short distance of her house, then he stopped. "This is it, then, Renee. Our final goodbye, my darling. This is the one I'll carry with me wherever I go, and you'll have to remember for always."

The tears, which had been threatening as their parting grew more imminent, spilled over. "Oh, Fergus," she sobbed. "Why did you join up? It said on the wireless they'd be starting conscription eventually, so why didn't you wait till you were called up and we could have had some more time together?"

Gently, he dabbed her wet cheeks with his handkerchief. "It's better this way, sweetheart, especially with how things are at home." Bending down, he bit her bottom lip lightly, in a teasing manner. "I'll never forget I was the very first for you. No matter what happens, even if you marry another man, nobody can take that away from me. I was your first, so you belong to me for ever and ever."

"I'll never marry anybody else," she vowed.

"That's what you think now, but you'll change. It's time you went home, or your mother'll be wondering where you are."

"Not yet," she pleaded, but he kissed her quickly and strode away from her, round a corner, out of sight. After spending a few minutes trying to compose herself, she walked on towards the house; slowly at first until she glanced at her watch and saw that it was half past eleven, then quickly as she reflected that there would be another scene with her mother when she went in.

However, only Tim, Mike and Jack were in the living room, drinking tea from the flasks Anne had prepared for them.

"Your mother went to bed about half an hour ago," observed Jack. "Will I pour out a cup for you?"

Hoping that nothing of what she'd been doing that evening showed on her face, Renee decided to postpone the moment of facing her mother. "Yes, please, if there's enough left for Fergus." She could have bitten her tongue out the moment she said it, because it proved she knew he wasn't home yet. Would any of them guess she'd been out with him? Jack hesitated for a moment before he unscrewed the cap of the thermos and, as he handed her the cup he'd filled, he shook his head accusingly.

He knows, she thought, but he won't tell. In any case, he didn't know the whole, tragic truth.

It was well after midnight before she went upstairs, and she could hardly believe her luck in finding her mother fast asleep. She undressed without putting the light on, then crawled into bed to save making any kind of noise. Her turbulent emotions kept her from relaxing, and at last, in a desperate attempt to calm herself, she counted the roses she could see dimly on the wallpaper in the moonlight straggling through the skylight window. She lost count several times, and had to start at the beginning again, and it wasn't until she heard Fergus coming in, just before one, that she settled down to try to sleep.

She was still keyed up, however, and was jerked back into anxious puzzlement a few minutes later, when it occurred to her that he was often out late like this. Where had he been for the hour and a half since he left her? Had he gone to another girl for comfort? Was it a girl, and not one of his mates, who lived in that high tenement in Market Street where he'd gone when they were coming back from the Bay of Nigg? That was the night Jack Thomson had come out of the Club Bar and had taken her home, and had given her a lecture on letting herself be taken in by Fergus. How could he have known what Fergus was doing, anyway?

She fell into a troubled sleep at last to dream that she and Fergus were making love and her mother was standing over them, shouting. The shrill voice cut through her nightmare. "Renee! You'll be late for work, if you don't hurry."

Thankful that it had been a dream, the girl jumped out of bed, and dressed at full speed. When she went into the dining room, she saw that her mother was in a state of agitated excitement. "Come and hear what Fergus has just been telling us. He's joined the army, and he leaves next Monday." Anne's voice was too bright.

Renee was grateful that Fergus had prepared her for this and relieved that her mother had forgotten how late she'd come home the night before. Feigning astonishment, she said, "That was sudden, wasn't it?" Keep calm, that's it. The shock and the leave-taking were over, but the pain would always remain. Jack and Tim glanced at each other as if a load had been taken off their minds, then they plied Fergus with questions. Mike took no part in this, and Renee thought that he was probably dreading the time his call-up papers would arrive and he had to take his leave of Babs Sandison.

When the four boarders left for work, Anne turned to her daughter. "I'm glad you weren't upset about Fergus joining up. It was the best thing he could have done, for all our sakes."

"I suppose so." The girl marvelled at her own fortitude. His departure would certainly save any further unpleasantness and suspicion between her and her mother. They would be able to live in peace, with no jealousy, but she doubted if she would ever forgive her mother for being her rival for Fergus's love.

That Tuesday evening was the first that Fergus had spent in the house for months, and he sat down with Anne, Tim and Jack, to play pontoon, while Renee did some mending. She had recently found, not far from the office, a little shop where she could buy chiffon lisle stockings for eightpence ha'penny per pair, which was a big saving compared with the one and eleven the Union Street stores charged for the thicker rayon pairs she had been wearing before. The chiffon was quite fine, and didn't ladder, but if a snag wasn't stitched as soon as possible, it developed into a huge hole.

About half past ten, Mike Donaldson arrived home looking very sheepish. "We're getting married, Babs and me," he announced, his eyes going round the assembled, astonished faces, daring them to laugh.

Tim and Jack jumped to their feet, almost capsizing the rickety card table, now covered with cups, saucers and plates.

"Good for you, Mike! She's the right girl for you." Tim slapped his brother on the back with a force that practically winded him.

Jack pushed himself forward. "That's great news! You've got my very best wishes."

Anne and Renee had also risen to their feet to offer their congratulations. "I wish you both every happiness," Anne said, smiling earnestly. "I hope you have a long life together, and, as the saying goes, may all your troubles be little ones." Her eyes twinkled mischievously.

Renee exploded with laughter as she realised the double meaning. "That's good, Mum, but honestly, Mike, I wish you all the best for the future. When's the wedding?"

"I'll have to arrange things with the Registrar, and have the banns cried in Babs's kirk and mine in Turriff, I suppose." Mike pulled a face, causing more amusement.

Fergus stood up then, and went over to the excited group. "You're a lucky man, Mike." He shook hands soberly and went to the door. "Goodnight, all."

"I wish I'd some drink in the house so we could celebrate properly." Anne looked wistful, because liquor was a luxury which she couldn't afford.

"It doesn't matter, Mrs Gordon. I'm happy enough as it is." Mike's beaming face was a testament to that.

"Are you going to buy her an engagement ring?" Renee wondered if staid Mike had remembered about such a thing.

"Aye. We're going on Saturday afternoon. Oh, I'll be staying here this weekend, Mrs Gordon, if that's OK?"

"You know it is," Anne assured him.

"What's the best jeweller to go to, do you think?"

Anne considered. "There's a few good shops in Union Street and George Street, and you'll likely have to try more than one if Babs is difficult to please." She laughed as Mike twisted his mouth and rolled his eyes in mock horror.

"What made you suddenly think of getting married?" asked Tim. "You never mentioned the idea to me."

"It was Fergus joining up that did it." Mike was serious now. "I'll likely be called up shortly and . . . well, I wanted to get everything settled before I've to leave Babs."

"I tell you what." Anne looked animated. "Invite her here on Sunday, and we'll have a special tea seeing you'll be here this weekend. It'll be a sort of belated celebration."

"I'll stop here the weekend, as well," Tim put in. "So I'll buy some beer and a bottle of whisky . . . and what do you drink, Mrs Gordon?"

"It's a long time since I had anything. It doesn't matter, really. Wait — get a bottle of sherry. That'll do for Renee and me, and Babs as well, like enough."

Jack joined the planning. "I'll give you money to buy some fancy cakes, or something, and I'll come back on Sunday afternoon instead of night. I can't miss this."

Mike's happiness seemed to pervade the house for the next few days, and most of the conversation was centred on his wedding. Even Fergus entered into the good-natured teasing that Mike had to undergo, and it was only very occasionally that Renee remembered, with dismay, that Monday was drawing nearer — the fateful Monday when he would be leaving, without having a chance to give her any further sign of his love.

CHAPTER ELEVEN

It was Sunday morning before Anne Gordon and Renee heard Mike's description of the ring Babs had chosen. He'd come in very late on Saturday night.

"The man in the shop said it was a half-hoop diamond," he said, grinning bashfully. "And it was exactly what she wanted. It was the first place we tried, and we got the wedding ring there, as well. The banns have to be cried for three Sundays. So the date's set for Saturday, the seventh of October at two o'clock in John Knox, Mounthooly — that's Babs's kirk."

"He's asked me to be best man." Tim tried not to look too proud. "And Babs's sister's going to be bridesmaid."

"That'll maybe lead to another wedding," Anne smiled.

"I haven't met her yet, but you never know." He winked at Mike and Renee.

"Aye, Moira's a real bonnie lassie, as well," Mike said, seriously, "and she's just a month or two younger than Tim." Renee felt a stupid twinge of . . . it couldn't be jealousy. It must be unhappiness because everyone else was so up in the clouds, and the next day would be the saddest one she was ever likely to experience.

The special tea was quite a celebration, with the whisky and sherry helping the conviviality more than a little. They all agreed that Babs and Mike were ideally suited, and the newly engaged couple had to put up with much teasing, until Anne was forced to caution Tim and Jack for their ribald remarks, which were becoming rather more than suggestive.

Fergus Cooper had not stayed in, and Renee noticed that the atmosphere seemed to be more free and easy without him, but, at last, Mike took Babs home, and Jack and Tim went to bed, slightly tipsy but in very good humour.

While Renee helped her to clear up, Anne said, "That went off very well, I think."

"Yes, it did. Mike and Babs looked really happy."

"He's a decent lad, Renee. I wish . . ." She checked herself, then went on, "I wish Jack and Tim would find nice girls, too, though maybe Tim'll fall in love with the bridesmaid at the wedding."

Knowing that her mother had been on the point of saying she wished that *she* would find someone decent, Renee wondered sadly what the future would hold for her. She could never love anyone else as she'd loved Fergus, and she'd always remember, as he'd said she would, that he was her first lover, but was it possible that she could ever care enough for another man to want to marry him? She didn't think so, and so she'd likely end up an old maid, working in Brown and Company's office in Union Street until she retired.

Anne broke into her thoughts. "It's time we were in bed."

Fergus was first at the table the following morning, although he hadn't returned home until long after the party was over, and he grinned when Mike and Tim, then Jack, appeared, obviously "under the weather", followed by Renee, also looking somewhat pale.

"You should have been there, Fergus," Tim remarked, after the previous night's jollifications had been discussed.

"Aye, I'm sorry I couldn't manage, but I'd a lot of things to attend to."

Renee's head ached; she would never drink so much again. It had been only sherry, but it was the first time she'd tasted it, and the three — or was it four? — glasses had gone straight to her head. The question of what Fergus had to attend to that had been so important did cross her mind, but she surmised he'd been saying goodbye to his friends, and she couldn't cope with trying to think about it.

He remained seated when the other three stood up to go to work. "I won't be coming with you, for Saturday was my last day at the yard. Cheerio, boys. All the best, and I hope your call-up papers get lost in the post."

"God, I've been that taken up with myself, I clean forgot you were leaving the day." Mike looked really repentant, and went over to shake hands. "Good luck, Fergus, and we'll be hearing how you get on?"

Tim leaned over to give Fergus another hearty handshake. "Aye, the best of luck to you — but we'll maybe meet up sometime when we're all in the forces."

Jack laughed as he came forward. "It's not very likely the four of us'll ever be in the same place at the same time, but you never know. Look after yourself, Fergus."

He grinned. "I'll do that, and I'll be thinking about you on the seventh, Mike, wherever I am."

Renee swallowed the lump which had risen in her throat, and rose to help her mother to clear the table. When she had to leave to catch her bus, she had to steel herself for the formal parting from the man to whom she had lost her virginity, and who would be taking her heart with him when he left.

"Goodbye, and good luck, Fergus," she said steadily, aware that her mother was watching them intently.

"Goodbye, Renee." He extended his hand and squeezed hers so tightly that she had to keep herself from wincing.

Immediately he released her, she picked up her handbag and went into the hall to put on her jacket. As she slipped her left arm into her sleeve, she slid her right hand into her pocket, with no real expectation of finding anything there.

Her heart leapt with joy when her fingers encountered a folded sheet of paper, but she withdrew her hand quickly. She decided to wait until she was on the bus before she read it in case her mother came through and caught her.

She was barely seated when she pulled it out and unfolded it.

Darling Monday Girl,

I'm writing this on a bench in the Victoria Park, thinking over the happy times we had here. It's Sunday evening and I can picture you enjoying yourself at Mike's party, but my heart is breaking at the thought of never seeing you again after tomorrow morning. That's why I couldn't join the celebration. I couldn't have sat and watched you all that time without being tempted to kiss you.

I wish you were here with me now, so I could hold you in my arms just one more time, but this is goodbye. Please think of me sometimes, because I will never forget you.

All my love for ever, and ever,

Fergus.

A tear ran down Renee's cheek as she folded the letter and put it in her handbag. She couldn't bring herself to destroy this precious love-letter, ever, but she would have to keep it in a place where her mother was never likely to find it. Under the lining paper in the chest of drawers! That would be perfect, because she always tidied out her own things, and nobody else would ever think of looking there.

She settled back in her seat, much happier than she'd been when she rose in the morning, because at least he'd been thinking about her yesterday. Well, she'd be thinking about him when the train left at twelve o'clock, whatever she was doing, and . . . But he wouldn't be leaving the house until about half past eleven, and that meant he'd have three hours alone with her mother. Three whole hours! What would they get up to, with three hours to say goodbye? Would he try to get round Anne again, and make her believe she was the only person for him after all? He surely couldn't be so treacherous, not after what he'd written in his letter. But he'd proved before that he was a confirmed liar, so was he to be trusted?

Renee's spirits had reached a new low ebb by the time she entered the office, and her pale face and dejected manner prompted Sheila Daun to ask, "What's up? You don't look very happy with yourself."

"Fergus goes away today. He joined the army." It took a great effort to talk about it.

"Oh, I'm sorry. He's the one you liked best, isn't he? But don't be so upset about it, he'll be back when he's on leave, and he'll write to you to let you know how he's doing."

Renee wanted to say, "He can't write, and he'll never be back, so I'll never know what he's doing," but it was impossible without going into long explanations which would shock and disgust the other girl. She tried to apply herself to her work, but her mind kept returning to the house in Cattofield, and what might be going on there. During their mid-morning teabreak, Sheila tried to cheer her up, but it wasn't until after twelve that Renee relaxed, with a guilty sense of relief that Fergus would have departed from Aberdeen altogether.

She made no mention of him at lunchtime, and neither did Anne. They spoke about Mike and Babs, about a possible romance springing up between Tim and Babs's sister Moira, about the celebration of the evening before, about anything except the person who was uppermost in their minds, and who had caused them both so much happiness and pain. When she returned to work, Renee still knew nothing of his ultimate leave-taking, but the great weight which had been pressing on her all forenoon had lifted. It was all over — the doubts, the suspicions — for ever, because he'd never be allowed to come back to the house now he'd left it.

Only the love and heartache would remain to haunt her.

CHAPTER TWELVE

The arrangements for his wedding were all that Mike Donaldson could talk about. "We can't afford a big do, and Babs's mother's a widow like you, Mrs Gordon, so there'll just be the four of us at the kirk, then we're going back to her house for a meal. She wanted to do that much for us, at least."

"Where are you going for your honeymoon?" Renee had romantic ideas of a bridal suite in a luxury hotel somewhere.

"That's another thing we can't afford," he said, ruefully. "I'm going to ask my folks this weekend if they'll let us spend our wedding night there. You see, I'd my holidays in the Trade's Week in July, when the yard was closed, so I'm only having the Saturday forenoon off, and I've to start on the Monday."

Renee felt very sorry for Babs, being denied a proper honeymoon, but perhaps she'd be happy enough just being in Turriff with Mike as his wife. As Anne had said, he was a decent man and he'd be a considerate husband.

On the Thursday after Fergus left, Jack and Tim succeeded, after much persuasion, in coaxing Renee to go to the Tivoli with them. "It's variety," Tim told her. "You'll enjoy it."

Anne put in her tuppence-worth. "Oh, yes, Renee, your dad used to take me there, years ago, and it's different from the pictures, completely different."

"Music-hall turns," added Jack. The girl reluctantly agreed to go, for she knew that Tim and Jack were doing their best to keep her mind off Fergus, and she was grateful that they had not fixed the outing for a Monday.

The Tivoli was in Guild Street, on the opposite side from the railway station, and on the bus going into town they told her about some of the famous acts which had appeared there in the past. The bus stop was quite a distance from the theatre, but they walked down Bridge Street and joined the queue which had already formed.

"We can only afford the gods," Tim remarked. "But it's not that bad." They reached their seats by climbing up a spiral staircase, up and up and up, until Renee thought they must surely go through the roof of the building, and she experienced a surge of vertigo when she stood at the top of the steep steps between the rows of seats inside the actual balcony. It was like looking down a near-vertical precipice, and she was afraid to move in case she lost her footing and catapulted right down and over the brass rail at the foot, into the stalls below. But Tim took her hand and went in front of her, while Jack held her waist to steady her from behind, and they descended slowly and carefully.

It was a marvel to the girl that she could hear the tiny performers on the stage so clearly. She laughed uproariously at the comedians, applauded the singers, cheered the acrobats and magicians, and was enthralled by the trapeze artists.

Going out wasn't nearly so bad but she did have one moment of panic when they were going down the spiral staircase, because the people behind seemed to be pushing and jostling. Jack understood the fear in her eyes when she turned round. "It's OK, Renee. Just keep holding on to the banisters and you'll be fine."

When they reached the street, she let her breath out noisily, making the other two roar with laughter. "That's the nearest you'll ever get to heaven," joked Tim.

The following Thursday they took her to His Majesty's Theatre, another first for Renee, where a repertory company was presenting a musical comedy. Once again, they went to the balcony, and had to pass the main entrance, where the patrons were flocking in for the upper and dress circles, the orchestra stalls and the boxes.

"I'd love to sit in a box, just once," she remarked after they were seated, and she'd had time to look around her. The occupants of the lower box at the opposite side appeared to be very wealthy, the men wearing evening suits and the ladies with fur coats draped over the backs of their seats. "Are they dear?"

Winking to Jack, Tim said, "Aye, the boxes are pretty dear, and you've to be wearing a fur coat before you're allowed in."

"Stop pulling her leg." Jack had seen the envy in her eyes, and felt sorry for her. "You don't need a fur coat, Renee, but the seats are dear. If I ever win the pools, I'll take you to a box in His Majesty's, and that's a promise." They all giggled, knowing that there was less than a million-to-one chance of such a thing ever happening.

The velvet drapes opened and the orchestra in the pit began to play while Renee read all the advertisements on the safety curtain, until it rose slowly to reveal a drawing-room scene. She sat on the edge of her seat, engrossed in the tale being unfolded by the actors and actresses, and was completely transported to the opulent world of Noël Coward.

The following morning, Renee was telling Sheila Daun about her theatre visit when Mr Murchie came out of his office, and they stopped speaking as he strode purposefully towards them.

"I've just received a memo from head office, girls. They've cancelled the rule about RSA. certificates being compulsory, so you won't need to enrol for evening classes this session. Apparently with the war on there may not be sufficient teachers in some parts of Britain to cover the syllabus for all the courses. You will be pleased to know, however, that the salary scale will remain as it is — increments each year until you reach the maximum."

Sheila was delighted. She had already passed the elementary and intermediate, but had been dreading the advanced. Renee felt only a great relief at not having to attend the grammar school during the coming winter. It would have been awful to come out and have no Fergus waiting for her. It was bad enough as it was, with not knowing what he was doing.

Mr Murchie had walked away, so Sheila nudged her. "Go on telling me about the play, Renee. It sounded good."

"It was, oh, it really was, and it was so well acted that you forgot you were only in a theatre. You thought you were actually there, in that drawing room with them." She sighed. "I wish I could have been an actress. I loved being in school plays, and the teachers said I was a natural." Which probably explained her ability to tell lies so easily, she reflected sadly.

On the Thursday before Mike's wedding, they all went to the Palais. The prospective bride and groom looked so deliriously happy that Renee felt like crying. Babs had taken her sister along to meet Mike's brother before they had to stand up as best man and bridesmaid in the church, and Renee noticed, later that evening, that Moira and Tim also had eyes only for each other. Love at first sight, obviously.

Jack, who was dancing with her, heard her long drawn-out sigh, and followed her gaze. "It looks like you'll have to put up with just me from now on, I'm afraid."

"There's no need to sound so sorry about it, I don't mind being with you." Her eyes were frank as they met his, because she could be alone with him if she wanted, now.

"Great!" He twirled her a complete circle, and partnered her for the rest of the evening.

At the opening bars of the last waltz, Tim appeared beside them, with Moira held by the hand. "I'm seeing Moira home, Jack. You'll manage to take Renee on your own, won't you?"

Renee didn't miss the wink he aimed at Jack, who replied, with mock-seriousness, "I think I might just manage that."

"We're leaving now," Tim went on, "because Moira doesn't want to be too late."

"Oh, aye?" Jack's eyes twinkled as the other couple walked away. "They don't want to go home in a foursome with Mike and Babs, that's what it is," he said, confidentially.

"I don't suppose Mike and Babs want them tagging along either." Renee felt quite at home as Jack's arms went round her for the last dance. The lights dimmed slowly, and he hugged her tightly.

"Are you disappointed about Tim?"

"No. Why should I be disappointed?"

"I thought you liked him better than me."

"You're just fishing, Jack Thomson. I like Tim, but I like you just as much."

"But you still like Fergus best, is that it?"

"Fergus is away now," she said carefully, wishing that he hadn't reminded her.

"Aye, but he'll be back when he's on leave, for he doesn't speak to his folk — or they don't speak to him — and your house is his only home now." Renee remembered then that Jack was unaware of the true reason for Fergus joining up, and of the fact that he had made it impossible for himself ever to come back to their house. She could see that Jack took her silence to mean that she did still love Fergus, but she couldn't explain.

"I've been thinking I'll maybe join up as well," he said, after a long pause. "There's nothing much for me in Aberdeen."

"Oh, no, Jack!" She found that she *did* like him, very much, even if the feeling wasn't quite deep enough to be called love, and she certainly hated the thought of him leaving.

"Would you care if I went away?" he asked softly, encouraged by her reaction.

"Of course I'd care." He seemed pleased with that, and they ended the dance with a big whirl, then said their goodbyes to Mike and Babs.

On the walk home, and in the middle of her telling him about a slight difference of opinion between Mr Murchie and Miss Esson, Jack said, out of the blue, "I care about you, Renee. Quite a lot." He kept on walking, his arm linked with hers, but his head still turned to the front.

"Oh." It was all she could say, although she'd suspected it for some time, and they carried on in silence for a while. Then he stopped abruptly and kissed her, a kiss which she returned with a fervour that surprised her.

It also surprised Jack. "I'll keep on hoping you'll learn to care for me properly, Renee," he said, but he dropped his arms and began walking again.

She noticed that he had avoided mentioning love, and was very grateful to him. It would have been far too soon. Before they went into the house, he kissed her again. "If Tim's to be going steady with Moira, will you still come out with me on Thursdays?"

"I think I could just force myself," she teased, not to give him the opportunity of becoming serious.

"That's a step in the right direction, anyway." He took her hand and they went inside.

"Mum! Why are you still up?"

Anne was sitting in front of the almost black-out fire. "I couldn't settle to go to bed. I wanted to know how you all got on, and what kind of girl Babs's sister is." She shifted the cups on the card table, showing how guilty she felt about being so inquisitive.

Jack beamed. "We all got on fine, and Moira Sandison's a very nice girl."

"She's as blonde as Tim, and a wee bit smaller," Renee added.

Anne looked expectantly at her daughter, but no more information seemed to be forthcoming. "Tim didn't come home with you, I see?"

Renee burst out laughing. "No, you were right. He fell for her, hook, line and sinker, and took her home before the dance was finished."

Anne looked satisfied. "I just thought that would happen," she said triumphantly. "Brothers often marry sisters, and romance must be in the air. The love bug'll bite you two next, no doubt." She looked at them archly. Jack turned red, proving to her that she was on the right track, but Renee said, "Oh, Mum!" in an annoyed voice, so Anne let the matter drop.

Saturday was wet, but the Gordons went to John Knox Church at a quarter to two, to watch the bride and groom arriving with their attendants. Jack had felt obliged to go home to see his mother because she hadn't been very well, and had expressed great disappointment at being unable to be with them.

The heavy rain hadn't dampened the high spirits of Babs and Mike, nor those of Moira and Tim, who were completely wrapped up in each other. The two spectators sheltered in a doorway until the bridal party re-emerged, then Anne showered the happy pair with confetti, while Renee went up to Tim and whispered, "Your turn next," before emptying her carton over him and the bridesmaid. Moira blushed, but Tim seemed rather put out.

When a taxi took the wedding group away, Renee and her mother waved until they were out of sight, then turned to go home.

"I don't think it'll be that long before Tim asks Moira to marry him," Anne remarked on the bus. "They looked head over heels in love."

"I believe they are, but Tim didn't seem to like the idea when I told him that it would be their turn next. They made a nice couple, though."

"Jack and you made a nice couple when you came home on Thursday night," Anne said carefully, waiting for the flat denial she expected her daughter to make, or the flare-up which might be her answer.

Renee, however, thought it best to let the remark pass without argument. "Jack's a nice boy," was all she said.

He *was* a nice boy — a very nice boy — and, given time, she might indeed come to feel more than liking for him now that Fergus was out of her life. Not a deep, devouring passion, perhaps, but a comfortable, loving relationship.

When Renee's thoughts turned to Fergus she pushed them resolutely from her mind. There was no point in dreaming of the unattainable, nor in dwelling on the past. That chapter of her life was over, and she was free to love anyone else if she felt like it. The trouble was that she didn't *feel* free yet.

It was only just over six weeks since Fergus went away. She'd gone out twice with Jack since Tim deserted them, and had skilfully diverted him any time he seemed to be getting serious. Her mother had made no more references to them as a couple, and Renee was quite content to let things jog along as they were. Tonight, Thursday again, Jack was taking her to the Palais, and she went home at teatime quite looking forward to being on the dance floor with him again.

Her heart lurched almost out of control when she saw the tall dark-haired figure in khaki talking to Jack and Tim in the dining room. "F . . . F . . . Fergus!" she stammered.

"In the flesh," he laughed. "You won't forget to close your mouth, will you? You look like a fish gasping for water."

She was so glad to see him that she didn't feel a bit annoyed at him for making fun of her, but just then,

Anne carried in a large ashet. "He's looking well, isn't he, Renee?"

He was looking divine, the girl thought, her legs trembling. "What . . .? How . . .?"

Fergus grinned. "I wrote asking your mother if I could come here when my square-bashing was finished — I've nowhere else to go — and she wrote back saying it was OK."

Annoyance, and anger, flooded up inside Renee now. Her mother hadn't said anything about it. How could she have been so underhand? And why had he never written to *her*, when he'd sworn, on his last night in Aberdeen, that he loved her and not her mother? He could have sent it to the office after all. The bile rising in her throat threatened to choke her, and she had to swallow repeatedly before she could speak. "That's good," she muttered at last.

Jack was studying her with an expression of resignation, and it crossed her mind that here was a way to pay Fergus back. Smiling sweetly at Jack, she said, "It's still all right for our date tonight, isn't it, Jack? I'm really looking forward to going to the Palais again." She was inwardly ashamed at using Jack for her own ends, but the wry smile which crossed briefly over his face told her that he understood why she was doing it.

"Oh, aye, it's still on." He turned to Fergus. "Renee and me are going to be tripping the light fantastic the night," he said brightly, then he glanced at Tim. "Are you and Moira coming as well?"

Before Tim had a chance to reply, Fergus pounced on the unfamiliar name. "Moira? Who's Moira? A girlfriend at last, eh, Tim?"

"Aye, we're going steady. She was the bridesmaid at Mike's wedding — Babs's sister — and I was the best man. We kind of hit it off the first time we met."

"So-o-o." The word was drawn out, and the sarcasm was aimed at Renee. "There's a lot of new romances starting up, I can see." The contempt in his eyes matched his sneering voice.

"Why shouldn't there be?" Renee was defiant, in spite of the sickness still deep down inside her. Was he trying to tell her that he'd be glad to get her out of his life? Was he pleased he'd got rid of one complication? By writing to her mother and not to her, had he been trying to prove his love to Anne? And how many times had he written? Renee forced herself to eat what was set in front of her, but her heart was as heavy as lead, and everything was tasteless.

"I'll give you a hand with the dishes, Anne." Fergus stood up when they were all finished eating, his use of the Christian name tormenting the girl even more. "So off you go, Renee, and make yourself look pretty for Jack."

She would willingly have killed him, then, for being so hateful, and for openly saying "Anne" again. He was just an unfeeling brute, and she shouldn't let his behaviour hurt her. She went to wash and dress, still seething at his treatment of her, and took extra care with her hair and her make-up simply to spite him.

Before she went downstairs again, she checked her appearance in the mirror, because she wanted to look her very best, to make Fergus jealous. The new, pale blue dress which she'd saved up for, and had bought last week, was quite stunning, she thought, and the small puff sleeves were sitting just right. The deep-blue embroidery on the bodice matched her eyes, and she felt she couldn't look any more attractive.

A very smart Jack was waiting for her, although his sandy hair, which he had plastered down with water, was already sticking up in what Anne called his "cow's lick". "You're looking very sweet," he said, smiling at her reassuringly.

"Love's young dream," sneered Fergus, exactly as he had said when he'd seen her kissing Tim months before.

Stung into retaliation, Renee said sharply, "At least it's all above-board," not caring that her mother, and Jack, would also know what she meant.

She had time to gather her shattered nerve ends together on the bus, because Jack seemed to understand that she wasn't ready to talk yet, but before they went into the dance hall, he took her hand and said, "He's not worth all your heartache, Renee. A two-timer like him? He's not fit to wash your feet. Enjoy yourself, lass, you're only young once."

She knew that he was speaking the truth, and she was still furious at Fergus. All right. Let her mother have him! She, Renee, was going to have a good time tonight, even if it killed her. She held her head high as they went through the door. Jack, also determined to let her have no time to feel bitter or let-down, was very attentive, and kept her laughing with his silly jokes. Gallant was the only word to describe him, she thought, and felt her spirits lifting, so much that she welcomed Tim and Moira warmly when they appeared some fifteen minutes later.

"Ooh, Renee, I like your dress," the other girl said. "I've to keep on wearing this old pink one. I've had it for ages, but I can't afford a new one yet."

"That one suits you, Moira, with your blond hair, and I'd to save for months and months to buy this. I got it in a sale at the Mascot, or else I wouldn't have had one at all. The lemon dress was an old one of my mother's, though I altered it a bit."

The two young men were looking at each other in amusement, but now Tim said, in a falsetto voice, "D'you like my suit, Jack? It's a 1937 model, but it's the latest style."

Jack smiled gravely. "And the black buttons just match your fingernails."

"Oh, you two!" Renee spluttered. "They're always the same," she informed Moira.

When Tim took Renee up to a slow foxtrot, he said quietly, "Now, I'm not interfering . . ." which made her heart sink again, because she suspected that he was about to deliver a lecture. "It's just . . . Jack thinks an awful lot of you, Renee, so don't lead him on if you're set on Fergus. That's all." He looked at her with his mouth screwed up, then added, "Uncle Tim's advice for the day, free, gratis and for nothing."

She gave a tight smile, and they danced in silence, apart from Tim's unmelodious humming of the tune, until they joined the other two, who had also been dancing together. During the next dance, Jack said, "You've gone all quiet again. Did Tim say anything to upset you?"

"No, not really. He was giving me some fatherly advice." She laughed suddenly. "Uncle Tim, he said, so it would be uncly advice. I'm sorry. I promise I'm going to enjoy myself."

"That's better. I don't like to see you unhappy."

Tim's joking, with Jack's assistance, made the rest of the evening fly past. Renee couldn't brood because she was laughing so much at their antics, and she was honestly sorry when it was time to go home. While they walked, Jack kept up a steady chatter, to which she responded in a similar light vein, but when they had almost reached the house, he stopped and slid his arm round her. It was at the same place where Tim had stood with her, and she felt her muscles tightening at the thought of being caught by Fergus again. But why should she worry about him now? He'd shown that he didn't want her any longer.

She received Jack's kiss gladly then, as a balm for her inner wounds.

"You've got guts, Renee, I'll say that for you," he said softly. "Keep going. He's only here for a few more days . . . I'm disappointed in your mother, though."

He knows, about everything, she thought. He must have guessed what had been going on, and was pitying her all the more. "Thanks, Jack," she said, simply, and they walked on.

Once again, Anne was still sitting in the living room. "Fergus has gone to bed, he was tired after his long journey." She couldn't meet Renee's eyes, and the girl felt fleetingly sorry for her, until she remembered how deceitful her mother had been in writing to him, and, even worse, that she had been alone with him all evening.

"We'd a really marvellous time, Mum. Tim and Moira were there, too, and we thoroughly enjoyed ourselves, didn't we, Jack?"

"Aye, it was great fun." He knew what this show of over-enthusiasm was costing her. "Where's Fergus sleeping?"

Since Mike Donaldson had married, Tim had been sharing the downstairs bedroom with Jack, to save work for Anne, but Fergus might have gone to his old room.

"He's upstairs." Again, Anne avoided looking at her daughter, who now realised why that room had been left unoccupied. She had wondered why her mother had not taken in another two boarders, but she must have known all along that Fergus would be back.

"I'll leave you two to take your tea," Anne said. "Use the red flask, and leave the tartan one for Tim, it's smaller." She rose and walked to the door. "Goodnight, Jack."

He held the door open for her. "Goodnight, Mrs Gordon." He closed it softly behind her, then came back to sit down.

"I'll pour it out," Renee said, waiting for him to push his cup and saucer across. "Do you think Tim's serious about Moira?" She concentrated on unscrewing the cap of the thermos flask.

He understood that she was trying to prevent him from touching on a more painful subject. "He says he's serious, and I think he means it. I thought at one time that you and him . . ." He looked at her quizzically.

"Oh, no." Renee smiled. "I told you before — I like him, but that's all."

"The same as you like me." Jack grinned and shrugged. "You told me that as well." He looked down at the contents of his cup. "I know we can't choose who we fall in love with, it just happens, but remember, Renee, I'll always be available for you to turn to when . . . at any time."

She stretched her hand out across the table and laid it over his. "I know, Jack, and I'm very grateful, but . . ."

"Aye."

They'd just finished the tea, when Tim came in, so Renee said, "Goodnight, boys," and left them talking.

The next few days passed without any awkward incidents — without any incidents at all — and Renee was coming to terms with the plain, unvarnished truth that Fergus obviously did not want to revive their previous relationship, but, on the Monday morning, after Tim and Jack had left for work, and Anne was in the scullery, he whispered, "Tonight. Half past seven, inside the Graveyard." Anne came back, so he didn't wait for any sign from the girl that she would be there.

Renee was left to stare at the half-slice of toast still on her plate. Her mouth was dry, her heart was hammering, there was an insistent pounding in her ears, and she hoped that her mother wouldn't notice her confusion. Luckily, Anne's mind seemed to be elsewhere as she gathered up the dirty dishes.

One of their neighbours sat down beside Renee on the bus, making it impossible for her to concentrate on her own thoughts, and she was kept busy all forenoon, so it wasn't until she was on her way home at lunchtime that she was able to consider the unexpected turn of events. What a cheek Fergus had! After sneering at her on Thursday, and ignoring her all over the weekend, he expected her to come running as soon as he snapped his fingers. Several times on the journey she decided not to meet him that night. Let him think what he liked. But she always changed her mind, and finally plumped for keeping the date, but only to listen to any explanations he could offer for his callous behaviour. She knew she was being stupid, that she was asking for trouble, that her heart would probably be broken again as it always was with Fergus Cooper, but she had to talk to him.

He wasn't there when she arrived home, and she was relieved that she could act normally with her mother. She took her dinner quickly as usual, because the travelling took up most of her lunch hour.

"I'll be going out with Phyllis tonight," she told Anne before she left. That should set her mother thinking, but she could put two and two together if she liked. Renee avoided letting her thoughts touch on Fergus during the afternoon. She was meeting him at half past seven, and there was no point in dragging her bruised feelings through the mill more than she could help.

At teatime, only Jack and Tim were in the dining room, arguing about football until their landlady came through. Anne eyed her daughter speculatively. "Fergus came home in the afternoon, but he went out again." Her face was tight and her voice was cold. God, they must have had another quarrel, Renee thought. Her mother must have really put two and two together and realised that she was going out with Fergus, not Phyllis. Anne must have tackled him about it, and that's why he hadn't waited for tea. Good! Her mother could have the sore heart this time, for a change, and could imagine what they were doing while they were together. Renee noticed that Jack looked hurt. He had guessed, too, but it couldn't be helped.

She came off the bus at the Graveyard, the affectionate name Aberdonians gave to the old kirkyard of St Nicholas' Church, their city's Mother Kirk, where the flat gravestones of long-dead citizens were used as a short cut from Union Street to George Street. The iron gates, although directly off the main thoroughfare, led into a quiet, calm oasis, far removed from the noise and bustle of Union Street. Fergus was waiting for her on a secluded bench, well away from curious eyes, and she would have walked right past him if he hadn't seen her coming and stepped forward. She stiffened involuntarily as his arms went round her, and turned her head away from his kiss. "No, Fergus. You can't expect to carry on as if nothing had happened. I want to know why you wrote to my mother and not to me. You swore it was me you loved, not her, but . . ."

"Renee," he interrupted. "Darling, listen . . ."

"No, you listen. I've had enough! I've been through hell and back over you, and I've had it! I'm finished!"

It wasn't what she'd intended to say. It had come out without her being conscious of even thinking it, but she was glad, and hoped she was wounding him as much as he'd wounded her in the past. Fergus seemed stunned by the tirade, but recovered quickly. "I know what all this is about," he sneered. "It's Jack Thomson. You're in love with him now, aren't you?"

"Maybe I am. What's it to you?"

"You're mine! You've been my Monday girl for . . ."

"Cut that out, Fergus Cooper! It's no use now. You made a mockery of that long ago, and all your sweet-talking won't make any difference."

His cajoling smile faded. "OK then, if that's how you feel. Your smarmy Jack can have you, but does he know he's getting second-hand goods? You can't change that, Renee. I was first."

She felt her gorge rising. "Shut up! Shut up! I don't know how you've got the nerve to . . . You can't hold a candle to Jack. He's everything you're not — decent, genuine . . . Oh!" She turned and walked away from him, so angry that she couldn't trust herself to say anything else.

He bounded after her and gripped her shoulder. "Go on, then. Tie yourself to him. You'll soon get fed up, and I guarantee you'll remember me every time he makes love to you on a Monday. You'll always remember that you belong to me, no matter who thinks he owns you."

She shook off his hand and stood breathing heavily. "I don't know if Jack has even thought of marrying me, but if he asks me I'll say yes, and you'll never cross my mind on Mondays or any other day of the week. As for being fed up with him, I'd be happy for the rest of my life as long as he kept on loving me, because I'd know it was just me for him, not hundreds of other girls, and certainly never my own mother."

"You couldn't be happy." Fergus stuck his face, contorted with rage, close to hers. "You need excitement, a proper he-man to keep you satisfied. You need me." His expression softened. "You can't send me away like this, when I might be killed any time."

She glared at him. "Don't try any of your tricks, Fergus, for they won't work any more. I've come to my senses at last."

That seemed to hit the target, because he said, sadly, "Your mother guessed you were meeting me tonight, you know, and we'd another barney. She didn't tell me not to keep the date, but she said I was never to come back to her house after I leave tomorrow." He looked at her pitifully. "She means it this time, Renee."

Her eyes flashed. "Good! Now, if you don't mind, I'm going home." She pulled away from him, and walked on along the path towards the side gate.

"I swear to you, Renee," he shouted after her, "every time *anybody* makes love to you on a Monday, you'll remember that I was first, and you belong to me. And there's nothing you can do about that!"

Ignoring him, and, without once looking back, she went down the steps and through the narrow gate on legs that were shaking violently. She felt empty, drained of all feeling, but she had broken his spell over her, with his own, unwitting, help.

After she crossed Schoolhill, and was walking up George Street, she realised that she was going in the direction of her grandmother's house. It hadn't been intentional, but she had to unburden herself to someone, and who better than her beloved granny, who had been perceptive enough, the first time she saw him, to assess Fergus for the rotter he really was? Unfortunately, her warnings had fallen on ears unwilling to listen. Sheer doggedness kept Renee going until she reached the tenement in Woodside, but she was still trembling as she climbed the stairs. By pure good luck, Peter McIntosh was out, and Maggie looked up in surprise when Renee walked in.

"What brings you here at this time o' night?" she asked, then one look at the girl's face in the light of the gas lamp on the wall told her that something dreadful had happened, and her voice became anxious. "Sit doon, my dearie, an' tell me aboot it."

"Oh, Granny!" Renee's delicate composure crumbled at the love and concern in the old woman's words. "You were right about Fergus. He *was* no good." She burst into tears and ran to the outstretched arms, then sank to the floor with her head on her grandmother's lap. Maggie let her sob her heart out, patting her head occasionally in sympathy, until the girl's shoulders stopped heaving and she held up her head, pathetically. The faded blue eyes looked down with compassion.

"Can ye speak aboot it, noo?"

Renee took a shuddering breath. "I've been stupid, Granny. Really stupid. I thought . . . he swore he loved me, but . . ." Her voice trailed away.

"Ye found oot that he didna?" Maggie didn't sound surprised, and waited for the rest of the story.

"It was worse than that. He'd been . . . making love to . . . other girls as well." Renee had almost given away her mother's secret, too, but covered up quickly.

"Aye." The woman's expression did not change. There was no disapproval or shock on her face as she took the girl's hand. "Lassie, ye're nae the first to be let doon like that, an' ye'll nae be the last. At least ye've seen through him noo."

"Yes, I have seen through him now, Granny. You warned me about him long ago, and so did Jack Thomson and Tim Donaldson, but I was sure he loved me, so I wouldn't listen."

Her grandmother smiled sadly. "Sometimes it's best if ye learn yer lesson the hard road. Ye'll nae mak' the same mistake again, will ye?"

"No, I'm sure I won't, but, oh Granny, it was awful. We'd a blazing row tonight, and we said terrible things to each other."

The grey head nodded. "Nae doot ye deserved them, the pair o' ye." She squeezed Renee's hand to let her see that she wasn't censuring her, and they sat silently, lovingly, until Maggie said, "He's hame on leave, then?"

"He goes away tomorrow, and I'll be glad to see the last of him. I'm sure he'll never come back to our house again, because Mum won't let him."

Maggie's eyebrows rose. "She ken't aboot you and him, did she?"

"Yes." Renee wondered how much she could say without Granny realising what had actually been going on in the house in Cattofield. "You see, I told her myself before Fergus went away the first time, because I wanted everything out in the open." Would that be enough to satisfy her grandmother's curiosity?

Maggie nodded wisely. "Now I understand. I was a bit feared that yer mother had mair than a soft spot for Fergus hersel'."

Their eyes met and held, until Renee looked away. "That's all finished now . . . I think . . . and I'm finished with him, too."

The old woman was quiet for a few minutes, then she said, "I'm goin' to mak' ye a cup o' tea, then ye'd better get hame, but mind this, Renee, a mother's a lassie's best friend. Dinna let that waster come atween ye."

She stood up and the girl rose off the floor to take out the dishes while her grandmother filled the kettle and lit the gas ring. They sat down at the table to wait for it to come to the boil, and Maggie suddenly looked anxiously at Renee.

"There's jist one thing I have to ask ye, lassie . . . Ye're nae goin' to ha'e his bairn, are ye?"

Renee shook her head. "No, Granny, I'm not. Thank God for that."

"Aye, thank God. Ye've got aff light, for things could ha'e been a lot worse."

When Renee was leaving, her grandmother said, "We'll nae tell yer mother ye've been here, eh?"

"Thanks, Granny . . . for everything. I feel better now." On her way home she congratulated herself that at last she'd had the courage to do what she should have done months ago. If only she had listened to Granny, and Jack and Tim, she could have saved herself all the heartache. Her step lightened as she went on. She felt purged, as if she had cast an evil demon from her soul. She smiled grimly. That was exactly what she *had* done. She had rid herself of a Svengali who had hypnotised her for far too long.

Fergus Cooper would be leaving tomorrow for good. Thank God he would never affect her life again.

Part Two

CHAPTER THIRTEEN

As the sound of John Boles' voice died away, Anne rose to wind up the gramophone. This twelve-inch recording of the "Desert Song" had been one of her late husband's favourites, and the song, "One Alone", especially, made her think nostalgically of Jim Gordon. She glanced across to her daughter, who was curled up on the settee, but Renee was too busy reading to be any company. They were alone in the house, Tim Donaldson and Jack Thomson having gone to visit Mike and Babs, and Anne's heart ached with longing for the life she had once known, and hadn't fully appreciated until it was gone.

Sighing, she lifted the record and drew her sleeve lightly round it to remove any particles of dust. She was replacing it on the turntable when she was startled by the ringing of the doorbell.

"I'll go." Renee jumped up eagerly. She had no idea who might be calling, but any visitor would brighten them up. The small dark-haired girl standing on the step was a complete stranger, and seemed nervous and apprehensive.

"Yes?" Renee asked, helpfully, because the girl appeared to be unsure of what to say.

"Is this where . . . er . . . Mrs Gordon lives?" The last three words came out in a rush.

"Yes, come in." Renee led the way into the living room, puzzling over who this girl could be, and what she wanted with Anne. "Mum, somebody wants to see you." She gestured to the girl to sit down, but the caller shook her head and remained just inside the door, one hand clenching and unclenching spasmodically at the front edge of her coat, so Renee shrugged and sat down on the settee again.

Anne switched off the gramophone and waited, but, when nothing was forthcoming, she smiled. "What was it you wanted to see me about?"

"Did . . . er . . . Fergus Cooper lodge here?" The almost-whispered words made both Anne and Renee look at her in astonishment.

"Yes, he did," Anne said, after a slight pause. "But he joined the army in September."

"I know." The girl was silent again and the other two kept looking at her expectantly.

"Has he been back on leave yet?" This time, the voice was a little stronger.

"He was here after his training was finished, and he went back about a couple of months ago." Anne's perplexed face had begun to show signs of anxiety. "Was it him you really wanted to see?"

The girl nodded briefly. "I . . . he . . ." She swallowed, then burst out, "I'm going to have his baby."

The two gasps were practically synchronised, and it was a few seconds before Anne said quietly, "Are you sure that Fergus is the father?"

"Oh, yes. I was never with anybody else, and he said he'd marry me, but then he just disappeared. I went to where he worked, and they told me he was in the army and gave me your address, because he would likely write to you. I waited for a few weeks, to give him the chance to get in touch with me, but he didn't, and my mother doesn't know yet, but I'm well over five months already and it's starting to show." She began to weep softly and sat down on the chair by the door.

"Is your name Lily?" Renee had remembered Fergus telling her that Lily was growing too serious.

The girl lifted her head. "No, it's Jeanette. Jeanette Morrison. Why? Did he speak about having another girl?"

Renee saw how upset she was by that possibility, and said, hastily, "No, no. That was a long time ago, probably before he ever met you." Another girl? she thought, ruefully. Dozens, if she was any judge, including herself . . . and her mother.

"Did he know about . . . this, before he went away?" Anne was asking.

"Yes, he did, and he promised he'd do the right thing by me, so the baby wouldn't be illegitimate." A remark which Fergus had made before he went away in September flashed into Renee's mind. When she had told him she hoped he'd given her a baby, his answer had been, "I've enough on my plate without worrying about that," which she'd assumed to be covering up his dread of being killed. No wonder he'd given that peculiar laugh. It must have been Jeanette and her pregnancy that had been filling his plate.

"I was wondering . . ." Jeanette gulped. "Could you give me his address? I have to get in touch with him."

"I'll give you the one I've got," Anne said, "but he'll likely have been shifted by this time. And even if he hasn't, don't be surprised if he doesn't answer any letters you send. I don't like having to tell you this, Jeanette, but he's an out-and-out rotter. He was involved with . . . a lot of other girls, and you're better off without him. Honestly."

"I have to try, anyway. You see . . . I love him, though I see now that he doesn't love me." Jeanette fished in her clutch handbag for a handkerchief, and scrubbed at her eyes. "I don't know how to tell my mum, and when she finds out, she'll likely throw me out on my ear."

"No she won't," Anne said quickly. "Go home right now and tell her. Mothers can forgive more than you think." She glanced at her daughter, her eyes conveying a message she'd been unable to put into words. Renee realised that she was being told she'd been forgiven for her previous secretive behaviour, and felt more affection for her mother at that moment than she had done ever since the terrible confrontation of the 3rd of September.

Anne stood up and went over to the sideboard. "If he doesn't answer your letter, Jeanette, get in touch with his commanding officer. Fergus Cooper should be made to face up to his responsibility." She took out a letter and tore off the corner with the address, handed it to the girl then crossed to the fireside and threw the sheet of paper into the flames.

"Thank you very much, Mrs Gordon." Jeanette dropped the address into her handbag and got to her feet.

On an impulse, Renee asked, "How often did you go out with Fergus?"

"Every Friday for about seven months. Why?"

"Oh, no reason, really, I just wondered." Fridays? So Jeanette wasn't the girl she had seen him making love to that Thursday night at the Bay of Nigg. He really had had a girl for every night of the week, and must have sworn to each of them that she was the only one for him. She felt nothing but sorrow that she'd been so easily taken in by him, but she brightened up when she saw his letter reducing to ashes in the fire. Her mother had proved that her attachment to him was completely broken, too.

Anne showed the other girl out. "If your mum does put you out, Jeanette, you're welcome to stay here, I've got plenty of room." She patted her shoulder. "But I don't think it'll come to that, just wait and see."

The tears came again to Jeanette's eyes, but she held her head up as she left. "Thanks again, Mrs Gordon."

"Poor thing," Anne remarked, when she sat down again. "You see what a lucky escape you had, Renee?"

Her daughter nodded gravely. It was lucky for her that she'd got him out of her system before this revelation, otherwise she'd have been tortured out of her mind now. The full impact of Fergus Cooper's faithlessness struck home to her, and she blessed the impulse which had led to her unplanned showdown with him — the denouement which had freed her from him for ever.

CHAPTER FOURTEEN

In the first week of April, Jack Thomson received his calling-up papers, and Renee wondered if he would declare his love for her before he left. He'd been taking her out every Thursday night for weeks, and she'd grown more and more fond of him, but, although he kissed her quite lovingly before they went into the house each time, he'd never again mentioned how he felt about her. She was almost sure that he loved her, and nearly as sure that he believed she still loved Fergus, but she couldn't explain anything to him without revealing the whole sordid saga of her obsession with Fergus and his treatment of her and her mother.

Because he had to leave on a Thursday morning, Jack asked Renee if she would mind making their last date on a Wednesday instead.

"No problem," she answered, flippantly, to hide how much she was affected by his imminent departure.

"That's right," he said, carefully. "There's no problem now." She was tempted to assure him that there was no problem at any time, now or in the future, because Fergus was out of her life for ever, but the moment passed.

On Wednesday, she was filled with hope that Jack would say something definite, this being his last night. He would go home to Peterhead when he had leave, so she might never see him again. At the Palais, after their third dance, she made up her mind to prod him a little, to give him the opening to say that he loved her, in case he was too shy to broach the subject himself. When the band struck up a slow foxtrot, she seized her opportunity.

"I'm going to miss you, Jack," she said, softly, while they moved slowly round the hall.

His arm tightened round her. "I'm going to miss you, too."

She tried to sound light-hearted. "You won't have much time to miss anything for a start, I suppose?"

"I'll always be thinking about you, no matter what I'm doing," he whispered.

Her heart started to beat faster. This was more like it. If only she could keep him on this track, he would end up by telling her what she wanted to hear. "You'll write to me, won't you?" she asked.

"If you want me to."

"Of course I want you to. I want to know where you are, and what you're doing, and everything about you."

"Do you?" He paused for a moment and looked at her seriously. "You'll write to me as well, and tell me everything that you do?"

"Yes, I will. I promise."

He was silent for so long that she said, "Jack?"

"I'm sorry, Renee. I'm not very good company tonight. I'm excited about going into the army, and yet

I'm worried about my mother. She'll be absolutely on her own if anything happens to me."

"Nothing's going to happen to you, Jack." She was very disappointed that he was thinking about his mother at a time like this, but a chill had run over her at the possibility of him being killed.

His laugh was harsh. "I'm just being morbid, Renee, I'm sorry. It's just . . . Oh, there's Tim and Moira." He removed his hand from her waist and waved vigorously to attract their attention.

Renee felt oddly relieved. She was slowly coming to the conclusion that she had read too much into Jack's kisses and the veiled hints of love which he had given her. Perhaps he had lost interest in her now that he had no rival for her affection? It would probably be best, then, not to let him see how much she really cared for him. When they joined Tim and Moira, after the foxtrot, she behaved as naturally as she could, and reflected that this had turned out to be another ordinary night at the Palais, after all her hopes of it being something special.

Walking home, she let Jack take the lead in the conversation, and they spent most of the time reminiscing over the various incidents which had happened since he had come to lodge at Cattofield. They spoke about Bill Scroggie going off to Canada — wondering why he had never written — about Uncle George's disappearance, about Mike's courtship and marriage, about Tim and Moira, speculating on whether Tim would ask his girlfriend to marry him before he was called up. When they neared the house,

Jack stopped at the usual wall, and Renee leaned against it, hardly daring to hope that the longed-for moment had come at last.

He looked deeply into her eyes for a few seconds, before he sighed and put his arms round her. "Renee . . ." His kiss was long and tender. "This is what I want to remember," he whispered, stroking her hair then running his fingers over her face. "You and me, standing together at this place . . . Oh, Renee, I wish I didn't have to go away."

"Me, too," she murmured. "But you'll be back, and there'll be other times."

He shook his head. "No, things'll be different."

"They won't, they won't. Oh, Jack, I lo . . ."

He covered her mouth with his hand before she could finish. "Don't say it, Renee. It's only because I'm going away."

She pushed his hand off her face. "No, Jack, it's not just because you're going away. I really do . . ."

"I don't want you to say it," he broke in, roughly, then his voice softened. "Can't you understand? You're making it more difficult for me." He turned and walked away from her, and she had to bite her lip to keep her from shouting out that she *did* love him, and that she didn't understand why he wouldn't let her say it.

He was waiting for her to catch up with him, and they walked to the house in an awkward silence. Jack looked uncomfortable when they went in and found that Anne was not in the living room. "I'll just say goodnight then, Renee," he muttered, "and we'd better make it goodbye as well, for we won't have a chance in the morning." He held out his hand, but her face told him how hurt she was by this formal parting, and with a jerk, his arms were round her and he was kissing her hungrily.

"Renee, my dear, sweet Renee," he murmured. "I'll never stop thinking about you."

"I'll always be thinking about you," she whispered, before his mouth came down on hers again.

As abruptly as he had started, he dropped his arms, and said, hoarsely, "No, Renee. I can't . . . it's too much . . . Goodnight."

He spun on his heel and left her, and she half collapsed on to the settee. She felt frustrated, her nerves were jangling, but she poured herself a cup of tea from the flask on the card table. She sipped it slowly, trying to figure out what had happened. She must really love Jack when she felt like this, or was it just a physical attraction? Was love only sex, anyway? Damn Fergus Cooper for taking away her innocence! Damn Jack Thomson for not following through and doing what he had so obviously wanted to do. No, she wasn't being fair to him. Jack was a gentleman, and wouldn't take advantage of the emotions which had been aroused at a moment of parting. And maybe, at sixteen, she was too young to cope with situations like this.

Wearily, she rose and went into the scullery to rinse out her cup. Anne was still reading when the girl went upstairs. "Did you have a good time?" she asked.

"Yes, thanks. Tim and Moira were there, too." Anne looked at her daughter sadly, and Renee knew that her mother had also hoped that Jack would declare his love tonight, but nothing more was said.

She didn't see Jack in the morning, because he hadn't come into the dining room by the time she had to go to work, and, in some inexplicable way, she was glad.

"Jack Thomson leaves today," she informed Sheila Daun when she went into the office.

The other girl looked sympathetic. "He's the one you've been going out with lately, isn't he?"

"Yes, but that's all finished now." Renee shrugged.

"If you're at a loose end, what about coming out with me some time?"

"Why not?" Renee had made her mind up that it would be best not to let herself get serious about any boy ever again.

When the girl went home at lunchtime, Anne said, "Jack's away, then. You know, Renee, he's a very nice boy."

"I know that perfectly well. Too nice, maybe."

Anne's eyebrows shot up, but she passed no comment.

"He promised to write," the girl said, then added, sadly, "but he'll likely stop when he falls for some ATS girl." Over the next few days, Renee began to wonder if she had truly been in love with Jack, or if it had been a reaction after her tempestuous break-up with Fergus and the shock of what Jeanette Morrison had told them later — a rebound? And her emotions had definitely been heightened by the idea of Jack leaving, as he himself had said. Anyway, he had made it quite clear that he didn't want anything more than friendship from her, so there was nothing to stop her from going out to enjoy herself with Sheila Daun.

She found that her colleague was very good company outside office hours, and they eventually came to an agreement that, if either of them wanted to let a boy see her home from whatever place of entertainment they happened to be at, the other one wouldn't object. Sheila was an outrageous flirt, and found an escort home nearly every time the two girls went out, to the cinema, the ice rink or the Palais de Danse, and Renee reflected mournfully, on her lonely walk home one night, that she must put the male sex off somehow or other, because no one ever asked to see her home.

As it happened, the next time they went dancing, a tall sailor stuck to her all evening, and, during the last dance, he said, "I'd like to walk home with you, if you don't mind?"

"It's a long way," she warned him, "and the buses have all stopped running." Why couldn't she just accept gracefully?

"That's OK," he beamed. "I never get much chance of walking when I'm at sea, so it'll be good exercise for me."

When they went out into the street, he said, "What's your name? I'm Bill Foster."

"Pleased to meet you, Bill," she laughed. "I'm Renee Gordon."

"How do, Renee?" He took her hand and they set off.

In a few minutes, he let her hand drop and put his arm round her waist. "Brr! The weather's freezing here. I'm just back from the Med and I feel it worse. You'll have to cuddle up to keep me warm."

She was slightly dubious about his intentions, but he kept walking briskly, and she relaxed. He'd only put his arm round her, after all. They were laughing and joking as they went along the different streets, then he started to hum "The Palais Glide". She joined in, and matched his steps when he began to dance, recognising that he had no designs on her. He was out for innocent amusement and that was all. She was rather taken aback, therefore, when they reached the familiar wall near her home, where Tim and Jack had both stopped to kiss her. Bill Foster had also thought it was an ideal place to stop, Renee having told him that her house was just round the corner, but she surprised him by extricating herself from his embrace and hurrying on.

"I only wanted to kiss you," he said plaintively.

"I know . . . but . . . goodnight, Bill."

Leaving him standing open-mouthed, she ran round to the house, regretting her behaviour as soon as she went inside. He had done nothing out of place — she hadn't given him the chance — and she should have allowed him to kiss her. It was only good manners, after him taking her home, and what were a few kisses, anyway? She would apologise to him the next time she saw him. But Bill Foster never returned to the Palais.

Jack Thomson's first letter had been mainly about his training, but the last paragraph had confused Renee. "I've been going to dances here, and I hope you're going out to enjoy yourself, too. I think about you quite a lot, and all our happy times together. Love, Jack."

He was telling her that he enjoyed dancing with other girls, yet he ended up by writing "Love". He didn't know his own mind. That was when she'd decided that she may as well have as good a time as Jack seemed to be having.

Each of his letters since then had told her about dances, concerts and of being asked into local people's homes, and he always ended by writing, "I hope you're having a whale of a time with all the fellows you meet. Love, Jack."

Renee gave herself up to having a whale of a time, and even had some hectic kissing sessions with the "fellows" she met, stopping them only when she thought they were going too far.

Anne, of course, disapproved of her daughter going out so often. "Renee's hardly a night in the house," she complained to her mother one Friday night, when her parents were visiting.

Maggie McIntosh sniffed. "Ye should be pleased she's nae sittin' at hame, Annie. She's young, an' she needs to be meetin' lads at her age. She'll settle doon when she feels like it, be sure o' that."

Anne was not appeased. "But it's a different one she's with nearly every night. God knows what they get up to, because she looks really flushed sometimes when she comes in."

Maggie chuckled loudly. "It'll be the same as what laddies an' lassies got up to when ye were young yersel',

I've nae doot, an' when we were young an' a', eh, Peter?"

Her husband lifted his head from the newspaper he'd just picked up. "Aye, an' what we got up to when we were young is naebody's business." His eyes twinkled mischievously.

"Oh, you two!" Anne sounded exasperated. "You're like sixteen-year-olds yourselves, and you're both nearly seventy."

Tim Donaldson was called up in May 1940, and, on his last day in the house, Renee gave him a little advice.

"You should ask Moira to get engaged before you leave on Sunday." He was going home to Turriff first before he had to join his unit in Nottingham, but she knew that he was seeing his girlfriend later that day. When he shook his head without speaking, she went on, "She could find somebody else after you're in the army. Aren't you worried?"

Tim pursed his lips. "I'll have to take that chance. I don't think it's fair to tie her down when I'll maybe never come back."

"Oh, Tim, that's a stupid thing to think," Anne said quickly. "I'm sure Moira wants to be engaged to you, and she wouldn't feel you were tying her down."

"No, I suppose she wouldn't, but I still don't think it's right, and it's her I'm thinking about." Tim looked grim. "Look at Babs. Since Mike's been called up, she worries herself sick if she doesn't get a letter from him nearly every day, and she's terrified he'll be sent overseas. She never goes out, just sits at home and mopes. I want Moira to find somebody else — well, feel free to find somebody else — if she wants to."

Renee looked at him sadly. "I thought you loved her. Men can be so insensitive."

"I do love her." He shrugged his shoulders. "But it's better this way."

Anne broke in to change the subject. "I'll have to find some more lodgers now. It's been taking me all my time to manage since Jack left, and I didn't feel like having somebody new here, but I'll have to, now. Would anybody at the yard need digs?" She looked hopefully at Tim.

"There's not that many single men left in the yard now, it's mostly women workers coming in." He raised his eyes to the roof in an expression of disgust.

"I don't fancy women lodgers." Anne couldn't really explain why she felt like that, it was just one of those things.

"It's time I was off," Renee butted in. "Goodbye, Tim, and good luck." She leaned across the table to shake his hand, and he gripped it tightly.

"Thanks, Renee. Is it OK if I drop you a line now and then, and you could maybe write to me?"

"Yes, Tim, I'd like that."

"Thanks again. I want to keep in touch and hear how Jack's doing, as well. Remember, Renee, he's a decent bloke."

"I know," she said, quietly, and was glad when Tim dropped her hand.

When she went home at lunchtime, her mother handed her an already opened envelope. "Read that."

Before she glanced at it, Renee had feared that it might be from Fergus Cooper, and prayed that he wouldn't be returning to upset her existence again. But the neatly written "Mrs Gordon" was not in his hand, so she pulled the letter out with relief, and glanced at the signature. It was from Jeanette Morrison.

Dear Mrs Gordon,

I told my mother when I went home that day and there was a big row, but she simmered down and talked my father round to let me stay at home.

I wrote to Fergus, and you were right, he never answered, so I wrote to his commanding officer and they're giving me an allowance. It's being kept off him, so he's been made to support me after all.

He's overseas, they told me, and I don't suppose I'll ever see him again, but I'm getting over it. I had a baby girl two weeks ago, and her name is Sheena, so I'll have to make my life round her now.

They gave me his parents' address from the army records, so I went to see them, to let them know what their son had done. They didn't seem all that surprised. His mother said she put him out because he wouldn't give her anything for his keep, and he made her life a misery, so I suppose I'm lucky that he didn't want to marry me. She was very kind, and gave me something to buy clothes for the baby.

Thank you for all your help and understanding.

Yours gratefully,

Jeanette Morrison.

"I'm glad her mum and dad let her stay with them," Renee said, as she slipped the letter back in its envelope.

"I thought they would." Anne looked enquiringly at her daughter. "What do you think of Fergus Cooper now? Have you really got over him?"

"Yes, Mum. I did see through him eventually. How do *you* feel about him?" It was an impertinent question, but she had to be sure that Fergus would never be allowed back in their lives.

Anne sighed deeply. "I was hurt and humiliated, like you, but I was older, and wiser, I hope, and I made the final break before you did. When he wrote — only the one letter — I felt sorry for him not having anywhere to go, so I said he could come here on that first leave. As soon as I posted the letter, I regretted it. I knew he couldn't be trusted, and when he arrived, I was surer than ever I'd made a mistake."

"Did he try to . . .?" Renee asked, purely out of curiosity.

"Yes, he did, and he was so cocky, and sure I couldn't resist him, it made me sick. I slapped his face, but he just laughed and said, 'Your daughter won't say no to me.' Well, I was absolutely furious, but I wanted to find out if that was true. I found out it was, when he told me on Monday morning that he was meeting you that night."

"Why didn't you say anything when I told you I was going out with Phyllis and you knew it was a lie?" The girl was angry with herself for being so naive as to agree to that meeting.

Anne briefly gripped her lips together. "What good would it have done, Renee? I'd only have made you more determined. I had it out with Fergus, though, and I called him every bad name I could think of, then told him never to come back here after he left the next day. And he knew I meant every word."

Renee's smile was humourless. "Yes, and he tried to make me feel sorry for him about that. I only met him to ask if there was still . . . something going on between him and you."

"So you didn't trust me, either?" Anne said sadly.

"I didn't know who to trust, Mum. I was so mixed up about you writing to each other after you'd sworn not to have anything more to do with him, I couldn't think straight. I was sure I loved him, even after everything, but when he tried to kiss me in the Graveyard, I couldn't . . . Oh, I don't know what it was, but I suddenly hated him. We began shouting at each other, and it was really horrible."

After a short silence, Anne said, "I can understand why his mother put him out. He's a real bad lot."

"That's what Granny said once." Renee recalled how upset she'd been about that remark at the time, but Granny had known what she was talking about.

Poor Granny. Her legs had given out on her altogether now, and she was unable to visit any more. Granda did all the shopping and most of the housework, but he wasn't all that fit himself and his chest bothered him quite a lot, although it hadn't made him give up his pipe. The girl felt ashamed of herself for not going to see them more often. Her mother did go occasionally, but Maggie had always been very good to her granddaughter, and had helped her to face the world after that last terrible night with Fergus.

Anne broke into her thoughts. "Look at the time, Renee. You're going to be late back if you don't hurry."

CHAPTER FIFTEEN

Because the firm of Brown and Company was concerned with food distribution, Renee Gordon and Sheila Daun were in reserved occupations, so there was no likelihood of them having to go into the forces, and they spent most of their evenings flirting with every soldier, sailor and airman they met.

Anne only rarely reprimanded her daughter, now — it was like water off a duck's back. Renee's war bore no resemblance to that of the young people in the services, although some of them were also having the time of their lives, including the four now ensconced in the Gordons' house.

Anne's reluctance to take female boarders had proved well-founded. After Tim left, she'd answered an advertisement in the local newspaper. "Homely board and lodgings required for four." Believing that it was the answer to her prayers, she'd been elated at the thought of both her rooms being filled at one fell swoop, if the men were suitable.

She'd been dismayed when four land girls turned up, but they seemed to be friendly and well-behaved and she realised that there was little hope of finding any male lodgers while the war was on. Pushing her doubts aside, she let them have the rooms on condition that they would take no male visitors into the house without letting her know, and that they would undertake to launder their own clothes.

The girls were every bit as friendly as they had appeared when she met them first, and never had any men callers. Kitty Miller and Flora Sims had taken the downstairs bedroom, and Hilda Matthews and Nora Perry were upstairs. They were a harum-scarum lot, apart from Nora, who was more reserved, and the bathroom always seemed to be occupied by one or other of them having a bath, washing her hair or rinsing out her "smalls". Furthermore, the rope which Anne had fixed up over the bath seemed to be forever festooned with stockings, every available surface in their rooms was draped with knickers or brassieres, drying or airing, and the mirrors on the dressing tables were spattered with liquid make-up and perfume.

They were good fun, however, and helped Anne around the house at times, and even kept her supplied with eggs and fresh vegetables, so she resigned herself to be thankful for small mercies. The house rang with shrill laughter, and discussions about boyfriends occupied every mealtime, so Anne felt it her duty one day to give the five girls some sensible advice.

"I hope you're all being careful when you're out with those boys of yours, and not letting them . . ." Her opening was met with howls of amusement.

"Oh, Mrs G.," gasped Kitty Miller at last. "You sound just like my mother."

Flora Sims spluttered. "Mine's always giving me lectures, too."

Hilda Matthews nodded vigorously. "So's mine — on the facts of life, she says."

"I'm glad your mothers have some sense, then." Anne felt slightly put out by their reaction. "I was only saying it for your own good."

"Yes, thanks, Mrs G." Nora Perry, the smallest and quietest of the four, sounded apologetic. "Don't mind this lot."

The other three had calmed down and seemed rather ashamed of their outburst. "Sorry, Mrs G. I know you were doing it with good intentions, but we're all careful. We're not going to land ourselves up the spout." Kitty smiled to show that she was quite sincere, in spite of the slang, and her green eyes pleaded for understanding.

Anne's heart melted. They were good girls, the lot of them, just a bit thoughtless. "That's OK," she said, "but just remember."

"We'll always remember." Hilda nodded her dark head, then glanced at Nora. "Right, Tich, race you to the bathroom."

There was a wild splatter, then Anne and Renee were left alone, looking at each other and laughing.

"Here endeth the first lesson," Renee said.

"I meant it for you as well," her mother reminded her. "You go out with so many different boys, too."

"I'm careful, Mum. More than careful — I abstain."

"I'm glad to hear it."

Tim Donaldson's letters to Renee were long and chatty, about his training and all the humorous incidents that had taken place between him and his fellow conscripts. She'd been very surprised, at first, that he also signed off by writing "Love", but he was a bit of a tease, and she knew that all his love was given to Moira Sandison, so she accepted it as a bit of fun. A letter from Jack arrived regularly every week, short notes, mostly, but her heart leapt when she saw his writing.

"I'll be coming on leave on the 4th of June," he wrote one day. "I hope it's OK if I give you a quick call before I carry on to Peterhead? It'll be late afternoon, so I won't have time to stop long, and if you've got a date, I'll understand. See you soon, I hope. Love, Jack."

She was pleased that he wanted to see her, but disappointed that it would be only a flying visit. Still, he might decide to come back during his leave, and there were only a few days to wait until he'd be in Aberdeen.

The next day, Saturday, was brightened up by Mike Donaldson appearing. Tim had told them in his letters that his brother was in the north-east of England, and that he'd been home for a few long weekends, but it was the first time Mike had come to Cattofield since he'd been called up.

"It's good to see you again," Anne said. "How are you getting on in the army, and how's Babs?"

Mike smiled. "I'd better give you my news right away."

Renee interrupted before he could do so. "Oho! Are we going to be hearing the patter of tiny feet?"

"Aye, you've guessed right." His face wore an expression of sheer pride, in spite of his embarrassment. "Babs is expecting in six months, about November sometime."

"That's great." Renee was beaming broadly.

Anne's face also wore a huge smile. "Congratulations, Mike."

"I only hope I'll still be in this country when it arrives," he said wistfully. "There's word of us being sent overseas."

Anne looked serious now. "We'll keep our fingers crossed for you both."

Poor Babs, Renee thought. If Mike is sent abroad, she'll have to bring their child up on her own. "Do you know where you'll be going?" she asked him.

"There's rumours it's the Middle East or North Africa, and that means we wouldn't get home again till the war's finished."

"Oh, Mike, what a shame if you've to miss seeing your baby growing." Anne was quite distressed at the idea.

"The war can't last all that much longer." Renee was still optimistic, not really having taken much interest in what was going on in any of the war zones.

Mike's mouth twisted in doubt, then he laughed to shake off his own fears. "There's nothing I can do about it anyway, except do what I'm told. It's the fortunes of war, I suppose."

When Anne went to make the obligatory pot of tea, he turned to Renee. "Any word from Jack lately?"

"Yes, and he'll be here on Tuesday, but he's only popping in for a wee while before he goes home to Peterhead."

"I won't have a chance to have a chinwag with him, then, for I go back on Sunday." He seemed quite disappointed. "Tell him I was asking for him, will you? He's a nice lad." He paused for a moment. "And Fergus? Has he been home on leave again?"

Renee was taken completely unawares, and feverishly searched for a reply. She'd forgotten that Mike, like Tim and Jack, had no idea of the outcome of Fergus's last leave. She realised that Mike was regarding her with some curiosity, and was extremely thankful when her mother came back. "Mike's asking about Fergus," she muttered.

Anne's eyes narrowed, then she gave a brittle laugh. "Of course, you wouldn't know, Mike, but he . . . blotted his copybook the last time he was here, and I had to tell him not to come back."

"Oh." Mike was obviously astonished and wondering what had actually happened, but he made a joke of it. "He came in drunk, and made a nuisance of himself, I suppose?"

"That's right," Anne said quickly. "He must have picked up bad habits in the army, and I wasn't used to that kind of thing. None of my other lodgers ever gave me any trouble, and I wasn't going to let him upset me like that."

She knew, as did Renee, that Mike had not been fooled, and that he had handed her the excuse to save her any further embarrassment, so she wasn't surprised when he let the matter drop.

"Tim should be home in a few weeks," he said. "According to Moira, anyway, though he does drop me a line now and then, as well."

"He writes to Renee sometimes," Anne remarked.

Mike nodded. "Aye, Moira told me. I think she's a wee bit jealous of you, Renee, and she half believes you're the reason Tim never asked her to get married."

"Oh, no!" Renee was still recovering from the shock of him asking about Fergus, but this was something she could put straight. "There was never anything between Tim and me, Mike. I like him and he was good fun, but we all knew it was Moira he fell in love with. Please tell her that, Mike."

"I've tried to tell her already, but jealousy's difficult to master, even if there's no grounds for it." He wrinkled his nose and smiled.

"He told us he didn't want to tie her down," Anne volunteered.

"He told Moira that, as well, but . . ." Mike suddenly stood up. "I'll have to go, though, or Babs'll be wondering what I'm up to."

"Give her our regards, and I hope she keeps well." Anne saw him to the door, then came back and sat down. "Mike's still the same, isn't he? He's always concerned about other people, and so thoughtful and dependable."

Renee's smile was wry. "He knows how to help people out of awkward situations, that's one thing."

Jack Thomson was in the house when Renee went home on Tuesday, and he greeted her with a kiss, quite naturally, in front of her mother, who smiled but said nothing. He held the girl away from him for a moment, saying, "You're even bonnier than I remembered you," then he crushed her to him once again. Anne walked through to the scullery to dish up the tea, but also to leave them alone for a short time.

"Oh, Jack, it's good to see you," Renee breathed, as soon as she could. "How are you?"

"Very well, thank you," he replied, formally, and they both flopped on to the settee, giggling.

"What have you been doing with yourself lately?" he asked.

She was disappointed that he was not being more sentimental, and said, in an offhand manner, "Oh, just this and that."

"I hope you're still going out to enjoy yourself, like I told you?"

"Yes, I am. I go out with Sheila from the office quite a lot. I wrote and told you — to dances, the pictures, the ice rink, walks even, if it's fine."

"Good. I'm the same." He looked at her squarely. "Life's too short to waste time dreaming, Renee."

She understood that he was telling her that love shouldn't enter into their relationship, and was suddenly angry with him. "I've met a few nice boys as well, and I've had a good time with them all." That might give him something to think about.

His smile was perhaps a little forced, but he said, "And I've met quite a few very nice girls, so we're quits."

The front door banged open, and he looked round in surprise at the clamour of footsteps and voices.

"It's only our land girls coming in," Renee told him. "I told you about them in my letters, remember?"

He nodded. "I'd forgotten for the minute. They're a lively lot, aren't they?"

Anne poked her head round the door. "Give me a hand, Renee, will you? That was the girls coming in, wasn't it?"

"Yes, they're home." Renee and Jack both rose and helped to carry through the various dishes to the dining room.

"I'd better be going, though," he said after a few minutes. "You'll be busy feeding your lodgers."

"Don't be stupid, Jack. I've put out a plate for you." Anne guided him to a chair. "Just sit down and eat."

Kitty Miller and Flora Sims were the first pair to come through. "Oooh! A real, live soldier. Bags me first refusal." Kitty sat down beside Jack, who turned pink.

"He's not booked, is he, Renee?" Flora sat down beside her landlady's daughter.

"No," Jack said, before Renee could answer. "I'm not booked."

"Carry on, Flora. You'll maybe have more luck with him than I've had." Renee couldn't resist it.

Her mother looked at her quickly, and then at Jack, who looked away and started joking with the two land girls. "Ah, here's Hilda and Nora," she said, when the last two appeared.

"I'm Kitty, and I staked my claim first," Kitty declared and slipped her hand through Jack's arm.

"Sup that lentil soup and behave yourself," Anne laughed.

The chaffing and teasing carried on throughout the meal, then the four boarders excused themselves from the table. As they went out, Kitty, who was last, turned and said, "Cheerio, lover boy. Hope to see you again."

"Sure thing," Jack said, winking to her.

Renee had been surprised, and a little jealous, at the ease with which he had handled the flirting, but remembered that he had been coming in contact with lots of different girls since he left Aberdeen, and must have learnt how to deal with it, the same as she had learnt how to cope with advances from the various boys she allowed to accompany her home.

At half past seven, Jack said, regretfully, "I'll have to go. I want to catch the eight o'clock bus. My mother's expecting me home."

"What a shame you can't stay longer." Anne glanced at Renee.

"He has to go home, Mum, and we've no spare beds."

Anne hesitated. It wasn't up to her to plead with him. "Will you manage to drop in again before you go back?"

"I'm sorry, Mrs Gordon. I just won't have time, for I've dozens of relations, and friends of my mother's, to go round, but I'll see you on my next leave. So long just now."

"I'll see you to the door." Renee made one last attempt to find out his true feelings for her.

"Cheerio, then, Jack, and look after yourself," Anne said.

On the doorstep, he gave the girl one gentle kiss then moved away. "Keep writing, Renee, please."

"You too, Jack." She watched him go down the path, then closed the door slowly and went back to the living room.

Anne looked rather surprised. "You weren't long."

"No, he was in a hurry." Renee sat down opposite her mother and picked up the newspaper, so Anne knew that she was being warned not to ask any questions.

When Renee went to visit her grandmother the following Saturday, she said, "Jack Thomson came to see us for a wee while on Tuesday."

"Oh, how is he?" Maggie McIntosh was always interested in everything the girl told her.

"He was looking great. Kitty Miller could hardly keep her eyes off him, and he seems to be having a high old time with the girls at Catterick."

"Is the green-eyed monster rearin' its ugly head, lassie?" The old lady laughed, but watched the girl carefully.

"A wee bit," Renee admitted.

"But you're havin' a high old time wi' the lads, as weel," Maggie reminded her. "It's jist the same, and ye're far ower young to be serious aboot onybody yet. Ye're still only sixteen."

"I'll be seventeen in September." Renee was indignant. "And you once told me you were only seventeen when you married Granda."

"Aye weel, but things were different in my young days, an' ye're surely nae thinkin' o' gettin' married, are ye?"

"No, I was just saying." Renee laughed at her grandmother's expression, and the woman joined in.

"Wile aboot for a puckle years yet, dearie, till ye get a man that's right for ye. I was lucky, for I got the best man in the world for me."

"Yes, you did, you lucky thing. How's Granda keeping?"

"He's nae bad, an' he loves bein' message boy for me. He's gettin' to be a dab hand at watchin' the prices. Naebody'll cheat yer granda." Maggie looked proud. "Is yer mother aye busy wi' her land girls?"

"Yes, they keep her going all the time, but we get some good laughs with them and their stories about their boyfriends. Not boyfriends exactly, just boys they meet. But Mum was saying she'll come to see you one of these days."

"Ony day, tell her. I'm stuck in the hoose fae morn to night, for my legs winna cairry me at a'. I need a stick to get to the lavvy, even. See, here it is, at the side o' my chair."

"You always keep cheery, though, and that's the main thing." Renee looked at her grandmother fondly.

"Ach weel, it doesna dae to let yer heart doon."

"No, Granny, it doesna dae." She laughed at her own mimicry.

When the girl was leaving, Maggie said, "Ha'e yersel' a good fling when ye're young. Ye'll meet yer Mister Right ane o' these days, jist wait an' see."

"Yes, I suppose so. See you next Saturday, Granny."

Renee walked home slowly. It was probably true. She couldn't have met her Mr Right yet. Jack Thomson apparently didn't feel ready to be serious about her, or he might not consider that she was his Miss Right. He was "wilin' aboot" like Granny had advised her to do, and taking his pick from a lot of girls.

The evacuation of Dunkirk occupied all their conversation in a short time, and Renee was thankful that Jack had not been involved, nor Tim, who was still in England, nor Mike, who, presumably, was on his way to the Middle East or North Africa, although the news from there wasn't any too good, either.

"I was speaking to a boy who got out at Dunkirk," Kitty said one morning. "They just had what they stood up in, most of them. They lost all their gear."

"Gee whizz!" exclaimed Flora. "That must have been terrible."

"Yes, he said it was something he wouldn't want to go through again. They'd been on the beaches for days, hoping they wouldn't be killed by enemy gunfire before they were picked up. He'd come to the Palais last night to try to forget, but it was haunting him. I could tell that."

"We don't know we're living, really," remarked Hilda. "It makes me angry to think of what these boys had to go through."

"They were the lucky ones," muttered Nora.

The others looked at her quickly. There had been something odd in the way she said it, but she said nothing more, so Anne changed the subject quickly. "Do any of you girls want to take a bath tonight? Because if you don't, I won't bother lighting the fire. It's sweltering hot today."

It was into July before Tim came on leave, and he took Moira to Cattofield on the Sunday afternoon. Renee recalled what Mike had said about Moira being jealous of her, and tried to allay the other girl's fears by stressing how much she was enjoying herself with all the different boys she met, or went out with. After a while, she was pleased to see that Moira, and Tim, looked very relieved.

"Jack was here a few weeks ago," Anne remarked, at a loss to understand why her daughter was going on so much about her boyfriends. The visitors wouldn't want to hear about that.

"Oh, how's he doing? I bet he's as fed up as me at still being in this country." Tim screwed up his face.

"He didn't say anything about that," Anne said, "but he seems to be enjoying life at Catterick."

He certainly does, thought Renee. "There's no word of you being shifted, then?" she asked Tim.

"Well, there's word of us being sent to the Shetlands, but I've been away on a technical course in Dagenham, so I don't know the latest."

"I hope he's never sent overseas," Moira said quietly. "Babs is really worried about Mike. Sometimes it's weeks between his letters."

"Is she keeping well?" Anne asked. "We were very pleased when Mike told us they were having an addition to the family."

"Yes, Babs is fine, but she says she's sure she'll look like a tank before the baby's born."

They laughed, and Anne said, "Tell her we send our regards."

When they went away, Renee was last in line in the hall, and Tim was just in front of her, so she whispered to him, "Have you changed your mind about asking Moira to . . .?"

"No," he interrupted. "I'm sure she expects me to, but . . ."

Anne turned round and ushered Tim past her. "Cheerio, and if you feel lonely any time, Moira, there's always an open door for you here."

Renee added, "Yes, we'll always be pleased to see you."

Moira slipped her arm through Tim's. "Thanks, but with Mum and Babs in the house, I never have the chance to be on my own, never mind feel lonely — though I do miss Tim."

When the young couple had gone, Anne said, "I wish Tim would ask that girl to marry him. They're made for each other."

"I know, but he told me just now that he hasn't changed his mind about it." Renee felt rather irritated with him. He stood a good chance of losing the girl if he didn't watch out. Just like Jack with her, although she wasn't sure if Jack really loved her as much as Tim loved Moira, if he loved her at all.

Anne had been ashamed when her daughter told her about Maggie's walking stick, and had resolved to pay more attention to her parents, so she accompanied Renee every Saturday afternoon now to the tenement in Woodside. Maggie was always very pleased to see them — Peter was usually out doing the shopping — and listened with great interest to the little stories they told her about their land girls and what they got up to.

First thing every week, however, she enquired about Jack Thomson, then about Tim Donaldson, then about Mike, and Renee took their letters for her to read — Mike wrote to Anne occasionally, so there were letters from all three men. After that ritual, Renee told her grandmother who she had been out with during the week. She couldn't speak too freely because of her mother, but Maggie could read between the lines.

She could tell that Renee was sailing near the wind with some of the boys at times, but forbore to issue any warnings or advice, knowing that the girl would take her own way, whatever she was told. And, anyway, Renee had learned her lesson over that Fergus Cooper, so she would surely never go over the score again. Maggie also sensed if her granddaughter felt a special attraction to any of her boyfriends — she would speak shyly of them and blush slightly — but nothing ever seemed to come of it.

Just after her seventeenth birthday, Renee quietly told her grandparents about a sick-berth attendant in the Royal Navy. "He's very nice, Granny, and he danced every dance with me. He didn't come home with me, because he'd to meet a special bus to take him back to Kingseat Hospital, but he's asked me to go to the pictures with him. He's nearly six feet, and broad, as well. His eyes are greyish-green and his hair's light brown, nearly auburn really, and lovely and wavy."

"A pin-up boy?" Maggie teased.

"What do you know about pin-up boys?" the girl asked in surprise. "But no, he's not just a pin-up boy, he's got something about him . . . I don't know, but he's really nice."

Anne was washing up their afternoon teacups, and her back was towards them, so the old lady leaned across and whispered, "Mr Right, maybe?"

Renee shrugged. "I only met him last night, Granny, so I can't tell yet, but he could be."

"Be sure, mind." Maggie sat back in her chair again, then asked in a normal voice, "What's his name, this sick-berth fellow?"

"John Smith."

The old lady laughed. "Weel, he didna try to impress ye wi' gi'ein' himsel' a fancy name, at ony rate."

"No, and that's one of the reasons I like him so much. He acts naturally, not like some of them I've been out with, trying to make me think they come from rich families and all that kind of rubbish."

"I'll likely be hearin' mair aboot this John Smith, then?"

"I wouldn't be surprised."

They smiled to each other, conspiratorially, as Anne came over to the fireside. "That's everything tidied up, Mother," she said. "It's time we were going home, Renee, to get the girls' tea ready."

"Thanks, Annie." Maggie looked up into her daughter's face. "You'll be back next week?"

"Yes, Mother. Father'll be in soon, won't he?"

"Aye, he usually comes back aboot half past four."

"Give him my love, and we'll see you next Saturday."

"Cheerio, Granny," Renee said as she walked to the door. "I'll keep you informed."

John Smith had asked her to go out with him the following Monday, but Renee kept Monday nights for writing letters, mending, and so on, so they had made it Tuesday instead.

He took her to the Capitol cinema, and held her hand all through the two films, then treated her to an ice cream in a soda fountain in Rose Street.

"I'm getting a lift at quarter to eleven, at the Queen," he said, as they came out.

"I'll walk down Union Street with you, and I'll get my bus outside Falconer's, that's just round the corner from the Queen."

The Queen — a statue of Queen Victoria, which stood at the corner of St Nicholas Street and Union Street — was a popular meeting place, and was a straight walk down Union Street from where they were. As they walked, arms round each other's waists, John told her that he belonged to Bristol.

"My dad's in the shipyard, a riveter, and my mum cleans offices." He glanced at her to see how she reacted to the information about his humble background.

She smiled at him. “My mum takes in boarders. We’ve got four land girls just now. What did you work at before you were in the navy?”

“I was an apprentice mechanic before I was called up.”

“Didn’t they let you finish your time?”

“I didn’t particularly want to. What do you do?”

“I work in an office, clerkess/typist. I’ll show you when we go past it.”

“Will I see you again, Renee?”

“If you like.”

He drew her into a shop doorway. “May I kiss you?”

She was astonished, but nodded. He was the first boy who had ever asked her permission, and it felt good to be treated in so mannerly a fashion. His kiss made her feel even more drawn to him, but he led her on to the pavement again and kept walking. Renee wished that he had at least repeated the kiss, but it was the first time they had been out together, after all, although that had never inhibited any of the other boys.

“How old are you, Renee?” he asked, suddenly. “You look too young to be going out with boys at all.”

“I’m seventeen.” Plus a few days, she thought, but she felt older than that, much older, and she’d had plenty of experience, good and bad, with boys.

“It seems terrible that I’m not seeing you home,” John remarked. “But it’s this business of getting back to Kingseat. They lay on a small bus for us, and if we miss it we’ve had it, unless we walk.”

"It's too far to walk." Renee was horrified at the idea, because Kingseat Hospital was about eight miles from Aberdeen. "You didn't have to walk back last Friday, did you?" She looked at him anxiously.

"Oh, no." He smiled to reassure her. "The bus leaves at 1a.m. on Friday nights to allow us to go to a dance if we want."

"That's all right, then."

They reached St Nicholas Street with five minutes to spare, so John snatched a few kisses before he boarded the Royal Navy bus. "Friday, outside the Palais, at half past seven?" he asked.

"OK." Renee crossed Union Street to wait for her own bus, but thought about John Smith all the way home.

She loved his wavy hair, his craggy face, his eyes — oh, his eyes! She'd be able to tell Granny on Saturday that she did think he was her Mr Right. Disconcertingly, the image of a sandy-haired boy with a cow's lick at the front came to her mind; a boy with laughing eyes which could turn serious and tender; a boy who wouldn't admit that he loved her.

She shook her head to be rid of the picture. Blast Jack Thomson! No, she didn't mean that. Forget about him, that was more like it. Think about John Smith again. Look forward to Friday. She decided that she would ask him to come to tea some day, on his day off. He would probably be glad of somewhere to spend his free time away from the hospital. Next morning, Renee asked her mother if it was all right if she invited him.

"Are you getting serious about this one?" Anne eyed her keenly.

"I might be — it depends," the girl said, cagily. She found it difficult to confide in her mother — not like Granny.

"Ask him any time you like, but be sensible. You haven't known him very long, have you?" Anne tried not to lecture.

"I'm going to know him better. We're going to the Palais on Friday."

When she went to work, Renee told Sheila Daun about John Smith. "He doesn't put on any airs, he even told me that he was only an apprentice mechanic before he went into the navy and became a sick-berth attendant."

Sheila burst out laughing, and Renee, rather piqued, snapped, "What's so funny about that?"

"From mechanic to sick-berth attendant?" Sheila giggled. "From patching engines to patching people? Don't you think it's funny?"

"Not really." But Renee smiled. "You'll meet him on Friday, if you're going to the Palais."

"That's right, of course, though I did catch a glimpse of him last week. He seemed a decent sort of chap."

John was very attentive to Renee on Friday night, while they were dancing and while they were sitting chatting to Sheila and the RAF corporal who had attached himself to her, and his eyes made her heart turn over every time he looked at her. When he was holding her closely during the last dance, Renee issued her invitation. "Mum says she'd be pleased if you came to tea, any time you've a day off."

She could feel the stiffening of his back, and her heart sank. "Whenever you like," she added, desperately.

He remained silent for a long time, then his hold on her slackened and he said carefully, "Thank you, but no. I make it a rule never to meet the mothers, or fathers, of any of the girls I pick up."

Renee gasped, and her eyes filled with tears as she jerked away from him and ran to the cloakroom. Once inside, she gave way to them and sobbed bitterly for a few minutes. Then she splashed her face with cold water and put on her coat. She opened the door slowly, but John Smith wasn't waiting for her as she'd feared, so she walked quickly to the exit. When she started her long walk home, she found that she was trembling. She'd known she would have to make the trek on her own, but had never dreamt that she would be in such a state. What a fool she'd been. John Smith was certainly honest. More than honest — he was absolutely brutal. She was just another of the girls he had picked up.

Her grief changed to anger suddenly. He was only a big, conceited lump after all, a practised ladies' man. She strode purposefully along Union Terrace, glancing at the statue of Robert Burns as she passed it. Another ladies' man. Love 'em and leave 'em. Her fury abated as quickly as it had started, and she gave a sad laugh. She was too vulnerable, that was the trouble. A few kisses and romantic looks, and she was hooked. John Smith had never said anything, or done anything, to her that could be construed as words or actions of love. He had asked if he could kiss her, and had done so several times, but that was all. She had been too eager, too intense, too hasty. If she'd only waited, it would have been . . . No, it was just as well that she'd found out about him before things went any further.

She turned the corner, and thought of her first nasty experience with a man. That had been a slippery-sided mountain which had beaten her, but this was only a mole-hill. Everything to do with John Smith had been in her imagination, and she had embarrassed him out of his usual gentlemanly behaviour by asking him to her home after such a short acquaintance. Her mood lightened as she carried on walking. She'd acted like a child, not a seventeen-year-old, and she deserved the slap-down she'd received. If John came to the Palais next Friday, she would apologise to him, but one thing was certain. He couldn't have been her Mr Right.

Her route took her between the Victoria and Westburn Parks, and with no street lighting during wartime, she felt slightly uneasy after she passed the last of the houses. To cover her fears, she began to whistle, and stepped out even more quickly than before. She arrived home at last, breathless and windblown, but in a far happier frame of mind than when she left the dancehall.

Maggie McIntosh looked expectantly at her granddaughter as soon as the girl went into the house the following afternoon. "How's yer romance wi' the famous John Smith goin'?"

Renee made a face. "It's gone. The romance that never was."

Anne seemed surprised. "He won't be coming to tea any time?"

"He certainly won't. I scared the living daylights out of him by asking." She joined in the older women's laughter, and the visit went on in the usual pattern.

Renee never saw John Smith again, either. "I blew it," she said to Sheila Daun, when she told her the whole story.

"I wondered where you'd disappeared to when the dance finished on Friday," the other girl said. "It's a pity, though. He seemed to be quite a decent sort."

"He was, I think. It was me that was silly. If I'd left things to develop naturally, he might have come to care for me. Maybe not. Anyway, I'm not broken-hearted, and I've learned another lesson."

"Good. Just remember it."

After she finished tidying up at teatime, one stormy night in November, Anne Gordon picked up the newspaper. The first thing she always turned to was the "Births, Marriages and Deaths" page, or as Peter McIntosh called it, "Hatches, Matches and Despatches", and sometimes even "Yells, Bells and Knells". She sat for a few minutes, then looked up in great excitement.

"Babs has had her baby, it's in the Births tonight. A boy. I'll have to get a congratulations card for her."

Renee was delighted. "That's great. Mike'll be a father at last. I bet he'll be pleased it's over, but what a shame he couldn't have been here. And God knows how old his son'll be before he gets home."

"It's sad, isn't it?" Anne's eyes misted. "But it's happening all over the country — all over the world, I suppose."

It was over a month later when they received Mike's letter. He told them the baby's name was Michael, and that he had been seven pounds two ounces at birth. "Babs says he's a perfect darling, and he's going to be spoiled rotten between his grandmother and his Auntie Moira. I wish I could see him, but there you are. That's war."

"Poor Mike," Anne remarked. "Having to keep on fighting out there in the desert and his son growing up without a father."

"He has a father," Renee corrected her.

"Yes, I meant not knowing his father, wise guy."

They fell silent. The news about the war in North Africa had not been good. Every day, the wireless told of fierce battles, and of the Allies having to retreat. Each knew what the other was thinking — would Mike ever come home to see his son?

CHAPTER SIXTEEN

Just before Christmas 1940, Jack Thomson paid the Gordons another quick call. This time there was no greeting kiss for Renee, merely a firm handshake, and she felt rather hurt. He was gradually drifting away from her and there was nothing she could do about it — or perhaps his love for her had also been in her imagination. She tried to act naturally when he was there, and found that they could talk and tease each other much more easily without the invisible barrier she had created before. Kitty Miller was on leave at the time, and had gone home to Yorkshire, and the other three land girls were more subdued without her effervescent presence.

The evening meal passed in companionable joking, even little Nora telling a few funny stories. In the couple of hours which Jack spent talking to Renee and her mother afterwards, he kept them amused with anecdotes about his army and social lives, and asked the girl to tell him about the servicemen she'd met. He left to catch the nine o'clock Peterhead bus, and again, Renee only received a handclasp at the door. The end of a phantom love-affair, she thought, and put it down to another lesson learnt not to count her chickens. She gave herself up to having a good time, but never allowed herself to become emotionally involved with any of the boys.

She exchanged confidences with Sheila — which boy had kissed them, which had tried to get fresh, which had said he was already married — and revelled in the moral danger they were courting. They had both become adept at fending off unwelcome advances, and the attempts, and the tactics they used to foil them, made hilarious telling.

To brighten up their spells of fire-watching duty in the office building, the girls sometimes asked the boys they had met the previous evening to come and sit with them, making it quite clear that, although there were two camp beds provided in the room, there was to be no hanky-panky, and the servicemen generally stuck to the rule. Renee kept up her correspondence with Jack and Tim, and told them about most of her escapades, making them as humorous as she could, and Jack retaliated by telling her about the girls who made it clear they were available to him, and those who rebuffed him. She felt a strong pang of jealousy at the first such letter, but gradually came to enjoy reading them. After all, there was no reason why Jack shouldn't be doing the same as she was herself.

Kitty Miller caused some excitement at the beginning of January, when she came back off leave and announced that she was engaged. Renee and the other girls showered her with congratulations and questions about the lucky man.

"He's a boy I went to school with." Kitty was uncharacteristically shy. "But he joined up and I kind of lost touch with him till I ran into him again on my last leave."

The ring was duly admired again, and the questions went on. What did he look like? How tall was he? What did he do in peacetime? When did they intend getting married? Anne sat silently until the clamour subsided, then she said quietly, "I'm very happy for you, Kitty. You're the last one I thought would settle down."

Kitty laughed uproariously. "Who said I'd settled down? When the tom-cat's away . . ." She caught Anne's disapproving frown and sobered. "No, you're right, Mrs G. My wild days are over."

Flora Sims tossed her auburn tresses aside. "Well, mine aren't, that's for sure."

"Nor mine," added Renee.

"Me, neither." Hilda looked at Nora, who looked away.

"I'm not as wild as you lot, anyway," she said softly. "I did have a steady boyfriend once, but he was killed at Dunkirk." They all remembered her remark about the "lucky ones", and their hearts went out to her.

Kitty voiced their feelings. "I'm sorry, Nora, really very sorry, but why didn't you tell us before?"

"I don't like speaking about it, though it's a bit easier now. I was frozen when my mother wrote and told me."

"You'll meet someone else," Anne said gently. "Don't let that tragedy ruin your life."

Nora smiled sadly. "I try not to."

Nora's sorrow affected Renee's thoughts that night. She had believed that she'd been treated harshly by fate, but the death of a man she loved was something she hoped never to experience. Not that there was any fear of that at the moment, because she had no steady boyfriend, but . . . how would she feel if Jack were killed? Even if he'd scrupulously avoided ever telling her that he loved her, she would be absolutely devastated. Then she realised that she would feel almost as bad if anything happened to Tim, or to Mike, and she'd never imagined herself to be in love with either of them. War, although she had been relishing it lately, was unpredictable. Tragedy could strike at any moment, so it was just as well to enjoy herself while she could.

Tim came to see them the following Saturday forenoon on his own, because Moira was working. She had been employed in the haberdashery department of the same large store since she left school, and was now second in charge.

"You should see young Michael now," Tim told them. "He's growing so fast, you wouldn't believe it."

"As long as he's healthy, that's the main thing," Anne smiled. "Doesn't seeing him give you any ideas?"

"Now, now, Mrs Gordon." He shook his head ruefully. "You should know me better than that, by this time. A child would tie Moira down, and that's one of the reasons I don't want to ask her to get married." Anne pouted and glanced at Renee, who raised her eyebrows in resignation. Tim would not be bulldozed into marriage.

"How's your mother and father keeping these days?" he asked his ex-landlady.

"Granny's not able to get about much," she told him sadly. "And Granda's failing now, too, with having to do nearly everything in the house, as well as the shopping, but they're full of spunk."

"They're good folk. I'm sorry to hear they're not in the best of health."

"They're getting on in years, of course," Anne reminded him. "We're going over there this afternoon, so I'll tell them you asked about them. Granny always asks if we've heard from you. What's been happening since we saw you last?"

Tim told them about his life in the Shetlands, where the soldiers were billeted in the huts previously used by the girls who followed the herring fleet to gut and pack the fish. At half past twelve, he stood up. "I'll have to go. I promised to meet Moira in her dinner hour. I'll see you the next time I'm home, though. You've been very quiet for a while, Renee. Having trouble with one of your boyfriends?"

She forced a short laugh. "No, there's nothing. I just feel a bit down in the dumps today." She couldn't explain to him that she'd been feeling sorry for Moira because Tim wouldn't ask her to marry him, and sorry for herself because she'd nobody to love her. When they went to visit Maggie in the afternoon, she was still full of spunk, as her daughter had told Tim, and it cheered Renee up quite a bit.

Her grandmother seemed to be pleased that Tim had been visiting, and was delighted that he had asked after her health. Then she looked at the girl and said, "Is there a boyfriend, the noo, Renee? You havena said onythin' about it."

"There's dozens, Granny," she giggled. "But nobody you'd give tuppence for."

The old lady looked relieved that Renee could joke about it, and asked about Jack, and then about the land girls, so the conversation was kept going for quite a while, until Peter came back from his weekly shopping expedition, earlier than usual.

It had been several weeks since Anne and Renee had seen him, and he looked more frail and tired than he had been then. His faded eyes lit up when he saw them, and he made them laugh about his price-comparing.

"I can get butter thruppence cheaper in Lipton's than the Home and Colonial, but their tea's dearer, so I get some things at one place an' some things at the other. Whichever's cheapest."

Renee laughed. "Good for you, Granda. You know more about prices than I do."

It was Anne who was quiet on the way home, and at last Renee said, "What's wrong, Mum? If you're worrying about Granny and Granda, don't. They're quite happy, you know."

Anne's anxious expression didn't alter. "Yes, just now, but what's going to happen when your Granda's not able to go out, either? He wasn't looking well today, and there'll come a time when the shopping's going to be too much for him. I wish I could take them into our house, but there's no room."

"I don't suppose they'd want to come, anyway," Renee said, sensibly. "They're too independent, but I could offer to do the shopping for him."

That made Anne laugh. "He'd always be telling you he could have got things cheaper than you."

Life in Cattofield continued on a fairly even keel, the weeks and months passing with monotonous regularity. The two ex-boarders came to see them, on their different times at home, and Renee began to regard them both in the same light — Jack being just another close friend, like Tim.

Her only wish now was that the war would soon be over, even if that happy event might complicate her routine existence. The land girls would leave, Tim would probably marry Moira, and Jack would . . . But would Jack want to return to Aberdeen and a dull job? And if he did, would he be her old friend again, or a stranger?

CHAPTER SEVENTEEN

On the last Sunday in May 1941, the Gordons were relaxing with the newspapers after their lunch, when someone came to the door.

"Who on earth can that be?" Anne hoisted herself lazily from her armchair. "It's not that long since Jack was here, and Tim was just a wee while after that."

Renee straightened up from her lolling position on the settee and smoothed down her old jumper and skirt, in case it was a male caller. She could hear her mother's excited voice as she brought the visitor through the hall, but she looked up without a sign of recognition at the bronzed face of the air force sergeant who came in. Even the Canada flash on his arm meant nothing to her.

The man took off his cap, and the fiery red hair stirred the girl's memory. "Bill Scroggie!" She jumped to her feet and shook his outstretched hand wildly until a shyness came over her. She should remember that she would be eighteen years old in just over three months, and that her dear old friend was almost a stranger to her now.

"He hasn't been in this country long," Anne informed her. "He's stationed in Lincolnshire, but he had some leave, so he came to see us."

Bill smiled. "Lena gave me strict instructions to visit you, but I'd have come even if she hadn't."

"We often wondered what had happened to you," Renee said.

"Yes, we wondered how you were getting on, and if you'd had any family." Anne's eyebrows went down in pretended displeasure. "You never wrote to us, you naughty thing."

His face sobered. "We did mean to write after we got settled down, but the man I was working for, an old bachelor, died about three months after we got there, so my job was finished."

"Oh, Bill, what a shame." She looked sympathetic. "And I believe jobs weren't so easy to come by in Canada in 1937."

"No, you're right there, Mrs Gordon, and we were put out of our house, for his nieces and nephews sold the whole place up. We couldn't find work where we were, so we kept on the move, and got lifts sometimes. We maybe got a job for a day at a little farm, and a decent meal, before we moved on again.

"I couldn't let anybody back home know how we were living. We were like tramps for over two years, and slept out in the open most nights, except in the winter. Some farmer's wife usually took pity on us if it was bad weather, and let us sleep in an outhouse or something. If we'd had the money, we'd have come home, but . . ."

His face clouded at the memory of what they'd suffered.

"Lena was the one thing that kept me going. She wouldn't let me feel sorry for myself, and she never blamed me for taking her away from Aberdeen."

Anne was quite distressed at what he was telling her. "Oh, Bill, what a terrible time you must have had."

"Our luck changed, though," he said quickly. "I happened to land at the right place at the right time, when they were needing a storeman at this big warehouse just outside Toronto. The boss belonged to Aberdeen himself, so I had the job as soon as I opened my mouth. Then, when he discovered that I was really a gardener, he introduced me to one of his friends who was looking for a man to take charge of a new branch of his horticultural firm in Toronto, and I was back on my feet again. We've managed to buy our own little house now — well, we're still paying it up — and we're quite comfortable."

"I'm glad to hear that." Anne was smiling again, pleased that everything had turned out so well for him in the end. "Have you any family, though? You never said."

"No, Mrs Gordon, we haven't any yet." He smiled. "At first, we . . . well, we couldn't afford any, and we hadn't a roof over our heads. Then, when I got this job, we were saving as much as we could to buy a house. When the war started, I wanted to come over right away and do my bit for the old country, but I hadn't long started working, and I wanted to see Lena settled, so I didn't manage to volunteer till the middle of 1940.

She wasn't all that keen on the idea, but she came round to it."

Anne's heart went out to the girl whose life had been so disrupted at a time when she had thought it ordered at last. "I'm not surprised she was against it, Bill. She'll be lonely in a strange country on her own."

"She's made quite a few friends now, and our neighbours are very good. Anyway, she's taken a job to keep her occupied till I get back." His eyes twinkled suddenly, and he laughed. "After that, we intend to have a big family, and that'll keep us both busy — night and day." He winked.

"You haven't changed, Bill." Anne smiled broadly.

"Neither have you, Mrs Gordon."

"Oh, come off it. Waist spreading, hair turning grey? I'm beginning to feel ancient."

Renee had been feeling too shy to enter into the conversation, but found her tongue at last. "Oh, Mum, you're only forty-one. That's not ancient old, just ordinary old."

"Thank you for those kind words." Anne roared with laughter. "I'll have to shift my ordinary old bones now, anyway. I've to get the tea ready for my four land girls."

"Oh." Bill looked crestfallen. "I was going to ask you about staying, Mrs Gordon. You see, I went to Lena's mother this morning when I came off the train, but she's still mad at me for taking her daughter away from her, so I thought you could maybe put me up for a few days, but if you've got four . . ."

"Bill Scroggie! You're welcome to stay here as long as you like," Anne said, indignantly. "You can sleep on the bed settee, if you don't object?"

"No, no, it's OK. I'll find somewhere in the town. I don't want to put you out."

"You're not putting me out. It's all right with me, if it's all right with you. We'll be delighted to have you."

"Thanks, Mrs Gordon. It's very kind of you, for I've nobody left in Huntly, now. My father died just weeks after we went to Canada, and my mother died five months after that. I didn't write to her after my chauffeur job was finished, but I sent a letter once I was settled in Toronto, to let her know we were all right, and one of her neighbours, the postie's wife, got my address off the envelope, so she wrote to tell me about my mother's death. It was an awful shock, especially when we'd just got ourselves sorted out."

"Poor Bill." Anne laid her hand on his shoulder. "You've had more than your share of troubles, haven't you?"

He shrugged philosophically. "Oh, well. I'll take you up on your offer of a bed, Mrs Gordon."

"That's settled, then. Renee, you keep Bill amused while I get on with the tea."

He looked at the girl properly then. "My goodness, there's a big change in you. I wouldn't have recognised you if I'd met you in the street. You're quite a sophisticated young lady now, not a little schoolgirl any more."

Her shyness returned, although their ex-boarder was not so unfamiliar as he'd seemed at first. "I didn't know who you were, either, till you took off your cap."

There was a slight, awkward pause, then Bill started the conversation rolling. "How's your Uncle George?"

She told him the story of George Gordon's abrupt departure, and about the debts he had left behind, and Bill was completely shocked. "Your mother's had a hard struggle as well, then? I'm sorry to hear that, for it was bad enough for her before. Have you heard anything from him since he went away?"

"Not one word."

"And what about young Jack? What's he doing now?"

"He was called up over a year ago, to the Ordnance Corps, but he writes quite a lot. I'll get his last letter for you to read." She took the envelope from her handbag and handed it to him, smiling when he hesitated to open it. "There's nothing private in it."

"He seems to be enjoying himself," Bill remarked when he handed the letter back.

"Yes, I'm pleased about that."

"He was never a boyfriend, then?"

"We went out together quite a lot," she answered carefully, "but there was never anything serious in it."

Bill regarded her quizzically. "He signs off 'Love, Jack'."

"So does Tim," she said hastily. "That's Tim Donaldson. He would be after your time, though. He came here with his brother, Mike, after Uncle George left. Mike got married before he was called up, and Tim's going steady with Mike's sister-in-law. So writing

'Love' at the end of a letter doesn't mean a thing. Not these days, anyway."

"It maybe doesn't mean anything with this Tim." He rubbed his chin with his little finger. "Most men find writing 'Love' an easy way to finish off a letter, but I got to know Jack pretty well when I was sharing the room with him, and I'd say he wouldn't write that lightly."

Renee blew out her cheeks. "He never gives any sign of . . . anything when he's here."

"That's just how he is." Bill didn't sound convinced that he was wrong. "What happened to . . . Fergus, wasn't it? The one that came after Lena and me were married? I saw him a few times when we were visiting. Is he still here?"

"He's in the army, too. He joined the Engineers the day after the war started." She could speak rationally about him now, though she much preferred not to.

"Oh? I didn't think he had it in him. I got the impression that he was just out for number one, if you know what I mean?"

"I know, and you're quite right, Bill. He never thought about anybody but himself."

He looked puzzled. "I wonder why he joined up as quickly as that. His kind aren't usually so self-sacrificing. He'd got himself in trouble over some girl, likely, and was taking the easy way out."

"Likely." Renee was amazed at Bill's correct assessment, but wished that he would change the subject, because it was well over a year since she had purged Fergus Cooper out of her system.

"What about you, Renee? Are you in the forces, do you work, or is it college?"

"I work, in a reserved occupation, worse luck, but it's quite interesting, really."

"You said 'worse luck'. Would you like to be in the forces?"

"I believe I would. It might be more exciting, though I enjoy myself pretty well as it is."

"What about boyfriends?"

"Nobody serious, and that's how I like it."

Bill regarded her thoughtfully. "It seems to me you've had a bad experience with somebody. Am I right?"

"Yes, and it was quite bad, but I was too young to realise what was going on until it was too late."

"Hmmm. Well, you're right to play the field and enjoy yourself, but be careful not to tie yourself down till you're quite sure it's the real thing. Love's the most marvellous thing in the world, as they say, but it can be a dodgy business sometimes, and not everybody's as lucky as I've been."

"Were you sure it was the real thing when you married Lena?"

"I was, and I've never regretted it. I love Lena as much now as I did the day I married her — more, maybe. When you've to struggle to exist, like we did, you grow closer together." He sighed. "I miss her, Renee, but I had to do my bit."

"What are you two so serious about?" Anne came in, wiping her hands on her apron.

"We were discussing love, Mrs Gordon," Bill smiled.

"Did you come to any conclusion about it?"

"Just that it's a dodgy business."

Anne looked alarmed. "Are you and Lena not . . . ?"

"We're perfect. I was just saying how much I missed her."

"She's missing you, too, I bet." Anne sat down. "I'll leave you to set the table, Renee, and remember, there'll be seven of us."

"I feel terrible about imposing myself on you like this." Bill sounded very apologetic.

"One more's not going to make much difference." Anne lay back against the cushions and Renee went to carry out her task.

When the four land girls came in they were delighted to see the handsome man in the Canadian uniform, and flirted madly with Bill, who lapped it up in amusement.

"Wait till I tell my wife about you lot," he giggled. "She'll come over on the next boat to keep her eye on me."

He turned to Anne when they went out. "They're a great bunch, very nice girls."

"You'll change your mind when you try getting into the bathroom in the morning."

"Yes," added Renee. "It's a good thing they leave the house before me, or I'd never get myself washed."

"I won't be in any hurry, though," Bill said. "I can wait till the rush is past."

On the following night, he took Anne and Renee to His Majesty's Theatre. Anne was quite overcome at being asked. "I haven't been out for an evening like this for . . . years, and I don't have anything fancy enough to wear."

"You'll look fine whatever you've got on," Bill assured her gallantly, and Renee felt a pang of regret that she'd never realised how drab her mother's life must be. She made up her mind to take her out occasionally in future.

"This must have cost you a fortune," Anne whispered when they were settling into their seats in the dress circle.

"I'm only repaying you for all the kindness you showed me when you were my landlady," Bill said seriously. "I'm very glad to be able to do it, belated though it is." After the show, he took them to a small cafeteria and treated them to a cup of coffee and a sandwich.

"Thank you very much, Bill," Anne said, when they were going home in the bus. "I've thoroughly enjoyed my night out."

"I'm happy about that, and it was my pleasure." On that wet, miserable Tuesday evening, Bill kept them regaled with stories about his experiences as a man of the road, and they marvelled at how he and his wife had survived. When he switched to the cheerier topic of reminiscing about his time as a boarder with them, they were soon chuckling at the memories of ten-year-old Renee being teased by Bill and Jack, and her futile attempts to get her own back on them.

Bill Scroggie left on Wednesday morning. After the four land girls had dashed out, he had gone into the dining room. "I think I'll have a day in Huntly, going round my mother's neighbours, for old times' sake, then I'm going to Edinburgh for a couple of days before I go back to the drome. Now, Mrs Gordon, you'll have to let me pay for my stay."

"Don't be silly!" Anne was outraged. "You're an old friend, and seven didn't cost me any more than six. Come to see us again, if you get the chance, remember."

"Right, I'll hold you to that," he smiled. "Goodbye, and thank you for everything. Goodbye, Renee, and remember what I told you."

"I will." The girl laughed self-consciously.

"If you've time, write and let us know how you're getting on, and where you are if you're posted." Anne went to the door with him and waved as he walked along the street. "He's a pet, isn't he?" she said to Renee as she closed the front door.

"Yes, he is. Lena's lucky," Renee sighed.

"She probably knows that, but Bill's a lucky man to have a wife like her, sticking by him through all his troubles."

Their life returned to normal, except that Renee now took her mother out once a fortnight, to the cinema or the theatre — not in the dress circle, which was far above her means — and Anne's gratitude made her ashamed that she hadn't thought of it before. Renee's own social life was still quite hectic, and she often took a lonely serviceman in for a cup of tea when he saw her home. She met several older men, in the Palais or in the snack bars she frequented with Sheila Daun, and somehow felt more at ease with them, although they were probably married and purely out for a bit of fun now that they were off the leash.

She also let some of them see her home, but made it quite clear that there was to be no pawing or messing about. Most of them were happy to have it like that, for the sake of feminine company for a short time, but one or two of them tried to find out if she really meant it. They found out, to their chagrin, that she did.

One night, about two and a half months after Bill Scroggie's visit, Renee found herself in conversation with an army sergeant in a cafeteria. He was definitely over forty, she thought, but he was polite and very easy to talk to, no flirting or innuendoes. He told her that he had been in the regular army, a widower who had been stationed at Aldershot before the war, with a grown-up son and daughter. "David's nearly twenty, and he's in the Artillery like me. Patricia — Pat — is in the ATS. She's just turned eighteen."

"I'll be eighteen in a couple of weeks," Renee told him. "Where are your son and daughter now?"

"Pat's just outside London, and she goes home every weekend."

"Who looks after your house, if you're a widower?"

"My mother moved in after Marjory died, so there's still a home for us all. David's in Shetland. Or he was, the last time I heard from him, but he's not very good at corresponding, so he could have been moved by this time."

"Were they quite young when your wife died?"

"It was five years ago, and they were both still at school, that's why their grandmother took over, because I was often away on manoeuvres and things like that. Since the war started, of course, I only get back when I'm on leave." He lifted his shoulders expressively.

"My father died when I was hardly ten," Renee told him.

"Oh, I'm sorry. Is your mother . . .?"

"Yes, Mum's still around, criticising me for going out so much." She grinned impishly.

"She has the right idea." His face was serious. "A lot of young servicemen are only out for one thing, and haven't the least intention of marrying the girls they play around with. I'm always telling Pat that in my letters."

Sheila Daun, sitting on Renee's other side, nudged her arm. "Chris here wants to see me home, Renee. Is it OK with you if I leave you now? There's no buses running because of the air-raid warning."

Renee had almost forgotten that the sirens had been howling when they came out of the cinema. "Yes, OK. I'll manage fine. I've done it before."

Her confidence wasn't as strong as she professed, and it was with a touch of apprehension that she watched her friend leave with the sailor. Aberdeen hadn't suffered a night raid for some time, but that didn't mean there wouldn't be one tonight. She felt a hand on her arm and turned round. The sergeant was regarding her apologetically. "I'm afraid I've spoiled your chance of an escort by sitting beside you, but may I offer my services? I promise I've no ulterior motive, just a craving for feminine company and a need to while away the time." His eyebrows lifted in question.

"I'll be all right, thanks." Renee didn't want him to feel obliged to accompany her. "I walk it quite a lot." Usually with a frisky young soldier or sailor, came the wry thought, and never during an air-raid warning.

"There's the alert as well as the blackout," he persisted. "I'd be much happier if I saw you safely home."

Why not? At least she wouldn't be on her own if enemy planes did come. "OK then, if you don't mind a double hike, because it's a good bit from here. Where are you stationed, though? It's maybe too far for you to walk back." She picked up her handbag and stood up.

"The distance won't bother me," he said, as they went up the stairs. "I'm accustomed to ten- and twenty-mile route marches. By the way, my name's Alfred Schaper. What's yours?"

"Irene Gordon, but I'm usually called Renee."

"I'm usually called Fred . . . or RSM," he replied, laughing.

The long walk, uphill for most of the way, passed very quickly, with them discussing films they had seen, Renee's work and Fred's service in the Artillery. Then she told him about the girls who boarded with them, and about the boys who had been there before.

"Your mother's had to work hard since your father died?"

"Yes, and she doesn't get out much. I take her to the pictures or the theatre once every two weeks, but that's the only entertainment she has."

When they reached the end of her street, she was saying, "It's just along here a wee bit," when the air was rent with the welcome sound of the all-clear.

"That's good," Fred remarked as they stopped outside her house — no gate nowadays, because that, along with the railings, had been taken away to be used for making war machinery. "I'll maybe get a bus somewhere along my return journey."

"I doubt it, it must be well after time for the buses to stop running altogether."

"Oh, well, no matter." Fred held out his hand. "I'm very pleased to have made your acquaintance, Irene Gordon, usually called Renee, and thank you for allowing me to walk home with you. It's been like having Pat with me for a little while."

"Thank *you*." She couldn't bring herself to call him Fred. "Will you be able to find your way back?"

"I think so. If I don't, I'll probably be wandering round Aberdeen all night," he joked.

"If you tell me where you've to go, I might be able to give you a shorter route."

"We arrived at the Torry Battery a couple of days ago."

"You're at the Torry . . .? Oh, no! That's about as far as you can get from here and still be in Aberdeen." Renee was quite shocked. "You'd better come in for a wee while, and have a cup of tea and a rest before you start off again."

"Thank you, Renee. I would like to come in for a wee while." He mimicked her accent, laughing as he followed her in. Anne jumped up in dismay when her daughter ushered in the stranger. She was wearing her old dressing-gown and her tattered slippers, and her hair was bristling with metal curlers, which would have mortified her at any other time, but her mind was occupied with something far more upsetting than her dishabille.

"This is Sergeant Fred Schaper, Mum," Renee explained. "He took me home because the warning was on and the buses were off."

"That was very kind of you." Anne held her wrapper together as she shook hands with the broad six-footer, but there was no real warmth in her manner.

"I'm very pleased to meet Renee's mother." Fred held her hand for a little longer than was necessary.

This did not escape the girl, and she realised suddenly that he was old enough to be her father, a thought which had not occurred to her before.

"I've to go back to the Torry Battery." Fred carried on the explanation for the girl. "Renee was kind enough to invite me in for a wee while." He imitated her again and smiled.

"For a cup of tea and a rest," she giggled. "I'll go and make some fresh, Mum."

"All right, and pour that out." Anne handed her the flask which had been sitting on the card table. "I'm sorry, Sergeant . . . er . . . Schaper . . ."

"Please call me Fred."

"I'm sorry I'm not presentable, but I was waiting up for Renee because . . ."

"Because of the air-raid warning?" he interrupted. "I quite understand, and don't worry about how you look. It's quite comforting to see a woman in curlers again."

"Fred's a widower," Renee said, coming back from the scullery. She felt happier calling him by his first name now that they were no longer alone.

"It wasn't just the air-raid warning that made me stay up," Anne said slowly. "You weren't home at teatime, Renee, so I couldn't tell you before. I'd a letter from Lena Scroggie, Bill's wife, by the second post today."

"That's good. Did Bill write and tell her he'd been here?" Renee's face sobered when her mother shook her head. "Is something wrong?"

"He's been killed, Renee."

"Oh, no! Not Bill! He was so full of life and . . . they were planning to have a big family after the war. Oh, Mum! How can things like that happen? Lena must be . . ." She stopped, too upset by the tragic news to say any more.

"Is this Bill a relative?" Fred asked gently, seeing how much the two women had been affected by the man's death.

"No, he used to lodge here before he was married, then they emigrated to Canada." Anne's voice trembled. "We never heard from them after they left at the beginning of 1937 — they'd a pretty rough time of it, apparently — then we had a visit from him about two or three months ago, over here with the Canadian Air Force." She gulped.

"I'm very sorry." His eyes were full of compassion.

Anne turned to her daughter again. "Lena thanked us for being so good to Bill when he was here. He'd written to tell her he'd spent a few days with us, and . . . I'm sorry, Sergeant . . . er . . . Fred, but I'm really upset about it. I shouldn't have told Renee in front of you, though, but I couldn't keep it in any longer." Anne wiped her eyes.

"I'd better go. I don't want to intrude on you at a time like this." He made to stand up.

Anne held up her hand. "No, no. Please stay. I'm all right now. It was just . . . coming so soon after we'd seen him, and . . . Renee, that kettle must be boiling by now. I think we could all do with a cup of tea."

The girl went to fill the teapot, and her mother looked at the man kindly. "What time do you have to be back . . . Fred? You're going to be very late."

"This was my day off, and I don't have to report for duty until eleven tomorrow forenoon, so I can have a lie-in if I like."

Anne hesitated, then said, "Look, it's nearly midnight, and if you don't mind roughing it, you could sleep on that bed-settee, and you'd get a bus in the morning."

Renee, coming in with the loaded tray, heard the surprising offer, and wondered if her mother had taken leave of her senses, letting a perfect stranger stay the night.

Fred, however, showed no astonishment, but accepted calmly and gracefully. "Thank you, Mrs Gordon. I'm used to roughing it after over twenty years in the army, but I'm sure the settee is very comfortable. I am quite prepared to hoof it, though."

"I can't let you walk all that way tonight, when you've been so kind to Renee. And please call me Anne. It seems silly me saying Fred, and you saying Mrs Gordon."

He beamed. "Right, Anne. You have another lodger tonight."

They drank their tea, then Anne said, "I think we'd better be going to bed, Renee. Get the spare sheets and things from the cupboard upstairs, and I'll make up the settee."

"Let me do that, Anne." Fred jumped up and removed the two small cushions before he swung the upholstered mechanism up and out in one easy movement.

"You won't have to worry about getting up early," Anne told him. "Nobody comes in here in the morning except me coming through to make the breakfast, and the house'll be cleared by half past eight, that's when Renee leaves. The other girls go out at half past seven."

"Righto. Thanks." Fred took the bedclothes from Renee when she came in. "I'll manage now. Off to bed, the pair of you."

In their bedroom, Anne said, "Where did you meet him? He seems very nice, but he's rather old for you, don't you think?"

"It was quite funny, really. Sheila and I went in for a milk shake after we came out of the pictures, and the place was nearly full up, so a sailor came and sat next to her, and Fred sat down next to me. They were chatting each other up, so he started speaking to me. I suppose he was sorry for me, being left out, if you see what I mean. Then Sheila said the sailor was taking her home, and Fred offered to take me. I was a bit worried about walking on my own with the warning on, so I let him. That's all."

"He's a fast worker, isn't he?"

Her mother's tone was so critical that Renee replied sharply, "He wasn't working at anything, Mum. He's a widower with a son of twenty and a daughter about the same age as me, and he didn't like the idea of me going home by myself." Her voice softened. "He said it was like having his daughter with him again. There was nothing more than that in it."

Anne smiled. "I'm glad. We'd better settle down, or else we'll all be lying in tomorrow."

In the morning, Renee and her mother took a second cup of tea after the other girls went out. Anne stretched over for the milk jug. "Your Fred's sleeping like a baby. He must have been very tired. I'm glad I let him stay the night."

"He's not my Fred. He's old enough to be my father."

"That's funny. That's what I thought when I saw him first. I don't know what he must have thought of me in that old dressing-gown and curlers."

"Does it matter?" Renee gulped the last of her tea. "You'll never see him again, I shouldn't think."

"No, of course not."

As Renee was putting on her coat in the hall, Fred came out of the living room with only his trousers on, his hair, greying at the temples, standing up in tousled spikes. "I meant to be up ages ago, but . . . I'm sorry, Mrs . . . er . . . Anne."

She laughed. "You were sound asleep when I was wandering in and out."

"I needn't bother asking if you slept all right," Renee remarked, picking up her handbag. "I have to go. Cheerio, Fred, and thanks again for seeing me home."

"It was my pleasure." He ran his hand over the stubble on his chin. "I'll be off shortly myself, as soon as I give myself a wash."

"I think there's a razor of Tim's or Jack's still lying in the bathroom cabinet, Fred, and you can't go without some breakfast," Anne was saying as Renee went out.

When she reached the office, Sheila Daun's first remark made her giggle. "Thank goodness you look normal. I wondered if I should leave you alone with that old sergeant, in case he asked to take you home then tried to get fresh."

"He did take me home, but he didn't get fresh," Renee told her. "He stayed all night on our settee, as a matter of fact, and I've left him at home with Mum. He's more her age than mine."

The other girl was rather disconcerted by this information, but, after considering it for a moment, she thought of another question. "Would you mind if he took a fancy to your mum?"

"No, of course I wouldn't. It's time she had some fun." Renee remembered that she had minded, a long time ago, when her mother had tried to have some fun, but . . . that was different. "It was a good thing he came in with me really," she went on, "because Mum had been waiting up to tell me that Bill Scroggie had been killed. Remember, I told you about him coming to see us — the one who's in the Canadian Air Force?"

"Oh, that's terrible. Coming all that way, just to be killed? It makes you realise that the war affects people all over the world. You don't think about it like that when you're having fun with the boys in the forces, do you?"

"No . . . but Fred being there stopped us from brooding about it."

When she went home at lunchtime, she felt an electricity in the air, a sense of excitement emanating from her mother, so she asked, "How did you get on with Fred, Mum? Did he get away all right?"

Anne concentrated on ladling out the soup. "Yes, he left at ten o'clock. He's a real gentleman, isn't he? Very correct, and he thanked me for my hospitality, and even offered to pay me. Of course, I didn't take anything."

"So that's another little episode over?" Renee couldn't resist voicing it as a question, because she suspected that there was something her mother wasn't telling her.

"He was sympathising again about Bill," Anne went on, still avoiding her daughter's eyes, "and he was so nice about . . . everything, that I've invited him to come to tea on Sunday."

"It's you that's turned out to be the fast worker, Mum." The girl was quite taken aback. She hadn't expected this.

"I felt sorry for him, Renee, and after what's happened to Bill, I felt I'd like to show someone else a bit of kindness, just in case . . ."

"Don't think things like that. But it was a good idea to ask him back. What did he say?"

"He was delighted."

"So, you're doing your little bit to help the war effort? Comforts for the troops, eh? I didn't know you were intending to do that." Renee was enjoying teasing her mother.

"You take lonely boys home sometimes, and it's the same thing, isn't it?" Anne sounded slightly guilty.

"I suppose so." Renee's mood had changed with the speed of lightning. "It was awful about Bill. I feel really sorry for Lena. Just after they'd begun to build a decent life for themselves, and . . . if she'd had any children to remember him by, it wouldn't seem so bad."

"It's maybe better that there aren't any children," Anne mused. "It leaves Lena free to marry again, with no encumbrances, if she ever feels like it."

Renee was quiet for a moment. "Mum, would you ever marry again, if you met somebody you really liked?"

"Don't speak rubbish!" A pink tinge had suffused Anne's cheeks, and she changed the subject quickly. "Will you be going out tonight?"

"No, I've suddenly thought of something I'd like to do instead." The girl smiled mysteriously, but although Anne looked inquisitive, she refrained from putting any questions to her.

Renee returned to work pondering over how she would really feel if her mother ever did want to marry again. It would be all right if it was to someone like Fred Schaper, but there were quite a lot of unscrupulous men about, and she didn't fancy having a wicked stepfather. Not that Anne ever met any men, but her daughter would have to make sure that it was Fred, and she'd have to be careful not to overdo it and spoil things. Before she went into the office, she went into Boots to buy a home perm. Step number one would be to give her mother a decent hairdo, even if it meant that she, herself, would have to forego at least one evening out, maybe more, because of the money she was spending.

That night, Anne protested all through the operation. "I'm not really needing this, you know. My hair would have been fine the way it was." But Renee could see that she was pleased with the finished result, and kept glancing in the mirror to admire her beautifully curled tresses.

"It's a bit tight just now, but it'll loosen out by Sunday," she told her mother.

On Saturday at lunchtime, she came home carrying a large paper bag. "It's an early birthday present, Mum," she said when she handed it over. "I thought you could wear it with your grey tweed skirt on Sunday. I bought it in Falconer's and they said they'd change it if it didn't fit, so you'd better try it on now."

"You shouldn't spend your money on me like this." Anne opened the bag carefully, and drew out a pale lilac twinset. "Oh, it's lovely." She ran her hand sensuously over the soft pure wool. "Thank you very much."

The short-sleeved jumper and matching cardigan fitted her perfectly. "Fred'll think I'm setting my cap at him with all this tittivating," Anne remarked self-consciously.

"He'll just think you look very nice." Renee thought that her mother was looking ten years younger, with her new hairstyle and the pastel shade of the twinset. Fred Schaper couldn't help but find her attractive.

When they were climbing the stairs to the McIntoshes' flat that afternoon, Anne glanced at Renee. "Don't tell Granny about Fred," she whispered urgently.

"Why not? There's nothing wrong about asking him to tea."

"I know, but . . . just don't tell her."

As usual, Maggie made them very welcome, and, after enquiring about Jack, Tim and Mike, she looked expectantly at her granddaughter. "An' who have ye been meetin' this week?"

Renee shot her mother a mischievous glance. "Well, Sheila Daun got off with a sailor when we went for a milk shake after the pictures, one night, and I was left speaking to a middle-aged Artillery sergeant with two grown-up children."

"Oh." Maggie showed her disappointment. "So ye'd to go hame by yoursel'."

It wasn't a question, so Renee smilingly waited a few seconds, to keep her mother in suspense, before she said, "How's Granda?"

"He's feelin' a lot better this week. Nae near so tired."

"That's good." Anne had let out the breath which she had been holding in case her daughter said something more about Fred. "We'd some bad news this week. Remember I told you we had a visit from Bill Scroggie a wee while ago?"

"Aye? I used to like him," Maggie remarked. "It was a shame he'd such a bad time in Canada till he got settled doon."

"Yes, it was . . . but Lena wrote to tell us he'd been killed." Anne sighed deeply. It was still difficult for her to believe.

"Oh, my! That's terrible." The old lady shook her head sadly. "How did it happen?"

"I don't know. Lena didn't tell us, but maybe she had never been told herself." Anne lapsed into a morose silence.

To take her mother's mind off the tragedy, Renee said, "Will I put the kettle on, Granny?"

"Aye, lassie, please. It's hard for me nae to be able to dae things for mysel'."

It was most unusual for Maggie to be sorry for herself, so Renee said quickly, "It's a good thing you've got Granda."

"Aye." Her grandmother smiled again. "I dinna ken what I'd dae without him, the auld gommeril."

Peter was still out shopping when they came away, so Anne knew that he must be feeling better, like her mother had said, and her anxiety about his health eased a little. "I shouldn't have told Granny about Bill," she said suddenly. "It just upset her. I should have had more sense."

"No, Mum. She should know. It's just life — or, rather, death."

CHAPTER EIGHTEEN

On Sunday morning, Renee brushed out her mother's hair and combed it into place, the curls now looser and softer round Anne's face, the odd strand of grey adding character.

"It really suits you, Mum. Watch when you're putting on your jumper, though, in case you knock it all flat."

"What a fuss." Anne felt that she ought to protest a little, although she was quite enjoying the attention.

At four o'clock, when Fred Schaper arrived, he was carrying a large bunch of flowers, which he handed shyly to Anne.

"Oh, thank you, Fred." She turned pink with pleasure. "It's the first time anybody's ever given me a bouquet. I'd better put them in water straight away." Her voice was high and breathless as she went into the scullery.

Renee giggled. "You've put her in a flap."

"I didn't mean to do that." Fred seemed quite worried.

"It's all right. She loved it. You got back to the Battery on Wednesday without any problems, I suppose?"

"No trouble at all. Your mother gave me instructions and I couldn't go wrong. A very capable lady, your mum."

"She's had a lot of practice looking after people."

"I could see that. Ah, that looks good." He looked approvingly at the vase Anne carried through, the blooms nicely arranged. "So do you," he added softly.

Her pink cheeks turned a deep crimson, and Renee felt elated. This was all going to work without any help from her, by the look of things.

The conversation ranged from food rationing to keeping boarders, from life in the regular army in peacetime to life in the army during the war, and Renee was content just to listen, putting in an occasional word or two to remind them that she was there. They did seem to need reminding. Her mother and Fred were so engrossed in finding out as much as they could about each other that the girl could almost hear the wedding bells ringing.

At a quarter to six, Anne said, "Come and help me to dish up, Renee. I think I heard the girls coming in a few minutes ago."

"Let me help, too." Fred followed them into the scullery and carried some of the items through to the dining-room table.

"This makes me feel really at home," he smiled, sitting down only after all the others were seated.

"I'm sorry there's no meat," Anne apologised. "We don't get very much, so we have to have meatless days. This is a vegetable pie — the girls keep me supplied with the veggies." She beamed at the land girls, who were reasonably quiet for a change, sensing, perhaps, that this serviceman was different, someone special to their landlady. Anne pointed to each one in turn, as she introduced them. "Flora and Kitty — they're downstairs — and Hilda and Nora are upstairs. Girls, this is Sergeant Schaper."

"It's RSM Schaper," Renee butted in. "That's Regimental Sergeant Major, isn't it?"

"It's Fred," he laughed, and tackled his pie with gusto. After a few minutes, he looked round him. "You're a lucky lot having a billet like this. I only wish we were so lucky in the army."

Flora nodded. "Yes, Mrs G.'s a gem." She laughed delightedly. "Gee whizz, I've gone all alliterative in my old age. G.'s a gem. Jar of jam. Jelly and junket . . ."

The other girls joined in, the challenge of the game overcoming their reserve with the man.

"Just a jiffy," Kitty squealed.

"Jack and Jill." Hilda looked for approval.

Fred was laughing loudly now. "Jumping Jehosophat!" he said.

Renee added her contribution. "Jumpers and jerseys."

Nora, the quiet one, had been thinking furiously, and came out with "Judge and jury."

Flora got to her feet and motioned them to be silent. They watched her as she put her fingertips together and bowed her head. "Gentle Jesus!" she boomed in a deep voice, then sat down with a thump amid hearty applause.

"Oh, stop it," begged Anne. "You're giving me the jim-jams."

Everyone laughed uncontrollably except Nora, who innocently asked, "What's the jim-jams?" causing Kitty and Flora to hold on to each other in hysterical mirth.

Hilda spluttered, "Mrs G. was just saying something to fit in, you dumpling."

Fred was the first to recover. "I think we've had enough hilarity. Let's get back to the serious business of doing justice to this beautiful meal. Home cooking's what I miss most of all."

"Yes, I suppose army food isn't very good." Anne wiped the tears of laughter from her eyes.

"It's not all that terrible, really, but nothing like this. Your pastry just melts in the mouth."

"It's not too bad," Anne said modestly, veiling the pleasure she felt at his compliment. Fred began asking questions about the work in the market gardens, and the four girls chattered away until the meal was over.

"We'll wash up for you, Mrs G.," Flora said. "That'll let you entertain your visitor."

"No, no. Off you go, we'll manage fine." Anne poured another cup of tea for Fred.

"You're spoiling me," he laughed.

"You deserve it." Anne turned to her daughter. "Right, Renee, we'll get the dishes done. Take your cup into the living room, Fred, we won't be long."

"No, I can't let you do all the work. You did the cooking." He emptied his cup and started piling dishes on to the tray. "You can wash, Renee, and I'll wipe."

"No, Fred." Anne tried to wrest the tray away from him. "You're a visitor. Renee and me . . ."

"Look, Mum." Renee stood up. "I'll settle it. You two can do the dishes, and I'll go up and tidy out the chest of drawers. You've been at me long enough to do it."

When she was climbing the stairs, she could hear them laughing as they carried everything out of the dining room across the hall. A promising beginning. The four girls went out shortly afterwards, and the whole house was suddenly silent. About twenty minutes later, Anne came into the attic bedroom. "Fred's suggesting that the three of us should go out for a walk. Are you nearly finished here?"

Although she'd pushed the last tidy drawer back into place a second earlier, Renee shook her head. "I've still a couple of drawers to do. Go by yourselves, I'll be finished by the time you get back."

"If you're sure you don't mind?" Anne took her coat out of the old wardrobe.

As soon as she heard the front door closing, Renee lay down on top of her bed. She had acted Cupid to the best of her ability, and it was up to them now.

An hour and a half elapsed before Anne and Fred returned, by which time Renee was downstairs listening to the wireless.

"It's a lovely night." Anne looked blissful. "You should have come with us."

The girl noticed her mother's bright sparkling eyes. "I think you enjoyed your walk better without me playing gooseberry," she teased.

"You know," Fred remarked, grinning, "I believe you're right."

Anne blushed. "We went down to the Westburn Park, then across the road into the Victoria Park, then home. We've done quite a bit of walking, and I'm desperate for a cup of tea."

Left alone with Fred, Renee commented on the difference between the two parks. "The Westburn Park's all right, really, with the burn running through it, and swings for kids. The Victoria Park's smaller, but nicer, I always think." It was a pity that it held such shameful memories for her, she reflected ruefully, and she hadn't ventured into it for years. Giving herself a mental shake, she told him a rather risqué joke which Sheila Daun had been laughing about a few days before.

When they were drinking the tea that Anne brought through, Fred said, "I've a proposition to make. I want to show my thanks for this lovely afternoon and evening, so I'm inviting you both out for a meal. I'm on duty Wednesday, but any other night you're free."

"It depends on Renee." Anne glanced at her daughter.

All the girl's nights that week were to be free. She'd spent all her money on the perm and the twinset, but she couldn't say anything about that. "Mum, it's good of Fred to include me in his invitation, but I'm sure it's you he wants to take out, not me. Am I right, RSM?" She winked to him quickly.

He understood and played his part. "Spot on." Then he added, "But I'd be pleased to have you along."

"I'd rather not come, thanks just the same. Two's company, but you make up your own mind, Mum."

Anne hesitated. "What would people say if they see me out with Fred on my own?"

Renee threw up her hands. "For goodness sake! You were out with him on your own tonight. Anyway, you've been a widow for eight years, and Fred's wife died five years ago, so there's nothing anyone can say."

"That's true, Anne." Fred touched her hand. "Please say yes, I really want to take you out."

Anne turned accusing eyes on her daughter. "You're up to something, I can tell."

"I think she's trying her hand at matchmaking," the man laughed. "And I'd say she's doing a pretty good job, but we should manage the rest ourselves. Which night will it be, Anne?" he coaxed.

After a moment of struggling between shyness and her attraction to the man, Anne said timidly, "Thursday?"

"Too long for me to wait."

"Tuesday, then?" She was absolutely thrilled by the implied compliment.

"That's better. Now where do you want to go? You know more about the eating places in Aberdeen than I do."

"To be honest, I don't. I've never once had a meal out in my whole life. Jim, my husband, always said he preferred my cooking, and after he died, I just couldn't afford it."

Renee took the tray back to the scullery, to give them a chance to make their arrangements, and pottered about aimlessly for a short time after she'd rinsed out the cups and saucers. When she returned to the living room, Fred stood up.

"I'll have to go, I'm afraid." He dropped one eyelid slowly as he went past her. "Thanks for all your help, Renee."

"I'll see you again, no doubt," she replied.

She hoped that the attraction wasn't entirely one-sided, but she didn't really think it was. Her judgement was proved correct when Anne came back from seeing Fred out, her face glowing with happiness. "He really likes you, Mum."

"Do you think so? Isn't he just asking me out to repay me for tonight's meal, like he said?"

"No, he's not. He wants to start taking you out all the time, a blind man could see that. He fancies you."

Anne blushed. "I quite fancy him . . . Oh, Renee, am I being stupid, at my age?"

"You're just beginning to live again."

On Tuesday evening, Anne fluttered about getting ready to go out for her meal, until Renee said, "You're going to be late, if you don't watch yourself."

"I feel like a young girl going out on her first date," her mother said, nervously, smoothing her skirt over her hips.

"Good luck, then." Renee shepherded her rather roughly into the hall. "Get your coat on, and go, for any sake."

At that moment, Flora Sims and Kitty Miller came out of their bedroom. "Ooh, Mrs G., you look ever so nice." Flora eyed her with admiration, and held up her hand with the thumb and forefinger touching, in a gesture of approval.

Kitty beamed all over. "Are you going out on a date?"

"Yes, she is," Renee said sharply, "and if she doesn't hurry, she'll miss the bus." She propelled her mother to the door.

"We're catching this one, too." Flora swung her bag over her shoulder. "Bye, Renee."

That was the first of many outings for Anne and Fred Schaper, and he became a regular visitor to the house, often spending the night on the settee if he didn't have to be on duty early the following day.

After three weeks, Anne decided that it was time to tell her mother what was going on. "I've been going out with a sergeant in the Royal Artillery," she said tentatively, as soon as she and Renee were seated in the flat.

Maggie's eyes widened in surprise, but her voice was not unkind. "An' where did ye meet *him*?"

Renee stepped in, to save her mother the embarrassment of explaining. "I told you about him, remember? He saw me home one night from a cafe, because he didn't like the idea of a young girl the same age as his daughter having to walk home in the blackout."

"His daughter?" The old lady pursed her lips. "He's a married man, is he?" There was a hint of disapproval in her voice now.

"He's a widower," Anne said quickly. "Renee took him in for a cup of tea, and I felt so sorry for him I asked him back on the Sunday for a proper meal. Then he asked me out to repay me, and that's how it started."

"An' how lang's this been goin' on?"

"Three weeks now. Fred's a gentleman, Mother, and hasn't done anything out of place." Anne sounded anxious to convince her.

"Fred? What's his last name?"

"Schaper. He comes from Pirbright, near Aldershot, and he's in the regular army. Do you think I shouldn't go out with him?" Anne waited. She desperately wanted her mother's approval, so that she could feel easier about her new friendship.

Maggie laughed. "Ye dinna need to ask my permission, Annie. Ye're auld enough to ken what ye're daein', an' to mak' up yer ain mind aboot it." Her daughter's rather disappointed face made her add, "But it's time ye had some enjoyment in yer life."

Anne smiled. "Thanks, Mother. There's nothing serious in it, but it's nice to have a male companion for a change."

Renee looked earnestly at her grandmother. "Fred *is* nice, I can vouch for that. I think you'd like him."

"An' what aboot yersel'? Is there a nice man in your life?"

"Not at the moment, but I'm living in hope."

"Is Father still keeping well?" Anne asked.

Maggie frowned. "Nae that great. He's got a real bad cough, but he winna gi'e up the pipe . . . mind you, I like the smell o' his Bogey Roll."

"Make him see the doctor if it doesn't clear up," Anne advised. "He shouldn't let a cough run on."

"Och, I'd be as weel speakin' to that table there as tell yer father to go to the doctor." Maggie laughed and the talk reverted to the usual catechism about Anne's boarders, past and present.

Jack Thomson's next visit made Renee resolve to stop considering him as anything more than a very good friend. She felt her heart stir at the sight of him and his dear "cow's lick", but, if he cared for her at all — only a tenderness she caught in his eyes once or twice suggested that he did — he would try to spend more time with her, not just a couple of hours on his way to Peterhead.

Anne, eternally hopeful, left them alone while she prepared the tea, but Jack spoke only of episodes in Northumberland, where he was stationed now.

At the table, Kitty Miller showed him her engagement ring. "I was hooked first, lover-boy," she laughed. "Though I can't understand why you're still footloose and fancy free."

Jack grinned and tapped his nose with his forefinger. "I have my moments, but I haven't been caught yet."

Although she laughed along with the others, Renee wasn't at all amused. This must be his way of letting her know that he was no longer interested in her, and it hurt. He helped to clear the table and dried the dishes for her, while Anne went through to the living room, shutting the scullery door behind her. Renee thought, wistfully, that her mother had more faith than she had, and a small vestige of hope flickered in her heart.

Doing her best to sound casual, she asked, “Do you have any girlfriends just now?”

“A few.” He was smiling, but his eyes seemed to be riveted on the plate he was drying. “It’s great to be free to have a good time with whoever you like, isn’t it?”

“Oh, yes,” Renee said, quickly. “I feel just the same.”

A full minute passed before he said, quietly, his head still averted, “You’ll be keeping yourself for Fergus, of course.”

This enraged her, and her dashed hopes made her snap. “For God’s sake, Jack, how often do I have to tell you? It was all over between Fergus and me nearly two years ago. I’ve never seen him since, and I don’t want to ever see him again.”

“Where is he just now?” he asked, softly.

“He was in the Middle East the last I knew, but I don’t care. The further away, the better.”

“Yes?” Jack’s scepticism was so evident that she could have slapped him. “He must have written to you if you know where he is.”

“It’s no good speaking to you, Jack Thomson,” she said, hotly. “You don’t believe me, whatever I say.” What was the point of explaining to him that it had been Jeanette Morrison who had found out where he was, and that Jeanette had borne his child? Jack was just as obsessed by the certainty that Renee still loved Fergus, as she’d been by the certainty that Fergus loved her — until he proved that he didn’t. The air was alive with tension, and she set each dish on the draining board with a thump, which did nothing to ease either her feelings or the situation.

After a few minutes, Jack said lightly, "I must tell you this, Renee, you'll have a good laugh. I was on late duty one night about three weeks ago, and when I went back to the billets there was a cake of chocolate lying on my bed. The lad next to me said the girl in the shop had sent it over for me, so I ate it all — it wasn't very big."

In spite of her anger, Renee wanted to hear why this had proved so funny. "Was it meant for somebody else?" Even if it had been, she thought, it wouldn't be all that funny.

His mouth twisted to the side. "No, it was meant for me, right enough, but it was Ex-Lax, not chocolate. One of the lads had taken off the paper for a lark. But I bet you can imagine what happened to me after."

Understanding now, Renee burst out laughing. Jack had eaten a whole cake of laxative chocolate, and she had no difficulty in guessing what had happened after that.

"I was on the trot for about a day and a half, and the pains in my stomach . . . Oooh!" He shuddered at the memory.

Her face sobered. "It wasn't really funny, though. It was kind of cruel, really. Why did the girl do it?"

Jack lifted his shoulders. "Oh, I used to tease her a bit, and she meant it as a joke. She didn't think I'd eat it. She was really upset when she found out what happened, and, of course, the rest of the lads didn't let me forget about it for ages."

When Renee saw him out, later, he shook hands and said gravely, "So remember, don't accept chocolate from boyfriends, for you never know what it could lead to." He walked down the path, chuckling, and she smiled as she went in to relate the incident to her mother. In bed, she reflected that it had been good to be laughing with him again. She didn't want to lose his friendship. After the war, he would come back, and who knew what could develop?

CHAPTER NINETEEN

After breakfast one Sunday morning just before Christmas 1941, Anne said, "Fred's bringing another sergeant with him this afternoon. He's had a 'Dear John' letter from his girl, and he's feeling pretty low."

Renee frowned. She hoped they weren't expecting her to cheer up this disappointed Romeo. "And whose brilliant idea was it to ask him here?"

"I felt sorry for him."

When Fred came in, he was accompanied by a tall, dark-haired man, a good bit younger than himself, with high cheekbones and a chiselled nose. "Glynn, this is Mrs Gordon and her daughter, Renee. Ladies, I'd like you to meet Glynn Williams."

"How do you do?" the other sergeant murmured shyly.

"Sit down, Glynn." Anne motioned to the settee, where Renee was now sitting sedately having been sprawled out on it before they arrived.

As she shook hands with the stranger, the girl looked up into the most gorgeous blue eyes she'd ever seen — fathomless pools of sadness, gleaming now with . . . could it be admiration? Her heart leapt so madly that she couldn't speak.

Glynn also remained silent while Anne and Fred chatted to each other, until Renee pulled herself together and turned to him. "How do you like Aberdeen?"

"It's a beautiful city, so clean and sparkling."

His lilting Welsh accent made her wish he would carry on speaking. She could listen to him for ever. "Are you regular army, too?"

"No. I was in the Territorials before the war, but I like army life."

"What part of Wales do you come from?"

"It's a little place you'll never have heard of, in Carmarthen. Porthcross, it is, between Llanelli and Llandeilo."

Renee clapped her hands in delight. "Say that again, please."

He wrinkled his brow. "Porthcross, between Llanelli and Llandeilo? Is that what you mean?"

"Yes. It's really lovely." She attempted to say the last two musical Welsh names, and he laughed at her mispronunciation.

"No, it's more like your Scottish 'ch' sound in 'loch'. Not exactly, but it's the nearest. Listen. Llanelli and Llandeilo." She tried again. "Chlanechly and Chlandylo."

"Not bad."

"Listen, Mum." Renee repeated the names with gusto, and Glynn nodded when she got it almost right.

Anne looked mystified. "What's that?"

"It's where Glynn belongs. A little place called Porthcross, between . . ." She took a deep breath and repeated the names once more. "Chlanechly and

Chlandylo. It's like a stream running over stones, isn't it? Really beautiful." She sat back, pleased that she had mastered the words.

Glynn was applauding her, and they all laughed, but she caught Fred giving her mother a meaningful wink. They were definitely trying to matchmake, but it was Glynn Williams they would have to work on. Renee Gordon was already hooked.

"I still don't know where any of these places are," she told him. "What's the nearest big town?"

"Llanelli's a fair old size, but Swansea's the nearest large city." His eyes held more than admiration now. Attraction, perhaps? They were completely at ease with each other now, and exchanged information about themselves until it was time to go through to the dining room, Anne and Fred having already attended to the dishing up and carrying in.

Flora and Kitty had been invited out to tea by a girl they'd made friends with at the skating rink, so only Hilda and Nora sat down with the Gordons and their two guests. Fred, of course, knew them already, and chatted to them companionably, but Glynn seemed uncomfortable in the presence of so many strangers.

At the end of the meal, Anne said, "Are you two going out tonight?"

It was Hilda who answered. "No, it's snowing, so we're going to have a quiet evening in. We'll stay in our own room, though."

"Don't let yourselves be cold," Anne told her. "Use the electric fire, that's what it's there for."

"We will, Mrs G., thanks." Hilda poked her room-mate. "Are you finished, Titch? Come on, then, upstairs — at the double."

Fred and Glynn insisted on washing up, so Anne and Renee went to sit by the coal fire in the living room.

"What do you think of him?" Anne spoke in a soft whisper, in case he would overhear.

"He's gorgeous," Renee whispered back. "If you and Fred are trying to pair us off, I'm more than willing."

Anne giggled. "He does look very nice, and you seemed to get on well. I'm going to ask him to come back with Fred on Tuesday night, so I hope you'll stay in."

"Wild horses wouldn't drag me out." Something that her grandmother had once said, ages ago, came into Renee's mind. "You'll know your Mr Right when he comes along." Granny, as usual, had known what she was speaking about. Renee did know that her Mr Right had come along. Mr Glynn Williams Right. She only hoped that he would recognise the fact, too. Although she was sure, beyond all doubt, that Glynn was the man who was meant for her, Renee told no one how she felt. She somehow believed that it would bring bad luck to talk about it.

Anne had no such qualms. As soon as they went into Maggie's house the following Saturday, she said, "I think Renee's smitten with Fred's friend, Glynn Williams. Remember, I told you he was coming to tea last Sunday?"

The old lady's eyes lit up. "A new romance, eh, Renee?"

"He's quite nice," the girl admitted, wishing that her mother wouldn't interfere.

Anne laughed derisively. "*Quite* nice? The understatement of the year. You should have seen them, Mother, sitting looking at each other like dying ducks." Maggie had recognised that this Glynn meant something to Renee. The girl usually babbled on about her boyfriends, and her reluctance to discuss him was significant.

"I invited him back on Tuesday along with Fred," Anne went on, insensitive to her daughter's reserve. "He asked Renee to go out with him on Wednesday, and they went out on Thursday and Friday, as well." She looked archly at Renee, but the girl kept her head down.

"Aye, it's grand to be young," Maggie remarked. "An' how's yer ain romance comin' on, Annie?"

"There's no romance between Fred and me," Anne said frostily.

"Oh, I thought ye were goin' steady wi' him?" Maggie's expression was innocent enough, but her eyes held a message.

Anne laughed as she realised that her mother was really telling her to go easy on Renee. "We're just good friends, Mother."

Peter McIntosh came home before Anne and Renee left, his face grey but his manner quite cheerful. "How's my two favourite lassies?" he joked, laying the heavy shopping bags on the floor.

"Just fine, Father." Anne studied him as he unpacked each item. "These bags must have been heavy for you?"

"They're nae aye so heavy," he wheezed, "but yer mother was needin' a lot o' extra things in for the New Year. Nae that we'll ha'e crowds o' folk comin' in, jist a few of the neighbours, but ye ken what she's like."

"I could go to the shops for you on Saturday afternoons," Renee offered. "I'd quite like to do it. You could tell me which are the best shops to go to," she added, hopefully.

He screwed up his face, then said, to the amazement of the three women, "Weel, I think I'll tak'ye up on that, lassie. I'm fair forfochen the day."

In spite of her concern for him, Renee spluttered with laughter. "Forfochen? What on earth does that mean?"

Maggie smiled at her perplexed face. "He means he's jist dead beat," she explained.

"Exhausted," Anne put in, to make quite sure that Renee understood.

"Oh." The girl's face cleared. "OK. I'll start next week."

"We'll nae be needin' muckle next week." The old man glanced fondly at his wife. "This woman's made me get in such a lot the day, it'll be weeks afore it's a' used up."

"Nothin' o' the kind," Maggie said drily.

When they rose to go, Peter went to the door with Anne, but Maggie put her hand out to detain Renee. "I'd like fine to meet this Glynn, lassie, if ye want to bring him sometime." Her smile was gently loving.

"I don't know yet if there's anything in it, Granny, but I'll take him to see you as soon as I'm sure."

"Aye. Awa' ye go, then, or yer mother'll be wonderin' what we're gettin' up to."

That night, Renee asked Glynn to take her to the ice rink.

"I can't skate," he protested.

"It's great fun, Glynn. Please?"

He gave in, and soon she was laughing at him each time he landed on his bottom on the ice. "Dry off on the radiators," she told him, as he was gingerly pulling his soaking trousers away from his skin. "And don't worry about it. I was the same when I came here first with Sheila Daun, but it doesn't take long to learn how to keep your feet."

Sheepishly, he dragged himself along the rail, then stood to let the heat penetrate to his frozen buttocks, and by the end of their session, he had mastered the art of putting one foot past the other and still remaining upright, although he didn't venture far from the rail.

On the way home, he kissed her for the first time, and Renee knew for certain that she had not been mistaken. This was the man for her. But, one swallow didn't make a summer, as they said, and that one kiss was not sufficient to let her know if Glynn felt the same. He was probably still grieving for the girl he'd lost, so it was up to Renee to make him forget, and to make him love her.

Should she ask him to visit her grandmother now? She recalled John Smith — the sick-berth attendant who had objected to meeting the mothers of the girls he picked up — and was thankful that Glynn already knew her mother, so that was no problem. But would he want to meet others of her family? Would he think she was putting pressure on him to declare himself? It would be better to wait until she was sure of him, before she issued Granny's invitation.

Glynn was on duty the next night, Sunday, so Renee spent the evening in her bedroom, to leave her mother alone with Fred Schaper. She could see that Fred was in love with Anne, but she couldn't make up her mind if her mother was in love with him, and knowing how she felt herself when other people tried to hustle on her relationships, she didn't make the mistake of interfering.

When she went downstairs at ten o'clock, she saw by Anne's pink confusion that Fred must have kissed her, and was very happy for her. On Monday, she was so glad to see Glynn again that she ran into his arms when he met her outside Brown and Company's office at five thirty. He looked surprised, but held her closely.

"I missed you yesterday," she told him.

"I thought about you all day." He kissed her slowly. "I was remembering that it was exactly a week ago since I met you." He held her away from him. "When Fred asked me to go with him, I didn't feel like meeting strangers, but I didn't want to offend him by refusing."

"Oh, Glynn, I'm glad you didn't refuse." Renee wished that he would hold her tightly again.

"I thought he was a sentimental old fool, going on about this woman he'd met through taking her daughter home one night, and I imagined some brassy young tart picking him up with the intention of getting a man for her equally brassy mother." He laughed suddenly. "How wrong can a man be?"

Renee was indignant at first. "That was a horrible thing to think, anyway."

"I wasn't in a particularly generous mood. Eiddwen, my girlfriend, had just written to tell me that she was in love with an Australian, and I thought my life was finished, but I took one look at you last Sunday, and came alive again. I loved you from the first minute I saw you, Renee. Could you learn to care for me?" His blue, blue eyes pleaded with her to say yes.

"I'll give it a try," Renee said flippantly, to tease him, then relented. This wonderful moment was not the time for levity. "Oh, Glynn, it was the same for me, love at first sight."

"*Duw*!" Glynn crushed her to him again, but suddenly became aware of the amused glances of the people passing by. "Come on, my lovely. Let's get the bus to your house."

Renee took Glynn to visit her grandmother the following Saturday, Anne obligingly declining to accompany them, and when she proudly introduced him, Maggie shook hands gravely. Peter stood up and followed suit, then they sat down, Renee being fully aware that her grandparents were reserving judgement until they found out for themselves what kind of man Glynn was. She wasn't in the least worried about it, because she was certain that they would soon come to like him very much. He told them that he had been in the Territorial Army, and that he had been employed by a firm which sold agricultural machinery.

"Will ye be goin' back to that after the war?" Maggie asked.

"The same sort of thing, I suppose," he said, "but not necessarily in Porthcross — that's in South Wales," he added.

After ten minutes or so, Renee knew, although he hadn't consciously tried to make an impression on her grandmother and grandfather, they had indeed been impressed by his natural manner, so she sat back and let them talk. When Peter went to the door with Glynn, Maggie again detained the girl for a moment. She gripped Renee's hand and said, softly, "He'll dae for ye, lassie, if ye're sure in yer ain he'rt."

"Yes, Granny, I'm sure he'll do for me. I've never been so sure of anything in my whole life."

The old lady smiled, a beautiful, sweet smile that touched Renee as much as the words which followed. "Ah, weel, ye've got my blessin', the pair o' ye."

"Thank you, Granny. That means a lot to me." Renee turned away quickly, before her brimming eyes overflowed.

"They're good people," Glynn remarked, when they were walking hand in hand along the street, "although I'd a problem understanding what they were saying sometimes, especially your grandfather."

Renee giggled. "I sometimes don't understand him myself." She wished she could tell him Granny's last few words, but was afraid he'd think she was rushing him. He'd said he loved her, and that was all she needed meantime.

Very shy with the land girls when he first met them, Glynn, like Fred, could now fend for himself in the crosstalk that went on round the dining table. Kitty, Flora and Hilda were the main culprits, and Nora felt obliged, at times, to stop them, often causing hilarity by the way she did so.

"What about putting bets on who'll be hitched first?" Kitty asked her three friends one evening. "Renee and Glynn, versus Mrs G. and Fred."

"Oh, that's a great idea. I'll keep the book." Flora whipped a small notebook out of her trouser pocket, and dug her hand in again to find a pencil.

"Don't be silly, girls." Anne's face was scarlet with embarrassment, as was Renee's, but Fred and Glynn seemed to lap it up.

"Half a crown on Renee and Glynn," squealed Hilda, ignoring her landlady.

Flora scribbled quickly. "What do you think, Kitty?"

Kitty pretended to weigh up the situation, looking from Fred to Glynn, then from Anne to Renee. "I'll put my half dollar on Mrs G. and Fred," she said at last.

"Nora?" Flora's pencil hovered. "What about you?"

The other girl considered, then said, reprovingly, "I think it's gone far enough. It's very bad manners, for one thing, and you shouldn't be making bets in front of the runners, for another."

Fred let out a loud guffaw and everyone joined in, much to Nora's mortification — she couldn't see what was funny — but Anne and Renee were both relieved when Flora slipped her pencil and notebook back into her pocket. For a fraction of a second, Glynn's knee touched Renee's under the table, but it happened so quickly that she couldn't be sure if he'd really meant to do it, or if it had been accidental. Was he trying to tell her that he didn't mind the girls speculating about a forthcoming marriage?

"They're an awful bunch." Fred leaned back when the four girls left the room. "All good, clean fun, though, nothing malicious or nasty."

Anne was glad that he could excuse the awkward incident, and she agreed with him that the girls had meant no harm.

The weekly visits to Maggie and Peter McIntosh continued, with Glynn escorting Anne and Renee if he was available, and accompanying the girl when she went into town to do the shopping for her grandparents.

When Peter was out of the room for a moment one day and Maggie was alone with her daughter, she said, "Glynn's a good laddie, an' Renee'll be fine if she sticks to him, but what aboot yer ain lad? I've never met him, Annie."

"Oh." Anne felt somehow reluctant to take Fred to meet her mother. "I didn't think . . . I don't know . . ."

"I'd like fine to see him."

So it was a foursome which made the journey to the tenement the following Saturday, and Fred Schaper was accepted by Maggie and Peter just as warmly as Glynn had been. The two men became so deep in conversation that they hardly noticed the return of the shoppers. Maggie beamed at all her visitors when they rose to leave. "I wouldna ha'e believed that a Scotsman, an Englishman an' a Welshman would get on so weel together." Her eyes were brightly mischievous, and she was pleased when they laughed at her reference to the jokes which were often told on the wireless.

"We foreigners aren't such a bad lot." Fred gripped the old lady's hand.

She laid her other hand on top of his. "So I've found oot."

Several hours later, when they were undressing for bed, Anne and Renee discussed their afternoon visit. "I must be getting better," the girl remarked. "Granda didn't tell me once that he could have got anything cheaper if he'd been doing the shopping."

Anne's mind, however, was operating on an entirely different track. "Granny and Granda seemed to get on well with Fred. I think they liked him, don't you?"

Her daughter smiled. "Yes, I'm sure they did. He's quite likeable, for an old man." She chuckled at her mother's indignant expression, then her manner grew serious. "And Granny told me, a week or so back, that Glynn and I had her blessing."

Sighing happily, Anne pulled her nightdress over her head. "God's in His heaven, and all's right with the world."

CHAPTER TWENTY

The June evening was beautifully cool after the almost claustrophobic heat of the cinema, so Renee suggested that they should walk home. Glynn had met her from work, and had taken her for a snack before they went to the picture house, so it was just after nine o'clock. They strolled at an easy pace, arms round each other, discussing the "A" and "B" films they had just seen, then Glynn said, "What they showed on the newsreel makes you think, though. What a hammering some of our cities are getting . . . God, Renee, I wish I could be doing something constructive, something to get back at Hitler, instead of idling my time away."

"You're not idling your time away. You're training people and preparing them to . . ."

"Preparing them to do something I want to do myself," he interrupted. "To fight the enemy. That's what I was trained for, not to be a bloody instructor." He fell silent, brooding. Renee was surprised at his vehemence. She hadn't realised that he felt like this, and hoped he would never have to leave Aberdeen. He shouldn't want to go, not if he loved her.

"But what about seeing those thousand bombers taking off to blast Cologne? It gives you a tight, satisfied feeling of revenge, doesn't it?" His voice sounded excited, with an air of triumph about it. This rather shocked her. She'd been sickened by the scenes of suffering in London, and it gave her no satisfaction to imagine the same thing happening in Cologne.

"It's innocent people that suffer," she murmured. "Women and children mostly, and they don't deserve to be killed, whether they're British or German."

He squeezed her waist. "You're a soft one, my lovely. Hitler's tried to bomb us into submission, and we're just doing the same to them. We can't knuckle down and not retaliate."

"I suppose not," she said, sadly. "It all seems so cruel, that's all."

"*Cariad*, I love you for your tender heart." Glynn turned his head to give her a light kiss on the cheek, then inhaled deeply. "It's a lovely night. Why don't we go into this park to have a seat for a few minutes?"

The Victoria Park! Panic struck at her heart. The thought of going through the gates and perhaps sitting in the same place as . . . It was more than three years since she'd come here first, but the memories came crowding back. Memories she didn't want to revive. Shameful, repugnant memories.

"No, Glynn," she whispered. "Not here. I used to come here before, years ago, with . . . someone else, and I don't want to be reminded of it."

He looked at her keenly. "All right, Renee, whatever you say, but won't you tell me about it?"

She shook her head miserably. "I can't."

"*Cariad*, I want to know everything about you. I've told you about Eiddwen, she was my only girlfriend before you, but I don't know anything about your past loves."

She sighed. "Not yet, Glynn. I will tell you some time, but not now, and there was only one with me, too."

"All right, my lovely." He didn't appear to be upset or annoyed by her refusal to confide in him, and they walked on.

When they entered the house, they found that Anne wasn't home. "Fred's on early duty tomorrow," Renee said, "so Mum's probably staying with him as long as she can."

Glynn pulled her down on the settee beside him, and stroked her brow, her nose, her lips, but when his fingers reached her chin, he kept them there, holding her head firmly.

"Renee, I love you." His eyes searched and his voice was low and throbbing. He had said it many times before, but this sounded different.

"I love you, too," she whispered, hoping that he wouldn't try to do what she suspected he wanted to do.

His grip on her face tightened. "Oh, darling, I love you so much it's torture for me." He swivelled round and slid his leg between hers. "If you only knew how much I've wanted to . . ." He sounded hoarse now, urgent, but she couldn't respond.

"No, Glynn, no! Mum'll be home any minute and . . ." She broke off, pushing his insinuating knee away from her.

But his mouth came down on hers fiercely and her senses reeled, though she struggled to free herself. She couldn't give in to him, much as she wanted to — as much as he wanted her to — in case he lost interest in her once he possessed her. This relationship had to be kept pure until they were husband and wife . . . if he ever did ask her to marry him. He shifted his legs and dropped his hands, looking at her in hurt surprise. "What's wrong, *cariad*?" His voice was tender again, loving. "I'm sorry. Did I frighten you? I was too rough. I want you . . . oh, God, I want you, but I'm willing to wait until we're married, if that's what you're trying to tell me. You *will* marry me, Renee?"

A sob caught in her throat. She wanted him so badly herself that it was agony to think of waiting, but she was determined to endure that agony so that he wouldn't think badly of her later. "Yes, I'll marry you, Glynn," she murmured. "I love you, and I want you, but we must wait."

"I'm not going to force you against your wishes, I love you too much for that. Will I arrange for a Registry wedding?"

"Yes, please, Glynn, as soon as you can." She gave in to his kisses then, but they grew rather passionate for her peace of mind, and she was glad when she heard her mother coming in.

Anne was delighted when they told her. "Wasn't it a good idea of Fred's to take you here that Sunday, Glynn? You'd never have met each other if he hadn't."

The young man beamed with happiness. "Yes, indeed, Mrs Gordon. I'll always be grateful to him for that. You've no objections to me marrying your daughter?"

"None whatsoever."

"That's good. Now, if I've to go to the Registry Office tomorrow, I'll need to get all the details." He fished in his breast pocket for a pencil. "Have you a sheet of paper handy?"

"You'll need your birth certificates," Anne told him. "I'll go and get yours, Renee."

"I haven't got mine," Glynn remarked as Anne went out. "But I think my army paybook should be sufficient evidence of my age and unmarried status."

"How old are you?" Renee had never thought to ask before.

"I'll be thirty in September."

Her jaw dropped. "I'll only be nineteen at the end of August."

They looked at each other uncertainly. Eleven years of a difference? Then Glynn chuckled. "You're still a child, but I'm quite happy about it, as long as you're prepared to saddle yourself with an old man?"

"You're not old, darling. What's eleven years?" Renee kissed the tip of his nose reassuringly.

They jumped apart when Anne came back. "Caught you!" she said, wagging her finger teasingly at them.

Renee stuck out her tongue cheekily as her mother handed the document to the young man. "Mum, we've just discovered that Glynn's eleven years older than me. It's funny, we never spoke about ages before."

Anne looked anxious. "Does it worry you?"

"No, I don't think so."

"That's all right, then. Age doesn't make any difference, really. Not eleven years, anyway, and it's on the right side. Of course, if you'd been thirty years older than Renee, I wouldn't have been so ready to agree to this, Glynn."

The wedding was arranged for Monday, 3rd August 1942, which was the first available date the Registrar could give them.

"So many young couples are getting married quickly now, in case the bridegroom is sent away on active service," he explained.

"Thank goodness we'll have a few weeks to come to terms with all this," Anne remarked, a few days later. Fred had gone home to Pirbright on leave, and Glynn was on duty, so the two women were alone in the house that evening.

"There's nothing to come to terms with," Renee said sharply. "We love each other, and that's all that matters."

"Have you thought of where you're going to live?"

"Oh." The girl looked thunderstruck. "We hadn't thought about that. There's no room here, is there? We'll have to look for a place somewhere."

"The only spare bed is that settee," Anne said sadly.

"It would do at a push . . . if we haven't found anywhere else by the time we're married." Renee was so deliriously happy that she would have settled to sleep on a church pew, as long as Glynn was there beside her.

After a moment's silence, Anne said, "I'd better tell you something."

A flash of dread shot through the girl. "Yes?"

"When I told Fred about you two, he asked me to marry him."

"Oh, Mum, that's great!" Renee's face reflected the relief and pleasure that the information had given her. "Will we have a double wedding, or do you and Fred want a separate day of your own?"

"I said no." Anne's lips were drawn together in a straight line, and her fingers drummed on her knee.

"Why? I thought you loved him."

"I do love him, Renee, but he's being posted shortly, and I don't want him to feel tied to me."

"You're as bad as Tim." One of her mother's words suddenly registered fearfully in Renee's brain. "Posted? Is Glynn likely to be posted, too?"

"I don't think so. Fred didn't say anything about that, anyway. They're not in the same . . . troop, unit, whatever they call it."

"Oh, I hope he doesn't have to go for a long time yet. But, Mum, you should have accepted Fred's proposal. You can't just let him go away. Are you sure about what you're doing?"

"Quite sure. I've been thinking about it for weeks and I knew Fred would ask me some time, and I had to make up my mind what to do. I've told him that I do love him, but I can't marry him."

"He might be killed."

"Oh, Renee, that's exactly why." Anne spread her fingers out on her knee and studied them. "I couldn't face being made a widow for a second time. Can you understand that?"

"I suppose so, but if you love him, you'd feel just as much grief and shock if he was killed, even if you weren't his wife."

"No, there is a difference. I can't explain it." Anne made her hand into a fist and hit her knee. "Don't keep on, Renee. I'd a hard enough time trying to make Fred understand. He wanted to tell his mother when he went home that we were going to be married, but I can't say yes."

"You're only thinking about yourself. Why don't you think of poor Fred?"

"I told him I'll marry him after the war, if he comes back and still wants me."

The girl let out an exasperated sigh. "That's just dangling a carrot. It's cruel."

Anne's taut nerves made her snap. "That's quite enough!"

They went to bed that night in silence, each regretting some of the things they had said.

That Saturday, Peter McIntosh produced a bottle of whisky when Renee and Glynn announced that they were going to be married.

"I've been savin' this up for a special occasion," he smiled. "But there'll never be a mair special occasion than this." He took out five tot glasses and laid them on the table. "Nae till the war finishes, ony road."

Maggie watched him unscrewing the cap of the bottle. "I canna stomach neat whisky, tak' oot tumblers for Renee an' Annie an' me, so we can ha'e water in oors."

Her husband shook his head impatiently. "Weemin!" he said to Glynn, but returned to the cupboard for the larger glasses. "Jist wastin' the good stuff," he muttered as he ran the cold water into them.

Glynn helped him to hand them out, then sat down with his own glass in his hand, waiting to see what would happen next. Peter had kept standing, and he held up his glass in a toast. "Here's to yer health an' happiness, Renee an' Glynn." He downed the contents in one go, and set the tiny glass on the table.

Even with water in it, the whisky was too strong for Renee, and she shuddered at her first taste of her national drink.

"Tak' it slow, like me," Maggie advised her, and raised her glass. "A lang, happy life together an' may good fortune smile on ye." She took a dainty sip.

"Your health and happiness." Anne barely wet her lips, but her face contorted, even at the diluted spirits.

"Och!" Peter sounded enraged. "They dinna ken how to drink whisky." He looked at Glynn, who was still twisting his glass in his hand uncertainly. "Swig it ower, like I did."

His first three words were incomprehensible to the Welshman, but the second three gave him the clue he was waiting for, so he took one large gulp, then spluttered as if he had choked.

Peter smiled in pity. "Ye'll ha'e to learn to drink like a Scotsman, laddie, if ye're goin' tae bide in Aberdeen."

"Leave him be," Maggie warned. "Dinna learn him bad habits."

When the visitors were leaving, Maggie beckoned to Renee. "What aboot yer mother an' Fred? Ony word o' them tyin' the knot?"

"Fred's going away shortly," the girl told her. "He did ask her to marry him, but she refused."

"Oh." Her grandmother's eyes widened. "That's that, then."

The old lady sounded quite disappointed, and Renee knew that she, too, had hoped that Anne would find happiness with Fred Schaper.

When Tim Donaldson turned up one evening during the next week, with Moira, he expressed his pleasure at meeting Glynn.

"Renee's been telling me about you in her letters," he said. "From the very first time she mentioned you, I knew she was serious about you."

Glynn smiled and held Renee's hand. "It's funny how fate works. We met because Fred took me here with him one night, and it turned out to be love at first sight for us."

"The same as Moira and you," Renee added, without stopping to think.

Tim glanced quickly at Moira, whose wry expression made him look away hastily. "Well, I wish you all the happiness in the world," he said.

Renee hoped that she hadn't upset the other girl by her innocent remark, since Tim was apparently still determined not to "tie Moira down", but Glynn proceeded to step in with both feet.

"Thank you, Tim," he smiled. "It'll be your turn next."

Tim frowned, but Moira said, carefully, "Tim doesn't think too highly of marriage, I'm afraid."

"It's not that, at all," Tim burst out suddenly. "It's just . . . I'm unsettled and I feel it's not fair to . . ."

Anne tried to pour oil on the troubled waters. "It's between Moira and Tim, and nobody should try to interfere."

"I'm sorry." Glynn's face had turned red, and he looked at Tim, not knowing what else to say.

The other young man laughed. "Don't worry about it, Glynn. It happens all the time, with Moira's mum, and all her relations. I'll likely give in one of these days, but . . . I don't like being pushed." He laid his hand on Moira's knee. "She knows how I feel about her."

The love in Moira's eyes showed how she felt about him, too. "I know, Tim, and it's not me who's doing the pushing."

"Are you still in the Shetlands, Tim?" Anne rescued him because she could sympathise with his feelings, for wasn't she doing the same thing with Fred? The atmosphere cleared and the talk gradually divided into two different conversations, Glynn and Tim discussing the war, and Anne and the two girls speaking about the progress Mike's baby son was making.

After the young couple left, Glynn said, "Tim's a good, honourable person, and I'm sorry I made things uncomfortable for him."

"You weren't to know," Renee said hastily. "He says he doesn't want to tie Moira down, but he's being cruel, really. Like somebody else I know," she added, bitterly, glancing at her mother.

Renee was quite upset when Glynn told her that he hadn't applied to have his leave changed. "I thought I should go to Porthcross, so I could tell Mam about you and the wedding," he defended himself. "It's going to take a lot of diplomacy."

"Haven't you written and told her?" She sounded shocked.

"I've told her I've been visiting your house with Fred, and about your mother and you, but not that . . ."

"I suppose you made out that my mother was a do-gooder, feeding lonely soldiers and making a home-from-home for them?" Her eyes were glittering like steel, now.

Glynn had the grace to look ashamed. "I suppose I did. But, darling, I didn't want to say anything until I was sure that you wanted to marry me." He paused for a moment, then obviously decided to tell her everything. "You see, she's still annoyed at me for not asking Eiddwen to marry me at the start of the war. Mam loved her like a daughter, and she says it's my own fault that Eiddwen fell in love with that Australian."

"But your mother'll surely be pleased that you've found happiness now?"

He shrugged his shoulders. "If it was with a Welsh girl, yes, but she hates the English . . ."

"I'm not English," Renee interrupted. "I'm Scottish, there is a difference."

"Not to my mam. Anyone who's not Welsh is a foreigner, as far as she's concerned. So it's better that I tell her about you face to face, so she can see how much I love you. Then perhaps she'll come to our wedding."

The girl's anger dissolved. "Yes, I see what you mean. You'll have to go to her, but it means that we won't be able to have a decent honeymoon, and I was really looking forward to it."

"We'll have a few days away," he consoled her, then he winked. "And nights."

She laughed then, knowing that the nights were to be far more exciting and fulfilling than the days, and as long as they were together, it didn't matter where they were.

Two days after Glynn went to Porthcross, Renee arrived home at teatime to find Jack Thomson in the living room. He stood up to shake hands with her, but she suddenly burst out laughing.

"What's so funny?" He sounded slightly put out.

"I was wondering what was different about you," she giggled, "and I've just realised . . ."

"Oh." He stroked his upper lip proudly. "My moustache, do you mean?"

"Is that what you call it?"

"That's what I call it, for that's what it is." He pretended to be offended, but his eyes were now filled with amusement, too. "At least, that's what it'll be in another few weeks. What do you think of it . . . honestly?"

Trying to keep a straight face, she studied him with mock seriousness. His cow's lick still stuck up from his sandy head, his face was still fresh and boyish, and the appendage he was nurturing, a thin uneven line, looked incongruous.

She fought back her mirth and said, "I suppose it suits you, Jack, but it was a bit of a shock, and . . . it's ginger!" She howled with laughter again.

"Renee!" Anne, who had come through from the scullery, looked reprimandingly at her daughter. "It's not that funny."

The girl was still helpless with laughter and Jack ruefully joined in. "It is that funny, Mrs Gordon. I've known it ever since I started to grow it."

"Why don't you shave it off?" Anne couldn't understand why he would keep it on if he didn't like it himself.

"It's a matter of principle, you see. A girl I know bet me that I wouldn't have the nerve to grow a bushy moustache, and I want to let her see that I have."

At the mention of the girl, Renee stopped laughing. "Are you serious about this one, Jack?" She hoped he was.

He screwed up his face. "Not really, but we have a good time together."

Anne went to answer the doorbell, and ushered in Fred. "I'll leave you to do the introductions, Renee. The girls'll be home in a few minutes."

Jack couldn't hide his astonishment when the girl said, "This is Fred Schaper, Jack. He's Mum's friend. Fred, this is Jack Thomson. You've heard us speaking about him."

The two men shook hands and smiled to each other, then Fred said, "I'll just go and help your mother, Renee."

The girl turned to Jack. "I wish you could have met Glynn, too, but he's off home on leave just now. We've set the wedding for the third of August."

"So you were serious about the Welshman?" There was no hint of jealousy. "You've mentioned him so much in your letters that I thought you must be." His smile was quite genuine. "I'm very pleased that you've found somebody at last, and I truly hope you'll both be very happy."

Renee hadn't realised how much she had dreaded telling Jack about her marriage, but his calm acceptance made a huge wave of relief wash over her. She had romanticised about him for years before Glynn came on the scene, but this proved that he had never had any deep feelings for her, thank goodness.

Everyone seemed to be in high fettle during the meal, Renee thought. Her mother and Fred were rather quiet at the start, but the merry atmosphere transmitted itself to them, too, after a while.

Jack was flirting madly with the land girls, and even lifted Kitty's left hand at one point. "You're still engaged, I see. You've completely broken my heart."

Kitty giggled. "I could break it off, if you made me a better offer."

Flora, on his other side, fluttered her eyelashes at him. "I'm ready, willing and able," she informed him. "And I've no other attachments."

"That's what I like to hear." Jack transferred his attention to her, and Kitty pretended to be offended.

"Your heart hasn't stayed broken for long," she pouted. "All you men are so fickle."

"You'd be better off with me," Hilda put in. She was sitting next to Renee, and stretched her hand across the table towards him. "Kitty's booked and Flora's only teasing you, but I could be all that your heart ever desired."

"I don't think so," Jack said quietly, giving Renee a long, enigmatic look.

She felt irritated with him and looked away. He had done it again — that soulful expression which made her imagine he cared for her — but he'd lost his chance. It was Glynn she was going to marry. It was Glynn she loved more than anyone else. Fred launched into a coarsely comic story which caused howls of laughter when it came to an end, except from Anne, who was very embarrassed, but Renee understood why he had done it.

Standing on the doorstep, when she saw Jack off to catch the bus to Peterhead, Renee felt awkward with him, even sorry for him, in a way. "It was good to see you again, Jack," she said, primly. "I'm sorry you won't be here for my wedding."

"I hope it all goes well for you," he replied. "I really mean that, Renee. I wish I could have met the lucky man, though."

"You probably will, the next time you're here."

"Probably . . . It's time I was going." He suddenly bent his head and kissed her full on the mouth. "It's the last chance I'll ever have," he murmured as he turned and walked away. Renee had been taken so unawares that she was left wondering if she would have allowed him to kiss her if she had known he meant to do it, or if she would have turned her face away from him. He had awakened a response in her that surprised and dismayed her. She hadn't thought she could be so much affected by any man other than Glynn now.

At the first opportunity after her bridegroom-to-be returned from Porthcross, Renee told him about Jack Thomson's visit. She felt that she had to get that past before they spoke of anything else, a confession which wasn't really a confession at all because nothing had actually happened.

Glynn raised his eyebrows. "From the way you spoke about him sometimes, I used to think that you were a bit too fond of this Jack."

"I like him," she said quickly. "I've always liked him, and Tim, too, but there's no need to be jealous of them."

"It was only Jack that bothered me."

"You can put him right out of your mind, darling. When I told him we were getting married, he said he was glad I'd found somebody at last."

Glynn put his arm round her. "I'm glad, too."

"Did you manage to persuade your mother to come to our wedding?"

His smiling face fell. "No, I'm sorry, Renee, but she was very, very angry about it. You see, Eiddwen had told her a few weeks ago that she was finished with the

Australian, and Mam was hoping . . . You know what mothers are," he ended hopelessly.

"I know, but she can't make you live your life the way she wants you to, Glynn. It's me you love now, not Eiddwen. Did you tell her that?"

"I told her until I was blue in the face, but it made no difference. Once we're married, she might come round to wanting to meet you, but . . ." He shrugged.

His woebegone face saddened her. "It wasn't your fault, Glynn darling, and it doesn't matter. We don't need her approval, anyway."

Renee tried not to show how bitterly disappointed she was. His mother's attitude seemed like a bad omen for their marriage. But that was ridiculous. How could anything go wrong between them when she and Glynn loved each other so much?

CHAPTER TWENTY-ONE

Finding accommodation was much more difficult than Renee had imagined. She answered a few advertisements, but the single rooms she went to see were unattractively poky, sometimes even dirty, and she couldn't expect Glynn to start their married life in a place like that. She began to think that they'd have to make use of the bed-settee, after all, although she'd meant that as a joke when she said it.

Five weeks before the wedding, however, the problem was solved for her. It was a Friday, and, as soon as the land girls came in at teatime, Flora Simms walked into the scullery.

"We're being shifted, Mrs G.," she said, mournfully.

"The four of you?" Anne wasn't all that surprised, because these girls had been with her for quite a long time, and nothing and nobody was static in wartime.

"Not only us four, the whole lot of us." Flora grimaced. "They're closing down the gardens, God knows why, and God knows what's happening. They never tell us anything. All I know is, we're being moved."

"Where'll you be going?"

"I'm going to somewhere near Montrose, Kitty's going to the Perth area, and Nora and Hilda haven't been told yet, but they won't be together. They've made a pretty good job of splitting us up." She blew a loud raspberry. "That to the powers-that-be!"

"When do you leave?" Anne was sorry that they had to go. They'd been very easy to get on with, and had been no bother, except for the bathroom situation at times.

"Next Saturday, and we're all down in the dumps about it. We've enjoyed our stay here, and you've been ever so good to us all, Mrs G."

"You won't be here for Renee's wedding. What a shame. I was going to lay on an extra-special meal."

"Just our luck! I must scoot now, though, and we'll have to rush our tea, because Kitty and I are meeting two Brylcreem boys . . . Don't look so disapproving, Mrs G. They know she's engaged." Flora almost ran out of the room.

When Renee heard that the girls were leaving, she made no mention of a plan which immediately jumped to her mind, but she talked it over with Glynn that evening and tackled her mother about it the next day.

"Mum, now there'll be two rooms going spare, Glynn and I won't need to look for anywhere else to live, will we? It's not very handy, though, with one upstairs and one downstairs, so I was thinking . . . what about you moving back down to your original bedroom, and we could have the loft. We could make the other room into a kind of sitting room, and that would give us a private little flat of our own upstairs." Her eyes were hopeful.

Her mother considered briefly, then said, "Yes, I suppose that would be quite a sensible idea, really."

"Oh, thanks, Mum. We'll pay for the two rooms, of course, and for our board."

Anne smiled. "We can work that out later on." She paused then asked, in an offhand manner, "Has Glynn invited his mother to the wedding?"

He had told them that his father had died a few years before, and that he had no brothers or sisters, so she knew that there was only his mother to worry about.

"That's why he went home," Renee replied, not wanting to admit the rest. "But she said she didn't feel able to make such a long journey." It was only a white lie, she reflected.

"I'd have thought she'd have wanted to see her only son being married." Anne's voice held disapproval.

"So would I." Renee still felt hurt and angry. "Maybe she doesn't like the idea of him marrying a girl she doesn't know." She could see that her mother was disappointed for her, and tried to assure her that it didn't matter. "It's Glynn I'm marrying, Mum, not his mother."

The house seemed empty and alien after the four girls left the following Saturday morning, and both Anne and Renee were glad to get out of it when it came time for them to visit the tenement in Woodside. Both Glynn and Fred were on duty that afternoon, and couldn't accompany them, so it felt like old times for the two women to be going on their own.

Maggie McIntosh smiled when they went in. "Did yer four lassies get awa' this mornin', Annie?"

"Yes, and I miss them already. They were good fun, weren't they, Renee?"

"They certainly kept everything going with a swing," the girl agreed.

"Will ye need to look for mair lodgers?" Peter asked.

Anne laughed. "I think you've guessed, Father. Renee and Glynn are going to take over the two upstairs rooms, and I'll move down to the back bedroom. We're going to start tomorrow to rearrange things."

"So it's turned oot for the best," Maggie said. "You winna be kept so busy wi' the lodgers awa', Annie, but watch an' nae strain yersel's shiftin' aboot at heavy furniture."

"Yes, Mother, we'll watch." Anne smiled affectionately.

"We'll dismantle Mum's double bed before we take it downstairs," Renee added, full of excitement at the move. "And the single bed I'm using just now can be stacked against the wall till we decide what to do with it."

Peter took his pipe out of his mouth. "I'd ha'e come to gi'e ye a hand, Annie, but I feel kind o' useless jist noo. I'm that easy tired, I jist dinna ken what's wrang wi' me."

Maggie smiled fondly. "Ye're nae so young as ye used to be, that's what's wrang, an' ye've enough to dae here."

"There's nothin' wrang wi' your tongue, ony road," he retorted.

"We'll manage, Father, don't worry yourself about that." Anne was concerned about him, and his slow and laboured movements, when he saw them to the door, gave her more cause for anxiety.

As they walked home, she said, "I hope your granda's OK, Renee. He wasn't like himself at all."

"No, and he didn't ask about the prices when I came back from the shops." The girl could see that her mother was very worried. "It's maybe just one of his down days. We all have them, don't we?" But his lack of energy and spirit had bothered her, too.

They walked on, not speaking for a few minutes, then Anne said, "We'll have to give all the rooms a good spring clean before we start shifting the beds."

"We should get on quite well tomorrow, then, seeing Glynn and Fred have the weekend on duty. We won't have to stop to make meals, or anything like that." She could hardly wait until the little "flat" was ready for her and Glynn to take over once they were married.

They worked hard all the next day in the back bedroom, scrubbing and cleaning as much as they could. They took down the curtains and stripped the bedclothes, to be washed on Monday. To Renee, it was a labour of love, and she could have worked on for ever, but Anne called a halt at five o'clock.

"I think we've done enough for one day, Renee."

"We could carry on for a couple of hours in the evening," the girl said, enthusiastically. "Once you've had a rest for a while, you'll feel better."

Anne sank wearily into her armchair in the living room. "There's no sense in killing ourselves, for there's plenty of time."

While Renee boiled two eggs each for their sustenance, by courtesy of the land girls but no longer to be forthcoming, Anne called through, "I've just been thinking. We'll have three single beds spare, once you're married."

Renee was pleased that her mother was keeping a double bed for herself. It meant that she did intend to marry Fred Schaper after the war. She pulled her mind back to the problem of disposing of the superfluous singles.

"Quite honestly, Mum, they're ancient. They've all seen better days. I've had mine since I was three, that's nearly sixteen years, and the other two . . . Well, Granny gave you one of her old ones when you started taking lodgers, and the other one you got at the same time was past its best then, and that was almost nine years ago. I think you should just throw them out."

Anne sighed. "I suppose so. We'd never be able to sell them, anyway, but it's such a waste. Surely there's somebody . . ."

"The Salvation Army!" Renee congratulated herself on her brainwave. "They always need beds and bedclothes. You won't need the single sheets and blankets any longer, either."

"That's a good idea!" Anne sat up, refreshed by the thought of helping someone in need. "I'll ask them to collect everything when Glynn and you are on your honeymoon."

“Some honeymoon.” The girl screwed up her face. “Still, it’s better than Mike and Babs had, remember? They just had one night, but we’ll have three. It’s a pity Glynn couldn’t have got the weekend off as well, then we could’ve had a week altogether, but it can’t be helped.”

She carried through the tray and placed it on the card table, then flopped down on the settee. She hadn’t realised how tired she was until she sat down, and said regretfully, “I think we’d better finish for the day, after all. We’ll be as stiff as boards in the morning.”

Anne sliced the top off one of her eggs. “I’ll wash the curtains tomorrow.”

“Leave the blankets and sheets till another day, then. I don’t want you laying yourself up before the wedding. You and Fred are our witnesses, remember.”

On Wednesday morning, Anne started upstairs, having finished the back bedroom completely the day before. The curtains were back at the sparkling window, the bedclothes, smelling fragrantly of fresh air, were folded neatly on a chair, ready for collection.

She set about this second room cheerfully, pulling over a chair to stand on until she unhooked the chintz curtains. Out of the corner of her eyes, she saw a man striding purposefully along the pavement towards her house, and her heart jumped with alarm when she recognised Mr Paterson, who shared the same landing as her mother and father in the Woodside tenement. Jumping off the chair, she ran down the stairs to open the door.

The man's face was grim, and he wasted no time in beating about the bush. "I've got bad news, Mrs Gordon, I'm afraid. Your father collapsed this morning, as soon as he rose, and he died before the doctor came."

She felt numb. "Oh, God! I knew he wasn't well when we saw him on Saturday. I should have done something." The full horror of the situation struck her then. "Now there's nobody to look after my mother, and she can't do anything for herself."

She was trembling violently, so Mr Paterson took hold of her arm. "Don't upset yourself about him, for the doctor said he wouldn't have felt a thing, but I promised your mother I'd take you back with me."

"Yes, of course, but I'll have to leave a note to let Renee know what's happened." As if in a dream, she took out the writing pad and a pencil, and wrote a few lines to explain her absence. She added a postscript asking her daughter to go to Woodside when she finished work at five thirty, then she went upstairs for her coat. When she went outside, her senses were too frozen to notice the beautiful sunshine.

As they walked quickly along, the man said, "I'll arrange things with the undertaker for you, if you like?"

"Oh, I didn't remember about that," she whispered. "Thank you. It's very kind of you and I'm very grateful."

"I'm afraid you're going to have your hands full with your mother," he said, sadly. "She's with my wife just now."

A new thought occurred to Anne. "How did you find out about my father?"

"Mrs McIntosh managed to struggle out of bed and on to the landing before she fell. My wife and I heard the sound and went out to see what it was, so we took her into our house."

Mrs Paterson was consoling Maggie when they went in.

"Oh, Annie!" the old lady sobbed. "I aye thought I'd be the one to go first, but here's me still livin', a helpless cripple, an' a decent God-fearin' man ta'en awa'. What am I goin' to dae withoot him?"

"You'll have to give up your house and come to live with me," Anne said decisively. "There's room now."

"We'd been thegither for near fifty year, Annie, an' I'm goin' to miss him. You've nae idea how much I'll miss him."

"Yes, Mother, I have." Anne gripped the old lady's hand. "I've been through it myself, remember?"

"So ye have, so ye have, but ye'd only been wed for aboot twelve year. Fifty year's a lang time to bide wi' a man. Ye get to ken what he'll da'e and what he's thinkin' even, an' it's like bein' one person, really."

Anne gulped. She was definitely going to have her hands full with her mother. She looked beseechingly at Mrs Paterson, who came to her rescue.

"You *will* go to live with your daughter, won't you, Mrs McIntosh? She'll take good care of you."

Maggie lifted her head pathetically, the tears still streaming down her face. "Aye, I ken that, an' I'll go, right enough. Thank ye, Annie, it's very good o' ye, though I wouldna come if I could look after mysel'. Oh, I wish it had been me that was ta'en."

Anne fought back her own tears. "Don't be silly, Mother. I know it'll be a big upheaval for you, but you'll soon settle down after a few days at Cattofield. We'll all get along fine, you and Renee and me." And Glynn Williams, she remembered, with a sinking heart. It was less than four weeks to the wedding. How on earth was she going to cope?

Maggie's voice, a little more composed now, cut into her thoughts. "I suppose ye'll ha'e to clear oot my hoose afore I gi'e it up, Annie? Ye'll nae ha'e room for ony o' my stuff."

"You can take whatever you want with you, Mother. I'll make room for it somehow."

"I'll tak' some o' that little ornaments I'm fond o', then. It would mak' me feel I had somethin' o' my ain beside me."

"If you're sure that's all you want, I'd better make a start to sorting things out as soon as I can. If I did a little bit every day, it shouldn't be so bad."

Anne knew that it would be distressing for her mother, but it would have to be done. There wasn't space in her house for all the furniture and the other things Maggie had amassed over the years.

The old lady remained with Mrs Paterson until after the undertakers had taken the coffin, with Peter in it, through to the bedroom, and Anne had changed all the bedclothes on the kitchen bed. Then Maggie was helped back into it, her daughter only having to remove the blanket which Mrs Paterson had wrapped round her when they found her lying on the landing in her nightdress.

When Renee came running in, just before six o'clock, she wasn't surprised that her grandmother was heartbroken, but she was shocked to see that the old lady looked on the point of death herself.

"What's happening about Granny?" she whispered to her mother, after expressing her deep sorrow at her grandfather's sudden call.

"I'll have to stay with her just now," Anne told her. "Will you manage to fend for yourself for a few days? The funeral's on Saturday. Mr Paterson next door arranged everything."

"I'll cope, don't worry, but who's going to look after her when the funeral's past?"

"She's coming to stay with us, it's all I could do." She looked at her daughter sadly. "I'm afraid Glynn and you can just have one room. I'll keep sleeping in the loft, so you can have the other upstairs bedroom. I'll have to clear out this house before I take Granny over to Cattofield, though."

"Oh." Renee's eyes filled with tears and she hastily blew her nose. "That really knocks it home, doesn't it? I'll come over to give you a hand in the evenings."

"Thanks. It'll take a while, I suppose. Do you want to see your granda now? He looks very peaceful."

Renee hesitated, remembering her vow on the day of her own father's funeral that she would never look at another corpse. "Would you mind very much if I didn't, Mum?" she said at last, feeling guilty and wondering if her grandfather would know.

"It's all right, if you don't feel up to it."

The funeral on Saturday was a gruelling ordeal for Anne and Renee. Maggie was inconsolable, and determined not to be taken out of the bed to be dressed. Maggie's sister, Teenie, and her other daughter, Anne's sister Bella, demanded various things out of the house as "keepsakes", and Anne let them take whatever they wanted because there seemed to be no point in quarrelling and causing her mother further distress.

Renee hadn't seen Auntie Teenie and Uncle Jimmy since Jim Gordon's funeral, almost nine years before, although Maggie had passed on any information she'd received in her sister's infrequent letters. She was shocked at how old they looked — much older than Maggie had looked before this tragedy, although the girl knew that both Teenie and Jimmy Durno were younger than her grandmother. Apart from her legs, Maggie had been a young seventy-year-old.

Renee smiled to Uncle Jimmy when he came over to speak to her.

"Yer mother was tellin' us ye're getting wed, Renee. I could hardly believe ye were auld enough for that."

"I'm old enough. I'm nearly nineteen now. I had a lovely holiday at Gowanbrae in 1933. I don't remember if I thanked you at the time, but I was only about ten, so I don't suppose it had crossed my mind."

"We enjoyed ha'ein' ye, lassie." He patted her head and moved away to speak to someone else.

Before they left, Auntie Teenie also found time to have a few words. "I'm really sorry aboot yer grandfather, Renee, an' yer grandmother doesna look very weel, either."

Renee swallowed quickly. "Yes, she's taking it pretty hard. Mum's going to take her to live at our house, once this place has been cleared out."

"I'm pleased to hear that." Teenie Durno's face softened into a hint of a smile. "It's terrible when ye're auld an' nae able to look after yersel'. It's a good thing me an' Jimmy's got a' oor faculties." She, too, moved on. Renee suddenly realised that this woman was no horrible old dragon, as she'd thought when she was holidaying at Gowanbrae. It was just her way, to present a forbidding face to the world.

Glynn Williams and Fred Schaper had been standing in the background, not wanting to intrude on the family's grief, but they followed the others into the bedroom when the minister spoke a few words over the coffin.

Renee was left on her own in the kitchen, apart from her grandmother, who seemed to be in a daze, and had paid no attention to any of the people who had come to pay their last respects to her husband. The girl was on the point of going over to her, to try to get through to her somehow, when she realised that Glynn had come back. He took her hand and she turned to him thankfully. "I hate funerals, Glynn," she whispered.

"No one likes them, my lovely."

"No, but I really hate them. I feel all tied up inside and my heart seems to be frozen solid."

"I'll thaw it out for you later," he murmured.

She frowned. "No, Glynn. Don't joke about things just now."

"I'm sorry, Renee." He was contrite. "I didn't think. You must be very upset. Your grandfather was a real character, and I came to think very highly of him in the short time I knew him."

She shot him a grateful glance, then the coffin was carried out and Glynn followed the other men down the stairs. During the next half-hour or so, the usual funeral-tea activity took place in the small kitchen before the women sat down to await the return of the men who had followed the hearse to the Grove Cemetery.

Maggie, propped up against the pillows, had watched all the preparations with an expression which suggested that she was completely unaware of the reason for them. When Renee glanced across, her grandmother reminded her of a shrunken, shrivelled skeleton, with fine parchment stretched over the bones, and her heart contracted as she moved towards the bed.

"Are you all right, Granny?" She laid her hand over the fragile one lying on the counterpane.

Out of deep sockets, the faded old eyes met hers sadly, but with fond recognition. "I'll never be a' right again," Maggie whispered. "I loved Peter from the first day we started the school thegither, Renee. He's been a fine, honourable man, an' I hope, from the bottom o' my he'rt, that you'll be blessed the same as I was."

"I have been, Granny. Glynn's a fine, honourable man, too, and I'm sure we'll be as happy as Granda and you were."

"As lang as ye keep lovin' an' trustin' each other, ye will be." Maggie closed her eyes, but Renee sat with her until the men came back.

Mrs Paterson, who had been helping Anne, told her that she would also lend a hand on Sunday with the clearing out. "I'm going to miss your mother," she said, when they were washing up after everyone had gone. "She's been a good neighbour to me for sixteen years, always cheery and willing to help, though we were never on first-name terms. It's best not to be too familiar, though, it often leads to friction."

Anne nodded. "You're welcome to come and see her any time."

By Sunday night, all Maggie's "bits and pieces" were packed into boxes, all, except one, to be taken to a saleroom along with the furniture. The carton containing her favourite little ornaments was to be transported with her to her new abode.

Mr Paterson said that he would see to the selling up, and he also organised an ambulance to take Maggie to Cattofield on Monday afternoon. "When the house is empty," he said, "I'll hand the keys to the factor, and that'll be the end."

Anne sniffed. "Yes, that'll be the end."

On Monday, the old lady was installed in a single bed in the back bedroom, but the upheaval and the journey, on top of the shock of Peter's death, took their toll on her. Over the next few days, they could see her slowly deteriorating. What was worse, she had lost the will to live, now that her life partner was gone, and she joined him exactly a week after the move.

Anne's remorse was unbounded. "I should never have taken her away from her own home. I should have stayed with her for another week, until she was stronger. Once she got over her first grief, she'd have picked up again, I'm sure."

"Mum, don't blame yourself. You were doing what you thought was best for Granny, and, quite honestly, I don't think that whatever you did would have made any difference."

Renee knew that she had to keep strong, to make sure that her mother wouldn't give in to the guilt she felt, to make sure that she kept her sanity.

Providentially, it seemed to the girl, Fred Schaper turned up unexpectedly about half an hour after the doctor had called to certify the death. He took over all the arrangements, and was a tower of strength to Anne, who had been on the verge of a complete breakdown, and was reluctant to let him out of her sight for any length of time.

Renee was extremely grateful for his presence, because she, too, would have been unable to cope had Glynn not been there to support her when her sorrow threatened to engulf her. It was he who had persuaded her to go through to the rearranged dining room — the ex-lounge where her father's coffin had once lain — to look at what was left of her beloved granny.

"Please go through," he had said quietly. "She looks so peaceful, it won't upset you, I promise."

She'd had to force herself to enter the room, but Glynn had been right. Her grandmother did look peaceful, and she was smiling as if she were happy that her struggle was over, and that she was to be reunited with her husband, so Renee did not regret breaking her long-standing vow.

On the day of Maggie's funeral, a macabre pressure seemed to exert itself over the whole house — a malign influence — and residents and visitors alike were affected by it. There was no talk, only brief murmurs of sympathy to the bereaved. No smiles, only stiff nods of recognition when relative met relative or friend met friend. No sign of real mourning, only a frozen acceptance of what seemed, now, to have been inevitable.

It was with enormous relief that Anne saw the last of them departing. Her legs gave way and she sat down suddenly, burying her face in her hands.

Fred sat on the arm of her chair and stroked her head. "Do you want me to stay, Anne, or will I leave you now to be on your own with Renee?"

She stretched out her hand to him, without lifting her head. "Don't leave me, Fred."

Glynn had left ten minutes earlier, because he had to go on duty, so Renee went upstairs to allow Fred to comfort her mother as much as he could. She sat on the edge of her bed, feeling absolutely empty. Granny and Granda were both gone. There would be no more cosy little chats on Saturday afternoons. No more little snippets of loving counsel. No shoulder to cry on.

She caught her morbid thoughts there. She would never need a shoulder to cry on again. She'd have Glynn to love, and to love her, and he would give her no cause for tears. She should really be happy that her grandparents were together again. It was what Granny had wanted. The girl felt easier in her mind now, so she picked up her library book and lay down to read.

When she went downstairs, after almost an hour, she was alarmed to see that Anne's face was drained of all colour, whiter even than it had been before, and that her sunken eyes were red-rimmed again. Renee glanced at the almost equally pale man, to find him looking at her apologetically.

"I've just told your mother that we leave the Battery tomorrow morning." Fred carried on, despite Renee's gasp of dismay. "We knew about it . . . we were told the day your granny died — that's why I came here so early — but you'll understand why I couldn't bring myself to say anything about it before. This was my last chance. I don't know where we're going."

"Oh, Mum! It's awful!" Renee clasped her hands together in misery. How could her mother cope with it, at this time?

"Everything's happening together," Anne whispered.

"I wish it could have been different." Fred stood up. "I'll have to go now, because we have an early start in the morning." He held out his hand to help Anne out of her chair. "I'll write to you, and if we're still in this country on my next leave, I'll come to see you."

She went to the front door with him, and Renee was left to wonder if this was the last calamity which would befall them. She couldn't think of anything else that could happen now, except . . . She prayed with all her heart that Glynn wouldn't be posted away from her. There had been no word of it yet, and her spirits had lifted a little by the time Anne came back. Renee saw by her mother's set expression that she couldn't talk about what had happened, so they went to bed, silent and uncomfortable with each other.

The following night, Friday, Glynn took Renee for a short walk, and was careful not to say anything to upset her. They had been strolling about fifteen minutes when she said, abruptly, "We'll need another witness, now Fred's away."

"It's all taken care of, my lovely," he assured her. "I asked Jim Black, another sergeant, and he's quite willing to stand up for us."

"Thank goodness you remembered, because it didn't cross my mind till just now." She turned her head away from him suddenly, her eyes apparently fixed on a distant object. "And another thing I just thought about . . . Now that Granny's gone, we'll be able to have the two rooms after all."

"Yes, of course, if your mother agrees."

She looked up at him again, repentant. "I shouldn't be saying things like that, so soon, should I?"

Glynn smiled. "I don't see why not, *cariad*. Your granny would want your happiness to come first."

Her relief came out as a soft sigh. "Yes, of course she would. She'd be pleased to see us so happy. Oh, Glynn, it's only a week and two and a half days till we'll be husband and wife. Are you as excited as I am?"

"I'm counting the hours, my lovely, but I know how mixed up you must be, after all that's happened lately."

They walked on again, unwilling to go home to Anne, who might possibly be tearful and reproachful.

When they did go back, however, Renee's mother was neither tearful nor reproachful, but was sitting thoughtfully by the fire. She looked up and smiled when they went in.

"I've just realised, Renee. You and Glynn can have the two rooms now. We've a whole week to get things ready, so if you give me a hand to dismantle the beds, and shift things, I can start cleaning the upstairs bedroom."

"Oh, Mum, thank you!" Renee was thankful that she hadn't been the one to broach the subject, and she flung her arms round her mother's neck.

"It's the only sensible thing to do." Anne was embarrassed.

On the afternoon of the Saturday before the wedding, Renee took her reluctant mother into town to choose their wedding outfits. Neither of them had fully recovered from the traumatic events of the past few weeks, but this was the only opportunity they had.

Anne Gordon could summon up little enthusiasm for anything, but tried to appear cheerful when they went into the various shops. There were no problems about clothing coupons, because neither of them had used any for some considerable time, and Renee chose a powder blue dress, with a silk-covered hat in a slightly deeper shade, and navy accessories, while Anne was just able to afford a black crêpe de Chine two-piece and hat. Renee paid for the black shoes, gloves and handbag for her mother, but insisted that Anne put a white polka dot ribbon round her hat to brighten up the ensemble a little bit.

They were both exhausted by the time they went home, but Anne had caught a little of Renee's excitement and seemed brighter.

On Sunday, Glynn Williams had to be on duty, so, after Renee had packed a few things into the travelling bag which Sheila Daun had lent her, she and her mother sat down to relax in their oldest clothes.

"We can't loll about like this after Glynn moves in," Anne remarked lazily.

Renee grinned. "I don't see why not. He'll have to see us for the couple of scruffs we are, sooner or later."

The excitement of it being the night before the wedding kept her awake for some time. She wasn't bothered about Glynn seeing her in old skirts and felted woollen jumpers — she'd never pretended to be a fashion plate — but what would he think when he saw her first thing in the mornings? With her face all pasty without make-up and her hair sticking up all over the place? But Glynn's hair would probably be the same, she consoled herself, and he'd be needing a shave. It was going to be fun learning about each other properly — the little intimate things.

Intimate! Her stomach churned with the thought of what would be happening in twenty-four hours.

CHAPTER TWENTY-TWO

The taxi, which Glynn had ordered, collected Renee Gordon and her mother promptly at quarter past two, and he was waiting at the door of the Registrar's Office with the other witness when they arrived in Bridge Street.

"You look beautiful, darling," he whispered to her, then introduced the other man. "Jim Black . . . Renee . . . Mrs Gordon. I don't know how he feels, but I'm beginning to shake all over with nerves."

The other sergeant laughed. "I was the same when I was married, but that was two years ago, so I'm a seasoned husband now. Your nerves will soon settle down, and in another twenty minutes or so, it'll all be over."

Glynn's eyes caught and held his bride's. "No," he said. "It'll be just the beginning for me."

After the brief ceremony, the taxi took them to a hotel in Market Street, Glynn having refused to allow Anne to "cook something special" as she'd proposed. When the meal was over, the four of them walked round the corner to the Joint Station, where the bride and groom were to catch a train to Edinburgh for their short honeymoon. Glynn held Renee's hand all the way, squeezing it occasionally now and then until she felt absolutely choked with emotion and almost burst into tears with the happiness that was coursing through her.

Her euphoria was somewhat blunted by the sight of her mother standing forlornly on the platform when the train pulled out, but Jim Black would surely see that Anne got home safely, and she would only be on her own for three nights. Glynn tugged Renee's coat when she turned to sit down, her heart again overflowing with love for him. The carriage was full, and, afraid that the other passengers would realise they were newly-weds, they meticulously avoided all contact with each other and tried to behave like a long-married couple.

It was almost nine o'clock when Mr and Mrs Glynn Williams emerged from Waverley Station, a cold wind whipping more colour into their cheeks, so they made their way to their hotel, had a drink and a cup of coffee, then went up to their room.

Renee turned to Glynn as soon as he closed the door, and they melted together in a kiss of love which turned rapidly to desire. Moving away from each other without a word, they began to undress, fumbling with buttons and fastenings in their haste.

"I haven't unpacked my nightie," Renee whispered.

"You won't need it tonight, my lovely." Glynn stood back from her. "Let me look at you."

She felt embarrassed and shy while he studied her body, as naked as his own. She hadn't stood like this since she was a small child waiting to be dried after a bath, and she wished that Glynn would allow her to get into bed. Suddenly, he stretched out his hands and led her across the room.

She lay down, shivering with anticipation and excitement.

"Oh, Renee, Renee, you're so beautiful," he breathed, exploring her with his mouth, his hands. "This is the happiest day of my life. I'll always remember it, every Monday. From now on, Monday will be my lucky . . ."

He broke off, surprised by the stiffening of her body, and the sudden coldness of her lips. He was even more shocked when she pushed him roughly away from her and burst into tears.

"What's wrong, darling? I'm not going to hurt you. If this is your first time, I promise I'll be very gentle . . ."

"What made you say that?" she sobbed.

"About it being your first time? I don't care if it isn't the first time for you, sweetheart. It's not my first time, either."

"It wasn't that. You said you'd always remember, every Monday. Why, Glynn? I've never heard you saying anything like that before." Her sobs became wilder.

He was utterly mystified and sat up, hurt and frustrated. "Renee, tell me what I've done wrong. I love you, there's nothing wrong in that. You're my wife now, and I want to make love to you. It's what I've been wanting to do ever since I met you, and I thought you wanted that, too."

Renee knew that she'd wounded him, but his mention of Mondays had brought back the awful memory of Fergus Cooper swearing that she would remember him every time anyone made love to her on a Monday. It wasn't Glynn's fault, and she sobbed all the more for hurting him.

He stood up to put on his trousers and vest, and threw his shirt on the bed. "Put that on," he said harshly. "I don't want you catching cold."

As she slid her arms into the sleeves, he picked up his jacket, thrown carelessly over a chair, and pulled a packet of cigarettes from the pocket.

Renee noticed that his hands were trembling as he struck a match and held it up, and she tried to stifle her sobs. Poor, poor Glynn. She loved him so much, yet she had dealt him the most cruel blow a man could suffer — she had refused him on his wedding night. He would never want to touch her again, never want to make love to her at all. Their marriage would be over.

Fergus Cooper's words had come true — his curse had worked. Her life was in ruins, and there was nothing she could do to salvage anything from the debris. In a few minutes, Glynn ground out his cigarette in the ashtray, and sat down on the bed. His back was to Renee, who longed to put her arms round him and tell him that her refusal had nothing to do with anything he had done, that it was her fault entirely. She couldn't move, but her weeping was lessening. At last, his attitude of dejection, complete and utter dejection, gave her the courage to stretch out her hand to touch his bare arm.

He turned round abruptly, and the deep pain in his eyes made her cry out, "Oh Glynn, I'm sorry! I'm sorry! I *do* love you."

He kept looking at her, like a dog that had been whipped, and she propped herself up on one elbow to put her hand over his, resting on the bed.

"It was nothing you did, Glynn, honestly. It was something you said . . ." She gripped his hand as he attempted to move away from her. "Something you said, which you meant as words of love, darling, but . . ." She couldn't finish. She felt sick and ashamed. Ashamed of what she had to tell him, because she *would* have to tell him now, to explain her actions.

She studied his tortured face and her love for him swelled up inside her. She owed him this explanation, even if he loathed her for it. "Glynn," she began, softly, "I have to tell you . . . I want to tell you . . . it's . . ."

"Is it about that man that you didn't want to remember?" he asked, gruffly. "The one you spoke of once beside the park?"

"Yes, darling. I wish I had told you everything that night. I might have lost you then, but even that wouldn't have been so bad as . . . And if you'd forgiven me then, this . . . would never have happened."

"I think you'd better tell me now, Renee." He sounded strained, defeated.

"Lie down beside me, Glynn, please."

He lay down, but it was as if he were a million miles away. He did not let any part of him touch her, and she felt cold and rejected, but knew that she must go on. She told him everything, beginning with the strange looks Fergus had given her from the time he had come to their house. Neither of them looked at the other, but when she came to the time Fergus had first made love to her in the Victoria Park, and had called her his Monday girl, she saw his hands clench, but he passed no comment.

"I was only fifteen, Glynn. I didn't really realise what I was doing, and he knew it. I loved him blindly, as if he'd hypnotised me into doing whatever he wanted."

She described how they'd met in secret, and how she had seen Fergus making love to another girl while she was out walking with Jack Thomson and Tim Donaldson. She knew that Glynn glanced at her then, but whether in disgust, pity, or disbelief at her naivety, she couldn't guess, and she couldn't meet his eyes to find out.

She told him of her suspicions regarding her mother, feeling like a traitor for dragging Anne into it, but it was necessary in order to explain what had happened later. When she told him about the ghastly confrontation which had taken place on the day the war started, Glynn laid his free hand over hers, and she knew that he felt sorry for her.

"Renee." He murmured only her name, but it gave her the courage to carry on.

"But that wasn't the end of it, Glynn." Her courage failed again, at the thought of what was still to be told.

He lifted his free hand and detached the other from her grasp. "Don't tell me you still carried on with him?"

She supposed that he would doubt her sanity when he learned that she had gone on meeting Fergus in secret, and letting him make love to her, but she had to tell him everything now.

"As I said already, that awful row happened on the day war was declared, and my mother ordered him out, but then she gave in and said he could stay till he found other digs. When I met him the next night, he told me he'd signed on for the army that day, and was leaving the following Monday."

Their eyes met for a second, hers apologetic and ashamed, his sad and apprehensive, as if he wondered how much more he could take. She carried on with her confession, how Fergus had made his last night as a civilian a memorable one for her. "Jack and Tim had both told me not to trust Fergus, and even Granny warned me he was a bad lot, but I couldn't help myself. As far as I knew, I'd never see him again, and I was broken-hearted."

"But you obviously did see him again?"

"He came back after his training was finished. He'd written to Mum, pleading with her, and she felt sorry for him because he'd nowhere else to go. His parents had put him out years before, you see, though we didn't know the truth about that until later. Well, I was very jealous because he'd written to her and not to me, but I couldn't say anything to him in front of Mum."

"And *was* your mother still involved with him, too?"

"No, she'd seen him for what he was, and knew he wasn't to be trusted, but she trusted me, unfortunately. I went to meet him that last time, hoping he could explain away all my doubts, even though I knew, deep down, that they were well-founded. But when I saw him sitting on that bench, smiling as if nothing had happened, I didn't want his excuses . . . I don't know, something snapped inside me, Glynn. I'd seen through him at last, and I wanted to hurt him as much as he'd hurt me so many times." Renee shook her head, as if to dispel the memories of the terrible things they had said to each other.

Glynn moved his feet, and rubbed his numb leg to restore his circulation. "Did it all end there?"

"Oh, yes. He must have realised he'd never be able to manipulate me again, and it was horrible. He shouted that no matter who I married, or made love with, he'd always remember that he'd been first, and so would I. His last words were, 'I swear to you, Renee, that every time anyone makes love to you on a Monday, you'll remember I was the first.' I never let a man ever get anywhere near making love to me again, Glynn, truly . . . not even you."

She looked up sadly. "Fergus hasn't crossed my mind for years, and I did want you to make love to me the night you tried, but I was afraid you'd lose your respect for me afterwards."

There was a lengthy silence, during which the young bride was afraid to say anything more. She knew that her husband was struggling with his own emotions, but would he turn to her in a minute and enfold her in his arms and murmur words of forgiveness and understanding, or would he turn away from her in disgust at her obsession with a worthless philanderer who had made her a puppet following his every command? Worse still, would he show his anger by walking out on her on their wedding night?

She couldn't bring herself to look at him, for fear of what she might see on his face, and turned her attention to the room, seeing it properly for the first time. The dark wardrobe and dressing table, not part of the same suite but close enough; the cracked wash-hand basin; the faded carpet with a few indeterminate stains; the green curtains, striped with almost white vertical bands where the sun had bleached them when they were open. Everything was clean, but impersonal. What a barren place for such a poignant drama! She drew a deep breath, a shuddering, body-wracking breath, and let it out in slow, difficult stages. Glynn had been silent too long. He couldn't forgive her, and she would have to accept that their marriage was over before it had begun.

The sound seemed to jolt him into consciousness. He turned his body a little towards her, still not touching her, and looked at her sorrowfully. "Why didn't you tell me all this before?" It was almost a whisper, but it conveyed the full extent of his misery.

"Glynn, I couldn't! I was ashamed of what I'd done. I wanted to pretend it had never happened, and I thought you'd despise me for being so gullible and . . ." Her voice faded away, and she looked at him, pleading with him to understand.

His eyes dropped, the black sweep of his lashes against his cheeks emphasising his pitiful pallor. "Renee," he said slowly, deliberately, "if he were to come back, after the war, would you . . . fall under his spell again and . . ?"

She sat straight up then, outraged that he could think such a thing. "No, Glynn! I never want to see him again. Never! I stopped loving him . . . I think it really was when I saw him with that other girl, making love in the very same place as he'd been with me."

"But it didn't stop you from going back again and again to him, and letting him . . . use you?"

She realised that this was what was most difficult for him to comprehend, and she could hardly understand it herself now. "Glynn, I can't offer any excuses. I can't explain, even to myself, why I was drawn to him like that in spite of what I knew about him. It was an obsession. I couldn't get him out of my system. I didn't want to believe he was unfaithful to me, even if I'd seen it with my own eyes. I always pushed that picture out of my mind, and pretended that it had just been a dream, a nightmare."

He lifted his eyes again, sympathetic, sad eyes, not angry. "You're sure your mother got him out of her system, too?"

"Yes, I'm sure, but what's that got to do with . . .?"

"I was wondering if this man could be the reason for her refusing to marry Fred Schaper."

"He told you he'd asked her? No, I'm sure Fergus had nothing to do with her not marrying Fred. She said she didn't want to take the chance of being made a widow again."

Glynn slipped back into his brooding silence, and Renee tensed herself to keep on persuading him that the hypnotic fascination which Fergus Cooper had held for her had been killed by Fergus himself in the end.

"Renee." His look was searching. "Why did you let our wedding go ahead for a Monday, when you knew . . .?"

"Glynn, I swear to you I didn't remember anything about that." She felt desperate. "I loved you so much, even fixing the wedding day for a Monday didn't remind me about him. He'd meant nothing to me for years, and I wouldn't have thought about him at all if you hadn't said that you'd always remember Mondays. That was what brought it all back to me."

He put his hands up to his face. "Oh, Renee, I want to believe you, but . . ."

"But you'll never believe that it's you I love and not Fergus," she finished for him. "I can understand that, Glynn, but please, please, listen to me. I love you more deeply and more truly than anything I ever felt for him." Her eyes shone with the truth of this, as she waited for him to reply.

"Oh, God!" he said, at last. "God, Renee, I love you with every part of me, and I can't bear the thought of losing you."

"You won't lose me, Glynn, darling, not if you want me — if you want to keep me. I can't bear the thought of losing you either."

He ran one hand wildly through his hair, then leaned over with his face close to hers. "I have to trust you, otherwise our marriage would be worth nothing." His tortured eyes burned into hers with a strength that almost frightened her.

"You can trust me completely, utterly, totally — I can't think of any more words to convince you, but it's true." She held her lips up to his, praying that he wouldn't turn away. There was no passion in their kiss, and no desire followed it. He cradled her in his arms until they fell asleep, both exhausted by the emotional ordeal they had just come through.

They rose late in the morning, almost too late for breakfast, and Renee could see the two young waitresses giggling in the corner of the dining room when they went in. She could imagine the jokes they must be making about the honeymoon couple having had a hectic night, and thought ruefully that they wouldn't think it was so comical if they knew what had really happened the night before in the second-floor bedroom. Glynn had hardly spoken to her since they woke, because they'd been rushing to be in time for breakfast, but he had taken her in his arms and kissed her tenderly before they left the room.

At the table, they discussed where they would go that day, acting like a couple who had been married for years, while Renee wondered if they would ever recapture the warm, loving, free-and-easy relationship they'd had before, and should have even more so now that they were husband and wife.

They went to the Palace of Holyroodhouse first, where she showed him where Darnley's conspirators had plunged their daggers into David Rizzio, thinking he was the Queen's lover. She had been in Edinburgh once before, when her father was alive, and even after more than ten years, she could still remember all that she had learned on that visit. History, especially the life of Mary, Queen of Scots, had always fascinated her, and Glynn was an interested listener. They walked up the Royal Mile, and spent the afternoon immersing themselves in the intriguing history of the Castle.

"This little room is where Mary gave birth to her son, who became James the Sixth of Scotland and First of England."

Glynn smiled. "It's very small, but I suppose it was only an old-time labour ward."

Renee was pleased that he seemed to have regained his sense of humour, and they moved on. Before they left the Castle, she took him into St Margaret's Chapel, built in 1076 by Margaret, Queen of Malcolm III, where a plan formed in the girl's mind, but she decided to keep quiet about it at the moment.

She would really have preferred to implement it here, but there were two other people in the tiny building and it wouldn't have been feasible. There was another place, though, she remembered, happily, which might be an even better setting for what she had in mind. She hugged her secret as they walked down the hill, only telling Glynn that they were on their way to visit St Giles' Cathedral, which they had passed on their way up to the Castle. To whet his interest, she told him the story of little Jenny Geddes throwing a stool at John Knox, the great preacher, because she disagreed with his teaching.

"Your Scottish history is every bit as turbulent as the history of Wales," he remarked. "Tell me, all the things you've spoken about today — do you remember them from being here with your father, or did you learn them at school?"

"A bit of both, I suppose, and I probably only remember what I found most interesting at the time."

They had arrived at the doors of St Giles and went through into the cool peace of the Cathedral. As they walked round, Renee said, quietly, "Sit down, Glynn, and we can ask God's blessing on our marriage." This was what she'd thought of back in the small chapel at the Castle, but she was doubtful now if even this would afford them a fresh start.

Giving her a quick, apprehensive glance, Glynn sat down and reached for her hand.

For several minutes they remained there, with heads bowed and hands held tightly, allowing the serenity of the holy building to take possession of them.

Dear God, Renee prayed silently, let Glynn forgive me for what I did when I was too young to know any better. Make him understand that he's my whole life now, and that nobody means anything to me except him. Amen.

As an afterthought, she added, I'll always be a good wife to him, and if he has to be sent away to fight, I promise to be faithful to him. Amen again.

When they stood up, she felt that they were truly husband and wife now, in the eyes of God as well as in the eyes of the world. A calm peace had entered her soul, and she trusted that it had been the same for Glynn.

She was overjoyed when he turned to her in the street outside and said softly, "I'm very pleased you thought about that, my darling. A registry office wedding doesn't exactly make you feel properly married, does it?"

They returned to the hotel in good time for dinner at seven, but while they washed and dressed, Glynn spoke only of what they had seen and done during the day, and made no move to kiss her or touch her in any way. Renee was bitterly disappointed. He still hadn't recovered from the shock of the previous night. He was friendly, amusing, but treating her as a friend, not as a bride. How long would it take him to forget . . . or accept?

After their meal, they went for a walk along Princes Street Gardens, which looked magnificent in the rays of the setting sun. When they came to the Scott Monument, Glynn stopped walking, but he kept his eyes on the Castle towering above them to the left.

"Renee, I'm sorry our honeymoon isn't going the way we expected," he said simply.

"I'm enjoying it," she protested. "I love Edinburgh."

"That's not what I mean, and you know it." He glanced at her quickly, then turned towards the solid dark silhouette again. "I've tried hard to come to terms with what you told me last night, and I've reached a conclusion."

"Yes?" She sounded alarmed. Was he going to tell her that their marriage had been a mistake? Was he going to suggest that they have it annulled?

"Either we go on as we've been doing all day, ignoring the problem, which would be intolerable for both of us, or else . . ."

"Yes?" she said again. "Or else?"

"Or else we'll both have to learn to forget about Fergus Cooper and what he did to you. That's the only way we can have a decent life together."

"I've forgotten already," she assured him, quickly.

Glynn bowed his head. "I haven't, Renee. I can't. I am trying, but I find it very difficult."

She touched his arm. "I know. But Glynn, please keep on trying. Please, just for me?"

He turned and drew her towards him. "We *can* make a go of it, can't we, Renee?" His eyes were earnest, anxious.

"I'm sure we can, darling." Her pulse was racing. It was going to be all right.

At last he kissed her, a long, tender kiss. "I'll try, Renee, for my own sake as well as yours, but you'll need to have patience with me. It might take some time."

Her heart began to sing. She would do her utmost to help him forget the past, and someday, very soon, nothing would come between them.

In bed, Glynn kissed her once more, and her spirits rose even higher, until he abruptly released his hold on her.

"I'm sorry, Renee. I can't. Not tonight. Not yet."

She could understand what he felt, but that didn't make it any easier for her. Was this going to be the pattern of all their nights together? Hurt and frustrated, she lay for over an hour listening to his steady breathing, before drifting into a troubled sleep.

On Wednesday, they took a bus to Cramond, and walked along the side of the River Forth, back towards

Leith. They ambled, slowly and easily, stopping now and then for a cup of tea or a snack in a little cafe, and arrived back at the hotel with an hour to rest before dinner. They lay, fully clothed, on the bed, silent but companionable, until it was time to get dressed.

In the evening, while they were climbing Calton Hill, Renee reflected that Glynn had become a master of small-talk, and wished with all her heart that he would say something romantic to her, for a change. He had been right yesterday. This honeymoon wasn't turning out as she had expected, but even looking out over the view below, she couldn't bring the subject up again.

That night was to be their last in Edinburgh, and Renee slid into bed hoping for a miracle. Glynn lay beside her, and she nestled in his arms while they talked about going home the next day, and how things would improve when they were sleeping in their own bedroom.

They'd bought an oak dressing-table and wardrobe the week before, to match the double bed which Anne had purchased when the Donaldsons came to lodge with her, and which had been moved into the attic bedroom. They'd also bought two rexine easy chairs to make their other room more like a sitting room, so that they would have their own little domain away from the rest of the house.

At last, Glynn said, "Goodnight, darling," and brushed her lips lightly with his before turning his back on her.

She could hardly believe it. He *wasn't* trying. He didn't want to banish her revelations from his mind.

She couldn't go on like this — she needed love, proper, total love. She lay, open-eyed and unmoving, remembering how she'd dreamt of this honeymoon with Glynn, of him being romantic, tender and passionate, not cold and distant, like this. Self-pity surging up in her, she wept silently for the fifteen-year-old virgin who had been hypnotised by a practised seducer, for the sixteen-year-old girl whose hopes and dreams had been riven apart, for the almost nineteen-year-old bride whose marriage was apparently doomed to be unconsummated.

If Anne Gordon suspected, when they returned to Aberdeen, that her daughter and son-in-law were not as happy as they should have been, she said nothing about it. They sat with her all evening, describing what they'd seen in Edinburgh, and assuring her that their honeymoon had been perfect.

When, at last, they went up to their bedroom, Glynn got into bed first and lay with his hands behind his head, watching Renee undress.

Aware that he was looking at her, she took her time, feeling like a cheap strip-tease artiste deliberately trying to kindle his desire. When she finally stood naked, she picked up her folded nightdress and shook it out slowly, hesitating before she pulled it over her head, and hoping that Glynn would tell her not to bother. But there was no reaction from him, so she put it on and slipped under the blankets beside him.

He made no move for a few minutes, then lowered his arms. "God, I'm tired. I'll have to get some sleep. Goodnight, my darling." He gave her the light kiss she was beginning to resent, then turned round, facing away from her, and within a short time, he was fast asleep.

Renee sighed and gave up. What was the use of hoping? Glynn had said that it would take some time, and he'd meant it. She felt quite tired herself, anyway, after the ordeal of the past three loveless nights, so she snuggled down and let sleep claim her almost immediately.

Glynn had to report for duty on Friday evening, and he left her with the usual hasty peck. He told her that he might be back on Saturday afternoon, but probably not, as he might have to be on duty for the whole weekend.

Renee wandered back into the living room and sat down opposite her mother.

"Is everything all right between you two?" Anne asked. "You look a bit under the weather."

"Everything's great," Renee lied. "We've just had a few late nights lately."

"Yes, of course." Anne's twinkling eyes revealed what she was thinking, and the girl felt like shouting the truth at her.

On Monday morning, Renee found Sheila Daun's good-natured teasing hard to take, but forced herself to laugh and joke along with her.

Glynn was helping Anne in the scullery when Renee went home at six o'clock, but they spent the evening in their own "sitting room" listening to the wireless he'd bought, and making light inconsequential conversation. At a quarter past ten, she went downstairs to make cocoa, and was surprised to find him in bed when she brought up the tray. Glynn finished his cup quickly but Renee sipped slowly, making it last deliberately. She hadn't shared the bed with him since Thursday, which had meant three nights without the tension he seemed to create, and was dreading his rejection again.

When she lay down beside him, however, he turned to her and cupped her breasts, gently at first, then more insistently until she gasped at his ferocity. He'd had time to consider, she thought happily, time to forgive her for her past indiscretion. His hands moved down her body, banishing any further thought, and she could feel his manhood straining against her as he pulled off her nightdress without a word.

She gave herself up to the exquisite delight of their very first, full mating, her own need now as great as his, her response to him uninhibitedly eager. "I love you, Glynn," she moaned.

"I love you too, my Monday girl," he said, harshly, his teeth grating against hers. Horrified and shocked, she tried to struggle away from him, but he kept her firmly pinned beneath him until he satisfied himself then rolled over and laughed vindictively.

"Did you think I could forget so easily?"

It hadn't occurred to her that it was another Monday, and she was nauseated by what he had done. She felt that she'd been violated, and was so furious that even tears would have been no relief.

"You callous, unfeeling brute," she said angrily. "I despise you for that, Glynn Williams."

"I can't be first with you," he said flatly, "but you're mine for the rest of your life, and it will always be Mondays, only Mondays."

"My God, Glynn, you're as cruel as Fergus was."

"It isn't cruel to make love to my wife for the very first time," he said, sarcastically. "I'm only trying to make sure it'll be me you'll always think of on Mondays, even if I'm not here with you."

A possible excuse for his behaviour occurred to her then. "Have you been drinking, Glynn?" Her mother had told her that he'd arrived home only a few minutes before she did herself.

"I had a few in the mess in the afternoon, but I'm not drunk."

"Well, how could you? Do you realise how much you hurt me by saying that?"

"Not as much as you hurt me last Monday night." His laugh was mirthless.

"Stop torturing yourself, Glynn . . . and me. I've told you, I love you. You, and only you. Not Fergus, not anyone else. All that was in the past."

He smirked slyly. "So you say, but it's significant that you always bring his name into conversation."

She turned away from him, feeling bitter. "That's not fair, and you know it."

He put his arms round her and made her face him again. His eyes were full of repentance as he said, misquoting, "Nothing's fair in love and war, I do love you, Renee. I love you with all my heart. I asked you to be patient with me, remember?"

"I remember, but it's difficult for me as well. You said we should both try to be sensible, to forget."

"I meant it, and I have tried, but I'll try even harder. I'm sorry, my darling."

His earnestness touched her, and she leaned forward to kiss him. "Goodnight, Glynn darling."

"Goodnight, my lovely." He fell asleep with his arms still round her but Renee lay awake far into the small hours, hating Fergus Cooper but thankful that he would never know the mockery her marriage had become because of him.

CHAPTER TWENTY-THREE

Over the next few weeks, Renee Williams learned the meaning of purgatory because Glynn made love to her only on Mondays, as he had threatened. She stopped protesting after the third week, and allowed herself to respond to him, in the hope, at first, that it would prove to him that she really did love him, but eventually out of her own need for him.

He was a good companion at all other times, and had made no objection to her carrying on her correspondence with Jack Thomson and Tim Donaldson, but she always showed him their letters, and her replies, to avoid any unnecessary jealousy springing up. She had written to both of them after the honeymoon, telling them how happy she was — what else could she say? — and Tim's answer had delighted her.

> I'm really pleased for you and I'm beginning to think I was wrong in not asking Moira to get engaged before I was called up. I've decided to pop the question the next time I'm on leave, so keep your fingers crossed for me.
>
> Love, Tim.

Jack's reply was more serious:

As I told you when I saw you, I'm glad you've found happiness at last. I wish you and your Welshman good luck, and good fortune in the future.

Your old friend, JACK.

Renee felt a sense of desolation when she read it, but perhaps he'd considered that writing "Love' would be out of place now that she was married, although that kind of nicety hadn't bothered Tim.

Occasionally, Anne received letters from Mike, passing on the reports Babs sent him about their son, but since he'd been posted, Fred Schaper had written to her only once, telling her that he was being sent overseas. It had been a light-hearted letter which he ended by saying, "Give my best wishes to Renee and Glynn, I hope their wedding went off without a hitch. From your more-than-just-a-friend, Fred."

Anne didn't know if her reply had reached him before he left England. "If my letter didn't get there in time," she said to Renee one day, "he might have thought I didn't want to write, and he'll be feeling very hurt about it. I shouldn't have taken so long to make up my mind about it."

"He'd surely have sent another letter just to make sure?" The girl felt extremely sorry for her mother, but her own life was far from perfect at the moment, too.

"He wouldn't have wanted to pester me," Anne said, sadly. "If only I knew where he was."

"He'll write when he arrives at wherever they've sent him. Don't worry about it, Mum."

No letters ever came for Glynn Williams. "Doesn't your mother ever write to you?" Renee asked, about three months after they were married. "Or don't you write to her?"

His eyes shifted guiltily. "I do write to her, but she can't forgive me for marrying you, so she sends her letters to the Battery. I think she tries to convince herself that I'm still single."

"Oh, that's just great!"

Her sarcasm made him wince. "Look, Renee, I'll take you to meet her on my next leave, if you can get off work. I'm sure she'll surrender to your charm as quickly as I did."

She regarded this as some progress, and gladly made enquiries the next morning. Mr Murchie, old Bill, was quite agreeable to letting her have a week off after the New Year, and she waited rather impatiently for the weeks to pass.

Unfortunately, two days before they were due to go to Wales, Sheila Daun broke her leg at the skating rink, and because Renee wanted Glynn to have a chance to reason with his mother, she persuaded him, with very little difficulty, to go without her.

"There'll be other opportunities for me to meet her, Glynn, but tell her how sorry I am that I couldn't go this time, and say that I hope I see her soon."

He looked rather ashamed. "Renee, I . . . you're so kind and understanding, in spite of everything. I wish I could . . ." Maybe this break from each other is what I need to . . ."

His inarticulacy gave her fresh hope. "Maybe it is, my darling, and all the time you're away I'll be praying that things work out for us."

On the day he was to travel to Wales, he kissed her warmly before she left for work. "I'll do my best to talk Mam round."

During the morning and afternoon, Renee often wondered where Glynn was at that minute, so she was astonished to see the army greatcoat on the hallstand when she went home at six o'clock. What had made him change his mind about going? She burst into the living room, but it wasn't Glynn who was sitting there.

"Jack! Oh, it's good to see you!" she cried before she could prevent herself. "You're looking well," she added, rather more primly.

"So are you, but you're a bit thinner. Are you living on love these days?"

"That's right." Conversation between them had to be light and impersonal. If he suspected that something was wrong with her marriage, he was liable to be sympathetic and want to know the whys and wherefores, and she could never divulge the true reason. She loved Glynn as much as ever, and he loved her.

Realising that Jack was regarding her curiously, she asked him what had been happening to him recently. They were laughing uproariously when Anne came through, and the jokes flew backwards and forwards until she held up her hand. "Enough! My sides are sore with laughing. You two get worse and worse."

"Sit down and have a rest, Mrs Gordon, and my friend'll help me to carry things through for you."

He winked to Renee, who stood to attention and saluted. "Yes, Sir Friend."

After their meal, Jack offered to do the washing up with Renee again, and they worked together companionably, keeping up their usual chaffing banter. In a short lull, Renee ventured to ask the question which often occurred to her. "Have you got a steady girl yet, Jack? I see you've got rid of the moustache."

He pulled a grotesque face. "Betty didn't like it after all, and, anyway, she started going out with a corporal, so a humble lance wasn't good enough. I wasn't all that bothered, though, and I've been out with quite a few girls since then, though I still enjoy a good night out with the boys."

"Once you meet the right girl, you'll feel different."

"The only girl for me . . . married somebody else." His voice was low, almost a whisper.

Renee avoided his gentle, caring eyes. "I'm sorry."

"No need. I'll get over it." He broke the tension by spinning another yarn, and they were soon giggling again. During the next hour and a half, Jack regaled the two women with tales of the happenings, serious as well as humorous, at his station and, before they knew it, it was time for him to leave.

He stood up regretfully. "The time's just flown past, but if I miss the last bus to Peterhead at nine I'll be stranded."

"You could come back and sleep on the settee," Anne told him. "You're welcome any time, you know that."

"Thanks, Mrs Gordon. I'll maybe take you up on that if I'm stuck some other time, but I should make it tonight. It's been good seeing you both again, but I'll have to run. I hope I meet your husband next time, Renee. He always seems to be on leave the same time as me."

They went to the door with him, and waved as he walked along the pavement. "He's a nice lad," Anne remarked when they went inside. "I used to hope . . ."

"Don't start that again. I'm a happily married woman."

"Are you?" Anne looked grave when she sat down. "Are you truly happy? It sometimes seems to me . . ."

"I'm truly happy." Renee smiled broadly, to reinforce her statement. She would be truly happy, except for one thing.

That night, alone in the double bed, her thoughts flew to Glynn. She hoped he could convince his mother to accept a Scottish daughter-in-law, but, most of all, she prayed that he could view their relationship in perspective from a distance, and realise how much he was endangering their marriage by his peculiar sexual behaviour. Most men could have coped with the situation, why couldn't Glynn? Jack would have forgiven her and buried the past, if he'd been her husband.

For heaven's sake, what was she thinking? That was a stupid and dangerous track to be on. It was Glynn Williams she loved, with every fibre of her being, not Jack Thomson.

When Glynn arrived back, the following week, he was in time to meet Renee outside the office at half past five. She ran into his arms, surprised and delighted to find him waiting for her.

"Why didn't you let me know the time of your train, darling? I'd have asked to be off early, and met you at the station. Oh, Glynn, I'm so glad to have you home."

"I'm glad to be home, *cariad*." He looked tired after the long, involved journey, but tucked her arm through his.

She snuggled against him while they walked to the bus stop. "What about your mother? Is she still against . . .?"

"She's a stubborn old thing, Renee, but I think she's coming round a little bit."

"I hope so." It seemed to her that he'd been away for years, but if his mission had been successful, even just the smallest bit, their parting had achieved something.

"I saw Eiddwen when I was there," he said, unexpectedly.

"Oh." Her happiness deflated like a burst balloon. "How did you feel about her?"

"Nothing, my lovely. Absolutely nothing. She's a very nice girl, but she's no more than a friend to me now."

This gave her new heart, and she bubbled inside with the anticipation of being in bed with him again.

Glynn went upstairs while she was helping Anne after tea, and was smoking in one of the rexine chairs, with his legs stretched out, when she joined him.

"Oh, Glynn, I really missed you." She went over and planted a kiss on his brow.

He pulled her on to his knee. "I missed you, too, my lovely, more than I thought possible. But I've had time to think since I went to Porthcross, and I'm easier in my mind about everything. It's you I love, as you are, not what you were, and I bitterly regret what I've done to you over the past few m —"

She stopped him with another kiss. "As long as you love me, darling. That's all I need to know."

"I love you with all my heart," he breathed, and she could feel his heart pounding against her breast. Her own heart was pounding, too, so when he whispered, "Come to bed," she let him lead her through.

"It's not eight o'clock yet, what if Mum hears us?" she murmured as he drew her jumper over her head.

"She'll know how much we love each other," he said softly.

It was wonderful! It was ecstasy. It was . . . Tuesday! Renee realised it with tremendous relief after their passion was spent. At last their marriage was turning out to be normal. It was worth spending eight lonely, doubting nights to have this at the end.

They made love every night for the rest of the week, and her happiness was unbounded. She could even be glad of Sheila Daun's broken leg, which had been the cause of Glynn having to go to Wales on his own. On the following Monday evening, Glynn was late home, and his face, when he did appear, told Renee that something was wrong.

"What's upset you, darling?" she asked, as soon as they were alone.

"Nothing's upset me," he snapped. "Can't a man have some peace in his own . . ." He stopped and frowned. "It's not my house, of course."

"These two rooms are our home," she reminded him. "I'm sorry. I didn't mean to be nosey."

He bent to take off his boots. "I'm sorry, too, for being so touchy. You were right. I've had a hell of a day, but I shouldn't take it out on you."

"Do you want to tell me about it? It might help."

"Not really, if you don't mind."

"OK." Renee knew how she felt herself sometimes, when things went wrong at the office, and probed no further.

Glynn was very quiet all evening, and she felt protective towards him. Poor darling, if only he would confide in her. As soon as they were in bed, he said, without looking at her, "I'm not in the mood tonight, Renee. You understand?"

"Of course I understand, and don't worry about it."

He gave her a light kiss which evoked a memory of their first few weeks of married life, and caused a touch of apprehension to stir somewhere deep inside her. No, it couldn't mean anything. He'd definitely come to terms with that old problem. The following night, his ardour was as fervent as she could have wished, and she forgot the misgivings which had returned to torment her.

It took a few weeks for Renee to realise that Glynn avoided making love to her on Mondays. He'd apparently given up trying to prove that she was his alone on Mondays, and was now afraid to touch her in case he was reviving memories of Fergus Cooper instead of obliterating them. Poor mixed-up Glynn, she thought, but at least the other days, and nights, of the week were happy for them, so she gave no sign that she knew of his fears.

He seemed pleased when Tim Donaldson arrived one Saturday afternoon with his fiancée, Moira, showing off the ring she was so proudly wearing.

After Anne and Renee had congratulated them, and said how glad they were that Tim had finally taken the plunge, Glynn said, quietly, "I hope you'll be as completely happy as Renee and I are."

His wife glanced at him quickly, but he was quite serious about it. His mind must gloss over their one, big stumbling block, she thought, and wished that he could gloss over what had caused it just as easily.

"We're getting married on Tim's next leave," Moira was saying. "I'll look for a flat somewhere before then."

"There's no room for us in Moira's mum's house," Tim told them. "Not with Babs and wee Michael there as well."

"Well, I hope you've better luck than I had," Renee said. "All the places I looked at had just one tiny room, and that wouldn't be much use if you wanted to start a family."

Tim smiled wickedly at a suddenly beetroot-red Moira, then turned to Renee and Glynn again. "What about you two? No sign of any addition yet?"

"Not yet." It was Renee's turn to blush, and she wished that she hadn't made the remark in the first place. She'd never discussed having a family with Glynn, though. Could that be their salvation?

In bed that night, she led up to the subject cautiously. "Tim and Moira are well suited to each other, don't you think?"

He nodded. "Yes, they are, just as we were."

She hesitated, wondering if his use of the past tense meant anything, but decided that it didn't. "And Babs is lucky having wee Michael. If anything happens to Mike, God forbid, she'd have his son to remember him by."

"I suppose that would be a comfort to her, although I don't imagine she'd really need anything to help her remember."

"Glynn, I wish I could have your child." It was out, and she watched him anxiously. He seemed to be wrestling with conflicting emotions, and was silent for so long that she laid her hand on his arm. "Glynn?"

He looked at her as if he resented her breaking into his thoughts. "No, I don't think it's a good idea. After the war, maybe, when we've got our own house, but not before."

She saw that it would be useless to argue and, to change the subject, said the first thing that came into her head. "Jack Thomson's coming home on leave again. I forgot to show you his letter, with the excitement about Tim and Moira."

"I've never met this Jack," he said, slowly, reflectively.

"That's right, of course. You were at Porthcross when he was here the last time. You'll like him, he's really nice."

He raised his eyebrows at that. "Another of your boyfriends, was he? Has he sampled your charms as well?"

"Glynn Williams! That was nasty and uncalled-for." She swallowed her anger. "Jack and I have always been good friends, but that's all."

"I'm sorry, darling, but I'm jealous of all the men you knew before I met you."

"You've no need to be jealous of anybody, especially not Jack. We'd some good fun together, but it was purely platonic."

He reached for her then. "I love you," he said, as if that explained away all his doubts.

Unluckily for Renee, her husband remained jealous of Jack when finally they did meet, although they spent only an hour in each other's company, because Glynn had been late in coming home — it was another Monday.

Jack shook hands vigorously. "I'm very pleased to meet Renee's husband at long last. You're a very lucky man, Glynn. She's a marvellous girl, one of the best."

Glynn winked at Renee. "Yes, she is," he said, "and I know how lucky I am."

The subject of their exchange wished that Jack hadn't passed the remark, but hoped that Glynn would take it as it was meant.

"Have *you* found the right girl yet, Jack?" she asked, smiling to show Glynn that she would be quite happy if he had.

"Not yet. I've come to the conclusion that I must be too hard to please." Jack shrugged his shoulders and laughed.

Renee and Glynn stayed downstairs until Jack left, about half past eight, then Glynn said, "I'm tired, Renee. I think I'll go to bed now. You can stay with your mother for a while, if you like, she'll be better company than I will tonight."

"OK." She tried to make it sound light-hearted, matter-of-fact, but Anne noticed that she was upset.

"Is there anything wrong between you two?" she asked when the man went upstairs.

"There's nothing wrong, Mum. He's tired, that's all." She couldn't meet her mother's eyes.

"It's just that . . . some days there seems to be a sort of awkwardness there."

"Yes, some days," the girl admitted. "We've got our ups and downs just like any other married couple. It's nearly a year since the wedding, you know." A year in which she had been up in the clouds then down in the depths so many times, that it was a miracle she'd survived.

"Is it a year already?" Anne sounded most surprised. "Time certainly flies." She waited a few minutes, then said, "Jack seems to thrive on army life. He's more handsome every time I see him, and he looks like a young boy still. He'll be a proper catch for some lucky girl."

"Yes, I wish he'd find someone and settle down." Renee truly meant what she said, and her mother was satisfied that her daughter loved her husband, and wasn't interested in Jack Thomson or anyone else.

Glynn was reading in bed when Renee went upstairs. She hadn't noticed before, but the bedlight above his head showed several strands of silver through his dark hair, and she loved him all the more for them. "Would you like a cup of tea, darling?"

He looked up at her and smiled. "If you wouldn't mind."

When she carried up the tray, he was sitting up, blowing smoke rings at the ceiling. "Your Jack's quite a fellow."

"He's not my Jack," she protested. "He's not anybody's Jack yet."

"He'll never settle for anyone else," Glynn said, quietly. "He's in love with you."

"Rubbish!" Renee was alarmed. Although she'd suspected the same thing many times before, she'd convinced herself that it wasn't true, and wondered how Glynn had reached his conclusion.

"Yes, he is. It's in his eyes every time he looks at you." Another smoke ring went spiralling upwards.

"Well, I can't help that, Glynn, if it's true, though I don't believe it is, and I've told you before, I don't love him. I love you, my darling, and nobody else but you."

"I should hope so." His voice had lightened, and he was smiling now. "Leave the cups, sweetheart, I'm waiting for you to come to bed."

It wasn't until he was asleep that Renee remembered that it was Monday night. Glynn had actually made love to her on a Monday again, after all these months. She lay drowsily happy, thankful that, at last, he'd got his fears out of his system.

CHAPTER TWENTY-FOUR

When Glynn came home the following day, he looked worried, yet excited. "We're being posted, a week today."

"Oh, Glynn. Where are they sending you?" Renee had known it had to come, but it was still a shock.

"We haven't been told yet, but there's a big movement of troops on, as far as I can gather, so there must be something in the wind. Anyway, I've got my leave, starting tonight, though I haven't been told if it's embarkation leave or not.

"Oh, God, I hope not." She felt sick, then suddenly she remembered something. "I'd a letter from Tim this morning, and he said that they're being shifted, too. You must be right, Glynn, something's definitely going to happen."

"That's it, then." Glynn sounded almost glad as he picked up his knife and fork. "We've been lucky having almost a year together, you know. Hundreds of men had to leave their wives shortly after they were married."

"I know," she said, "but it's not much comfort."

That night, they lay talking for a long time, assuring each other of their love and trust, and voicing their hopes for the future — a not-too-distant future. They had made love before they began to talk, they made love again when they ran out of things to say, but Renee's mind kept strictly separate from her body. Sexual satisfaction did not quell her fears for his safety.

Mr Murchie was very understanding on Wednesday morning, when Renee told him that Glynn was to be moved away from Aberdeen, and let her have the rest of the week off to be with her husband. They spent the time exploring the city, and Renee was dismayed to find that she knew less about the history of her own home town than she did of Edinburgh, but Glynn was very impressed by the sparkling, granite grandeur of Marischal College, and the ancient splendour of King's College and St Machar's Cathedral.

Their nights were usually fully occupied, too, and Renee knew that her husband was trying to give her something to remember when he was far away from her. She would certainly never forget these wonderful, precious hours.

Monday was their last night together, and Glynn made sure that it was the best yet. Their rapturous unions were repeated until they were both exhausted and fell asleep locked in each other's arms. In the morning, she clung to him, unwilling to let him go, until he forcibly removed her arms. "You'll be late for work," he murmured. "I promise I'll write every day, darling."

"So will I," she vowed.

"I love you, my darling."

"I love you, dearest Glynn." One last, lingering kiss, then she dragged herself away, but her eyes were full of tears as she walked towards the bus stop.

Renee had accepted the parting by the time she went home at lunchtime, Anne was pleased to notice, having worried that she would be disconsolate at Glynn's departure. "It won't be long before he's back on leave," she said, brightly.

"I know, Mum, but I'm going to miss him, and if he's sent abroad, it might be long enough before he gets home."

"Lots of other girls are feeling exactly the same."

"That doesn't help me, or make me feel any better," the girl said, bitterly.

Next day, Renee came home to find her mother sitting in the armchair, red-eyed, and twisting a damp handkerchief in her hands. The girl was alarmed and went straight across to her. "What's wrong, Mum?"

Anne pointed to a letter lying on the mantelpiece. "It's from Pat Schaper," she said shakily. "Read it."

"Oh, Mum," Renee said, after she had read the first few lines. "I'm very, very sorry."

Fred Schaper had been shot dead in Libya. His captain sent on his personal belongings, and his daughter had written ". . . and there was a letter from you in his wallet. He was happy in Aberdeen, and was most disappointed that you wouldn't marry him. He told me, before he was sent overseas, that he wished the war were over, so he could go back to you. I'm very sorry, Mrs Gordon. I know you'll be just as upset as we are by my father's death."

Renee raised her eyes sadly, as she laid the letter down. "I don't know what to say to you, Mum. It's really terrible, and I know how you must be feeling."

A sob caught in Anne's throat. "I wish now I *had* married him when he asked me. We'd only have had a short time together before he was sent away, but . . . Now I've nothing to remember, and nothing to look forward to."

"Mum." The girl's arms went round her mother. "You've got the memories of all the happy times you spent together, and Fred understood why you wouldn't marry him then."

"We'd have had happier times if we'd been man and wife. Oh, Renee, he was a good, good man."

"I know that, and he loved you. Always remember that."

Renee offered to run to the telephone box to ring her office and tell them she wouldn't be back in the afternoon, but Anne wouldn't hear of it. "I'll be all right, honestly. I've done my weeping — all forenoon. It's crazy. I refused to marry Fred in case he was killed, and now that it's happened, I wish I'd said yes."

"It's only natural, Mum." Renee hadn't the heart to remind her that she'd been warned at the time that she would feel like this if anything happened. "Well, if you're sure you don't want me to stay with you, I'll have to think about getting back. I'll just make a quick cup of tea before I go."

"Oh, Renee." Anne looked at her regretfully. "I'm sorry. I didn't make any dinner for you, and you must be starving."

"No, it's all right. I couldn't eat anything, anyway. A cup of tea's all I want." When she left the house, about ten minutes later, Renee said, "Don't brood, Mum. You can't change things, you know."

When Glynn's letter arrived, a few days later, it gave little information. One sheet of paper was all he had written.

My Darling,

We're somewhere in England, I can't say more than that. We came here in a huge convoy and it was a very tiring journey. I miss you every minute, and I'm aching to hold you in my arms again. I can't write much, because they keep us very busy.

All my love, dear wife,

Glynn

It was Renee's first love letter from him. She read and reread it a dozen times that day, and felt ashamed of being so happy when her mother was still mourning for Fred Schaper.

For just over three weeks, Renee and Glynn kept their promises to write every day, then his letters began to miss a day. He apologised, and kept repeating how busy he was, so she forgave him and carried on writing each evening.

She took her mother out at least once a week, having had great difficulty, at first, in convincing Anne that she must face the world occasionally, and the outing relieved the boring monotony of their flat lives. It gave them something, other than Brown and Company and the problems of food rationing, to talk about.

Glynn's letters were now coming once a week, and his wife followed his lead and wrote every Sunday night. He still wrote of his undying love, as she did to him, but the magic seemed to have gone out of the correspondence.

When Tim and Moira were married, Anne and Renee went home feeling more downhearted than ever. The bride had looked so wonderfully happy when she came out of John Knox Church — where Mike and Babs had also been married — and the groom so proud, that they both realised, more deeply than ever, how empty their existence was.

A welcome diversion for the two lonely women came with a visit from Jack Thomson, the day after Tim's wedding. He had them laughing in no time with his stories, and they blessed him for his timely appearance.

"Have you heard from Glynn lately?" he asked Renee.

"Yes, he writes every week," she said, cheerfully now. She had also kept writing to Jack at irregular intervals, the usual friendly letters.

"How about you, Mrs Gordon? Are you still hearing from . . . Fred, wasn't it?"

Renee rushed in, to save her mother. "Fred Schaper was killed, Jack." She wished that she had told him about it when she was writing, but she'd thought it was best not to.

"Oh, I'm very sorry." Jack's head went down, and there was an awkward silence.

Anne was first to break it. "You'll be staying for tea, of course, Jack?"

"Thanks. If it's all right with you?"

"Of course it's all right. I hadn't really thought about what we were going to have, but I can rustle up something."

She "rustled up" an omelette, using dried eggs, and while they were eating it, Jack asked, "How's Tim? Are you still hearing from him?" He grinned mischievously when they told him that Tim and Moira had been married the previous day. "Poor Tim. Caught at last."

"They looked very happy," Anne remarked.

"I'm sure they did." He was serious now. "Tim's another lucky man. Moira'll make him a good wife."

"What about you, Jack?" Anne smiled kindly. "Is there no sign of you being hit by Cupid's little arrow?"

He shrugged. "Cupid's given up on me, I think."

Renee felt his eyes on her, and her heart skipped a beat. It felt good to think that a man was in love with her, a man other than her husband . . . It was time Glynn was back, she thought, hastily. It shouldn't be long now. He'd been posted just after Jack was here the last time, so he must be due home soon.

When he was leaving, Jack said, quietly, "This is the last time I'll see you for a while. It's strictly hush-hush, but there's troops training all over the south of England, and it's rumoured all leave's to be stopped."

"Oh, no," Renee said anxiously. "I hope Glynn gets home before that."

"I hope so, too, for your sake." Jack looked at her quickly. "It looks like the big push this time — invasion, I think, but mum's the word."

"Renee," Anne said, "you haven't been out all day and it's quite a nice evening. Why don't you walk along to the bus with Jack and have a breath of fresh air?"

"Good idea." Renee went to get her jacket.

Jack's face had lit up. "Cheerio then, Mrs Gordon."

"Good luck, Jack. We'll be hearing from you, but look after yourself."

Renee walked along the pavement beside the young man, feeling rather ill at ease at being alone like this with Jack after such a long time.

"We've walked this road together quite a few times before," he remarked, making her more uncomfortable than ever.

"Yes," she managed to laugh.

"B.G.," he said, with a wry smile.

"B.G.?" She was genuinely puzzled.

"Before Glynn." He turned to her, and she could see for herself what her husband had meant about Jack's love for her showing in his eyes.

"There's the bus coming," she said quickly, as they turned the corner. "You'll have to run."

"I'll get the next one." He took her arm and piloted her, in the opposite direction from the bus stop, to a small lane where they were out of sight of the main road. "Why did you marry him, Renee?"

She felt cornered, with her back against a wall and Jack standing in front of her expecting a straight answer. "I fell in love with him," she said quietly.

"Why didn't you wait for me? You knew I loved you, didn't you?" He looked at her steadily. "I've always loved you, ever since I came to lodge with your mother and you were only a kid."

She knew she should try to move, try to break this up, but there was still some sort of tender feeling in her heart for this man. "You never told me you loved me, Jack," she said, after a moment. "Not in so many words."

"I thought you loved Fergus Cooper," he said sadly. "You *did* love him, couldn't see past him, for all that he made a fool of you."

"I know, and Tim and you both warned me, and my granny, but I couldn't help myself. I was being used and I didn't know, or maybe I just wouldn't admit it. But I did get him out of my system, the last time he was here. We'd an almighty row and I told him how much I hated him."

"Did you now?" His voice was slightly sarcastic though he was smiling. "And what did he say to that? Knowing Fergus, he wouldn't have taken that lying down."

Renee hesitated. "I may as well tell you everything. It doesn't make any difference now."

She started at the very beginning of her association with Fergus Cooper, and poured it all out, faltering only when she came to their first intercourse. She made no attempt to excuse herself for anything that had happened, and Jack let her carry on, his face impassive. When she came to a halt, after describing the final, horrible meeting, she looked at him pitifully. "I suppose you're shocked to learn I wasn't the sweet, innocent girl you thought?"

He shook his head. "I knew what was going on, Renee. He told me about his other girls, boasting about them, and he even boasted about . . . your mother and you."

"Oh, no." She felt sick suddenly. "He told you about Mum and me, too?"

"He knew what I felt about you, and he told me to keep off. He was an out-and-out rotter, and I tried to warn you."

She hung her head. "I couldn't see past him at that time, but I'd begun to realise I felt something for you before I finished with him. I even told him that night, that he couldn't hold a candle to you, that you were decent and caring! Everything that he wasn't."

"Thank you for those kind words." His smile was crooked.

"I was in love with you, Jack, when we were going out together, but you didn't say anything to me before you were called up."

"I wanted to, Renee. God, I wanted to, but I couldn't believe you were over Fergus."

"Jack," she said softly, knowing that what she was about to say was foolish, and could lead to complications, "if you'd asked me to marry you at that time, I'd have said yes."

With a quick intake of breath, he placed his arm on the wall behind her and leaned over her. "What a bloody fool I was. To think you could have been mine all this time. How many years? Three, at least, nearly four."

"I suppose it must be." Her knees were buckling under her, and she thought he must hear the banging of her heart against her ribcage.

He let his hand slide down the wall on to her shoulder. "I'm not going to ask you to be disloyal to your husband, Renee. I had my chance and let it slip through my fingers, but I don't think he'd mind if you let me kiss you, for one last time?"

The girl pushed aside all thought of how much Glynn *would* mind if he knew about it, and held her face up for Jack's long, tender, smouldering kiss, which, unexpectedly, opened the floodgates of their pent-up emotions.

"Renee, my darling, darling, Renee," he whispered. "God! I wish I could turn back the clock."

"So do I," she murmured, forgetting, for the minute, her marriage vows and her husband, or perhaps deliberately not wanting to remember them.

They clung to each other, exchanging desperate, hungry kisses, until Jack stepped back, letting his arms fall to his sides. "No, this is too much for me, Renee. I've dreamt about this so long, and I've wanted you, like I'm wanting you this very minute, but . . ."

She flung caution, and her principles, to the wind. "I want you, too, Jack."

"No," he almost moaned. "We can't. Remember Glynn. He's a good, decent man, and I can't do that to him."

Their tormented eyes locked, their need for each other crying out to be relieved. "I'll always remember this, Renee," Jack said, brokenly, at last. "It's a memory I'll carry with me wherever I go and whatever happens to me. But you're married to Glynn, and there's an end to it."

"You're right," she whispered sadly. "I'm married to Glynn, and I do love him, as much as he loves me, but . . . I love you, too, Jack."

"Say it again, my darling."

"I love you, Jack."

"That's something I never dreamed you would say to me, not since you were married, anyway, and it'll stay with me for ever." He leaned forward and kissed her forehead. "You don't know how happy you've made me, but I'll have to leave you. Your mother'll be wondering why you're away so long. I've missed the last bus to Peterhead, as well. What a pair we are."

They stared at each other for a second, then burst into near-hysterical laughter. "What'll you do, Jack? Mum said you could sleep on our settee, remember, so will we just go back?"

"Oh, no." His smile faded. "I couldn't face your mother just now. She'd see straight away how much I love you, for I couldn't hide it tonight, not after . . ."

"Where'll you go, then?"

"I'll get a bed in a hostel, or something, and go home in the morning."

"Will you come to see me on your way back from Peterhead?"

"No, darling, I'd better not for all our sakes. Yours, mine, and especially Glynn's." He pulled her out of the lane, but a bus was drawing in to the stop, so he had no time to say anything more than, "Goodbye, Renee. I love you."

"I love you, Jack." She watched him sprinting across the road and jumping on to the moving vehicle, to be carried away from her. Sanity returned then, and she walked slowly towards the house.

As she closed the front door behind her, she switched on the hall light and looked at her watch. It was nearly ten, and they'd gone out at half past eight. Her mother would know that something had been going on. Hoping that the cool night air had cooled down her burning cheeks, she held her head high as she entered the living room, praying that she wouldn't be faced with a barrage of questions.

Anne was sitting in her dressing-gown, but her face was devoid of any accusations. "I was beginning to think something had happened to you, Renee. Where on earth have you been all this time? Did you go into town to see Jack on to the country bus?"

The excuse was a life-saver to the girl. "Yes, Mum. There was a bus coming when we went to the end of our street, and I went on without thinking. I'm sure Jack was glad of the company, though." More lies, she reflected, when she'd thought she was done with them, but she couldn't tell her mother the truth.

She went upstairs, not daring to write her usual Sunday night letter to Glynn. She couldn't think straight, after what had happened between Jack and her. In bed, she relived the time they'd spent in the lane. It *was* possible to love two people at once, she realised, but it usually meant that at least one of them would be hurt, maybe both.

She did love Glynn, that was still true, and she loved Jack, she had just rediscovered, and the only thing she felt guilty about was the falsehood she had told her mother. She shouldn't have done that. She should have been honest and told her exactly what had happened, because they'd done nothing really wrong.

Yet a small voice inside her reminded her that it wasn't due to her that she hadn't committed adultery, and she flushed at the memory of her desire for Jack Thomson.

CHAPTER TWENTY-FIVE

1st June, 1944

Darling Renee,

It's bad news, I'm afraid. All leave has been cancelled, but I can't say any more. It might be a long time until I see you again, and I'm really sick about it. We got a 48-hour pass last week, so I went to Porthcross again, as I didn't have time to come to Aberdeen. Don't worry if you don't hear from me for a while, but remember that I'll always be thinking about you, and that I love you with all my heart.

Your adoring husband,
Glynn.

Renee looked at her mother across the breakfast table. "Jack was right. All the leave has been cancelled, so Glynn won't be coming home for a long time. I wish he'd been able to come here instead of Porthcross, though."

"At least he went to see his mother." Anne felt very sorry for her daughter, but tried to be sensible.

"Yes, and I bet that had pleased her." Especially when he hadn't had time to come to see his wife, Renee thought viciously, then realised that she was probably doing the poor woman an injustice.

Would Glynn have seen Eiddwen again while he was there? This was something which had worried Renee each time he'd told her he'd spent a quick weekend in Wales. His mother could have tried to throw them together, hoping to renew the old romance.

Could Glynn have fallen in love with Eiddwen again? Was he, like Renee herself, in love with two people at the same time? The thought hurt, and she knew how much it would hurt Glynn if he ever found out about Jack. She vacillated between regretting what had happened in the lane, and being glad that she'd sent Jack off happy, to face whatever lay ahead of him.

She was sure now that Glynn's mother would never accept her. He didn't refer to it at all now, but he had told her in previous letters that he'd tackled his mother when he was there, asking her to invite Renee to Porthcross, to get to know her, but her answer had always been no.

Renee's thoughts returned to what this letter was really telling her. Glynn must be involved in this "big push" which Jack had mentioned, this invasion, and he would be in great danger. She turned cold at the idea of Glynn being killed. Even the memory of the heartaches he had caused her during most of their marriage — his inability to cope with her association with Fergus Cooper — couldn't extinguish the flame of anxiety she felt for his safety now.

"Don't be so upset about it, Renee." Anne's voice brought the girl out of her reverie. "I'm sure Glynn's going to be all right, even if he is sent abroad." Her cheerfulness belied the sudden, tragic sadness which came into her eyes, and Renee remembered that her mother had good reason to be bitter about the war. Poor Fred Schaper.

And Bill Scroggie was dead, too, although that had happened in this country, and they had never learned the cause. She shivered at the thought of how precarious the life of a serviceman was in wartime, and prayed that nothing would happen to any of the soldiers she knew. They were all good men, like Fred and Bill had been.

The day after she received Glynn's letter, the news was broadcast on the wireless, and splashed all over the front pages of the newspapers, that the Allies had made landings in Normandy on the 6th. It was the "big push", an invasion on a scale that no one had foreseen. Renee followed the daily reports of advances, of setbacks, of losses, of victories, thinking all the time of Glynn, Jack and Tim — and of Mike, too, who would probably be amongst those making their way up through Italy.

It was four agonising weeks after D-Day before another letter came from Glynn. He wrote that she had likely heard about the invasion, and assured her that he was well. He ended his brief scrawl, "I miss you, darling. Your loving husband, Glynn."

Her thankfulness at knowing he was safe was only temporary, because she realised he was still facing danger every day, every hour, every minute, and she fervently hoped that he would understand how worried she was and write as often as he could.

A few weeks elapsed before she received another letter from him, another short scribble, hoping that she was well and sending love. One sentence threw her into a panic. "I'm still alive — just!" Things must have been pretty bad when he wrote that.

A visit from Moira Donaldson didn't help matters. "Tim's been wounded," the agitated girl said, as soon as she went in. "I'd a letter this morning, but somebody else wrote it for him because it's his hands that have been hurt. He's going to be sent to a hospital in this country as soon as he's fit enough."

"Oh, Moira! That's terrible," Renee burst out, while Anne said quietly, "I'm sorry."

"I'm not." Moira looked defiant. "I'm not sorry if it's taken him away from the fighting. I won't have to worry any more about him being killed, you see, and his hands will heal in time, I hope." Her expression changed. "Does that sound awful to you? That I'm glad he's been wounded?"

"No, no, Moira," Anne assured her. "I can quite understand how you must be feeling, and thank you very much for coming to tell us about him."

"I thought you'd like to know straight away, Mrs Gordon, you've always been so good to him. I've written to his mother and father, but I just had to get out of our house. I can't say what I really feel in front of Babs, when she's still so worried about Mike. Oh!" She became embarrassed. "You'll be worrying about Glynn, of course, Renee. I'm sorry, I just didn't think. Have you heard from him lately?"

"A few days ago. He doesn't get much time to write, but even a line or two lets me know he's still alive."

"I know exactly how you feel." Moira nodded.

When the other girl left, Renee thought sadly of Jack Thomson, who was also involved in the bitter struggle being fought in Europe. She had heard nothing from him since she had kissed him goodbye in the lane. Why hadn't he written to her? Surely he couldn't have been . . .? No, no! He just hadn't had time to write, that was all.

Two more letters came from Glynn over the course of the next three weeks, but still no word from Jack, and Anne had heard nothing from Mike Donaldson for some time, either.

"Of course," she said to Renee one day, "he'd write to Babs any minute he's got, and she'd have let us know if anything had happened to him."

The anxious days crawled past, with the two women glued to the news bulletins on the wireless as often as possible, although they didn't know which field of the struggle either Glynn or Jack were in.

"No wonder some wives go off the rails," Renee remarked, after six long weeks of looking in vain for a letter from her husband. "This suspense is getting me down."

At lunchtime three days later, her face blanched when her mother handed her an official envelope which had been delivered after the girl had left to go to work, and she turned it over and over in her hands.

"Would you like me to open it for you?" Anne asked, solicitously, having been tempted to do so many times before her daughter came home.

"No, I'll do it myself." Renee slit the envelope with trembling fingers and drew out a single, typed sheet. She began to read it aloud, her voice faltering and fading to a whisper by the time she had finished. "We regret to inform you that 15792, Sergeant Williams, Glynn, Royal Artillery, has been reported missing."

"Oh, dear God!" Anne's arms went round her daughter as she held on to the back of the nearest chair.

"Oh, no!" Renee said, her eyes wide with disbelief. "It's not true! It can't be true!"

"It must be true, before they sent the letter," Anne said, gently. "And it just says 'missing' not 'killed'." Anne tried to sound optimistic, but her spirits were as low as the girl's.

"He could have been killed, though, if he's missing." Renee's whole body was shaking violently now, and her face and lips were blueish-white.

Anne recognised the signs of shock. "I'll go and make us a cup of tea." She went to put the kettle on, and came straight back. "There must be some hope, you know, or they'd have put 'missing believed killed'."

Renee stared at her blankly then said, "Yes."

"You must keep hoping. Never give up hope."

"No." Her voice was flat. Anne made the tea very sweet and carried through the two steaming cups. "Drink this. I've put sugar in to help you."

Grimacing at the unaccustomed taste — she'd stopped taking sugar in tea when it became scarce —

Renee sipped it obediently, and the colour gradually returned to her cheeks.

"Would you like to go to bed? I could fill a hot water bottle for you?" Anne hovered anxiously.

"No, thanks. I'd rather sit here."

"I'll turn off the oven, I think." The woman knew that neither of them would feel like eating the shepherd's pie she'd made.

Renee kept wringing her hands until her mother could stand it no longer. "I'll go along to the phone box and tell them you won't be back to work this afternoon. Sheila's got a different dinner hour from you, hasn't she?" When the girl nodded, Anne went on, "Will you be all right till I come back?"

The girl seemed to rally for a minute. "I'll be all right, but don't be too long."

"I'll be back in a jiffy."

When Anne passed on the sad news to Sheila Daun, the girl expressed her dismay, then added, "I'll tell Old Bill she won't be in. He's quite good, really, so there won't be any bother."

"Thanks, Sheila."

Renee was sitting in the same position when Anne returned, sunk back against the cushions as if her spine had caved in.

"That didn't take long," Anne said breathlessly. "Sheila's going to tell your boss, and she said to give you her love and say how sorry she is about . . ."

Renee lifted her head. She had been thinking while her mother was out, and now felt the need to unburden her soul. "Sit down, Mum. I want to tell you something."

The words came spilling out: the tragedy of her wedding night in its entirety; the loveless nights of her honeymoon; the Monday-night punishments which Glynn had inflicted on himself and her.

Anne's face had tightened in agony and disapproval during the recital of Renee's secret, passionate meetings with Fergus Cooper, but at the mention of Glynn's cruel behaviour, her expression softened in pity for her daughter. "Why didn't you tell me what was going on?"

"I'd to bear with him and work things out for myself, it was all my fault. He was eaten up with jealousy because I'd let Fergus use me over and over again, even after I'd seen him making love to another girl, and knew he was a rotter. That was really what he found so difficult to understand."

Anne rose and went over to sit on the pouffe beside the girl's chair. "I'm not surprised he didn't understand that, and I didn't realise exactly what Fergus had done to you. I knew you couldn't see past him, but I didn't know how much he was to blame for everything. He always swore it was you that wouldn't let him alone, and pestered him until he had sex with you. I'm sorry for believing him, Renee, and doubly sorry for the part I played in your misery for a while."

Her daughter regarded her sadly. "It wasn't your fault. Fergus could make any woman believe whatever he liked to tell her. I found that out myself, later . . . Mum, I went to meet him the night before he went away the last time."

"I know."

"That's when it all blew up. I wanted to let him know how I felt and I'd a blazing row with him. I wouldn't have had anything more to do with him, even if he hadn't gone away."

"He told me he finished with you." Anne's eyes were apologetic for her credulity. "But by that time, I didn't trust him as far as I could see him, and I'd already told him never to come back to this house."

"He told me that, trying to make me feel sorry for him." The girl's voice was low. "I said I was glad."

Anne sat up straighter on the low seat. "But Glynn's a different matter. I thought there was something wrong between you, then you'd seem happy again for a while and I couldn't make it out."

Renee explained then about Glynn switching from Mondays only, to any night except Mondays. "I was perfectly content all the rest of the week, you see, and I really did — do — love him."

"Was that twisted behaviour still going on when he was posted?"

"No. He came home one Monday night — the night Jack Thomson was here, remember? — and he took it into his head that Jack was in love with me, and he was so jealous that I think he forgot it was a Monday and made love to me. There was no difficulty the rest of the week, either, and the next Monday was his last night here, and we made love that night, too. I was really happy that he'd got Mondays out of his system."

Anne looked right into her daughter's eyes. "He's never been home since then, of course, so you won't really know if he did get over it, or if it was the circumstances on those two Mondays that made him . . ."

"I don't know, Mum, but I've got to keep believing he'd got over it, the same as I've got to keep believing he'll come back."

"He will come back, I'm sure of it."

"Have you been shocked at what I've told you, Mum?"

Anne lifted her shoulders. "I suppose I have, I can't deny it. Not all of it came as a surprise, of course, but the rest was a bit of a shock. I'm glad you told me, though."

Renee waited a moment before she said, firmly, "I've more to tell you, I'm afraid. I have to get everything out now I've started, and this'll probably shock you just as much."

"I doubt if anything else is going to shock me today." Anne let out a short, bitter laugh. "Go ahead."

"Remember the last time Jack was here? Just before the invasion? And you told me to walk with him to the bus stop?"

Her mother's expression changed from curiosity to grim apprehension. "You were away for nearly an hour and a half, and you told me you'd seen him on to the country bus?"

"That wasn't true. We spent the whole time in that little lane round the corner."

"I thought you couldn't have taken an hour and a half to go into town and back. My God, Renee! You didn't . . . ?"

"No, we didn't, but it was Jack that said no. I would have, in a flash, if he'd wanted me to."

"Renee Gordon! No, it's Williams now. Did you forget that?" Anne looked more shocked by this last confession than by anything which had gone before.

"Only for a few minutes, but Jack didn't. That's why he wouldn't carry on. It only started with him giving me a goodbye kiss, and it sort of got out of hand after that, until Jack called a halt." The girl hesitated, then made up her mind that she may as well confess everything. "I love Jack, too."

Pursing her lips, Anne gave a low whistle. "You've really got your life in a muddle, haven't you? I used to wish, years ago, that you'd fall in love with Jack, but . . ."

Renee sighed. "I *was* in love with Jack years ago, but he wouldn't admit that he loved me. I guessed he did, from little things he said, but he never came right out with it. He told me, that night in the lane, that he always believed I'd never get over Fergus."

"He knew about you and Fergus, did he?" Anne seemed surprised.

"He knew all along, ever since it started, really, and Fergus had boasted to him about . . . me, and told him to keep off. Anyway, I told him I'd have married him if he'd asked me before he was called up."

"Your love life's been one long mix-up, then?" Anne's smile was a little crooked.

"I suppose it has. I thought Jack didn't love me, and I went mad amongst the boys for a while."

"I remember," Anne said, dryly.

"And then Fred Schaper brought Glynn here and I fell in love with him." Renee's face suddenly crumpled. "Now Glynn's missing, Fred's been killed, and I don't know what's happened to Jack." She sobbed loudly, and her mother let her weep. It was the best antidote for the shock she'd just received, and for all the worry she had gone through previously. When she calmed down, Renee said, quietly, "You must despise me for all the awful things I've done."

Anne shook her head. "I pity you. You made your own life a misery for most of the time."

"I know. I've been very stupid, haven't I?"

"You should have told me about the trouble you and Glynn were having. I wouldn't have been able to do anything, but you'd have felt better, not bottling it all up. I'm glad everything's out in the open now . . . I suppose it is all out?"

"Oh, yes." The girl summoned up a watery smile. "There's no more skeletons in the cupboard."

"Thank goodness for that . . . Could you eat something now, do you think, seeing you've got everything off your chest?"

"You know, I believe I could."

Anne insisted on sleeping with her daughter that night. "Just so I'll know you're all right," she explained.

Renee's emotions had been ripped apart since she had read the fateful letter, and when she became tearful her mother tried to comfort her as best she could.

"You've come through quite a lot in your life, you'll come through this, too. Once Glynn comes back, you'll be able to laugh at yourself for worrying so much."

"If he comes back," Renee whispered.

"Yes, he'll come back. He's all right, I tell you. Now, go to sleep. You'll feel better in the morning."

Anne slipped out of bed quietly next day, to let Renee sleep on. They would understand in the office if she didn't go in today. It was ten past twelve before the girl made her appearance downstairs.

"Why didn't you waken me, Mum?"

"You needed the rest. I was going to shout to you when the dinner was ready. It'll be about half an hour yet. Would you like a cup of tea while we're waiting?"

"Yes, please. My mouth feels like it's got half Aberdeen Beach in it." Anne laughed, pleased that Renee could joke a little. She was definitely going to see it through.

As year-long week succeeded year-long week, with no word about either Glynn or Jack, Renee tried to appear cheerful, although all hope was fading fast within her. At last, almost three months after Glynn had been reported missing, she received notification that he had been seriously wounded, and was now in a hospital in England.

"Thank God!" she murmured, through dry lips. "At least he's alive."

"I told you." Anne was smiling as they turned and hugged each other.

"He must be very bad, though, or else he'd have written to me himself," Renee said anxiously, after a few minutes.

"He'll write as soon as he can," her mother comforted her.

The Allies were now forging ahead in Europe, and the wireless and newspaper reports gave some hope that the war would soon be at an end, and the two women, like millions of others, were happier than they had been for some time.

They were very pleased when Tim Donaldson called one evening, with Moira, to let them know that he was home. His hands were still bandaged, but the doctors were apparently satisfied with the way they were healing.

"He nearly lost his right hand, you know." Moira could talk about it calmly, now that it was clear that such a calamity would never occur.

"The operations and grafts were all successful," Tim told them, "but I've to attend Outpatients here once a week for a while."

"That's good news." Anne beamed at them. "I'm very happy for you both."

"Me, too," added Renee. "And I hope it's not long till Glynn can write and tell me how he's doing."

"Oh, you've heard from him?" Moira had been afraid to ask.

"No, he hasn't been able to write himself yet, but I had notification that he was wounded, that's all I know."

"But you know he's not missing any longer. That's good." Moira laid her hand on Renee's.

"Is there any word of a house for you two yet?"

"Oh, yes, I nearly forgot to tell you." Moira giggled. "I found a small flat to let in Chapel Street, just two rooms, with the lavatory on the stairs, but it's very nice.

We're starting to buy furniture and things, and I suppose it'll take a while before we get everything as we want it."

"I should be able to help with the decorating once they give me the all-clear at the hospital," Tim said.

Anne laughed. "You don't know what you're taking on. We painted and stippled the two bedrooms a few weeks back, and it was some job, wasn't it, Renee?"

"You can say that again." The girl had actually been very glad of the task to help take her mind off her worries. "How's Mike? Has Babs heard from him lately?"

Tim nodded. "She gets letters occasionally, not much in them, of course, but at least he's still writing. She worries about him a lot."

"I know what it's like," Renee said with feeling.

As they were leaving, Tim said, "Is there any word of Jack Thomson yet? Moira said you hadn't heard from him for a long time."

Anne glanced at her daughter, then answered for her. "No, there's nothing yet."

Tim looked thoughtful. "I'd have thought his mother would have let you know if anything had happened to him. After all, he lodged here for years."

"That did cross my mind," Anne said slowly. "But it's nearly four years since he was called up, and she maybe thinks we're not interested now."

"He came to see you when he was on leave, so she must know you'd want to hear about him. Well, we'll have to be off. You'll let us know when you hear from Glynn, Renee? And from Jack?"

When Anne came back from seeing them out, she said, "Tim's looking quite well, considering. Moira'll just have to feed him up."

"He made me think, though." Renee took the writing pad from the top drawer of the sideboard. "I'm going to write to Jack's mother, to see if she knows anything about him."

"I'd better do it." Anne grabbed the pad and sat down at the card table. "It wouldn't look right if you did it, being a married woman. Have you your fountain-pen handy?"

Renee rummaged in her handbag to find it, and they composed the letter together — a short note, couched in gentle terms, not to cause Mrs Thomson needless worry or grief.

"I'm not too sure about this," Anne observed, after she licked the flap of the envelope. "I wondered about doing it before, but I thought I'd better not. Jack's maybe trying to be honourable by not writing to another man's wife, especially after he's told her he loves her."

"He wouldn't stop writing because of that." Renee's mouth set in a thin, obstinate line.

"He knew how you felt about him, but he knows you still love Glynn, so he could have thought he was betraying Glynn if he kept on writing to you, reminding you."

"I suppose that's the decent kind of thing Jack would think," Renee admitted. "But I still want to know about him."

Mrs Thomson replied by return post. She'd heard from Jack up until about six weeks ago, telling her that he was quite well and not to worry.

Her letter went on:

> Thank you for your concern for my son, because I am worrying about him now, it's been so long since I heard. I'll let you know as soon as I get a letter, to set your mind at rest. Jack was very happy when he lodged with you, he was always speaking about you and your daughter. I hope her husband recovers quickly from his wounds. Thank you for looking after Jack so well when he was working in Aberdeen, and God grant he comes home safely.
>
> Yours in friendship,
> Wilma Thomson.

Renee's hopes had plummetted to rock bottom by the time she reached the end. "That's it, then. His mother was hearing from him, so he must have just stopped writing to me. He must have wanted me to believe he'd been killed."

Anne chose her next words carefully. "It might be best for you and Glynn if Jack didn't come back."

Renee gasped with horror. "That's a horrible thing to say! How could you, Mum? I thought you liked him."

"I do like him. I love him like a son, but . . . life's not going to be easy for him, or for you, if he comes back to Aberdeen after the war. You'd have to make a complete break with him, otherwise it wouldn't be fair to Glynn."

"I realise that." Renee spoke slowly. "It's something that's been torturing me for quite a while. I worry about it, but I wouldn't wish him dead."

"I wasn't wishing him dead," Anne snapped. "That's not what I meant at all."

"It sounded like it to me," the girl said, pettishly.

"Listen, Renee. His own mother hasn't heard from him for weeks now, and it's a possibility you'll have to face. You know, you weren't being fair to Jack that night. He'd already accepted that you were married to somebody else, and that he'd lost you, but you gave him new, false hope."

"I didn't plan it," Renee protested. "It just happened."

"I suppose it was mostly my fault for telling you to go to the bus with him." Anne had been regretting that suggestion ever since her daughter had told her what transpired.

When Glynn Williams did write, at last, it gave his young wife further cause to worry, about more than the ominous shakiness of his hand.

> I was unconscious in a French hospital for weeks after they found me, apparently. My leg was shattered, but they're speaking about fixing me up with a new one if things don't work out right. I couldn't write before, because my right arm was wounded, too, and by the time I was sent to England, I wondered if it would be best to let you carry on thinking I was dead.

I asked a nurse to write to my mother, and the next thing I knew, Mam had sent Eiddwen to cheer me up. This place is only about an hour's journey from Porthcross.

"Damn his mother!" Renee exclaimed, in the middle of reading the letter out loud. "She wants to split us up."

"How on earth do you make that out?" Anne sounded mystified. "She was only sending somebody to visit him. She maybe didn't feel up to going herself."

"She hadn't wanted to go herself. She was disappointed that Glynn didn't marry Eiddwen, and she's trying to get them together."

Anne sighed, but said, "Go on. What else does he say?"

Renee bent over the letter again.

I was very glad to see her, and I told her what I'd been thinking, but she said I wasn't being fair to you and made me write. I hope you haven't been too upset, never hearing from me for so long, but I'm still undergoing a lot of treatment, and my innermost thoughts are all jumbled up. I don't want you to come here, because I really couldn't face seeing you just yet.

The girl looked up again. "He's been able to face seeing Eiddwen again, though."

"He'd no choice about that," Anne said gently. "Does he say anything else?"

Renee glanced down quickly. "'I hope you are keeping well. Love, Glynn.' That's all."

"At least he's sent his love," Anne pointed out.

Renee remembered Bill Scroggie saying that most men found it easy to end a letter by writing "love", when she had told him about Tim and Jack writing to her. She kept the thought to herself, and agreed with her mother, rather reluctantly, when Anne said that she would have to await developments.

On the 8th May 1945, just a few days later, the war in Europe came to an end, and both women wept at the welcome news, but it was another three long weeks before Glynn Williams wrote again. His handwriting was steadier, and he told her first about some of the treatment he was receiving.

Then he went on: "Eiddwen has been very good. She comes nearly every second evening, and she's a great tonic. I don't know how I would have coped with all this, if she hadn't been around."

Renee let the pages drop to the table. "I can see what's happening, you know. He's falling in love with her all over again. That's what she wants, and so does his mother."

Anne's eyes were full of sympathy. "Just think, though. Wouldn't you rush to help an old boyfriend if he was wounded and in hospital near you, hundreds of miles from his wife? You'd do it for Jack, if he was in that position, wouldn't you?"

"That's different. I love Jack."

"That girl more than likely loves Glynn."

Her daughter was silent, considering this, then admitted to herself that it was probably true. "If I knew Jack was in hospital somewhere, I'd go to him straight away," she said at last. "Like I'd have gone to Glynn, if he'd let me."

"Yes, Glynn was wrong in telling you not to go." Anne's tone suggested that she was angry with her son-in-law for causing this extra, unnecessary suffering to his wife. "A man in his physical and mental state could easily imagine he's in love with the person showing him care and devotion. Does he give any explanation?"

Renee carried on reading aloud.

> I've told Eiddwen how much I loved you, still love you, and she understands. I'm telling you, now, how much I loved Eiddwen, how much I love her again. I hope you can bring yourself to understand and forgive.
>
> Believe me, my dear, this is the best way. It wouldn't work with us. I can't forget that terrible scene on our wedding night, for I touched the depths of Hell. I never recovered, and I made your life a hell with the way I behaved afterwards.
>
> Our marriage was never normal, and I think the burning anger and jealousy which was with me on that first night would return to haunt me over the years if we were together. I loved Eiddwen long before I met you, and she made one misjudgement, which I can freely forgive. My life with her could be happy and carefree, but I haven't said one word

of this to her, and I don't intend to unless you agree to divorce me.

I want to marry her, so please consider this carefully. Put all the blame on me, and try not to think harshly of . . .

Glynn.

Renee heaved a shuddering sigh when she laid the letter on the table, her hand trembling in agitation.

"You'll divorce him, of course?" Anne eyed her keenly.

"Why should I? That girl's not going to get my husband."

"Not even if your husband wants that girl, not you?"

"No! I've suffered enough, Mum." The girl's face had tightened.

"He was in love with her when Fred took him here first," Renee reminded her. "He maybe never got over her. He saw her when he went to Porthcross after we were married, remember? The time I was supposed to be going with him, but Sheila broke her leg and I couldn't go. And he likely saw her every time he popped up there when he had short passes before D-Day."

"It's more or less the same with you and Jack Thomson," Anne observed, quietly.

The girl paused. "Yes, I never thought of it like that. I'm the pot calling the kettle black, you mean?"

"Exactly, and you'll have to forget about Jack, or accept it if Glynn decides he loves this girl more than he loves you."

"I'm going to lose both of them. I can feel it." Renee's eyes filled with tears. "Something must have happened to Jack, when there's been no word from him or his mother."

The girl's doubts about Glynn were to be answered when he wrote the next time.

> Renee,
>
> Reading between the lines in your last letter, I can tell that you're jealous of Eiddwen. I wish I could say you're mistaken, but you're not. I've turned this over and over in my mind, because I knew I was going to hurt one of you whatever I did, and I'm sorry that it has to be you.

"I'm sorry, too, Renee," Anne murmured, "but you have been expecting it, haven't you?"

"I suppose so, but it's not a nice feeling to think that you're about to be thrown away like yesterday's newspaper."

Anne raised her eyebrows. "He'll never come back to you, even if you don't divorce him."

"She's not going to have him." Renee gripped her mouth.

"She has him now. Be sensible about it."

The girl picked up the letter and read it through again, silently. "He says he still loves me," she said pathetically as she put it down once more.

Anne patted her hand. "Yes, but he also says he can't go on with the marriage. Face facts, Renee. Give him up. You can't cling to Glynn just because you've lost

Jack. You'll get over this, and start to make a new life for yourself. You'll find somebody else, you're not twenty-two yet."

Her daughter was still stubborn. "I don't want anybody else."

"You might, someday."

Renee's thoughts turned sadly to Jack. If she could only get in touch with him . . . no, that wasn't possible. He must have been killed, it was over a year since she had seen or heard of him, and she was completely alone. She came slowly to the conclusion that what her mother said was true. It was pointless trying to hold on to Glynn, when she knew she would never see him again, either.

She sat down that night and wrote a long letter to him, expressing her feelings for him and regretting what she had done to him by telling him of her sordid past life, letting the words flow on to the page as they came into her head.

After the fourth page, she laid down her pen to read over what she had written, before she would let him know that she agreed to the divorce. Suddenly, with a snort of derision, she picked up the sheets of paper and ripped them into tiny fragments. Then she started to write again. "Glynn, I'm sorry about everything. I will give you your divorce, and I wish you and Eiddwen every happiness. Renee."

She folded the single page, slipped it into an envelope and wrote the address boldly. This was the end for her, the end of all her hopes and dreams. She would have to forget Glynn — and Jack — and make a fresh start, on her own.

"I've agreed," she told Anne, and held the envelope up before she went out to post it.

"I'm glad."

Next morning, Renee made an appointment on the telephone to see a solicitor during her lunch hour, to set the wheels in motion to end her marriage.

Mr Miller, a small, dapper man with a sympathetic face, and brown hair balding at the temples, asked her some very personal questions, which she negotiated skilfully without mentioning her association with Fergus Cooper, but indicating that Glynn had been obsessively jealous and, in consequence, had shown some peculiar sexual behaviour. She said, also, that he had now left her for another woman. It wasn't the whole truth, but she couldn't file for divorce unless she seemed to be the innocent party.

The solicitor made copious notes while she talked, and then, as he wrote for quite a long spell without saying a word, she looked round his small office, full of leather-bound law tomes. The musty smell in the tiny space became overpowering, and she was very relieved when Mr Miller laid down his pen amongst the clutter of documents and forms on his desk.

He leaned back in his chair. "It will be a few months before you'll be called to the Divorce Court in Edinburgh, I'm afraid, Mrs Williams. The war broke up so many marriages, there's a large backlog of cases to be heard."

She stood up to go, and he smiled. "It will be a traumatic time for you, my dear, but when it's over, you'll be free to find new happiness."

When she went out into the street, she stood for a moment, thankfully breathing in the fresh air and reflecting, sadly, that there would be no new happiness for her. A tide of anger swept over her suddenly, when it occurred to her that Fergus Cooper had wreaked his ultimate revenge.

CHAPTER TWENTY-SIX

Spirits in Cattofield were brightened up one miserable Saturday afternoon in November 1946 by a welcome visit from Mike Donaldson, now home for good, accompanied by his wife and their four-year-old son, Michael.

After the delighted greetings were over, Mike apologised to Anne Gordon for having stopped writing to her. "We came up through Italy, after the North African campaign was settled, and we didn't get much time to ourselves. I managed to scribble a line or two to Babs now and then, but that was all."

Anne's smile was understanding and forgiving. "Don't worry, Mike. I knew Babs would have let me know if you'd been wounded, or taken prisoner, or anything like that."

"He nearly *was* taken prisoner once," Babs put in.

"Och, they're not wanting to hear about that." Mike brushed the experience lightly aside.

Anne respected his obvious reluctance to speak about it. "When did you come home?"

"Last Tuesday, but I've been getting to know my son, here." His eyes rested adoringly on the small boy who was standing between his mother and father, and the chubby face looked up and grinned.

Babs laughed. "They've been together every minute. I can hardly get Michael to leave his daddy, even at bedtime."

Renee had been just as effusive over Mike's return as Anne when he came in first but now she sat silently, pleased that he was reunited with his wife and son, but reflecting on her own plight. She would never be reunited with either of the men she loved, and the thought intensified the dull ache which was always present in the pit of her stomach, and which she had almost learned to live with.

She glanced at the man and woman on the settee. Babs was the picture of happiness, and, even holding her child's hand, still looked like a young girl. Mike's face was older, much older than when he went away, and his hair was pure white now, not blond. His striped demob suit was rather ill-fitting, but he, too, seemed deliriously happy, hardly taking his eyes off his wife except to look lovingly at his son.

Swallowing, Renee tried to concentrate on the conversation. Babs had been telling Anne about their plans to look for a place of their own, and was saying, "You see, it's not fair to Mike for us to be living with my mother after all he's come through."

"No, it's not very satisfactory being in somebody else's house," Anne said, sympathetically, "not with a little boy."

Mike shrugged his shoulders. "It wouldn't worry me, Mrs Gordon, as long as we were all together. I'm just thankful to be home again, all in one piece."

Babs turned to Renee. “Have you had any better news of Glynn? Tim was telling us he’d been wounded. Is he recovering all right now?”

Renee hadn’t been prepared for this. She had taken it for granted that her mother would have forewarned them at the door, but presumably she had been too pleased to see Mike.

“Yes, he’s recovering gradually,” she replied in a steady voice. “Enough to ask for a divorce, anyway.” Their shocked silence made her wish that she hadn’t been so flippant.

Babs visibly gathered her wits together. “Oh, Renee, I’m very sorry.”

“Don’t be. It was a bit of a bombshell at first, but I’ll get over it. I’ve arranged it with a solicitor, so all I have to do now is wait.”

“Well,” Mike said quietly, “it’s maybe all for the best.” He changed the subject quickly, embarrassed for her sake. “Tim’s getting on quite well now. The doctors say he should be able to go back to his old job in a week or two.”

“That’s great!” Renee didn’t have to force herself to sound happy about this. “And you, Mike? Will you be going back to your old job as well?”

“I haven’t been to the yard yet. I’ve been enjoying my family too much, but I’ll go next week. I think it’ll be OK though, because I heard they’re taking all the returning warriors back. Not that they all returned, of course,” he added, sadly.

No, Renee thought, they didn’t all return, and Jack Thomson was only one of many. She was rather surprised that Mike hadn't mentioned him, but he probably knew about it.

Anne stood up and moved towards the scullery. "You'll have a cup of tea?"

"No thanks, Mrs Gordon. We had one before we came out. We've a few friends to go round yet, and we're going to Turriff tomorrow to see my mother and father."

"They're potty about young Michael, too," Babs laughed. "It's a wonder he's not spoiled, with Mum and Moira and Tim all running after him."

When they stood up to leave, they kept talking for another five minutes before they actually went out, promising to let Anne and Renee know when they found a house, and when Mike and Tim started work. At the door, Mike turned to Renee. "I was sorry to hear that there's never been any word about Jack."

She kept a firm grip of herself. "Yes, it's very sad."

She sank on to the settee when she went inside, but Anne said, "I think we'll have that fly-cup ourselves."

Renee was thankful that another day's work was over, as she ran down the stairs and opened the door on to Union Street. The pavements were still covered in slush which was hardening into ridges with the keen frost, and she was glad she had put her boots on in the morning. Still standing in the doorway, she opened her handbag to take out her purse and extracted some coppers for her bus fare.

Turning up the collar of her tweed coat, and holding her head down against the piercing January wind — she stepped out on to the pavement. A pair of legs seemed to be blocking her way, but when she moved to one side to avoid them, they moved along with her.

"Renee."

The all-too-familiar, unwelcome voice made her head jerk up and a great sickness welled up in her as she found herself looking into the near-black eyes of the last person on earth she wished to see. "Go away," she said, coldly. "We've nothing to say to each other now. You should realise that."

"Please, Renee?" His old charm was turned on as he laid his hand on her shoulder.

She shrugged it off, angrily. "I don't know how you've the nerve to come back, Fergus Cooper."

"You know why, I love you." If she hadn't known him for what he was, his earnest words, and humble pleading look, would have made her capitulate blindly, but she'd suffered too much because of this man. She glared at him, her icy, clinical eyes taking in every detail of his appearance. His dark hair curled in exactly the same way over the collar of his cheap raincoat, his sensuous mouth was open just far enough to reveal his pearly-white teeth, his hypnotic eyes were caressing her, but they'd lost their spell and she felt nothing but contempt for him.

Brushing past him, she moved towards the bus stop, praying that she wouldn't have long to wait.

"Don't go, Renee." He hurried to walk alongside. "I've had time to think about what I did to you, and I'm really sorry. It was always you I dreamt about in the desert, and six years is a long time. You can't turn your back on me now."

"Can't I?" She kept on walking. Why wouldn't he leave her alone? Her stamina was at a low enough ebb without having to cope with this.

"I swear I've changed. It was always you I loved, but I wanted other excitement as well. I know I was a rotter, but I'll be faithful to you now, if you say you still love me."

She stopped abruptly, and he stood, uncertainly, a step ahead. "Why was it you that came back?" she asked, bitterly. "The world could do without scum like you, Glynn's been seriously wounded and Jack's been killed. Both of them good men, not like . . ."

"Jack Thomson killed? I'm sorry to hear that, he was a decent bloke." Fergus seemed to be genuinely affected. "But who's Glynn?"

"He's my husband." It was safer not to tell him about the impending divorce. There was no need to let Fergus know that his curse had worked. Let him think she was happily married; that might get rid of him, if he had any decency in him whatsoever.

He was studying her sadly. "I never really imagined you marrying another man, Renee, except Jack, maybe, for you were always chummy with him, and he fancied you, but nobody else."

"Well, you were wrong, weren't you? Just go away and leave me alone." She had taken a few steps before she remembered something she hadn't thought about for years, and halted again. "What about Jeanette

Morrison and your daughter? Or had you conveniently forgotten about them?"

"Jeanette? She got a girl, did she?"

"Didn't you even know that?" Renee's voice dripped with cold sarcasm.

"I knew she had the baby — I've been paying for it for years but I didn't know it was a girl." His wary expression changed, and he grasped her hand. "Can't you divorce your husband, Renee, so we can . . .?"

She took a deep breath and wrenched her hand from his grip. He had touched on her most vulnerable spot. "No, I can't! It's no use! If you're a reformed character, like you say, go to Jeanette. That's the only decent thing for you to do."

He let out a protracted sigh. "How am I going to bear it, loving you and knowing you're married to somebody else?"

"You'll live!" Her tone was cutting.

"So it's goodbye for ever?"

"For ever . . . and I really mean it."

"Goodbye for ever, then . . . Monday girl." His voice was softly seductive.

Her stomach lurched, and she struggled to avoid showing her shocked reaction to his blatant effrontery. She wouldn't give him the satisfaction of seeing how much it affected her.

Filled with chagrin because even his last two calculated words had failed to break her down, Fergus sketched a mocking salute, then walked away. Renee was still trembling when she reached home, and Anne was hotly indignant when she learned about the encounter.

"I don't know how that man had the nerve to . . ."

"He's the nerve for anything, Mum," the girl interrupted. "I told him he should go to Jeanette Morrison and his daughter, but I doubt if he'll take my advice." Nine days later, however, Anne received a letter which astonished and touched her, but she handed it to Renee without saying anything.

Dear Mrs Gordon,

I thought you would like to know that Fergus came back, after all this time without a word. He asked me to marry him, and I said yes because I still love him. He says he can't settle in Aberdeen now, so we're going to the south of England somewhere after the wedding — maybe Southampton or Portsmouth. I'm very happy, for I'm sure he does love me, and he thinks the world of Sheena. I won't write to you again, but I'm looking forward to my new life.

Yours,
Jeanette Morrison (soon to be Cooper)

"Well!" Renee raised her eyebrows. "So he did do it, after all. And maybe having a wife and a daughter'll be enough to keep him on the straight and narrow. I'm pleased for her, anyway."

Anne nodded her head. "All's well that ends well. And it'll maybe all end well for you, too, one of these fine days."

Her daughter made a moue. "I can't see how."

When Renee went to bed that night, she looked round her attic bedroom, remembering how her mother had suggested that they redecorate it. There was no wallpaper to be had, so they'd painted the walls in pale grey then used bits of sponge to dab on a pattern in lilac, and it still looked fresh and professional. What a pity that Glynn had never seen it. It had been done while he was still missing, she recalled sadly — at the time when she was still trying to convince herself that he hadn't been killed. Well, he hadn't been, but he was lost to her as irrevocably as if he had. His conscience wouldn't be pricking him, of course, because he probably believed that she would have turned to Jack Thomson for comfort, but Jack was really dead.

The irony of it all suddenly hit her. Of the three men she'd ever loved, why had Fergus Cooper been the one who came back to her after the war — the one who had caused her so much heartache and trouble, the one she'd prayed would never enter her life again? And now, he was to be starting a new life, in a new city, with a wife and daughter. Jeanette Morrison's dream had been realised, although she might live to regret it; Glynn had found true love at last, but Renee Williams, née Gordon, was left with only memories, good and bad. Then the tears came — hot, burning tears, which didn't even begin to cleanse the bitterness from her soul.

Fortunately, she soon became caught up in the excitement of Sheila Daun's preparations for her wedding. The groom-to-be, Chris Darborne, was the sailor she'd met the same night as Renee had started talking to Fred Schaper. They had done most of their courting by mail, with only occasional meetings over the years, for a few days at a time, but Chris, like Tim Donaldson originally, had been unwilling to tie his girlfriend down until peace was restored to the world. Sheila was ecstatically happy, and could concentrate on nothing but the forthcoming nuptials in March. She had asked Renee to be matron-of-honour, and stressed the fact that Chris had two brothers, hinting that the girl might find solace with one of them. Her colleague, however, felt that her capacity for love had been exhausted, and refused to rise to the bait.

A week before Sheila's great day, on a Saturday morning, Renee and her mother were debating on whether or not it was too wet to go out shopping, when the doorbell rang. Anne went to answer it, and the girl could hear her talking animatedly to someone before heavy footsteps sounded along the hall. Renee looked round idly when the living-room door opened, then jumped up and ran to throw herself at the tall figure who came in with his arms held out, his adorable "cow's lick" standing out from his sandy-coloured head.

"Jack! Oh, Jack!" She was laughing and crying, and the force of her hurtling body made him rock on his feet.

"Steady!" he grinned. "I've brought somebody with me that I'm sure you'd like to meet."

Her face fell, and her heart, racing from seeing his beloved face again when she had thought him dead, almost stopped beating. He must be married, and was about to introduce her to his wife! That was why he'd stopped writing. She stepped away from him when she realised that a stranger was standing in the doorway with her mother — a small woman with bright eyes and a beaming face. My God, the girl thought, she's old enough to be his . . .

"Renee," Jack was saying, "I'd like you to meet my mother."

Mrs Thomson shook her hand vigorously. "I've been wanting to meet you for a long time. My Jack's been in love with you for years, since long before he went in the army. A mother's intuition's never wrong, you know."

Renee looked from her to Jack in amazed wonder, her confused brain not taking in what was happening. She'd given up all hope of ever seeing him again . . . and he couldn't possibly know that her marriage was over, so why had he brought his mother to meet her, and why was the woman saying these things?

Jack laughed at her puzzled face, knowing exactly what was running through her mind. "Don't look so flabbergasted, Renee, my darling. It's not a ghost you're seeing. I'm alive and kicking, and I haven't got second sight, either."

Anne moved nearer. "I wrote to Jack's mother after you decided to let Glynn have his divorce, Renee. I always knew, deep down inside, that Jack was safe and well, and I was sure he'd go home to Peterhead someday." Her daughter's grateful expression made up for all the weeks she had spent wondering if she had done the right thing.

"Oh, Mum, I'll never be able to thank you enough."

"Mind you," Anne said, ruefully, "I wasn't too sure about it when I did write. You hadn't heard from Jack for years, and there had been no word from Mrs Thomson that he'd written to her, either, or was home, and he might have been killed for all I knew. But some sixth sense kept telling me he was still alive."

The young man's face was much more than just alive when he said, "I'd have come straight to Aberdeen last night, when Mum told me about the divorce, but I'd to wait till this morning to get a bus. Even my love for you couldn't give me wings."

Renee gave a tremulous laugh and he placed an arm round her. "And this terrible woman wouldn't let me come on my own," he added, turning to put his other arm round his mother, while Renee pulled Anne into the tight group, too.

Mrs Thomson laughed with delight. "Of course I wouldn't let him come on his own. I wanted to see you, Renee, to make sure you really loved my Jack."

"I do, Mrs Thomson," the girl cried. "I really do love him."

The woman held up her hand. "You don't need to tell me, it was in your eyes when you turned round first and saw him."

The two mothers exchanged knowing smiles when they moved out of the circle, leaving Renee and Jack gazing at each other, completely oblivious to everything except their love and their happiness at being together again.

Anne's eyes were moist when she said, softly, "Take Jack up to your own sitting room, Renee. I'm sure you've plenty to speak about that you don't want us old fogeys listening to."

Renee dragged her eyes away from Jack. "We do have things to say to each other, though it wouldn't matter if you two mums heard them."

"Get up the stairs and show him how much you missed him," Anne ordered, her smile broad.

Mrs Thomson nodded. "You too, Jack. You've a lot of wasted time to make up for."

"What choice have we?" Jack pretended to look helpless as he led her to the door. Once upstairs, he turned much more serious, even looking apologetic as he sat down. "I'm afraid I owe you some sort of explanation, Renee."

She stood in front of him, alarmed by his solemn manner. "No, darling. You don't have to explain anything. You're here, and that's all that matters."

He shook his head. "Please listen to me. I *have* to tell you everything. We must be completely honest with each other." Her blood ran suddenly cold. What on earth had he done that he felt compelled to confess?

He began slowly. "After I saw you the last time, I was so happy about you saying you loved me that I couldn't think straight."

"I didn't want you to think straight. I told you the truth."

"I know you did, but the more I thought about it, the more I was convinced that you only said it on an impulse. You were married to Glynn, and you still loved him, so I began to feel that I'd been a proper heel. That's why I never wrote to you again."

"I thought you'd been killed."

"That's what I meant you to think. If I was out of the way, you wouldn't have anything to complicate your life. I carried on writing to my mother though, till even that reminded me of you, because she'd guessed, long ago, how I felt about you, and often asked about you in her letters."

"Oh, Jack. Didn't you realise that she'd be nearly out of her mind with worry? And me, too?"

His mouth twisted. "I never meant to come back, Renee. You'd both have believed I was dead, and you'd have got over it come time. When I was demobbed, I went to London and found a job, the same as I was doing here. Then I met a girl, started going steady with her, and even set a date for the wedding."

A knife turned in her heart. "What went wrong, that made you come back, after all?"

During a slight pause, he stared into space, then he looked at her earnestly. "I couldn't get you out of my mind, Renee, that's what went wrong. Every time I kissed her, it was you I was kissing. When I made love to her, it was you . . . I couldn't go through with it, so I told her about you, but if she'd kept me to my promise, I'd have gone ahead and married her. She could see it wouldn't have worked, though, and called it off."

His voice wavered a little. "She was a decent girl, and I felt really awful about letting her down like that."

Renee was torn between being thankful that he'd come back, and being jealous of the unnamed girl that he'd made love to, when he'd never made love to her, and who must have awakened something in Jack before he'd said he'd marry her in the first place. But, if he could accept Glynn having been in her life, and Fergus, surely she could forgive him for something he'd done while he thought she was unavailable to him.

Jack carried on, steadier now. "I packed my bags and came home. I meant to get a job in Peterhead and never come near Aberdeen again. I'd done enough damage to people's feelings, and I didn't want to come between you and your husband."

"And then your mother told you about my divorce?" She couldn't understand why his eyes were still clouded.

"I could hardly credit it, at first, and I was impatient that it would be morning before I could come to you, but I had all night to think about it. Renee, is it because of me you're being divorced? Did Glynn find out that I love you, and that you'd said you loved me?"

The imaginary knife made another twist. It was her turn to confess, but would Jack understand about what had happened between Glynn and her? "It wasn't because of you, Jack," she said, slowly. "It was because of Fergus Cooper."

"Fergus?" His anxious face contorted with horror. "Have you started up with him again?"

"No, no, it wasn't that. It was . . . I told Glynn, on our wedding night, all that had gone on between Fergus and me, and he couldn't understand or forgive."

She went over the trauma of the Monday nights with Glynn — how he'd tried to destroy Fergus's claim on her, and how he'd come to avoid Monday nights altogether — and Jack listened without a word, his face impassive, his eyes fixed on her as if he were in some kind of trance.

This is it, she thought, sadly. This is the end of Jack's love, too. How could he possibly feel the same about her after hearing all these sordid details? But she had to tell him, before he could understand the situation. Steeling herself, she carried on.

"When Glynn went missing, I was nearly frantic." She bit her lip with the remembered pain. "I hadn't heard from you since that night in the lane, and I thought you'd both been killed."

He broke his silence at that. "Oh, Renee, I'm sorry. I didn't realise what I'd been putting you through . . . But he wasn't dead, either?"

She swallowed. "No, he wasn't dead."

"Why did he suddenly ask for a divorce?"

"He'd been seriously wounded, you see, and he was sent to a hospital in England when he was able to be moved. That's when everything really ended. He wouldn't let me go to him, but his mother sent his old girlfriend to visit him, and you can guess the rest. He fell in love with her all over again, and wanted to marry her. He wrote that our marriage would never work, because he couldn't forgive me for . . ." She shrugged. "He asked me to divorce him by putting all the blame on him, and I agreed."

During the short silence which fell, Renee held her breath. It was asking too much of Jack to expect him to ask her to marry him now that he knew everything.

He was smiling, however, when he leaned across and took her hand. "I'm glad it wasn't because of me." Her apprehensive face made him add, "Darling, I'm not like Glynn. I knew all along what was going on between Fergus and you, and I never blamed you for it."

"Thank you for saying that."

"It didn't change the way I felt about you, any more than what you've told me now about Mondays has changed it, but I have to ask you this, to set my mind at ease. Renee, if Fergus comes back, would you fall under his spell again, like you did before?"

She shook her head quickly. "He did come back, a few months ago, but I just felt sick when I saw him, and told him to leave me alone. He'll be married, by this time, to a girl he left pregnant when he joined up, and they've gone to live somewhere in the south of England. She wrote and told us about it, and she knows about him being a rotter, so their marriage might succeed. I hope so, anyway, and I'm glad he did the honourable thing for once in his life."

Jack squeezed her hand. "There's one last thing I have to ask you, my darling, and please don't be angry about it." He seemed slightly reluctant to come out with it, but finally said, "How will you feel about Mondays, after we're married?"

A stab of anger did shoot through her, until she realised that this had to be dealt with before they could have complete understanding. "I love you, Jack, and I'll never think of anybody but you, on Mondays or on any other day of the week."

He pulled her down on his knee, and kissed her until they were forced to surface for breath. "Oh, Renee, if you only knew how much I've longed to do that," he whispered huskily.

As his lips touched hers again, she jerked away, her eyes widening in dismay. "I've just thought! We'll have to buy a new bed. You won't want to use the same one as . . ." She turned scarlet as her voice tailed off.

His grimace was one of relief at the insignificance of her embarrassment. "Renee, my pet, we're not innocent young things any longer. If I can share your bed for the rest of our lives, it wouldn't bother me if you'd had the entire British Army, Navy and Air Force in it, including the Marines."

"Jack Thomson!"

Her shocked expression made him chuckle so infectiously that she had to join in. "Oh, I'm glad we can still laugh about everything together." She touched the dimple at the side of his mouth, lovingly.

"We'll always laugh together, Renee, no matter what happens." This time, his kiss was tender and reverent. "Now, I think we should go downstairs, to prove we haven't been up to anything we shouldn't . . . not yet, anyway."

They were still smiling when they entered the living room, where the two mothers turned round expectantly.

"Have you done all your talking?" Anne smiled archly. "And got everything sorted out?"

"Not quite!" With a theatrical flourish, he went down on one knee in front of Renee, his "cow's lick" rather spoiling the image of romantic suitor he was trying to project. " 'Pray, will you marry me, my pretty maid?' "

She giggled, then made a deep curtsy. "'Yes, if you please, kind sir, she said.'"

He stood up and hugged her. "You see," he confided in a loud stage whisper, "we'll have to make it legal to please the two mums."

Anne sighed with contentment. "Thank God you two got together at long last."

"I think God meant them for each other all along," Mrs Thomson observed, gravely.

Jack spluttered. "I'm sure He did, but He took His time about letting us know."

The house was filled with laughter, for the first time in almost three years.

Also available in ISIS Large Print:

Rachel's Secret

Susan Sallis

An engrossing and heartwarming novel from this beloved bestselling author

In 1943, two schoolgirls, Rachel and Meriel, best friends in the Gloucestershire city where they have grown up, amuse themselves by tracking down imaginary German spies. It all seems a harmless way of whiling away the long school holidays . . .until their game turns into a frightening reality, the consequences of which affect their whole lives.

Rachel becomes a reporter on the local paper while Meriel, a GI bride, goes to live in Florida. But the bonds that hold them together can never be broken, as the secrets and scandals which first surfaced in those far-off wartime days eventually come to light.

ISBN 978-0-7531-8162-1 (hb)
ISBN 978-0-7531-8163-8 (pb)

A House by the Sea

Elvi Rhodes

Ever since the death of her beloved husband Peter, Caroline's life in Bath has not been the same. Friends, though sympathetic, have moved on, her daughter is so far away and life just seems to be passing her by.

An impulsive moment sees her buying a dilapidated house in Brighton, a place that holds happy memories for her, and soon she is ensconced in a new life in her house by the sea.

But things are never that simple. Caroline's decision is met with outrage and incredulity from those who care about her and at times there seem to be insurmount-able obstacles ahead. Can she overcome these difficulties, find happiness in her new life and even leave a little room for love?

ISBN 978-0-7531-8208-6 (hb)
ISBN 978-0-7531-8209-3 (pb)

Lands Beyond the Sea

Tamara McKinley

By the 1700s, the Aborigine had lived in harmony with the land in Australia for 60,000 years. But now ghost-ships are arriving, and their very existence is threatened by a terrifying white invasion.

When Jonathan Cadwallader leaves Cornwall to sail on the Endeavour, he is forced to abandon his sweetheart, Susan Penhalligan. But an act of brutality will reunite them in the raw and unforgiving penal colony of New South Wales.

Billy Penhalligan has survived transportation and clings to the promise of a new beginning. But there will be more suffering before he or his fellow convicts can regard Australia as home . . .

ISBN 978-0-7531-8038-9 (hb)
ISBN 978-0-7531-8039-6 (pb)

Two Men and a Maiden

Winifred Foley

Forced to find another job to help support her family, Laura leaves the Forest of Dean to take up the position as maid to a Jewish family in London. She quickly settles in to life with the Cohens, befriending the daughter Rachel and catching the eye of both unmarried sons, David and Adam.

After a tragic incident, Laura returns home to the Forest of Dean, where she marries a promising young footballer. But after his untimely death, a surprise comes knocking. A surprise that signals a wonderful new life for her.

ISBN 978-0-7531-7970-3 (hb)
ISBN 978-0-7531-7971-0 (pb)

Jam and Jeopar

Doris Davidson

Was it the raspberry jam that finally killed her?

Revenge, lust, hatred and murder envelop a small Aberdeenshire village in Doris Davidson's latest novel

Wealthy 87-year-old spinster Janet Souter takes pleasure in raking up scandal, old and new, about her neighbours. She also relishes refusing her two nephews the money they desperately need to bolster their struggling businesses. So when she acquires some arsenic to deal with rats in her garden, she decides to test them: whichever attempts to kill her will be her sole beneficiary; if both do, they will each get a half share of her substantial savings. Naturally she takes precautions to ensure that her life will be in no real danger, but news of her newly acquired poison spreads round the village, sowing the seeds of murderous intent in several people. And one of them will succeed in silencing her vicious tongue forever . . .

ISBN 978-0-7531-7848-5 (hb)
ISBN 978-0-7531-7849-2 (pb)

...sh a wide range of books in large print, from ... to biography. Any suggestions for books you ...uld like to see in large print or audio are always welcome. Please send to the Editorial Department at:

ISIS Publishing Limited
7 Centremead
Osney Mead
Oxford OX2 0ES

A full list of titles is available free of charge from:

Ulverscroft Large Print Books Limited

(UK)
The Green
Bradgate Road, Anstey
Leicester LE7 7FU
Tel: (0116) 236 4325

(Australia)
P.O. Box 314
St Leonards
NSW 1590
Tel: (02) 9436 2622

(USA)
P.O. Box 1230
West Seneca
N.Y. 14224-1230
Tel: (716) 674 4270

(Canada)
P.O. Box 80038
Burlington
Ontario L7L 6B1
Tel: (905) 637 8734

(New Zealand)
P.O. Box 456
Feilding
Tel: (06) 323 6828

Details of **ISIS** complete and unabridged audio books are also available from these offices. Alternatively, contact your local library for details of their collection of **ISIS** large print and unabridged audio books.